EARTH'S HOPE

DYSTOPIAN URBAN FANTASY

ANN GIMPEL

Edited by
ANGELA KELLY

Illustrated by
FIONA JAYDE

CONTENTS

EARTH'S HOPE

EARTH RECLAIMED, BOOK THREE

Dystopian Urban Fantasy
By
Ann Gimpel

Power so old, deep, and chilling it hurts to think about it will overrun Earth if nothing changes. Targeted, furious, and fighting back, Aislinn runs wide open, gathering allies and putting her life on the line.

Aislinn Lenear has traveled a long road since the dark gods invaded Earth better than three years ago. After seeing her father slaughtered in front of her, and her mother sink into madness, Aislinn built strong walls around her heart. First her bond wolf, and then Fionn MacCumhaill, changed all that, but she and Fionn are far from home free.

Four of the six dark gods are still sowing destruction, and they've joined forces with Lemurians, a desperate lot, running just ahead of the tide of their own mortality. In a bold move, they try to coopt a group of young dragons, and very nearly succeed. Dewi, the Celtic dragon god, and Nidhogg, the Norse dragon god, banish their brood to the dragons' home world, but they refuse to stay put.

In a fast-paced, tension-riddled closure to this dystopian, urban fantasy series, Earth's Hope sweeps from Ireland to the Greek Islands to the Pacific Northwest to borderworlds where the dark gods live. Fionn's and Aislinn's relationship is strained to the breaking point as they struggle to work together without tearing one another to bits. Fionn is used to being obeyed without question, but Aislinn won't dance to his tune. If they can find their way, there may be hope for a ravaged Earth.

The world of magic and mythology comes to life, the prophecies so fascinating it's easy to lose onself in Ann's stories and forget everything in the real world. Definitely a hit right out of the park. InD'Tale Magazine

Earth's Blood

I fell in love with these characters and their world in the first book Earth's Requiem and more so in Earth's Blood!!! The characters and world is so detailed that you feel as though you are there and for me that means it is an amazing book! Cupcakes and Books

Top notch read!! Do yourself a favor a pick this book up! Fury8 Bibliophile

Book 2 is just as fantastic as the first! Please note to read Earth's Requiem (book 1) first as it would answer many things and keep you better connected to the wonderful world that has been created. Just as the first book this one grabs you from the start and pulls you into a wonderfully created world with a tension filled plot, beautiful descriptions and easy to love characters. Book Bliss Blog

Aislinn & Fionn have a wonderful relationship that tends to grow as the story progresses. Rune is a wolf that makes you wish you had one just like him for yourself. This story is sex, romance, and adventure all rolled in to one. If you haven't read this author yet, make sure you add her to your list. This is my third book of her's that I have read & I haven't read another author since I started reading her books. She's awesome that she gives away free copies in exchange for a review. Ann Gimpel is a can't miss.

Why have you not started this series yet?! It's truly magnificent. This series covers several genre's in one. Romance, action and a couple different cultural mythos and lores packed into one fantastic series. All the characters are just brilliantly laid out.

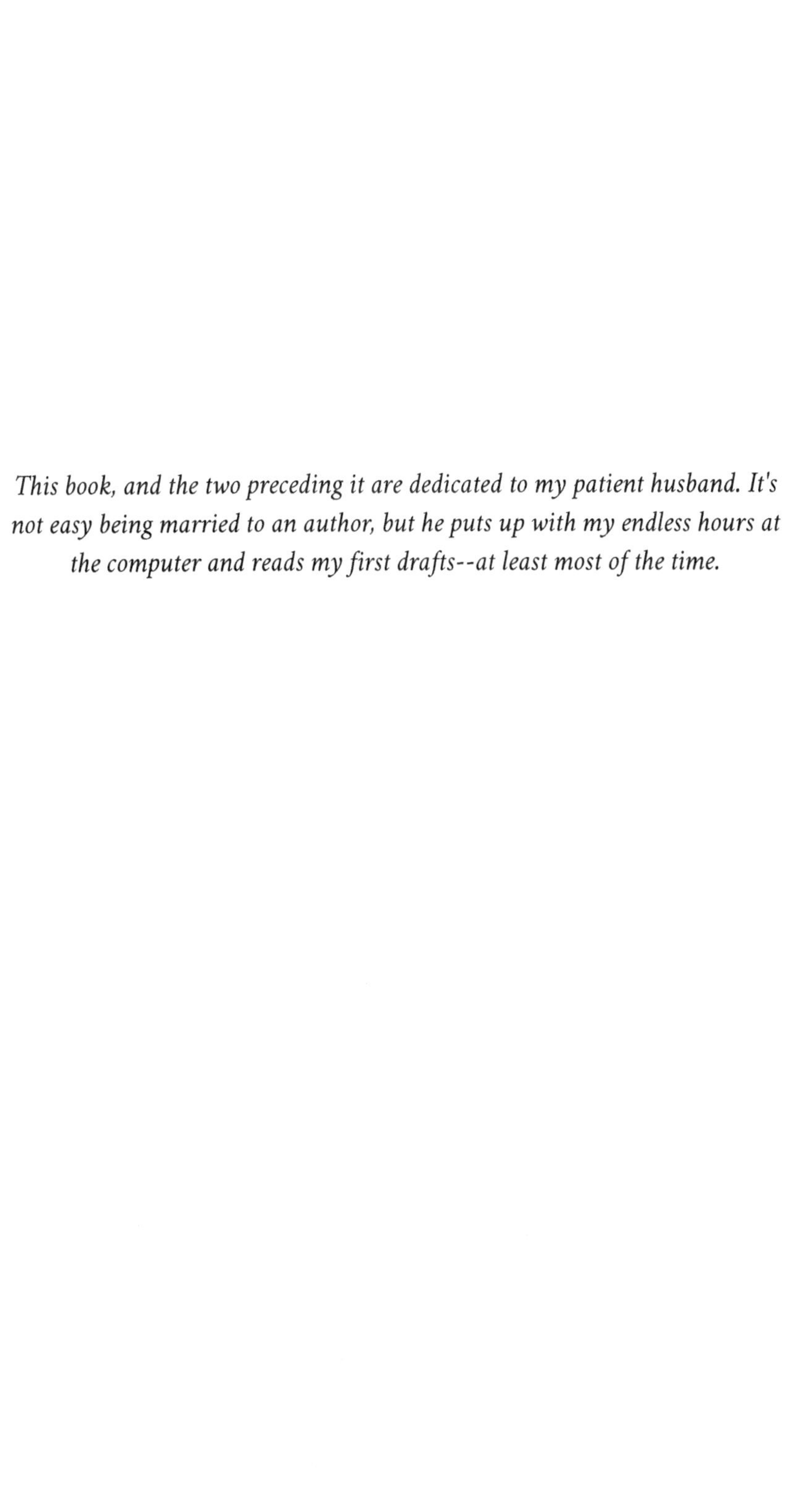

This book, and the two preceding it are dedicated to my patient husband. It's not easy being married to an author, but he puts up with my endless hours at the computer and reads my first drafts--at least most of the time.

CHAPTER 1

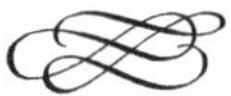

*D*ewi's blood-red wings cut through cold, blustery air. Day edged into evening, and the western horizon would soon be awash in the muted tones of a winter sunset. The dragon traveled without thought, following Nidhogg's dark bulk as he flew in front of her. For a time, she'd kept pace with her mate, the Norse dragon god, but the sight of their dead child cradled in his forearms smote her, and she'd dropped back to where the dark gods' treachery didn't smack her dead in the heart. Perrikus and Tokhots had kidnapped two of her younglings. One was safe, but the other had bitten Tokhots and succumbed to his poisoned blood.

Fire burst from Nidhogg's mouth, followed by steam. His grief was shifting to anger. Too bad hers couldn't do the same. Dewi rotated her head atop her sinuous stalk of a neck. Today she felt every single one of her better than two thousand-year life span, and her mistakes haunted her. Life had been simpler before mankind developed a fondness for machinery and electronics. Back then, everyone still believed in magic and treated her with the reverence that was her due as the Celtic dragon god, but the world had changed. Humans no longer jumped when Celtic gods—like her—snapped their fingers.

Smoke burbled past her double rows of teeth. Not that the electronic age was a problem anymore. The dark gods had joined forces with Lemurians, alien beings from the lost continent of Mu, and stripped the planet of all human life they couldn't turn to their advantage. They'd done a damned thorough job of it too.

Dewi was falling behind, so she flew faster. Not fast enough to pull in front of Nidhogg, though. It was pathetic, not dragonlike at all, but Dewi clung to sanity by a thread. If she didn't watch it, despair would get the better of her, and she'd set the countryside below on fire.

"What are you doing, woman?" Nidhogg trumpeted.

Dewi's eyes snapped open and she looked around. Lost in her thoughts, she'd veered off course to the east. "Sorry," she called and flew faster until she drew alongside the coal black dragon who'd been her mate for millennia. He turned whirling green eyes awash in pain her way. Dewi shook her head and said firmly, "This is my fault. I should've—"

"Stop." He narrowed his eyes. "We can't go back. You think I don't feel guilty for what happened to our child?" More fire streamed from his nostrils. "I was so spellbound to have you by my side again, I deluded myself into believing nothing wicked would befall us. How could it? Hadn't we paid enough?" Bitterness underscored his words.

"Hush, love." Shaken out of her own sorrow by Nidhogg's distress, she sent healing magic across the air between them.

"We will find time for talk," he said, "but now I need your help crossing the barrier into our borderworld."

"Of course." Dewi wove magic around them, strengthening the air currents beneath their wings. She'd been overjoyed and astonished when Nidhogg breathed life into dragon eggs she'd turned into a shrine. Between delight at being reunited with Nidhogg after his centuries of imprisonment, and the sudden reality of eight baby dragons, she hadn't fully settled into motherhood. The small dragons were so endearing—and unexpected—she'd coddled them, denying them nothing.

In hindsight, she should have been more vigilant. While her back was turned, the dark gods had filched two of her precious brood from beneath her nose, with help from the Lemurians. Thank the goddess Fionn and the MacLochlainn had stepped in and saved one of her purloined children. They'd tried to save them both, but had been too late. Aislinn—the MacLochlainn—might be headstrong, but she was courageous and loyal. Dewi hadn't thanked her enough, something she'd remedy just as soon as they returned to Fionn's manor house in Inishowen.

Dewi peered through the gathering gloom of the dying day. She couldn't see across the barrier quite yet, but she knew what lay beyond it. Dragons had been forged in a fiery world. Long ago, most dragons raised their young there, but she and Nidhogg—and the eight younglings he'd resurrected from their egg casings—were the last of their kind. New eggs percolated in her belly, but it would be weeks before they'd be ready to incubate, and a year beyond that before they hatched.

"Pay attention!" Nidhogg's deep voice held an uncharacteristically sharp note. "Your mind is wandering."

"I said I was sorry." Steam curled from her mouth. "This isn't easy. I want to be back in Inishowen with our other younglings."

"You think I don't?" More smoke followed his words. "Would you have us pile one sin atop another? We must honor our lost child by bringing her home."

Dewi didn't answer. Each of them was so mired in grief it was a miracle they were able to be civil. She pushed more power into her spell. They were close to the magical barricade separating Earth from the dragons' homeland. The air darkened and developed an iridescent glow. Power tinged with an electrical jolt zinged off her wingtips; the air smelled singed with a hint of ozone. "I haven't been here since we lived in the Old Country," she murmured.

"That long?" At least the funereal quality had left his voice. "Why?"

The anger that had eluded Dewi earlier slammed into her like a runaway train. Fire boiled from her belly and erupted through her mouth. "Because," she snarled, "there were hundreds of years when I was convinced I was the only dragon left alive. Why would I want to return to our world—unless I planned to die?"

"You gambled when you tried to free me that first time." Nidhogg's tone was soothing, gentle. "In your place, I would have done the same."

"I may have gambled, but I lost," she moaned. "I tried my damnedest to liberate you from the dark gods, but I wasn't strong enough, and I abandoned my clutch of eggs when I went after you. It was a hell of a choice. You or our children. In the end, I lost both." She shook herself from nose to tail tip, and scarlet scales rained from her hide.

"I love you for trying to save me." He turned his head and gazed at her. "You did rescue me. It just took a few hundred years longer than you'd hoped." He hesitated through a couple wing beats. "I've never been so happy to leave anywhere as I was to escape that wretched borderworld Perrikus calls home. Ruler of power and energy, my ass. Petty despot, more like. He only kept me alive to siphon my magic, so he could keep his pathetic excuse for a world from withering. That idiot D'Chel didn't help matters. He'd stop by my prison and gloat until I wanted to smash his face in and shove those perfect teeth of his down his throat."

"How did you know dragon's fire would reanimate our eggs?" she asked. "If I'd known it was that simple, I'd have done it long ago."

"I didn't. Not for certain. I'm much older than you, Dewi." He blew a gentle tongue of flame her way. "It's entirely possible I'm the oldest living creature on Earth. I hold bits and pieces of things, images that float in my mind. We had nothing to lose."

Dewi thought about the shrine she'd made of her clutch when she returned without Nidhogg after her first rescue effort. She'd mourned so deeply, the eggs were surrounded by mounds of precious gemstones from her tears. "I suppose you're right," she murmured and stopped. No reason to admit she'd also kept the eggs as a reminder of her own fallibility.

"Brace yourself." Nidhogg's wings beat so fast they became a blur.

Dewi shuttered her inner eyelids across her corneas. The dragons' world was a place of heat and light. Moments later, familiar smells buffeted her, singeing her lungs until she inhaled deeply, breathing past the pain. A charred landscape spread beneath her, beautiful in its barrenness. Red, orange, and black scorched dirt stretched in all directions.

Dragons could go for long periods with no food and little water. Their home world had only a single spring, and it had always proven sufficient for the dragons and small herds of wildebeest-related ungulates they fed on. Most of this land was a continuous string of volcanoes ringed around caves. The spring was deep within the cave system. Double suns were just falling beneath the western horizon, turning the sky a deep crimson, like a bloody gash across the world. Soon the only light would be from the ever-present fires.

"We will offer our daughter to the flame," Nidhogg said and inscribed circles in the thick, smoky air as he headed for a stark volcanic crack. Dewi followed him down. Some part buried deep within her welcomed the barren world, recognized it as part of her making. Nidhogg touched down, and Dewi joined him on the cracked, dry ground of their borderworld. He held out their daughter's body.

Dewi took her child and clasped the small dragon close. She would have grown up to be golden; even in death, her red scales had continued to change color. Dewi bent her head and brushed her jaws over her youngling's scaled head. "I'm so sorry," she said. "So very sorry. I wish I'd had time to get to know you."

"She would have been special," Nidhogg broke in. "Just like her mother."

Tears gathered, welled, and spilled into the dust. Pearls, diamonds, rubies, and emeralds sparkled at Dewi's feet. She gazed into Nidhogg's eyes. "I will always blame myself for this. Just like I blamed myself for making the wrong choice and leaving our eggs to search for you." She blew out steam and fire-streaked air. "We'll move beyond this, but those bastards will not get any more of our children."

"I hope you're correct." Nidhogg narrowed his spinning green eyes. "We've thrown down the gauntlet. Not just you and me, but the Celts and humans like Aislinn, humans with power. The bond animals are in this too."

"I suppose they are." Dewi thought about Rune, the wolf bonded to Aislinn, and Bella, the raven bound to Fionn. Hunters bonded to animals, infusing them with magic, or drawing out latent power that was already there. Human magic came in five iterations: Hunter, Mage, Seeker, Healer, and Seer. Most humans had two magics, one primary and one weaker, but Aislinn held all five. Fionn did too, just like all the Celtic gods.

"Dewi." Nidhogg laid his snout alongside hers. "There's never been a war without casualties. You may not come through this. I might not. Certainly, people we love will die."

Dewi bristled and clutched her child closer. "No more of my children. Not on my watch."

"No matter how vigilant and well-intentioned you are, it could happen." He straightened. "We fight to save Earth. We have no choice. Tomorrow is far from a certainty. Hear me when I tell you I welcome death as a free dragon. Dying by inches over hundreds of years in that stinking pen on Perrikus's world was agony. No matter what comes to pass, it won't be worse than that."

Alarm sluiced through her, and she shifted so she faced him. "You can't die. I just got you back."

Compassion streamed from his eyes. "I feel the same way about you, Dewi, my love, my heart. Remember they said we'd never last? That the Norse dragon god and Celtic dragon god would be at each other's throats?"

Dewi nodded. "Now that you mention it, yes, I do remember." She snorted and smoke rose above her head. "Proved them wrong, didn't we?"

"Yes, love. We did." He held out his forelegs for their daughter. "Let us pray and send her to her rest."

The sound of his chanting in their ancient language rose and fell around her. After a time, he kissed their daughter and handed her to Dewi one last time. Nidhogg didn't have to talk. He glanced at Dewi and then at the jagged crack at their feet, which belched sulfuric fumes. Dewi joined her voice with his for the final stanzas of the lament for the dead. Once they fell silent, she hunkered forward and dropped their daughter's body into the bowels of the dragons' borderworld.

No matter what Nidhogg says, I am never burying another of my young. Never.

"Come." Nidhogg's deep voice rumbled next to her. "So long as we are here, we should visit the caves and make certain the everlasting spring still flows." He spread his wings and beat the air with them.

Dewi had been ready to teleport into the caves, but flying was better. They'd be able to lay eyes on their world, assure themselves it hadn't been disturbed. Not that it was likely. Wards wrapped their borderworld, powerful magic that would incinerate anyone who wasn't a dragon.

Dewi took to the skies; once airborne, she scanned familiar landmarks and felt a bittersweet tug. Humans would never understand the attraction of the dragons' home. Neither would the other Celtic gods. She'd always felt she lived two lives, particularly once she believed she was the last dragon. Longing rose in her like a hot tide. If she had a choice in the matter, she'd bring her children back here and settle in with them and her mate. Let the humans and Celts sort out the mess with the dark gods. She could raise another clutch of eggs, and they'd be well on their way to repopulating the Earth with dragons…

Nidhogg circled to land, touching down in a flurry of dusty, reddened dirt. Dewi blew steam to clear her nostrils and lumbered near where he stood.

"We could bring the younglings here—" she began, but he silenced her with a harsh look. Fire plumed from his open mouth.

"The same thought crossed my mind, but we will not do that. How could we live with ourselves if we turned our backs on honor? More importantly, what kind of lesson would that teach our children?"

Shame burned hot and viscous in her chest, and Dewi looked away. "Once our younglings are a month old, the Celts will want to use them in battle."

"They would be within their rights." Nidhogg's tone was devoid of inflection. "Our children will be capable of fighting once their scales harden." He shook his head, and steam flew in all directions. "No one gets an exemption, Dewi. Not me. Not you, and not our children."

"I'll be chained to the eggs in my body once I've laid them. I don't know how I'll manage being stuck in our cave in Ireland knowing how thin a margin we hold."

"I've been thinking about that." Nidhogg raised his snout. "You will hold the eggs within you. Until the outcome of the coming battles is more certain, we will need you in battle."

"But how can I do that?" Dewi stared at her mate as if he'd lost his mind. "Last time we produced a clutch, the eggs came when they did. I couldn't have stopped them anymore than I could have turned back time."

"It's numbers. So long as you have fewer than fifteen fertilized eggs within you, you control when they emerge."

Dewi rolled her eyes. "Why do you know that and I don't?"

He shrugged, his black scales jangling against one another. "Maybe because I paid attention when the females got together. What this does mean, though"—he eyed her meaningfully—"is no more mating. We can't risk creating more eggs."

"Not sure I like that," she muttered and clanked her jaws together. "Let's get going with the caves. We've already burned up the better part of a day getting here, and we told Fionn and Aislinn we'd be back in two."

"I don't like the not mating part, either." Nidhogg winked broadly. "But it will create an incentive to plow through to the other side of things and secure Earth once and for all."

"I heard the tail end of that." Arawn, Celtic god of the dead, terror, and revenge, strode out of the mouth of the cave system. Black robes cloaked his tall, slender frame. Black hair hung loose to his waist, and his dark eyes glittered dangerously.

Dewi puffed smoke in surprise. "How did you get here? This world is closed to all but dragons."

"I'm surprised ye have to ask. The Halls of the Dead link to every borderworld, even this one." Arawn narrowed his eyes. "It got me around the problem with your ward system."

"So I suppose a better question," Nidhogg cut in, "would be why you felt the need to intercept us."

"Neither of you have been to these caves for a verra long time," Arawn spoke deliberately, enunciating each word until Dewi felt like strangling him.

"Your point?" she snapped.

"A handful of dragons yet live—"

"That's scarcely possible," Dewi huffed.

"Hush, dear." Nidhogg straightened his spine until he hit his full eight-and-a-half-feet height and shifted his gaze to Arawn. "I suppose you're going to tell us why you kept their existence a secret."

The dark-haired god shook his head. "Nay, I will let them tell you that themselves. I merely wished to prepare you. They are here at my behest and have remained so out of deference to me. I saw no reason to alert our enemies to their existence after Perrikus imprisoned you." A rare smile split Arawn's gaunt face, displaying very white, very even teeth. "I must return to Inishowen. I presume I will see you there soon."

"Thank you." Nidhogg inclined his head.

Dewi gnashed her teeth, not believing her mate was actually thanking Arawn for his deceit. "You could have told me," she gritted at Arawn. "I can keep secrets."

"Unless ye'd been taken," Arawn pointed out. "And tortured."

"Damn you, you arrogant Celtic ass," she sputtered. "I suffered terribly."

"Aye, but ye dinna die." The god of death's dark gaze flashed menace. "Enough. We all made sacrifices, and I fear we are far from the end of them." He raised his arms skyward, shimmered, and was gone.

"Get hold of yourself." Nidhogg nudged Dewi with his shoulder. "Let's get moving. I want to see which of our kin remain."

"Traitors, the lot of them," she hissed.

Nidhogg pivoted on his powerful hindquarters until he faced her and grabbed one of her forelegs with a taloned foot. "You will hear them out," he pronounced. "Only a fool makes judgments without facts."

Ouch.

Shame nudged anger, not totally displacing it, but at least making room for something beyond indignation. She yanked her foreleg free. "I promise to listen, but if I don't like their answers—"

"Neither of us will take action without consulting the other." He skewered her with his gaze. "Agreed?"

"Agreed." She aimed for neutrality, but a sullen undernote crept beneath the word just the same.

CHAPTER 2

Fionn, Celtic god of wisdom, creation, and protection, wanted to slam a fist down on the huge oblong table in his kitchen, but he restrained himself. The carved oak table could have accommodated twenty-five, but today just him, two other Celts, and four humans sat ringed around its scarred surface.

"Let's play this one again from the top," Fionn said, making an effort to remain in his seat. What he wanted to do was bolt from the room. Let the others come up with a plan if they were going to pick his to bits.

"Temper, temper," Bella cawed from her perch atop the door.

Fionn eyed his bond raven. "I'll thank you to keep your thoughts to yourself."

"Thank away." The bird fluffed her coal black feathers and nailed him with her beady avian gaze. "In the end, I'll do as I please."

"Aye, ye always do." Fionn turned his attention back to the group. Gwydion, master enchanter and warrior magician, sat at one end of the table. His sky blue robe was sashed with a leather belt that held pouches with a variety of herbs and powders in them, and his intricately carved wooden staff was propped against the wall behind him.

Blond hair was braided in a Celtic warrior pattern, and his blue eyes held a somber note.

Bran, god of prophecy, war, and the arts, wore his usual battle leathers. They clung to his heavily muscled body like a second skin. Blond hair fell halfway down his back, and his copper eyes danced with suppressed mirth. He tilted his chin in response to Fionn's gaze.

Fionn narrowed his eyes. "I doona see the humor here. Mayhap ye might enlighten me."

Bran shrugged. "Ye are used to getting your way. 'Tis interesting watching you grapple with compromise."

"Glad to provide entertainment," Fionn gritted through clenched teeth. Bran's words skirted dangerously close to the truth. Fionn was used to working alone, or with other Celts who tended to share his worldview. He hadn't counted on this bunch of humans to have differing opinions.

And did I think they'd bow and slaver and thank me for my wisdom? Fionn winced at his folly in expecting passivity.

"This isn't helpful," a woman from the far side of the table said. "We have our difficulties too, but if we don't work through them, we may as well hang out a white flag and tell the dark gods and those Lemurian bastards to come get us." Red hair hung to her shoulders, and the skin around her clear, green eyes was pinched with concern. She wore faded green pants and a nondescript sweater with many patches.

"You're Corin, right?" Fionn asked. "Sorry to ask, but..."

"Yes, I head those with the Mage gift." She took a measured breath. "One of the problems here is you're immortal. We're not. It makes us cautious, since we don't get do overs."

"Neither do we," Bran drawled in his conciliatory voice. "We can be sorely injured, so much so we end up waiting out our immortality in the *Dreaming*. 'Tisn't such an enviable position."

Corin frowned. "I'm sorry, I thought—"

"So long as I've put my foot in it," Fionn broke in, not wanting to go into the intricacies of Celtic immortality, "we never did go around the table for introductions. I'd asked for the leaders from each of the human magics. I recognize Daniel from Castle Balloch, but not the rest of you."

A stocky, blond man with deep green eyes nodded from across the table. He was dressed in tattered trousers and a plaid wool jacket. "As if any of us could forget the night we strung up that Hunter traitor, Travis. Damned shame about his civet, but we couldn't salvage him, either." Daniel thinned his lips into a disgusted line. "As I'm sure you guessed, I represent Seekers."

"Ye must be a Hunter," Gwydion cut in, angling a glance at a tall, slender woman with long black hair and a tawny mountain lion curled up behind her chair. Black skirts pooled around her, and a teal tunic covered her upper body.

"What tipped you off?" Her blue eyes shone with merriment.

For one sour moment, Fionn considered mentioning that she and Bran would make quite a pair since they saw humor in a bleak situation, but he kept his thoughts to himself. As if the cat could read minds, it leveled its amber gaze his way and growled.

"Surely ye have a name," Fionn prodded.

"The cat is Tabitha," Bella quorked from her perch. "She said her human is named Eve."

The dark-haired woman shifted in her chair and laid a hand on her bond animal's head. "Spilling secrets again, eh?" The cat growled a second time.

"We waste time sparring." The other occupant of the table spoke up. "I am Timothy, and I represent the Healers who are here." Curly brown hair shot out from his head at odd angles, and his hazel eyes held warmth. He wore robes much like Gwydion's, except his were black.

"Where's Aislinn?" Gwydion asked. "She was supposed to represent Seers."

"Not quite sure who that might be," Corin muttered, "since she's the only human I've ever known with that gift."

"Aislinn's babysitting the dragons," Fionn said. "They respond better to her than to anyone else, so she volunteered." Rune, Aislinn's bond wolf, had been far less anxious to take on the task, but she'd vetoed his request to hunt. Aislinn was Fionn's mate. She'd be his wife if things ever slowed down enough for Gwydion to marry them. His heart swelled with affection and longing when he thought of her lush body and prickly disposition. Win, lose, or draw, she was his, sharp edges and all, and he wouldn't have things any other way.

Fionn pushed to his feet and went to the pantry where he retrieved two bottles of mead. Returning to the table, he plonked them down and went in search of glasses. As he worked, he said, "The best I can tell, we are of three minds about our next steps. Some of us want to go after the other dark gods. Others want to target the Old Ones, or Lemurians as I've always named them. The third contingent wishes to solidify our power base and let the enemy come to us."

"Aye," Bran nodded, "'tis a fair encapsulation."

"Mayhap we might come up with pros and cons to each approach." Gwydion stood about the same time Fionn found his seat. The master enchanter tipped one of the mead bottles, pouring the fragrant liquid into a glass. He drank, set the glass down, and got paper and a pencil from a drawer at the far end of the kitchen.

"Not sure I see the point," Eve said. "We favor biding our time and the three of you"—she pointed an index finger at Fionn, Gwydion, and Bran—"would take a more offensive approach."

"All right." Fionn started to bring the mead bottle to his mouth, remembered his manners, and poured himself a jot. "What is the benefit to waiting until we are set upon?"

"Before ye answer," Bran jumped into the conversation, "consider they may never attack us directly."

"Why wouldn't they?" Daniel asked.

"If they can gain control of Earth, all except for this corner of Inishowen, they may well call it even," Bran noted. "We've proven difficult to fight, and the dark ones are lazy."

"I still say we have no choice," Fionn snapped. "If we can immobilize more of the dark gods, our task will be done. The Lemurians are a dying race. 'Tis why they allied themselves with the dark ones. They lived in those infernal tunnels beneath Mount Shasta for centuries with nary a problem that rose above ground level."

"So you're thinking they'll sink back into oblivion?" Daniel asked.

"'Tis exactly what I'm thinking," Fionn concurred. Since no one contradicted him, he kept talking. "Aislinn did away with Slototh, god of filth and all that's discarded. Dewi discombobulated Tokhots with dragon's fire. She injured Perrikus on his home world, but he recovered."

"You can't kill them," Eve protested. "It's one of the reasons we feel it's a waste of time to take them on in battle."

"Aye, lass, ye canna kill them," Fionn said, "but ye can cause them enough damage they think twice about bothering you again."

"Assuming Slototh and Tokhots, his trickster buddy, are down for the count," Gwydion said, "that leaves Perrikus, D'Chel, Majestron Zalia, and Adva."

"Refresh my memory," Corin said. "Perrikus controls power and energy, but what about the others?"

"D'Chel is the god of illusion. Adva controls portals, and Majestron Zalia is Perrikus's mother. She's their de facto queen, and her blood is just as poisonous as Tokhots's was," Bran said.

"We likely wouldna have to take all of them on," Fionn noted. "Once we were down to one or two, I believe they'd withdraw to their borderworlds and leave us be for a few centuries."

"So," Eve narrowed her eyes, "if we took out two of them that might be sufficient?"

Daniel shook his head. "I don't like it. There are too many unknowns. The Celts are certain the Lemurians will fade into obscurity. I'm not so certain."

"Why?" Gwydion arched a brow.

"If they're dying, do you expect they'll allow themselves to dwindle into nothingness without a fight? They were the Third Race."

"Yon human may have a point," Gwydion said. "They hatched up that plan to bond with the dark gods to save themselves. Just because it dinna work the way they planned, they may have other tricks up their sleeves."

"We need consensus," Fionn ground out. "There isna any more data that will open some magic door to something we have yet to come up with."

Corin stood and closed her teeth over her lower lip. "I will discuss this with the other Mages. My suggestion is we reconvene tonight. I don't know about the rest of you"—she tossed her head, and her gaze moved from Daniel to Eve to Timothy—"but I'm not willing to volunteer my people for slaughter unless they go willingly."

She strode across the kitchen and went out through the door leading to the great room of Fionn's sixteenth century manor house. After a slight pause, the other three followed her, with the cat bringing up the rear. Bella cawed something, and the cat made a sound between a purr and a snarl in return.

"What was that about?" Fionn asked his raven.

She fluffed her feathers. "You don't want to know."

That did it. Fionn jumped from his chair so fast it made a squealing noise as its legs scraped the wooden floor. He ended up directly below Bella. "Aye, I most certainly do want to know."

Bella made a great show of preening her feathers with her razor-sharp beak. "Tabitha thinks the Hunters may leave."

"Fucking great," Bran muttered.

"Aye." Gwydion blew out an exasperated sounding breath. "Here I thought we were a gnarly lot when it came to 'getting to yes.' We're pikers compared with humans."

"Get down here." Fionn patted his shoulder and the bird fluttered into place, her talons digging deep into his shoulder muscles. He walked back to the table, grabbed a mead bottle, and took a long swallow.

"What's our next move?" Bran inquired caustically. "Since what we're doing seems to be working so well."

"Mayhap we should ask Aislinn," Fionn said. "She's human, so she might have better luck second guessing them."

"That's exactly the problem." Gwydion seized the bottle from Fionn.

"What is?"

"We dinna treat the humans in this part of the world verra well," Bran clarified. "They have no reason to trust us."

Fionn grimaced. Though he'd spent most of the last few hundred years in North America, he was equally guilty. Three-and-a-half years before, when the Lemurians had weakened the gates between the worlds and allowed the dark gods access to Earth, he'd laid low right along with all the other Celts. They'd stood by—and done nothing— while the Lemurians had marched millions of humans into a radioactive vortex. Aislinn had called him to task soundly for that particular lapse. Once she'd gotten done with him, Fionn felt ashamed.

The Lemurians' excuse had been all humans without magic were worthless, an unnecessary drain on planetary resources, but the truth was much closer to something quite different. Even with an infusion from the dark gods, the Lemurians' power was limited. It took all their capacity to marshal humans with magic to do their bidding. There wasn't anything left over to control masses of other humans who would likely have staged a rebellion.

"Ye're a mite on the quiet side," Gwydion observed.

"'Tis because Bran hit the nail on its head," Fionn admitted. "They doona trust us, and I doona blame them. Were I in their place, I wouldna trust us, either."

"If we had time," Gwydion spoke slowly, "we might wait for trust to develop naturally."

"Time is a luxury we doona have," Bran said.

"Worst case," Fionn muttered, "we gather the other Celts and do what we have to." A thought surfaced, and he glanced from Gwydion to Bran. "Do you two agree with my strategy of targeting the remaining dark gods?"

"'Twould be best if we did a bit of both." Bran pushed to his feet and went to glance out a window.

"Say more." Fionn snapped his fingers.

Bran snorted and turned to face Fionn. "What? Am I your dog now to be clucked at?"

"I wasna clucking, I was snapping."

"Fine." Bran shoved his long, heavy hair behind his shoulders. "The Old Ones are weak. We could take enough of them out in a single campaign to send them scurrying back into Taltos for the duration."

"What would that buy us?" Gwydion asked.

"They helped Tokhots and Perrikus kidnap the youngling dragons," Bran said. "Doona underestimate them. They have a group intelligence, and it makes them slow to move, but dangerous once they do."

Gwydion narrowed his eyes. "Mayhap ye have a point. After all, Aislinn got rid of Slototh single-handedly, so 'twill not necessarily take numbers to decimate the dark gods, particularly not if the dragons help."

Breath rattled from Bran. "Aye, and I'd nearly forgotten about that. How do ye suppose Arawn's getting along telling Dewi about the other dragons?"

Gwydion shrugged. "He's not back. It might mean she immolated him with dragon fire."

"What other dragons?" Fionn felt confused.

"Och, and ye dinna know," Gwydion said.

"Dinna know what?" Fionn clenched his teeth together as annoyance built.

"Once Nidhogg was captured, Odin threw a fit and said if *his* dragon wasn't free, no dragon should be."

Bran picked up the tale, "Arawn got wind of Odin's plan to target the dragons and sequestered four of them on the dragons' borderworld." He shrugged. "It never occurred to us Dewi would avoid the place for so long."

"And ye dinna tell me, why?" Fionn asked.

"Because ye were closer to Dewi than the rest of us, and we were afraid ye'd tell her," Gwydion said.

"Mmph. Why dinna Odin go after Dewi?" Fionn asked.

Gwydion's eyes widened. "Because she's a god just like him."

Fionn stood and joined Gwydion on the far side of the kitchen. "I'm sick of problems. Give me solutions."

Gwydion mock bowed. "So sorry, your lordship."

"Aye." Bran chuckled softly. "The verra next solution that hops into my head is yours."

"This isna funny," Fionn snapped.

"Nay. 'Tisn't," Gwydion agreed.

Fionn might not have noticed if he hadn't been focused on Bran, but the mage shut his eyes and his body stilled for the space of a few heartbeats. When his coppery eyes opened, they held a grim cast.

"What?" Fionn asked.

"Prophecy be damned," Bran said. "I'm often wrong, particularly for things like this, but I fear the dark willna give us a choice."

Adrenaline shot through Fionn, leaving a bitter taste at the back of his throat. "What did ye see?" he demanded.

"Nothing specific. The Lemurians are far from storming your castle gates, but I felt them closing. They know if they wait until the baby dragons grow past a month, their odds of winning plummet."

"Arawn should be back soon," Gwydion said. "Once he is, I say we seek out the humans, apologize all over the place for our past sins, and map out a defensive strategy in case we're attacked."

Bella squawked and launched herself off Fionn's shoulder, flying toward the open doorway. "Where are ye going?" Fionn demanded.

"To tell Tabitha it's not safe for them to leave."

"That bird has good instincts," Gwydion said.

The raven, who'd flown past the doorway, returned, hovering in the air. "At last!" she cackled. "Someone believes in me. Maybe you'd like to take over as my bonded one?" She flew close to Gwydion and brushed her beak through his hair.

"Doona be ridiculous." Fionn snatched his bird out of the air and held her between his hands. She pecked at him, but not hard enough to draw blood.

"A bit more appreciation would be nice," she said.

"Aye, and there are things I'd like as well," he countered, "but we're stuck with one another." He raised the raven to eye level. "Would ye like me to catalogue your sins?"

"Not particularly." Bella looked away.

"I dinna think so." Fionn let go, and the bird made a low, sweeping circle before she flew out of the room.

"Thanks," Gwydion said, his voice weary. "Ye spared me telling her I dinna wish a bond animal."

"She might have pecked your eyes out," Bran said.

Fionn nodded his agreement. Bella was more than capable of something like that. "I'm going to find Aislinn," he told the others. "She's probably outside next to the moat, since the small dragons like to swim."

"We'll come with you." Gwydion shot a glance Bran's way. "Won't we?"

"Aye." Bran stood. "I could use a dragon fix. Let's see, we only need about one more week afore they're cannon fodder."

"Doona let Dewi hear you call them that," Fionn said and strode from the kitchen. If the Celtic dragon god had her way, her younglings would never get anywhere close to battle. Nidhogg was more reasonable, but in the end they were his children too, and he'd sacrifice himself to protect them.

CHAPTER 3

*A*islinn sat next to the moat, bundled against the chill of an early evening. Winter days were short this far north, and the ever-present damp soaked into her bones. Seven young dragons cavorted in the water. Rune had been in the moat with them, but he'd tired of their antics and now lay by her side, tongue lolling as his thick black and gray pelt dried. Thank Christ, Dewi and Nidhogg would be back within a few hours, and then they could take over.

She sank her hand into Rune's fur and he leaned into her touch. Her wolf had taught her about two magics she never suspected she held: Hunter and Healer. She'd always seen herself as a Mage with weak Seeker traits, but Rune had cornered her one day and demanded she bond with him. Shortly thereafter, he'd been critically injured, and she'd found ways to keep him alive. Fionn had shown her how to access the Seer gift. Insofar as she knew, she was the only human with all five magics, and she still wasn't certain how she felt about it.

One of the red dragons leaped from the water, wings flapping, and dive-bombed her, showering her with slimy moat water.

"Ewww." Aislinn sputtered the dank water away from her lips.

"Play with us," the female dragon demanded.

"It's almost time for bed." Aislinn tried to sound stern, but she had the same problem with the younglings that plagued Dewi. They were so damned cute, it wasn't easy to pull rank.

"Bed?" echoed from six other dragonlings. They vaulted from the water and converged on her, nearly crushing her beneath their bulk.

"Get off me," Aislinn cried. "You're heavy."

"Yes," the one black dragon announced proudly and nudged Rune with his scaled snout. "Once I rode you. Soon you'll fit atop my back."

"Don't count on it," Rune snarled.

Aislinn snickered. Flying atop a dragon wasn't the wolf's favorite activity. He tolerated it when he had to, but avoided it when he could.

"How's it going, leannán?" Fionn strode down the greenway separating the moat from his castle.

Aislinn scrambled to her feet and shook water out of her hair. Her beige trousers were thick, boiled wool and fairly resistant to moisture. A cloak woven from the same wool wrapped around her body. She'd found the clothes in one of many trunks in Fionn's attic. He couldn't recall who they'd belonged to, but she assumed it was an earlier wife or girlfriend since he'd been born in 1048.

"Good, you're here." She squinted through the gloom. When he got close enough for her to see his face, the welcoming smile died on her lips.

"Aye, well at least someone is glad of my presence."

"Didn't go well, huh?" She held out her arms. He walked into them and wrapped his around her.

"Nay. Mostly the humans want to wait until we're attacked. Bran wants to annihilate the Lemurians first." He tightened his arms around her shoulders. "I want to bash our way through the dark gods until they get fed up enough to retreat, but I canna do it by myself."

"We'll help." The black dragonling tried to wriggle between Fionn's and Aislinn's bodies. His scales caught on Aislinn's pants.

"We will, we will," other young voices chimed in.

"The dark ones killed our sister," the black dragon went on, his piping voice serious. "We want revenge."

"Mother won't let us fight," a green dragon spoke up. "She already said so."

"Father disagreed," the red dragon who'd invaded Aislinn's lap said.

She'd gotten better at telling them apart, but it would be a relief once they named themselves. In all, there were two red females, three green males, the black male, and a copper male.

"I fear all of us will get our chance in battle afore this is over." Gwydion, flanked by Bran, walked into their midst. "Come with me. Time to give Aislinn a break."

"Will you tell us a story?" the copper dragon demanded.

"Yes," a red dragon clapped her clawed forelegs together. "You tell the best stories."

"I'll be your bard tonight." Bran made a sweeping bow. "Mayhap you'd care to hear about how dragons came to be."

"Yes!" the red female shrieked.

"Follow Bran," Gwydion urged. Once the dragons were in motion, some flying, some walking, he rolled his eyes and brought up the rear.

"Thanks," Aislinn shouted after him.

"Ye owe me, lass," he called over one shoulder.

Aislinn leaned her head into the nook between Fionn's neck and shoulder. "Would you like to walk a bit before we go inside?"

"Aye, lass. Now ye mention it, I'd like that verra much."

"Do you suppose we could go as far as the sea?"

"I thought we'd remain within my wards—"

Bella flapped out of the darkness and landed on Rune's back. "We're coming," she announced.

"Of course we are," Rune seconded. "My bonded one would never consider leaving me behind."

Aislinn stifled a snort. The bond animals had their own network and frequently shared things among themselves that they'd never tell their humans. Apparently Bella had complained about Fionn ditching her, and the wolf was reminding her of that in a less-than-subtle manner.

"Since we're all going," Aislinn cut in before Fionn got into another argument with the cantankerous raven, "let's do this. I sat for so long, I'm cold." She wriggled out of Fionn's embrace, reluctant to leave the warmth of his body.

"Would ye like me to find you a warmer wrap?" Fionn asked.

She shook her head. "I don't want this to be a big production number. Mostly, I want to work the kinks out of my legs before we go to bed. Thank Christ Dewi will be back by the middle of tomorrow."

Fionn hooked a hand beneath her arm and guided her toward the wall that rose all around his manor. He'd had the mansion built in the fifteen hundreds to exacting specifications. Flat, gray stones comprised the outer wall; they fit together so precisely it was nearly impossible to detect their edges. The house itself was built from huge wooden beams and river rock. Five stories, with turrets and a tower and leaded glass windows, it looked like something out of a movie set.

Aislinn fell into step beside him, grateful for her long legs that let her keep pace easily. They passed beneath one of four curved gateways set into the outer wall and out onto open moorland. Humans who'd been assigned sentry duty nodded as they passed. The salt tang of the sea deepened, tickling her nostrils. For a moment, she felt homesick for the dry air of the American west where she was from. Rune jumped to one side, jaws snapping, and came up with a small, wriggling creature.

"I shall hunt too," Bella declared and launched herself off the wolf's back. The black of her wings melted into the shadows until Aislinn couldn't see her anymore without magic.

"Why's she unhappy this time?" Aislinn asked.

"What it comes down to," Fionn replied, "is she doesn't enjoy sharing me. Aye, she likes you well enough. Not like your mother, who she detested, but jealousy still gets the better of her."

"She's good to have by our side in battle, though." Aislinn licked her lips and tasted salt from perpetual mists that hung in the air. "Speaking of which, I assume there's another pow-wow with the humans."

"Aye, that there is. If nothing else, we must craft a defensive plan should we be attacked."

"Not if, but when," she cut in. "I can't put my finger on it, but time grows short. I feel it here." She laid a hand over her chest.

"Ye and Bran, both. He says the Lemurians are closing, and I presume the dark gods are masterminding whatever they're up to."

Rune growled from around his impromptu meal. *I'm ready.* He shifted to mind speech because his mouth was busy.

Aislinn waited for the raven to jump in, but either Bella was out of earshot, or biding her time. The roar of breakers on sand got louder as they closed the distance to the beach. Fionn stopped walking and spun her in his arms until they faced one another. He murmured a string of Gaelic endearments just before he closed his mouth over hers.

Aislinn wove her arms around Fionn's muscled torso and opened her mouth to his insistent tongue. Need flared, hot and urgent, but Fionn always had that effect on her. From the moment their bodies had first slammed together, passion drove reason from her mind.

She'd lost her father to Perrikus and D'Chel the night they'd pierced the veil separating Earth from their borderworlds. Lemurians had killed her mother a year later, and Aislinn had vowed to never let another soul get close enough to hurt her if something hideous happened to them. She'd held firm for two years, but first Rune and then Fionn, had walked into her life and changed everything.

Too late. It's too late to worry about it now. Her breath quickened, and her nipples formed hard peaks where they were squashed against his chest.

Fionn dropped his hands lower and cupped the curves of her ass, pulling her hard against an obvious erection. She tore her mouth from his. "So, do you just want to fall into the wet grass and get it on?"

He made a decidedly male sound deep in his throat. "Not a bad idea, leannán. I can make us a dry place with magic." He butted his hard-on against her pelvis. "At least we'd have a shred of privacy. No telling who'll burst into my rooms back in the house."

"No kidding. Do you suppose the dragons have figured out how to work their way past the deadbolt?"

"Och, lassie. Now ye mention it, I caught the black one using magic to do just that earlier today." He tugged one of her arms from around him and pushed her hand over his engorged flesh. "We willna be long. Think of the adventure aspect." Muted humor ran beneath his words.

Aislinn tilted her head back and gazed into his sky blue eyes. His long, blond hair was braided in an intricate Celtic pattern the men favored. Classic bone structure—with a high forehead, sculpted cheekbones, and a square jaw—wouldn't have been out of place on a statue of Adonis. At six feet two, he was just a shred taller than her. Her throat thickened with emotion, and she asked, "Do you know how much I love you?"

"Aye, mo croi, because I love you just as much. I canna imagine my life without you in it." His cock jumped against her curved fingers.

"Och, 'tis just that MacLochlainn bond thing." She aped his brogue.

"'Tisn't and ye know it. Your mother loved Gwydion, yet she was bound to me through the same stricture."

"I was teasing." She stroked him through the thick wool of his trousers. "Sure, we can make love—"

"Mistress!" Rune's mind voice was sharp, urgent.

Fionn's head snapped up, and he swung his head from side to side, scenting the air. "Fuck!"

"What is it?" Aislinn sent her Mage gift spinning outward, trying to sense whatever Fionn and her wolf felt.

"Harpies."

Fionn let go of her, and she felt him draw warding around them. The air warmed with the feel of his power, and her skin tingled. Fionn's magic carried many faces, and she thought back to the first time he'd shielded her from harm in a thick pine forest in Northern California. She leaned toward him and murmured, "You mean those women-bird things are real? Did the dark gods send them?"

"Aye, they're real, but probably not connected with the dark ones.

Add your magic to mine. They're too close to make a run for the manor."

Aislinn wove threads of power into the warding around the three of them. "Where's Bella?"

"I doona know, but she can take care of herself." Fionn spoke tersely. "Damn! It's been hundreds of years since they've shown themselves."

Deep evil touched the edges of Aislinn's power, different from anything she'd ever felt before, and she straightened her spine. "They're strong. How can we fight them?"

"Depends which ones show up and what they want."

"Goddammit, Fionn. You're talking in riddles, and I need information."

"What? Ye want a crash course in mythology?"

"If it will help me understand what we face, yes." Aislinn's temper, always a weak point, flashed white hot.

"There are three. Aello, or sea storm, Ocypete, or swift flying, and Celaeno, or dark one. My best guess is they doona care for the dark gods' energy and have their own ideas for how to address the problem."

"Smart." A multi-toned voice that reminded Aislinn of the Lemurians echoed out of the darkness.

"He always was," a second voice chimed in.

"Holy crap! You know them?" Aislinn demanded, not liking the shrill note in her voice. Next to her leg, Rune vibrated with outrage.

"Of course." Fionn sounded exasperated. "We're in the Old Country. The gods all know one another. I told you, magic runs stronger here."

Light showered around them, and two glowing figures burst into view. Close to six feet tall, their upper torsos resembled human women. Long, tangled blond hair partially hid their naked breasts. Feathers started about stomach level, and their lower bodies were birdlike, with long curved red talons tipping each foot. Energy pulsed from them. When Aislinn looked closer, she saw coal black wings folded over their naked, human backs.

"Aello and Celaeno. Welcome." Fionn half bowed, never taking his eyes off the pair.

"Polite won't save you." One of the Harpies grinned and licked her lips.

"Save me from what?"

"We're not interested in a pitched battle between you and the dark gods and the Lemurians," the other of the pair spoke up.

"Fine." Fionn shrugged. "Do something about it."

"We are." The grin widened, and Aislinn saw pointed teeth. "If we take you out of the equation, it will at least slow things down."

Fionn loosed a string of Gaelic curses. "Ye're mad, Aello, but then ye always were."

The grinning Harpy leveled molten silver eyes at Fionn. "You didn't feel that way when you shared my bed."

Aislinn gnashed her teeth together. This just got better and better. "Did you fuck all of them?" she gritted out.

"What difference does it make?"

Guess I got my answer. Aislinn wrestled her temper into détente and stepped forward. "Nice to meet you—" she began.

"Save it, human," the other Harpy broke in.

"Oh, really?" Aislinn bristled. "You must be Celaeno. You could help us. Surely you don't want Earth to fall into the dark gods' hands."

"What we want is for all this"—Celaeno swept her arms wide—"to go away. It disturbs the magical currents—and our rest."

Breath whistled from between Fionn's teeth. "Where do the rest of the Greek gods stand?"

"Like whom?" Aello inquired archly.

"For starters, your father, the sea god, Thaumas. Or your mother, the nymph, Electra."

"They live in the Aegean." Aello narrowed her silver eyes. "We haven't seen them in several hundred years."

"Ye're hedging," Fionn said, and placed his body between Aislinn and the Harpies.

"Knock it off." Aislinn moved back by his side.

"He's right to protect you from us," Celaeno said. "We could snuff out your pathetic existence with a thought."

Rune snarled and launched himself at the Harpies. Before he got even close to striking distance, a blast of magic picked him up and tossed him twenty feet backward.

"Control your bond animal," Aello said, "if you wish him to live."

The wolf leaped to his feet and shook himself all over. Before he could charge again, Aislinn snapped, "Rune. To me." It would piss the wolf off because he couldn't refuse a direct order from her, but it was better than having him cut down before her eyes.

This time, Rune's snarl was for her as he stalked to her side. When she settled her hand on his head, he jerked from beneath it.

"Come with us." Aeollo's voice, directed at Fionn, was liquid honey.

"I don't think so." Aislinn squared her shoulders. "He's mine."

"If I come with you, then what?" Fionn asked.

"Your woman and her bond animal will be allowed to return to your home," Celaeno spoke smoothly.

"Bullshit!" Aislinn spun so she stood in front of Fionn facing him. "Not an option. We face this, whatever it is, together."

"But we don't want you, human," one of the Harpies said.

"Of course you don't." Aislinn twirled and faced them. "Not if you're thinking of seducing him again."

Aello laughed, and her mirth cut into Aislinn's heart like sprinkles of grated glass. "I wouldn't be so certain just who seduced whom, human." She snapped her fingers and tossed her hair over her shoulders displaying her full, white breasts to advantage. "We waste time. There are only two outcomes. Either you join us, or fight us."

"There might be three." Aislinn spat the words. "We could get lucky and kill you."

Fionn placed his hands on her shoulders and pulled her back to his side. "Nay, leannán, 'twould never happen. Not against two. Harpies are soul stealers. Not mine, but they prey on human souls."

"Shall we?" Celaeno extended a hand, her fingers tipped with curving red talons.

"Hold." Fionn's face could have been carved from stone. "I want your word that Aislinn, Rune, and my bond raven will have safe passage between here and my house," Fionn said.

"No!" Aislinn shrieked. "I—"

"Hush." Fionn cut her off. "We doona have a choice, lass. Tell Gwydion and Bran exactly what happened. Arawn and the dragons too, once they return."

"But when will you be back?" Aislinn cried.

"He won't," Aello said.

Magic flashed and the place where Fionn had stood lay empty. Smoke roiled, stinging her nostrils and eyes. Aislinn pulsed destructive magic in a wide enough arc to disable damn near anything, even though she knew in her bones the Harpies were gone.

"Goddammit!" Aislinn pounded her fist into a nearby fencepost. The pain cleared her head.

Rune nipped her leg. "Hurry."

"Where?"

"Fionn bought our freedom. Don't throw his gift away."

She ground her jaws together until she was surprised her teeth didn't shatter. "I was going to go after him."

"Do you know where to find him?" the wolf asked.

"No." The word tore out of her.

"Maybe Gwydion or Bran will." Rune pushed his snout into her thigh. "Come on. Before those bitches change their mind and return."

At the very edges of her hearing, Aislinn heard shrill, tinkling laughter that sounded a lot like Aeollo. She shook her fist at the night sky. "Fine. I'm leaving, but this isn't done. You can't have him."

She took off through the night running as fast as she could with Rune right beside her. Just before she passed beneath the manor house outer wall, Bella landed on her shoulder, cutting deep with her long, sharp talons.

"Stop it!" Aislinn grunted. "That hurts." But the bird didn't loosen her grip.

Aislinn pelted past the moat and up the greenway to the set of stairs leading to the front door. As soon as she got inside, she raised her mind voice to a shout. *"Gwydion! Bran! Find me now."*

CHAPTER 4

*D*ewi lumbered into the cave system on the dragons' borderworld right behind Nidhogg. Limestone walls rose around her and stalactites and stalagmites glistened in light reflected through the cave's entrance. Soon it would be pitch black except for the faint glow she and Nidhogg emitted. The cave system was extensive; it could easily take two or three hours to wend their way to the fountain at its center.

She was still seething that something as important as not being the last living dragon had been hidden from her. By now she'd figured out the Celts wanted her right where they'd sent her: to spy on Lemurians from the infernal tunnels beneath Taltos. Had she known other dragons lived, she'd have left her post in search of them.

Bastards! They used me.

"Sorry for eavesdropping on your thoughts," Nidhogg lowered his voice, "but you have to be rational."

"All I can say," she muttered, "is I'm having one hell of a hard time imagining what would keep our kin locked on this world. Arawn said the dragons remained because he wanted them to. Since when do we kowtow to the Celts?" Fire streamed from her mouth. "Dragons owe their allegiance to me."

"And me." Nidhogg's tone was mild.

"You were gone forever," Dewi said.

"So? Calling on dead gods is a time-honored occupation."

"You're not funny."

"I wasn't trying to be," he countered. "Remember our agreement."

"Which was?"

"You will not harm anybody unless we have fully discussed it and are in agreement."

"I won't have to harm them." Dewi blew fire-streaked smoke out her nostrils. "If I command it, they will throw themselves into the caldera. Even dragons will burn if we're in there long enough."

"When did you grow so bitter?"

"When the Celts refused to help me rescue you, and I lost both you and our children." She swallowed back an acrid taste coating her throat. "Once I'd lost everything, it was impossible not to be...bitter."

They walked in silence for a long time, winding lower and lower into caves that flowed into one another. The temperature increased incrementally as they moved downward. Nidhogg picked up the pace when they got close to the bottom. Dewi heard rustling and smelled the other dragons before she saw them. She inhaled their scents and recognized each of them.

"At least this explains something," she muttered.

"What?" Nidhogg asked.

"When I needed assistance once you'd been captured, I called upon our own kind first. It didn't take long, since there were only eight dragons left. The four who lived near our cave were impossibly old and feeble. When I tried to locate the four I sense down here—Kra, Berra, Royce, and Vaughna—I couldn't find them. It didn't make sense at the time, but I was so flummoxed about you being gone I couldn't figure it out. It never occurred to me they'd gone AWOL. I assumed they'd been killed." She punched a wall with her foreleg in frustration.

Finally, she rounded the last corner. Huddled in an enormous oblong chamber littered with wildebeest bones were four dragons, one red, one green, one copper, and one black. Nidhogg ground to a halt just inside the final cavern and thundered, "Explain yourselves."

The copper dragon, Kra, rose on his hindquarters, his dark eyes whirling pools. He bowed first to Nidhogg and then to Dewi. "We knew Dewi would come eventually," he began, and steam billowed above his head. "We believed Nidhogg dead until Arawn told us differently earlier today."

"What else did you know?" Dewi asked.

"How angry you would be," Kra replied.

"Then why remain here?" Nidhogg cut in. "I was imprisoned by the dark gods for hundreds of years. If any of you had been available, Dewi might have rescued me far sooner than she did."

Fire belched from Dewi's mouth. She wanted to launch herself at Kra, rip his throat out, but she forced herself to remain by Nidhogg's side. "Answer him," she growled.

Kra focused his gaze on Nidhogg. "Have you been to Asgard since your return?"

Nidhogg shook his head until his scales rattled. "I haven't been to Asgard, or spoken with Odin, since he threatened me."

"Threatened you with what?" Dewi clacked her jaws together. "You never said anything about it."

"Oh but I did, just not directly. He said if I mated with you, he'd hunt us down and kill our young."

Fire roiled from Dewi's belly and burst through her mouth. "That bastard! I'll hunt him down and—"

"Which is exactly why I was vague about the particulars," Nidhogg broke in. "Odin didn't mean it. That man always had a nasty disposition. I figured he'd get over himself if we gave him a wide berth." Steam and smoke rose from his nostrils. "Perrikus captured me about twenty years after Odin threw his temper tantrum."

"Aye." Berra, the red dragon, moved to Kra's side. Dewi recalled they were mated.

"Once you'd been kidnapped"—she shot a meaningful glance at Nidhogg from whirling golden eyes—"Odin came unglued. He rampaged through Asgard and Valhalla and said if *his* dragon was gone, no dragons should survive."

Suddenly Dewi understood, and felt thunderstruck by the revelation. She clacked her jaws together and said, "Since Arawn knew your whereabouts, he must have rounded the four of you up and brought you here." At Kra's nod, Dewi went on, stuttering with fury. "He had no right. He didn't ask my leave, or for my help. It was my job to protect you. Mine." She scraped a taloned foreleg against a nearby limestone formation, reducing it to dust, and then pulverized another.

"At first, Arawn said we wouldn't be here for very long." Royce stepped out of the shadowed section of the cavern, bringing his mate, Vaughna, with him. Royce straightened, and his black scales chittered against one another.

"So much time passed, I feared the god of the dead forgot about us," Vaughna cut in. The green dragon narrowed her copper eyes. "Royce and I left on a reconnaissance after we'd been here a few years. The first person we encountered was one of Odin's spies."

"Crap!" Dewi leaned forward, fearing the worst. "You didn't."

"We had no choice," Vaughna said. "If he'd lived, he'd have reported back to Odin."

"But the covenant forbids us from killing humans who haven't harmed us," Dewi protested, aware how feeble the words sounded. "Never mind. It's not relevant. Why didn't anyone tell me about this? Why didn't Odin harm the other four dragons? The ones living near me."

"They were old," Kra said. "Nearly at the end of their lives. Odin probably didn't think them worth bothering with."

Dewi remembered how feeble they'd been, and how sad and apologetic, when she'd asked for help hunting Nidhogg. They'd even declined egg nanny duty to keep her clutch warm, saying they no longer possessed enough heat. It hadn't been long after that when they'd teleported for the last time, returning to the dragons' border-world to die. They'd been gone when she returned without her mate.

With her clutch gone cold, Dewi had almost returned to the

borderworld herself, intent on self-destruction. No one who had kin left could possibly understand what she'd gone through. She'd never gotten used to being the only dragon. Even joy at discovering Aislinn, a MacLochlainn bonded to her through ancient ritual, hadn't tempered the grief that shrouded her with numbness.

I'd have done away with myself if I weren't such a coward.

"I'm leaving," Nidhogg said.

"What?" Dewi stared at him, incredulous. "Where are you going? Our brood needs you."

He laid his snout alongside hers. "You'll have help caring for them. Bring these dragons back to Fionn's. I'll join you once I've had it out with Odin. He overstepped his bounds when he targeted our kind to get even with Perrikus for kidnapping me."

"You think?" Scorn saturated Dewi's voice. Fury left an ashy residue in her mouth, and she shook herself to contain her anger. An idea took root, and she nuzzled Nidnogg's neck, infusing compulsion into her words. "Kra knows where Fionn's manor house is. They scarcely need me as an escort. Maybe—"

"No." Nidhogg's eyes whirled faster. "You're not coming with me."

"Why not? These four dragons are my subjects. He had no right to terrorize them and force them into hiding for centuries."

"Oh, believe me, he'll hear that." Nidhogg's tone dripped menace. "And more. This is between Odin and me. Technically, I'm his subject, but I won't be after we get done."

Berra stepped in front of Dewi and bowed low. "My humble apologies for not letting you know we yet lived. I thought you'd show up here, and we could tell you then. Except you never did."

I can't very well tell them I avoided our world because it would have made it too easy to take the coward's way out of my pain...

"Apology accepted," Dewi grunted through stiff lips.

Vaughna lumbered to Berra's side, her coppery eyes aglow. "We'd love to see your younglings. Because things on Earth were so uncertain, we didn't think it wise to create new dragons if they were just going to end up sport for Odin and his Viking horde."

"We could remedy that." Kra strode behind his mate, caught her eye, and winked lewdly.

Dewi smirked in spite of her ire. Men. No matter what race, they were all the same, with sex-saturated brains.

Nidhogg backed away from her. The air shimmered and thickened, smelling of a newly lit fire, as Dewi felt him summon teleport magic.

"Be careful," she said.

"He can't kill me," Nidhogg said. "I'm one of the gods." He skinned dark scales back from his teeth and smiled with all the warmth of a scimitar. The air around him took on a glittery aspect, and he whisked out of sight.

Dewi looked at the other dragons. It was impossible to be angry with them. "Bet you're ready to leave," she said.

"More than ready," Royce concurred.

"Rather than return to your caves in Norway, why not move into the ones near mine in Inishowen? That way we can support one another. Odin isn't our primary foe."

"What do you mean?" Kra blew a gout of flame.

Dewi shook her head. Apparently Arawn hadn't been any more forthcoming with this group than he'd been with her. "We have much to catch up on. Let's teleport out of here. We can talk once we're at Fionn MacCumhaill's. You do remember where he lives?"

"Of course." Kra's tone was prickly. "My long stay here hasn't addled my mind."

Dewi ignored his barbed comment. "How about the rest of you? Do you know where we're going?"

"The northern tip of Inishown, not far from the sea," Royce rumbled.

"Near enough. You'll sense my energy once you get close. See you there." Dewi gathered power, reaching deep into the magic that thrummed through the dragons' world. No point wasting her own magic when she had a ready source near to hand. What had taken the better part of a day to fly to, took only a few moments to cover using a teleport spell.

She burst through the veil separating her world from Earth right atop Fionn's manor house, spread her wings, and floated to the ground in one of the many courtyards. It was morning, but still dark since the sun didn't rise much before nine during the cold months. Before she landed, she trumpeted a command to her young to join her.

It wasn't her brood, but Aislinn who stomped out of the house to greet her. "Finally!" Aislinn grunted, sounding very out of sorts. Her long, flame-colored hair hung in tangles to her waist, and fury blasted from her golden eyes.

"My younglings! Are they—?"

"They're fine," Aislinn interrupted. "Everything isn't about you."

Dewi blew out a frustrated breath, tinged with flames. "Are you going to tell me what happened, or are we going to joust with one another? Four other dragons will be here soon, and—"

"You told me there weren't any more."

"I didn't think there were. I have a bone to pick with Arawn about that."

"Fucking Celts," Aislinn snarled.

Dewi snorted. "Och, so you're beginning to see them in that light too?"

"Don't forget you're one of them." Aislinn screwed up her face as if she'd bitten into a rotten lemon.

"Child." Dewi folded her forelegs across her scaled chest. "We can spar, or you can tell me what happened."

Rune bounded from the shadows around Fionn's manor house and planted himself in front of Dewi. Bella flew through the air and landed on the dragon's shoulder.

"They took Fionn," the raven shrieked.

Trepidation gripped Dewi and sent icy tentacles winding around her spine. "Who?" she demanded and twisted her head to look at Bella.

"Harpies," Rune answered.

"This just gets thicker and thicker," Dewi muttered. "Why? What would they want with him?" She sent a penetrating glance Aislinn's way. "What did Gwydion say? Or Bran?"

"It's terribly convenient, but neither of them knows shit," Aislinn said.

"Damn it! I haven't laid eyes on a Harpy since the fifteen hundreds. Which ones showed up?"

"Why does it matter?" Aislinn asked sullenly.

"You have to find him," Bella quorked. "We must leave now."

Dewi sought the bird's mind with her own and sent soothing magic her way. "We can't go anywhere until we know where to look." Dewi switched her attention to Aislinn. "It matters if Celaeno was one of them."

"She was." Angst and frustration streamed from Aislinn, forming a bubbling mass of energy around her. "Why did you ask?"

"Momma! Momma's back!" All seven younglings picked up the chant, streaming from a side door in the manor house. Dewi bent and opened her forelegs. The baby dragons pushed, bit, and shot fire at one another as they fought for a choice spot next to their mother.

"You didn't answer me," Aislinn shrieked. "While we're at it, where's Nidhogg?"

Dewi straightened with dragons clinging to her body. "Celaeno is the dark one. She's the brains behind the Harpies and by far the most dangerous. Did they tell you why they needed Fionn?"

Aislinn spat on the ground. "Somehow they think if he's out of the way, the war with the dark gods will vanish. What a crock! If Celaeno's their mastermind, she's not a very smart one. A bigger problem, though, is Aello. She fancies Fionn back in her bed."

Breath whistled through Dewi's teeth. "I'd forgotten about that. I don't believe he spent very long with her—"

"I don't give a flying fuck if he spent a hundred years with her." Aislinn picked up a handy rock and threw it so hard it shattered against the manor house wall. "I don't want him with her now."

Wing beats sounded, loud against the still of the new day, and Aislinn and the wolf gazed skyward. The other dragons floated to the ground and formed a rough circle around them. Hackles raised the length of Rune's back and he growled.

"They're friends," Dewi said to reassure the wolf. Clearly he was reacting to Aislinn's ill temper.

"How could they be?" Rune demanded. "You told us there weren't any other dragons."

Kra inclined his head at Rune. "I greet you, bond wolf. My name is Kra. The red dragon is my mate, Berra. The green is Vaughna, and the black, Royce."

"Where did you come from?" Rune persisted.

"They were on the dragons' borderworld," Dewi said. "Nidhogg and I found them when we went there to bury our daughter."

"Yes, but what were they doing there?" Aislinn asked. "And why didn't you know about them?"

"We were hiding from Odin, so he wouldn't kill us after Nidhogg was kidnapped," Kra answered.

"Great! That clears things right up," Aislinn muttered.

"We want to hear about our sister," the black youngling spoke up.

"Yes, you must tell us of her ending," a red youngster said. "She was brave, and we must sing of her courage so we will never forget her."

Tears pricked behind Dewi's eyes. So much to do, it was difficult to determine what needed to happen first. Aislinn clearly expected her to drop everything and go in search of Fionn. The four adult dragons needed to be brought up to speed, and she wouldn't rest easy until Nidhogg returned. Goddess only knew how long he'd be closeted with Odin. On top of everything, her brood was well within their rights to want to hear about their sister's final moments.

Bran, Gwydion, and Arawn marched out of the gloom.

"When did you get back?" Aislinn extended her arm toward Arawn.

"Just now."

"All right." Dewi blew a fiery breath and pointed at Bran. "You tell these dragons everything about the Lemurians and the dark gods." She narrowed her eyes at the master enchanter and considered blasting him with flame for not treating more equitably with Aislinn earlier. "Sit with Aislinn," she told Gwydion. "Tell her what you know about the Harpies, and work out a plan to get Fionn back."

"Somehow I believe I know what ye have in store for me." The god of the dead straightened and pushed his dark hair behind his shoulders. He'd exchanged his dark robes for battle leathers, which clung to his lithe frame.

You have no idea. "Get on my back," Dewi commanded. "You and I need to talk."

"I'm leaving," Bella cawed. "I know when I'm not wanted." The raven spread her wings and floated to Rune's back.

Arawn pulled magic and vaulted across the space between them, landing neatly between Dewi's shoulders. "Ready when ye are, madam dragon."

"Humph. MacLochlainn!" Dewi focused her gaze on Aislinn. "Take care of my brood until I return. Berra and Vaughna will help you."

CHAPTER 5

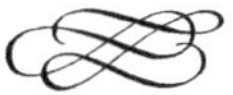

"What the hell?" Aislinn sputtered. "She sounded like an army general."

"Ye havena seen that side of her afore. Or at least not much of it," Gwydion noted dryly.

"I've seen her act like a high-handed bitch," Aislinn countered, "but not like just now. This was different. She was cold as ice."

"She's angry because Arawn hid the other dragons from her," Bran said.

"Do you know why?" Aislinn asked.

Bran made a sound midway between a snort and a grunt. "Aye, lassie. She canna keep secrets, that one."

Aislinn rolled her eyes. It was true that Dewi was an irrepressible gossip. Secrets weren't even a remote part of her makeup. Her thoughts boomeranged back to Fionn. "I don't need to know why Odin was so angry that Arawn felt the need to hide the dragons. We have to get Fionn back."

"The dragon's orders make sense," Bran said. "I'll catch this group up." He spun and trotted a few feet away. "Gather round," he gestured at the four newly-arrived dragons with both hands, "this willna take all that long."

"We're dragons. We would hear what you have to say too," the black youngling, clearly the brood's alpha, announced in his clear, ringing voice.

"I dinna say ye couldna be a part of this." Bran smiled, and it turned his solemn face into a thing of rare beauty.

Aislinn looked away, missing Fionn so much her insides cracked into a million jagged shards of misery.

She gazed into Gwydion's clear, blue eyes, so like Fionn's it was uncanny. "Help me get him back."

"I will, lass. Ye were so overwrought earlier, ye wouldna listen to reason."

Rune trotted close with Bella on his back, and Aislinn placed a hand atop his head. He felt good next to her, warm, solid, and comforting. "I was too listening, but mostly you didn't have any answers."

Gwydion drew her into the shadows of the manor house and dropped onto a stone bench. He patted the place next to him. Aislinn sat and Rune curled at her feet with the raven still clinging to him. Once she'd settled, Gwydion said, "No one's seen the Harpies since the early fifteen hundreds. They retreated to the Strophades Islands in the Aegean. Rumor had it the Eumenides joined them."

Aislinn drew her brows together. "Aren't those the Furies?"

"Aye, 'tis their Greek name, but all the deities and monsters had both Greek and Roman names. It dinna mean there were two of them, merely that different people saw the same creatures and named them according to their own language and customs."

"So all those mythological beings are real?" She thinned her lips and pressed them together.

"I'm surprised by such a question from you, lass." Gwydion sent a sharp glance her way. "If Fionn and I are real, why wouldna everything else be as well?"

"Crap! I have no idea. Living in the States my whole life, things like that never came up."

"Mayhap not *things like that.*" Understated cynicism ran beneath his words. "Merely Lemurians and dark gods."

Aislinn looked askance at him. "Don't forget their filthy minions like the Bal'ta." She shuddered as she thought about the apelike men that had nearly been her demise on more than one occasion. She sucked in a tense breath and spread her hands in front of her. "Okay. I get it. Every fucking nightmare I ever had is real. How do we get Fionn back?"

"Ye werena listening."

"Don't lecture me, goddammit!" She clenched her jaw muscles in frustration.

"I told you the Harpies live on islands in the Aegean. Unless my information is incorrect, that would be where they took Fionn."

She surged to her feet and pulled magic so quickly it made her nauseous.

Gwydion was by her side in an instant. He laid a hand on her arm and chanted a single word that cut the power filling her. "Ye canna run off half-cocked, lass. They'll kill you."

She jerked her arm away. "I've been in rough spots before. Rune and I will figure it out."

"And me," Bella cawed. "You're not leaving without me."

Gwydion blew air through his mouth in a whistling hiss. "Waiting isna your style, but Fionn would have my balls if I let you throw your life away."

"If you have a better idea"—Aislinn sheathed her power and rocked back on the balls of her feet—"let's hear it."

"Better, lassie." The master enchanter sent an appraising glance her way. "We wait for Dewi and Nidhogg to return. I suspect Nidhogg is having it out with Odin, and Dewi is flaying the skin from Arawn's bones, but neither should take long."

"Once everyone is back, then what?"

"Back up a step. What exactly did the Harpies say?"

"Something about not liking their peace disturbed and that they saw Fionn as some sort of epicenter. If they could remove him from the action, their lives would improve. They didn't seem to get that the dark gods were key players."

"Mmph. That might be good news—if they're telling the truth, and all they want is to be left alone."

"Good news how?" Aislinn stared at him. None of this seemed like *good news* to her.

"If we can provide peace, they'll side with us. If the dark gods promise the same, they'll side with them. They never were verra intelligent, but then none of the Infernal ones were, except perhaps Medusa and Tantalus."

Aislinn snapped her fingers under Gwydion's nose. "Focus. I don't need a history lesson."

"Aye, but ye do. Ye'll be much better equipped if ye understand your adversary."

She walked in a tight circle and returned to face Gwydion, hands on her hips. "I'm leaving to find him. Now. You can deal with all the rest of who fucked whom over without me."

"That wouldna be verra smart."

A wheedling tone entered his voice; she recognized a mild compulsion spell and threw a ward around herself.

"You will not force me," she ground out, "to do anything."

Bran closed from behind her. "I'm done with my part of Dewi's assignment." He jerked his chin back toward the dragons where the adults had hunkered in the thick grass to play with Dewi's brood.

Aislinn glanced at the riot of scale colors and heard the adults crooning to the younglings in the dragons' tongue. A place deep inside her cracked open. If she hadn't been so insufferably stubborn, she wouldn't have lost Fionn's child. Her empty womb mocked her. Maybe being alone was her destiny—until she was killed battling the dark.

"I've been listening with half an ear," Bran went on. "Gwydion is correct. Ye must wait until we are all reassembled. 'Tis possible Nidhogg or Dewi will know far more about the Harpies than we do. Nidhogg in particular, since he is truly ancient."

"Dewi doesn't know anything," Aislinn muttered. "I already asked."

"Ye willna like to hear this," Gwydion's voice was soothing and she recognized more magic, "but if Aello wants Fionn for herself, he'll be safe enough."

Aislinn doubled up a fist, but Gwydion caught her arm before she could swing at him.

"I told you, ye wouldna like it, but it means Fionn's life isna in any immediate danger."

"Fucking great," she spat. "You won't let me leave, and now you just told me that conniving bitch has her sights set on Fionn."

"Ye knew that afore he said aught," Bran pointed out. "The Harpy told you." He shrugged pragmatically. "Not only are they not particularly intelligent, they never were good with subterfuge."

Rune bolted upright, displacing the raven who cawed her displeasure and flew to a nearby window ledge. "Lemurians," the wolf snarled, and hackles rose along his spine.

Aislinn sent magic thrumming outward and felt like the worst kind of fool. While she'd been arguing like a thwarted ten-year-old, a Lemurian horde had gathered outside Fionn's gates. "Can they fight?" She pointed at the dragons.

"I surely hope so," Bran said.

"What are their names if I need their attention?"

"The black one is Royce and the copper one is Kra," Bran said. "They're males. Their mates are Vaughna, who's green, and Berra, who's red."

Kra trumpeted, and Berra herded the young dragons through a side door into the manor house. Once they disappeared, she spun, clearly intent on taking up a post to defend the entrance.

Rune growled and skinned back his lips, showing his fangs. The muscles in his haunches bunched, but Aislinn knelt next to him. "Not yet," she said. "We need a coordinated approach." Broadcasting her mind voice, she called Corin, Daniel, Eve, and Timothy. *Organize your people. Come to the front of the manor house. We're under attack!*

"Exactly what I was trying to get across about Fionn," Gwydion muttered. "A coordinated approach where we doona fragment our efforts."

"I don't need a sermon." Aislinn speared him with her unwavering gaze. "You're the damned warrior magician. Come on. Craft a battle plan. Now. They're almost upon us."

Humans poured out of the house and from the manor's many outbuildings. Grim-faced and determined, they formed groups according to their gifts. Cronin, Daniel, Eve, and Timothy marched to Aislinn.

"I sense Old Ones," Timothy snarled. At Aislinn's nod, he made a sour face. "Bastards."

"Tell us where we can do the most good," Eve said. Tabitha flanked her, lips etched into a growl. Magic bubbled around the humans, creating interlocking wards.

"At least there're no dark gods." Bran spat into the dirt. "Or they've done a stellar job of cloaking their presence."

"What about Fionn's wards around the manor?" Aislinn demanded. "Won't they protect us?"

"If enough Lemurians gather forces, probably not." Gwydion's voice held a harsh edge. He grabbed his staff, carved with runes, and spread his arms. Power eddied around him, and his face became stern. A loud cracking noise pounded against her ears. Aislinn squared her shoulders and moved to face the cataclysm pressing against the magic she'd shielded herself with.

"Kra! Royce! Vaughna!" Gwydion cried. "Full power. Doona hold back. Berra. Make certain no one enters the house."

"I'll help with that," Bella squawked. "I'm small enough to fit inside, and I can alert you if I need help."

"While ye're at it, make certain the brood stays in one place, probably the kitchen." Gwydion reached a hand skyward as if to stroke the raven who perched ten feet above his head and called, "Thank you."

"Don't mention it." Bella disappeared through an open window.

Gwydion narrowed his eyes and focused on Cronin, Daniel, Eve, and Timothy. "Will you follow my direction?"

"Aye," Daniel said. "I speak for Seekers."

After exchanging glances, the other three nodded, but Aislinn sensed their reluctance. The Celts had hung them out to dry here in the U.K. No wonder they'd be suspicious and uncertain about taking orders from one.

Gwydion drove his staff into the dirt; it crackled with blue-white light. "Hunters and Healers attack from the left. Mages and Seekers, take the right flank. Kra, Royce, and Vaughna will strike from the air. Arawn, Bran, and I will harry them from the front. Fight well."

"What about me?" Aislinn asked.

Gwydion glanced at her. "Stay near me, lass."

She snorted. "Rune and I will go where we can do the most good."

The master enchanter opened his mouth to argue, but closed it a moment before Aislinn felt thick, sticky magic roll over her warding. Everyone fanned out to discharge Gwydion's orders.

Her eyes widened. Lemurians streamed toward them. There must've been fifty or sixty, and they weren't bothering with illusion, probably to conserve their power. They looked like what they were: seven foot tall reptiles who walked upright on their hind legs. Their scaled hides were gray-green, and their whirling eyes reminded her of the dragons'. When she'd gotten sucked into working for them— because her only alternative was death—they'd looked like very tall humanoids with masses of thick, golden hair. They'd always swathed their bodies in robes and favored heavy silver and gold jewelry, but their eyes had never changed.

She loosed power and watched it bounce off the nearest Lemurian. *Not going to work.* Aislinn switched to mind speech. *"Last time I fought these things, their warding was only in front. Rune and I will sneak around behind them."*

Power bubbled from Gwydion and Bran, and they funneled it into the thick of the Lemurians, but didn't have any better luck than she'd had. The dragons shot fire at their enemy, but the Lemurians were just as impervious to flame as the dragons. For one wild moment, Aislinn wondered if they'd had some long-ago common ancestor.

"Lass!" Gwydion's mind voice was terse. *"Call Dewi back here. I've tried to reach both her and Arawn, but neither are answering. Mayhap your MacLochlainn bond will serve us better."*

"Once I've done that, cover me."

"Agreed, but only if ye agree not to tell Fionn I allowed you to march into the lion's den."

Aislinn felt for the threads that bound her to the dragon and plucked them. "Get your ass back here now. We're under attack."

She hunkered next to Rune. *"Remember how we took them in the corridors beneath Castle Trim?"* One sharp nod told her he did. *"We're going around to the back of their lines. I'll do my best to shield our presence with magic, but once we've killed the first one, they'll be onto us."*

"I'm ready."

Her throat thickened. Rune was so loyal it smote her. He'd follow her into certain death because not fighting by her side was incomprehensible to him. Aislinn gave him a quick hug, sprang upright, and wove magic into a shield to mask their power and render them invisible. The battle raged around her, and the air thickened with smoke, dragons' fire, and the coppery, metallic stench of blood. The humans stood tall, fighting courageously. Even after everything, they hadn't lost their pluck. Proud to be a part of her kind, she targeted a pair of Lemurians and sprinted to what she hoped would be a decent vantage point.

DEWI DIDN'T BOTHER MAKING her landing elegant. So what if it rattled Arawn's bones? She took them across the Irish Sea to a crumbling castle in Scotland and snarled, "Get off me."

"As madam dragon wishes." Power flashed and the god of the dead ended up standing in front of her with his arms crossed over his chest. In contrast to his mild words, his dark eyes glinted dangerously.

"Explain yourself." Fire streamed from her mouth, and she didn't take care to divert it. Arawn rolled his eyes and warded himself.

"I could have done so back in Inishowen," Arawn said. "This side trip was entirely unnecessary."

"Your opinion. Not mine." More fire; a small wooden building went up like a torch. "I'm waiting."

"Ye canna keep secrets," Arawn said. "'Tis that simple. Plus, ye were in a fine muddle once Nidhogg disappeared and ye lost your clutch. Half mad as I recall. It wasna the time to tell you Odin targeted your dragons to even the score because Nidhogg was gone."

"I would have confronted that slimy poor-excuse-for-a-god and burned him to a cinder. That ridiculous Valhalla of his too."

Arawn nodded. "I rest my case. 'Twas precisely why we decided to remain silent."

"We?" Dewi's temper escalated another notch.

"Aye. Bran, Gwydion, and myself."

"Of course," she growled. "The dynamic threesome. Why didn't you include Fionn?"

"He was closer to you than the rest of us after Nidhogg was taken. We worried he'd soften and tell you." Arawn hesitated. "Ye've forgotten how distraught ye were."

Oh no, I haven't. More fire spewed from her mouth as she regarded the god of the dead.

Arawn uncrossed his arms and let them swing free. "Look at the bright side—" he began.

"What bright side?" Fire splashed off Arawn's ward, leaving dark, singed places.

"Ye have four living dragons who would likely have been maimed or dead if I hadna intervened."

Anger burned so hot, she almost couldn't contain it. "You think I was incapable of protecting them?" she demanded.

"Of course not. If ye'd set your mind to it. Ye've already said ye'd have gone to Asgard and called Odin out. Between him and his Valkyries and Vikings, ye'd scarcely have emerged unscathed." Arawn shook his head. "Even if ye lived through that confrontation, Odin would have targeted you too. He left you out of his original plans out of deference for you being one of the Celtic gods."

"And you know this how?"

"The information network used to be much more accurate before men filled the air with electromagnetic radiation. Odin figured if he left you and the geriatric dragons near you alone, he might escape notice killing the other four. Actually," Arawn furled his brows, "ye should thank me."

"Because you hid the presence of my subjects from me and allowed me to go half-crazy with believing myself the last of my kind?"

"Nay, because I ferreted out Odin's plot in time to subvert it."

Dewi stomped around what was left of the castle's side yard. "Were you ever going to tell me?"

"Och aye. And verra soon. Once Nidhogg was safely returned to us, I figured he could take on Odin, plus we needed Kra and the others for the battles to come. The more dragons, the better our chances of prevailing. 'Twas why the miracle Nidhogg crafted by dousing your eggs with dragon's fire and resurrecting half the clutch was so welcome."

"Mmph." Smoke streamed from her nostrils, but Dewi's temper, always quick to kindle, was settling.

"I am not the enemy, Dewi. Ye waste valuable energy. We must locate Fionn. I wasna back long, but long enough for the others to tell me he'd been snatched by Harpies."

"Get your ass back here now. We're under attack," reverberated in Dewi's head.

Aislinn.

A chilling clearness wiped the last of Dewi's fury aside. "Get on my back."

"Where are we going now?" Arawn inquired caustically.

"Oh, shut up. I've forgiven you."

"Ye could have fooled me."

"Aislinn just told me they're under attack. We're teleporting back there."

"Why dinna ye say so?" Arawn materialized between her shoulder blades. "Doona put us down right in the courtyard—"

"I don't need your instructions." Dewi summoned teleport magic. "Just make certain nothing happens to my MacLochlainn once we return. Or any of my children."

CHAPTER 6

*N*idhogg wished he had more time to select his words, but the golden walls of Asgard rose around him while his mind still seethed. He took advantage of the few extra moments before he landed to clear the fury scouring his nerves. Rationality was the key to dealing with Odin. If Nidhogg let his emotions loose and allowed the fire in his belly to blaze from his mouth, he'd have been better served to stay with Dewi and the other dragons. He spread his wings and settled onto the cobblestoned courtyard. Valhalla, the warriors' hall, lay off to one side. Lesser buildings peppered the well-kept grounds. Nothing had changed in the hundreds of years since he'd stormed out of the Norse stronghold.

Startled Vikings stared at him, and one ran into Valhalla as if Hellhounds chased him. The vast structure's lower levels held the dead, but contrary to popular mythology, Odin, Thor, Freya, and other living Norse gods and Vikings utilized the castle's upper floors. Nidhogg saw the sense in it. Why waste all that golden glory on the dead? He settled his wings across his back, not expecting much of a wait.

Odin emerged from the castle as if he'd been shot from a cannon and pelted down stone stairs. As always, he wore battle armor with twin brass drinking horns slung across his burly chest. Blond braids fell down his back and he smiled through his thick, red-blond beard. He extended both hands when he got close to Nidhogg, and exclaimed, "You're back! How did you escape? Damn my eyes, but it's glad I am to see you again."

"Unfortunately, the feeling isn't mutual."

The smile on Odin's broad face faded, and he narrowed his blue eyes. "After all this time, you still haven't forgiven me?"

"I might have," Nidhogg measured his words, "except you piled more sins atop your original one."

"I've rethought my position about Dewi—" Odin began.

Nidhogg held up a foreleg. "It scarcely matters. I didn't need your approval when I mated with her, and I don't need it now. You knew the dark gods took me, but you didn't lift a finger to try to help."

"Och, lad. I was still angry about Dewi."

"What about the four dragons you planned to kill?"

Odin's gaze skittered sideways. "Plans aren't deeds. How did you find out about that? It's very old news."

"Arawn discovered it and took steps to protect them."

"All right." Odin took a step back, drank from one of his horns, and crossed arms thick with muscle over his chest. "You sought me out for a reason. What is it?"

"Two reasons, actually. Dewi and I have younglings. One will become the next Norse dragon, but for that to happen, I need your word you will leave Dewi and me in peace. Earth is under siege. Nothing is certain."

"What do you mean under siege?" Odin lowered his blond brows into a thick line that cut across his forehead.

Nidhogg clanked his jaws together. "I don't have time to explain, but I'm guessing you haven't left here in ages."

"You'd be right. The world's become a damned depressing place. No one believes in the gods anymore."

"The ones who stopped paying homage to you are mostly dead."

Nidhogg's voice could have etched glass. "So you needn't worry about them any further."

Shock registered on Odin's sharp-boned face. "What killed them?"

"The six dark gods invaded Earth three years ago."

Odin thinned his lips into a hard line. "I wondered when those bastards would surface again. Pah! I imprisoned all six of them here in Asgard for millennia, but they escaped. It took almost a thousand years after that, but the Celts helped and we corralled them on the borderworlds."

Nidhogg knew the tale. Thor had been even drunker than usual one night and had freed the dark gods by mistake. Saddled with guilt, he'd been the one to spearhead finally purging them from Earth. Nidhogg considered jibing Odin about still whitewashing his son's role in that fiasco, even after all this time. Instead, he muttered, "Lemurians weakened the gates between the worlds."

"Those pesky reptiles?" Odin shook his head in disbelief. "They never created mischief before. As I recall, they were so relieved to have a retreat point once Mu imploded, they disappeared into that city of theirs beneath Mount Shasta and didn't bother a soul."

"Yes, well, they were dying and needed an infusion of power." Nidhogg blew steam from his mouth. "I must leave. If you wished to gather a group of warriors and venture forth, I'm certain we could use your firepower."

"You said two reasons." Odin flashed a grim smile. "What was the other one?"

"I want your guarantee, bound by your blood, that you will never plot to destroy another dragon."

"If I refuse?"

"I will hunt you until you're closeted with the dead beneath Valhalla." Nidhogg paused. "And there will never be another Norse dragon." He gazed at the crowd that had gathered around them and raised his voice. "I recognize many of you. I flew to war with the Valkyries, and played with your children. Dragons are an integral part of Norse tradition, but I will not be hunted, nor treated with anything less than absolute respect."

He returned his attention to Odin. "This is a onetime offer. I would have your answer."

Odin drew a blade from a leather scabbard that hung by his side. He held a hand in front of him and made a deep cut in the ball of his thumb. Once his blood flowed, he turned his hand so it dripped onto the stones beneath his feet. "Dragons will always have safe passage in Asgard. I give you my word, I will never harm one, nor plot to do so. Nor will I interfere in dragon affairs."

Nidhogg bent and placed a foreleg beneath Odin's extended hand. Once blood dripped onto his talons, he brought them to his mouth and licked them. The dragon straightened and gazed right at the Norse god. "A blood bond forfeits your freedom if you break it. I shall hold you to your word."

"Somehow I don't doubt you will."

Ready to be gone from Asgard, Nidhogg summoned teleport magic. As his spell bubbled around him, he narrowed his eyes. "We really could use your help."

"I shall gather my elite warrior group. Once we're on your side of the barrier that keeps Asgard hidden, I'll let you know."

"Do that." Nidhogg set his spell in motion and the shining city of Asgard dropped away. By the time he heard the unmistakable din of battle raging around him, it was too late to alter course, so he constructed a ward and took in a scene from Hell playing out beneath him.

Lemurians.

Nidhogg did a quick count and came up with close to eighty. Where had all of them come from? Odin had been correct when he'd called them *pesky reptiles*. Who would have guessed they'd turn into deadly enemies?

Dewi and Kra managed the left flank from the air, while Royce and Vaughna held the right. The Celts were evenly spaced throughout the field, with magic blazing from their outstretched hands. Humans added firepower from both flanks; their faces held a gritty determination, and they fought with skill and fortitude. Maybe the Celts had been wrong to discount them as not worth bothering with.

"You're back!" Dewi screeched into his mind and flew toward him.

The other dragons joined her. Just as well. They were much more effective adversaries when they tag-teamed their aerial efforts. Fire spewed from Nidhogg—and bounced off the Lemurians' scaled hides.

"Save your power." Kra flew abreast of him.

"My children?" Nidhogg asked.

"Safe within Fionn's manor house." Dewi took up a position on his other side. "Berra and Bella are guarding them."

Magic flashed bright white at the far side of the field. Nidhogg stared at the spot as Aislinn and Rune leaped on two Lemurians, taking them from behind. Rune sank his teeth into a Lemurian's neck and was obliterated in a geyser of red and green blood. Aislinn had a harder time. The Lemurian she'd targeted threw her off its back. She rolled to her feet, her teeth bared in fury.

"Come and get me, you son of a bitch."

Half a dozen Lemurians closed around Aislinn forming a circle.

"Shit!" Dewi cried. She banked and flew right above the group where she rained fire on their heads, taking care to avoid Aislinn and the wolf.

Rune circled the group, slicing through Achilles' tendons with his teeth. As Nidhogg watched, he understood the Old Ones' warding only covered their fronts. Fire still wouldn't hurt them, but magic could.

"We'll keep the rest of them busy," Kra said. "Maybe if we kill a few, they'll leave. My memory is they aren't particularly brave."

"Thank you." Nidhogg latched onto the fury he'd wanted to loose at Odin and flew to Dewi's side.

"Land. If we launch killing magic from behind them, it should do the trick," Nidhogg instructed.

"Our angle is better from up here." Fire blasted from Dewi's mouth.

"They're vulnerable from behind. Not fire, woman. Magic."

"Got it." Dewi plonked heavily to the ground not far from Aislinn and screamed her fury.

Aislinn drew the short dirk she always wore in a sheath hanging around her waist. She drove it forward, but it bounced off the Lemurians' warding. Nidhogg felt when the warding around Aislinn first developed cracks and then fissures. Humans tried to batter their way past the circle of Lemurians to help her, but couldn't get through.

Nidnogg landed next to Dewi. "We've got to get her out of there."

"Can we help?" Daniel asked. His round, fair face was streaked with blood and soot, and he was panting.

"It's better if you stay back," Nidhogg said. "That way Dewi and I won't have to worry about hitting one of you by mistake."

Dewi pounded magic into the nearest Lemurian. He shrieked as scales and skin boiled from his bones. Before he was even close to done dying, Dewi snatched his body aside, and waded into the circle.

"Get on my back," she shouted at Aislinn.

Aislinn dropped her warding and catapulted atop Dewi. Rune kept racing around the outside of the circle doing as much damage as he could. The Lemurians didn't seem to understand he'd hobbled them by biting through tendons and ligaments until they tried to move and couldn't.

"I'm taking her out of here," Dewi called to Nidhogg.

"The hell you are, "Aislinn snarled. "I'm fighting. If you won't fight with me, I'll jump right back down."

"You stubborn little twit," Dewi cried. A jolt of Lemurian power hit her in the flank and she screeched in outrage.

"Pay attention and fight," Aislinn cried. "Take us around to the back where my magic can penetrate."

Grumbling, Dewi backed out of the circle, spewing fire as she went and adding smoke. The air grew so thick, Nidhogg shut his inner eyelid. They needed an organized approach. Why the hell hadn't Gwydion come up with an attack plan?

Nidhogg screamed, "Fall back. Meet in back of the house." Just to make certain everyone heard him, he followed the command with the same one in mind speech.

"What are you doing?" Aislinn shrieked at Dewi.

"Following orders," the dragon said. "'Tis something you don't do terribly well. Nidhogg is right. We need a strategy. For that, we must be in the same place. Otherwise, we'll be here a week from now still fighting these bastards." She spread her wings and flew fifty feet above the manor house yard.

"Protect Rune," Aislinn said, her voice shrill. "We just left him alone down there."

"Fuck!" Dewi wheeled until she was over the wolf. Power exploded and a snapping, snarling Rune dropped into Aislinn's lap.

"I had no idea you could do that," Aislinn said, struggling to contain the freaked-out wolf.

"I have a lot of other tricks up my sleeve you haven't seen, either, Missy. Don't forget it. See to your wolf, he's tearing holes in my back."

"This won't take long." Nidhogg shouted across the air between them.

Moments later, the five dragons and three Celts ducked behind the bulk of the manor house. Humans trickled in, joining them.

Rune still hadn't calmed much. He vaulted off the dragon's back the second she touched down. It was tough to understand him between snarls and growls, but he faced off with Dewi and said, "Never again. Do not do that to me ever again. Do you understand?"

Aislinn picked her way to the ground and wrapped her arms around her wolf. "It was just magic," she protested. "I asked her to save you."

"I didn't need saving. And that magic felt like a red hot poker from my shoulders to my ass. I'll be lucky if my balls don't fall off."

"Ingrate," Dewi muttered.

"You're making it worse." Nidhogg shot a pointed glance at his mate."

"Enough." Gwydion faced the group. "If Nidhogg wouldn't have ordered a retreat, I was verra close to it."

"Where are they?" Aislinn glanced over her shoulder. "Why didn't the Lemurians follow us?"

"They're communing, plotting their next move too." Bran pinched his lips into a sour expression. "That hive mind deal they have going isna verra efficient."

Aislinn let go of Rune and strode to Corin and Daniel, nodding solemnly. "Thank you so much for helping. Losses?"

"Not too bad." Corin dragged a hand down her face, leaving a grimy streak. "Three dead and two injured. None of the bond animals were hurt."

"Excellent." Aislinn hugged her.

After a surprised moment where she stood stiff and still, the other woman hugged her back.

Watching the exchange, Nidhogg nodded to himself. Perhaps Aislinn held the key to mitigating the hatred that flared from the humans' eyes every time they looked at a Celt. Rather than viewing her as a turncoat because she'd mated with Fionn, they might come to view her as a symbol of possibilities…

He turned his mind to their current dilemma and said, "The only way to take the Lemurians out is one by one. Problem is there are more of them than us, so some of us need to keep them busy while the rest of us pick them off."

"That will take too long," Gwydion countered. "We've been at this for an hour, and Dewi only killed one of them."

"I killed one and then another, and then one more, and disabled a bunch," Rune said.

"My cat and some of the other bond animals saw what Rune was doing," Eve said, "but it's damnably hard to get close enough to those bastards to damage them." She eyed Rune appraisingly. "You have steel balls, wolf."

He skinned his lips back in a snarl. "If I have any left."

Arawn bent and patted his head. "Too bad we all canna simply bite their ankles, laddie."

Rune growled. "Do not patronize me."

"Sorry. I dinna mean to."

"Listen up!" Gwydion sounded hard-pressed. "This may not work, but I say we focus the unmaking spell on a group of them. It should blow through their wards and smear them to kingdom come."

Bran eyed him as if he'd lost his mind. "If it works. That was what we were tampering with when ye and I ended up on Perrikus's borderworld—trapped."

"'Twas the strange energy in that house," Gwydion grunted. "It sat on psychic fault lines and perverted my magic."

"Quick tutorial," Timothy barked. "Is that the one where you mix mostly fire with a bit of earth and stoke air in once it's percolating?"

Gwydion jutted his chin upward. "Aye. 'Tis the air part that's tricky. If ye add it too fast, the whole thing can blow up in your face."

Aislinn bolted upright and trotted to where she could see around the corner of Fionn's house. Rune stuck to her like a dark, furred shadow.

"Holiday's over," she called. "They'll be on us before I can count to three. Son of a bitch," she muttered and Nidhogg felt her summon power and anchor herself within in.

"Are you with me?" Gwydion asked.

"We'd be fools to quit now," Corin said.

"Who do we target?" Royce asked.

"The first bunch that shows their nasty, reptilian snouts." Arawn's voice held a flat, dead tone. "I tire of this." He raised his voice in a chant, and Gwydion and Bran joined in.

It took a moment before Nidhogg recognized both the language and the incantation. It was Enochian, a perversion of Celtic mixed with Hebrew, but the combination held massive amounts of power. He added his magic to the mix, as did Dewi. The humans picked up the chant and magic jumped to their command.

Kra took to the air with Dewi, Royce, and Vaughna. The four engaged in an aerial ballet, dive-bombing the Lemurians to divert them from what the Celts were cooking up. Nidhogg was impressed. The dragons other than Dewi may have been absent, but they'd maintained their intuitive edge during their lengthy exile. Power blasted from the Lemurians. So much power, it shocked Nidhogg. They hadn't been this strong just a few moments before.

Truth chewed a hole in the back of his mind. "Hurry," he urged. "One of the dark ones must be close."

Gwydion focused his gaze on the dragon, blue eyes pulsing with tension, and nodded, but never stopped chanting. The air developed a shimmery hue, and cracks formed in the damp earth as power oozed upward. Between them, Gwydion, Bran, and Arawn shaped the energy as it rose to their call. When it became an amorphous, pulsing mass, they heaved it at the nearest group of six Lemurians.

Nidhogg held his breath. Would it bounce off, just like his fire had done? For a long, wrenching moment, nothing happened, and then audible cracks, piercing as gunshots, rose in a rapid tattoo that pounded his sensitive hearing. As if it were sentient, the mass pressed forward, coating each Lemurian once its warding dissipated.

The timber and pitch of the Celts' and humans' chanting escalated. All of them were shouting, and sweat streaked their faces, creating runnels in the soot and grime that smeared across their flesh. Their muscles bunched into hard knots as if they fought a physical foe. The Lemurians were slow to respond, but then they always had been. It was probably why their race was dying out. Just before the first one exploded in a shower of red and greenish blood, sinew, bones, and bits of grit, its kin recognized their doom and tried to run, but the unmaking spell had them in its grip and they couldn't get away.

One by one, the six lead Lemurians shattered, splattering everything within reach with gore. Rune and the other bond animals were in their element, lapping up blood and guts. Nidhogg would have smiled, were their situation not so tenuous.

"Do it again," Gwydion shouted. "Borrow power from the Earth if you need to."

Breath hissed through Aislinn's teeth. "At this rate, it will take days to knock off these sorry sons of bitches. Can't we hurry it up?"

"Ye should thank the goddess we found something that works," Arawn panted.

The threatening sensation that had bothered Nidhogg earlier rose to the fore. He smelled the dark god before he saw him and stepped forward, fire flashing from his mouth. "Perrikus, you old dog. I know you're here. Come to gloat? Oh, wait a minute. I'm not under your dastardly thumb anymore."

Looking as fresh as if he'd just stepped off a New York runway, the dark god sauntered around the corner of Fionn's manner house. Auburn hair swirled around him, falling in waves to his waist, and his golden skin glowed. He turned sparkling green eyes Aislinn's way and reached for her, but she jumped aside.

Rune launched himself at the dark god, but before he got within three feet, Perrikus waved a lazy hand, and the wolf's arcing jump ended with him falling hard into the dirt.

Aislinn thrust herself between her wolf and the dark god. "Leave him alone."

"Just as feisty—and desirable—as ever, I see." The dark god licked his chiseled lips. He turned his nose upward, scenting the air. "What? Your Celt boyfriend doesn't seem to be here. Excellent." He rubbed his hands together. "What he doesn't know won't hurt him, eh?"

Aislinn turned away, but Nidhogg caught the scent of her arousal. The dark gods were sex incarnate. No one could withstand their pull.

Dewi landed and pushed to Aislinn's side. "She is bound to me as well, scum-sucker. You'll have to go through me to get to her."

"Us too." Timothy and Daniel flanked Aislinn.

"Och, you're easy," Perrikus said to Dewi. "All I have to do is dredge up Slototh's Minotaur to keep you occupied."

"Dewi," Nidhogg bellowed. "You didn't."

"Later," she shot back. "Next time you think I'm dead for a few hundred years, let's see how long you stay faithful."

"That's hardly the point—" he sputtered, puffing fire-laced smoke as fury roared through him. Dewi was his. *His.* No other creature had a right to touch her.

"It's exactly the point," she countered, spinning to face him. "I thought you were dead. *Dead.* You hear me? What? Was I supposed to live out my next few thousand years in celibacy?"

"Stop it!" Aislinn shrieked. "This is how they win. By turning us against one another."

"She has a point." Dewi tossed her head, fire streaming from her mouth. She skewered Nidhogg with her dark gaze. "If you must dissect this, I say we do it later."

Nidhogg turned away, recognizing wisdom in his mate's words. But a small, wounded place burned deep inside him. Maybe they'd hash it out. Maybe they wouldn't. Balanced against what they faced, its importance dwindled. He spewed fire at Perrikus, recognizing it as displacement for his anger and hurt.

The dark god screwed up his impossibly handsome face and laughed, sidestepping the flames with the grace of a dancer.

CHAPTER 7

*A*islinn shrank away from Perrikus, hoping to lose herself among the Celts and humans. Her breath caught in her throat, and her body was primed for sex, nipples achingly hard and pussy awash in liquid heat. Damn the dark gods to Hell. They all had that effect, at least on her. As if they'd cast her in a porn flick where all she could think about was spreading her legs for the first man to show up with an erection.

"Steady." Timothy spoke low into her ear."

She forced deep, even breaths, but it didn't help. An arm latched around her shoulders from behind and she shoved it away, hissing and spitting like a scalded cat, before she realized it wasn't Perrikus.

Bran's touch was cool, measured. He came around to the front and leveled his copper gaze at her. "Doona fash, lassie. But I fear the plot thickens."

Dewi glowered at Perrikus, and blasted him with fire, but it crackled against his warding and sloughed off. "Mind your own affairs," she ground out. "Too bad I didn't injure you worse when I had the chance."

He tilted his chin with a jaunty smile. "I'll give you points for boldness, dragon. I never would have suspected you'd pull your mate out of my prison." Perrikus waved a hand. "At first, I was more cautious, but when centuries passed, I assumed—"

"Got lazy, more like," Nidhogg broke in. He blasted the dark god with fire too, which spoke to his level of frustration, since he had to know it wouldn't do any good.

Aislinn closed her teeth over her lower lip until she tasted blood. Pain had a salutary effect. It couldn't have been easy for Nidhogg to hear about Dewi's dalliance with the Minotaur. Aislinn winced; she'd been stuck inside Dewi's body during that particular fall from grace, and the murky kinkiness of it still gave her nightmares.

Rune slunk to her side, still growling and she asked, "Are you all right? Did the fall hurt you?"

"My pride. What I wouldn't give to sink my teeth into that bastard."

"I heard that," Perrikus called and danced from side to side in a macabre parody of a prizefighter. "Come and get me, wolf. I could use a bit of sport."

Aislinn lunged for Rune's neck and held him back. "He's baiting you."

"But..." The wolf whined a protest.

"No." Aislinn's conscience smote her. Rune was bonded to her, so he couldn't challenge a direct command. She didn't play that card often because it was so inequitable. Rune snapped his jaws millimeters from her face, and she realized he hadn't forgiven her for the last time she'd pulled rank.

Gwydion, Bran, and Arawn advanced until they formed a line between Dewi and Perrikus. "You want something," Gwydion growled. "What is it?"

Perrikus smiled and was transformed into such a profanely beautiful creature that his golden skin actually glowed as if illuminated from within. Aislinn took a few steps toward him before she understood she was caught in thrall and forced herself to halt. The dark god had noticed, though, and leered knowingly at her from in between the Celts and Dewi's bulk.

Damn him!

Much as D'Chel had done on one of the borderworlds, Perrikus latched his gaze onto hers and ramped up the sexual energy pulsing from him until an orgasm coursed through her, leaving her legs weak and shaky.

"Go in the house." Gwydion's voice rang with command, but Aislinn ignored what was probably a prudent suggestion.

"I'm stronger than that," she panted.

"Like hell, ye are," the master enchanter said.

Pain shot up her leg. When she looked down, Rune's jaws were around her calf. She sank a hand into his thick neck ruff and said, "Thank you." The wolf didn't answer, just bit harder. He'd done the same thing before to keep her mind clear enough to reason.

"I asked you a question." Gwydion stared at Perrikus. "If ye're not planning to answer it, we may as well get back to wiping out your Lemurian sacrificial sheep."

"Hush," Perrikus said in a stage whisper and grinned engagingly. "Once they find out, the gig will be up."

His supercilious attitude blasted past Aislinn's cautions, and she wrenched her leg out of Rune's jaws and scurried forward. "They know. They're not stupid. It's just that they think differently than we do, and they were desperate. Only the truly hopeless would hook up with the likes of you."

"You're defending them?" Perrikus's cultured tones rang with incredulity. "They would have killed you."

"So would you," she countered and crossed her arms over her chest. Lust shivered through her body, and she shook herself all over. "Stop that."

"But you're so desirable. D'Chel and I have created some particularly rich fantasies with you as the star."

"I'll just bet you have," she ground out, surprised her back teeth didn't crack from pressure.

"Enough," Gwydion huffed and cut through the air with his hand.

"I've dealt with you longer than I want to. You want something. Either spit it out or move aside."

"Fair enough." Perrikus shook hair behind his broad shoulders. Rather than his usual translucent robes, he was garbed in battle leathers, much like Bran and Arawn. The beige skins clung to him, outlining every nuance of his magnificent build.

Aislinn felt her gaze being drawn downward and was unable to interrupt its trajectory until Rune clamped his teeth onto her calf again. Thank fucking Christ he timed his bite before she laid eyes on a cock she remembered all too well.

"Hurry this up." Arawn rolled his eyes. "Even the dead in my kingdom move quicker than you."

"It's simple, really." Perrikus spread his hands in front of him as if he were at the head of a boardroom table in an upscale business preparing to present closing arguments. "Give me the girl, and I'll take my reptiles and leave you in peace. I'll even see that the Harpies let Fionn go."

Aislinn lurched forward, intent on scratching out Perrikus's dancing, green eyes. Gwydion caught one of her arms and Bran the other. "But he's behind the Harpies snatching Fionn," she shrieked, so furious the pull of the dark god's sexuality shrank to nothing. "He just said so."

"Get yourself together." Gwydion spoke into her mind. *"Now."*

"At least that explains why Harpies showed up after all this time," Dewi spoke up. "Let me guess. You rousted them, promised them a taste of your body, and they jumped to do your bidding."

"Close." Perrikus licked his well-shaped lips and rearranged his body until each muscle stood out beneath his leather clothing. "D'Chel and I entertained them. It was a bit odd and extremely... unconventional, but we're good at pleasing women, no matter what species they happen to be."

"And did ye promise them peace?" Arawn inquired.

"Of course." Perrikus's smile widened.

Aislinn closed her hands into fists and forced a rationality she was far from feeling. "If I go with you, you'll free Fionn?" she asked, barely recognizing the strained voice that issued forth as her own.

"Silence," Dewi shouted. "You'll do no such thing."

"No kidding." Timothy spat into the dirt. He and Daniel moved close and poured power into her to augment her own.

"It makes sense," Aislinn argued, frantic to get Fionn away from the Harpy with the seductive silver eyes who had such fond memories of him in her bed. "Once Fionn is back, you can rescue me. I've held my own against that one"—she smirked and flicked her fingers at Perrikus—"and against D'Chel too. Don't forget, I'm the one who took Slototh out of the game."

"Hear that?" Perrikus extended both hands her way. "She will come with me willingly. You all heard her."

"She dinna say she would." Arawn's voice cracked like a whip. "She merely inquired further regarding the terms of the bargain ye propose."

Aislinn swallowed. It was a fine point, but an important one. Once she gave her word, no one—neither Celt nor dragon—could save her.

"Come, beautiful one." Perrikus beckoned and drove lust her way until the only thing filling her mind was the outline of his cock straining beneath its leather covering. "I've dropped my wards just for you."

If Gwydion and Bran hadn't been holding her, Aislinn would have walked right into Perrikus's arms. Her magic, even augmented with Daniel's and Timothy's, wasn't strong enough to resist the dark god's pull. The rational part of her brain shut down; all she could think about was opening her legs to the magnificence jutting from between his thighs. Wing beats rustled. They interrupted her concentration on the vision of masculine perfection standing twenty feet away, so she didn't pay much attention.

"What the fuck?" Perrikus shouted.

The tractor beam that had her in its sights shattered. With her mind her own again, Aislinn watched Perrikus batting at something.

Bella.

The bird had come out of nowhere and drove her sharp beak into everything vital she could reach. So far, blood streaked down the dark god's neck and from an eye socket. Aislinn panted, her mouth dry and bitter as ashes. Perrikus had almost had her and it hadn't taken any effort at all. None. He'd snapped his fingers, and she'd made cow eyes at him and been willing to do anything he wanted.

Goddammit. I am not that weak.

Or maybe I am. Even the thought about how wonderful it would be to toss her freedom on the slag heap for Fionn had been planted.

By Perrikus.

Dewi jumped into the breach before Perrikus could ward himself again and scorched him with fire. Nidhogg joined suit. The air around the dark god developed a fiery hue.

"Hurry," Aislinn screamed. "He's making a portal to leave."

The words had no sooner rolled off her lips, when the space where he'd been standing held nothing but smoky air.

"You can let go of me now." She jerked free of the Celts and humans and stomped to where she could see the Lemurians. They milled about, rudderless, and she blew out a disgusted breath. Without leadership, it would take time for the reptilian hive mind to figure out what to do next.

"Strike," she called over one shoulder. "There will never be a better time." Rune would follow her. So would Bella with her bloody beak, who clearly felt quite full of herself. Without waiting to see if she'd have further backup, Aislinn raised her hands, called power, and loped toward the nearest Lemurian. He exploded into bits, which told her everything she needed to know. Perrikus had been somewhere behind the scenes, masterminding everything including the Lemurians' shielding.

Above her, dragon wings cut through the air. Fire and magic gushed from Nidhogg, Dewi, and the other three, mowing through Lemurians as if they welcomed immolation. Humans fanned into the field, wielding death as power streamed from them. Aislinn embraced the pure, cold fury pouring through her. It cleansed her of the taint left from Perrikus and his sick, mesmerizing sexuality. She picked Lemurians randomly, pretended each was Metae, the Lemurian magelord who'd conscripted her into the Lemurian ranks. She'd fought for them for two years, believing they were on the same side, allied against the dark. Discovering the Old Ones had been in league with the dark gods the whole time still rankled, as did the knowledge she'd been used.

I sold myself to them in exchange for my life. Bitterness pooled in her gut, and she killed another Lemurian. The air around her became charged with a surfeit of magic. It thickened until she struggled to breathe.

"They're leaving," Rune said.

"Smart of them," Bella cawed from her perch on what was left of a dead body.

They can't leave. I'm not done. Fury, disgust, and disbelief at how close she'd come to giving in, shook Aislinn to her core. The air cleared, and she stood in the midst of stacks of smoking, stinking corpses. Arawn trotted to her side.

"Into the house with ye, lass. A good bath and some mead are in order."

Aislinn turned away, ashamed. "I don't deserve anything. You don't know how—"

"Aye, but I do." He hooked a hand beneath her arm. "Ye and the animals will come inside now." Gwydion joined them, exchanging glances with the god of the dead.

"Make certain the humans have whatever help they need." She met Gwydion's troubled gaze.

"Aye, lass. They fought bravely and helped control the unmaking spell we cast. Ye have my word. We shall honor their dead and see they have whatever healing and assistance they need. Into the house." He repeated Arawn's command.

Aislinn recognized compulsion beneath his words, but she was too heartsick and weary to fight it.

∿

Fionn rested his back against a withered pine tree about fifty yards from the water on a white sand beach. Aello sat cross-legged, facing him. Her bare breasts, milk-white with strawberry nipples, gleamed in sunlight, and her blond hair had been brushed until it gleamed with coppery highlights. He reached for his power for the umpteenth time, but it skittered just beyond his reach. Jaw clenched, he fought desire that clawed at him. Aello's scent, musky with sandalwood undernotes, wafted through the air, making things that much worse. Scents carried memories, and hers was so unique, he'd never forgotten it.

"You want me," she purred. "Even if the front of your pants wasn't belled out like a kite, I smell your lust."

"Wanting and acting on it are two different things," he growled. "Besides, ye're forcing my hand with magic, yet ye stripped me of my own so I canna protect myself. I love another, and I willna break my vows to her."

"What vows? You never married her."

"Vows I made with my heart and soul."

Aello whistled long and low. "Principles. Since when have you ever bothered with them? I recall when you fucked anything female that twitched her twat your way." She cupped her breasts in her hands and twirled the nipples into peaks. "We had a lot of fun, you and me. I'm hurt you forgot about me. Except you didn't, not really."

Fionn glanced away. Watching her touch herself did dangerous things to his cock, which had been hard ever since she'd plunked them on this remote stretch of beach and bombarded him with magic designed to break him down and lure him into her bed. He assumed they were on one of the Strophades Islands, but wasn't certain since he couldn't use his magic to check.

"Be reasonable," he sputtered. "Aye, we had a bit of fun, but 'tis been hundreds of years. Surely ye've found others to satisfy your fancy."

"Aye," she aped his brogue, "but none like you." She rose slowly, balancing on her bird hindquarters, spread her wings, and fluttered to his side, not stopping until she was pressed full length against him. Her breasts flattened against his chest, and she ran her tongue down his neck.

He curled his hands into fists hard enough for his nails to cut into his palms. He wanted to punch her, but restrained himself. If he injured Aello, the others would flay him alive. Even if they weren't here now, they'd find him and make his life—and probably Aislinn's—hell.

"I'm having a hard time believing you pined after me all this time and finally hunted me down." Fionn pushed her away from him and squatted, still with his back against the tree. Maybe his bent knees would provide a barrier to keep her away from his crotch. His heart thudded against his ribs, and his cock was on fire. "Even without power at my disposal, I sense something deeper afoot."

"Do you now?" Her silver eyes gleamed conspiratorially, and he remembered she was almost as hopeless in the gossip department as Dewi.

The air off to the side of them took on an incandescent shine, and Celaeno stepped through a faint portal, accompanied by Ocypete. Between them, they dragged Aello toward the gateway. "What?" she sputtered, and folded her wings more firmly across her back.

"Come with us," Celaeno said. "Your pet isn't going anywhere." She shot a saccharine smile at Fionn, who kept a poker face. For a moment, it looked as if Aello would argue, but then she joined her sisters without a backward glance.

Breath hissed through Fionn's clenched teeth once he realized he was alone. He pushed upright and arranged his cock so it wasn't bent double, straining against his pants. Simply having her gone was enough to take the edge off his unnatural sexual hunger. It had taken an enormous amount of self-discipline to not sweep her into his arms and bury himself inside her. Half a snort blew past his lips. He remembered her all right. Some of the weirdest, most inventive sex of his long life had been with the Harpy. Her unusual anatomy had been responsible for part of it, but the larger share had come from her insatiable nature. Usually, he could outlast any woman, but she'd hounded him until he begged for a respite, for mercy.

He pushed himself into a lope and traveled down the beach, meaning to go as far as he could. As he ran, his mind cleared. It hadn't been coincidence the other Harpies showed up the second he'd begun grilling Aello for information. Surely they must know as well as he did how incapable she was of holding secrets.

There's something they doona wish me to find out.

Another thought surfaced. The Aello he remembered would have fought her sisters tooth and nail if they'd ordered her away from something she wanted. That she left with nary a protest spoke volumes. She'd been toying with him, but why? To what end?

Frustrated, he quickened his pace and tried to reach his power again. If he had even a small amount, he could teleport out of here. This time, without Aello sitting watchdog over him, he got closer to his segregated magic. Maybe if he focused with everything he had...

Fionn headed for a thick grove of olive trees atop a nearby hill. Olive trees were sacred. They'd help concentrate his efforts. In the depths of his being, he suspected Aello and her sisters were part of a plot to separate him from Aislinn. If that were true, the only ones who could be behind it were the dark gods. They'd wanted Aislinn forever because of her magical strength and planned to use her as a broodmare.

Impotent rage hammered him, and his gut twisted into a burning hornet's nest. If something happened to Aislinn because he wasn't there to protect her...

Have a spot of faith. Gwydion, Bran and Arawn will care for her. Dewi and Nidhogg too, right along with Rune. She has plenty of guardians.

Aye, but she's a stubborn lassie. She may well give them the slip and try to come after me, which might spell disaster. She doesna understand how vulnerable she is alone.

Fionn shut his eyes for a moment. His thoughts—accurate and dead on the money—sliced right through him and made his heart ache with worry. Aislinn was just as likely to run headlong into danger as she was to heed it. Once she got her Irish dander up, she stopped thinking. She'd told him she operated that way because if she thought too hard, or too deep, it would immobilize her.

"The next time I see Aello," he muttered, "unless I get verra lucky and escape, I'll ask after Perrikus, D'Chel, and Adva. She willna have to say a thing. I'll see truth reflected in her eyes."

CHAPTER 8

*A*islinn let herself float in the deep bathtub in Fionn's suite of rooms on the third floor of the manor house. She'd fallen on her face and slept for a few hours first. It hadn't been enough because her head ached and her eyes were stinging and gritty, but worry about Fionn drove her from their bed. She'd filled the tub nearly to the top, and then summoned magic to warm the water, a trick she learned from Fionn.

Rune curled on the cream-colored Italian marble floor near the door, and Bella perched on the sink, cleaning blood from her dark feathers.

"You were very brave," Rune told the bird.

Bella preened beneath his praise. "Anyone would have done the same thing," she said. "After all, he dropped his warding."

"Anyone whose bond human hadn't ordered them not to approach him," Rune snarled.

"Oh for Christ's sake," Aislinn sputtered. "I'm sorry already. Give it a rest."

Rune stood and padded to the edge of the tub. "What do we do next?"

Good question. "I have no idea what everyone else's priorities will be, but I'm going after Fionn." She pulled the drain plug and got to her feet with water sluicing down her body. Climbing the two steps at the end of the sunken tub, she snatched a towel and wrapped it around herself. Before her wolf could make another snarky comment, she eyed him. "You're coming with me. Bella too, if she wants."

"Of course, I want." The bird clacked her beak shut. "Fionn is my bonded one."

Aislinn wrapped her head in another towel, chucked the damp one she'd used to dry off over a rack, and strode into the bedroom where she rummaged through a dresser she'd claimed for her things. Nothing was clean, but she dragged on dark, serviceable pants, a black wool shirt, and a heavy, plaid, woolen jacket. The towel slipped off her wet hair, so she picked it up off the floor and tossed it over a chair. Aislinn glanced at her boots and groaned. Each one was split up one side, but they were all she had. If she couldn't come up with replacements, and damned soon, she'd be effectively barefoot. Not good for fighting.

Before she finished donning thick, woolen socks and lacing her boots, a heavy fist landed on the other side of her door. She sent magic outward and recognized Gwydion's energy. Rune trotted to the door and nudged the deadbolt with his nose until it snicked open.

"Thanks, laddie." Gwydion, garbed in a dark blue robe sashed with red, ambled into her room.

"I suppose I should thank you for knocking"—Aislinn narrowed her eyes—"but I'm not going to."

"There's food made in the kitchen." He mock bowed. "Consider this your personal invitation to breakfast."

"Awesome, since I missed dinner. And yesterday's lunch, now that I think about it." She laid a hand over her concave belly and realized she was starving. Finished with her boots, she got to her feet. "You saved me the time to find you. Once I've eaten, I'm going after Fionn." Aislinn tipped her chin defiantly, daring him to contradict her.

"Oh ye are, are ye?" One corner of Gwydion's mouth twisted into half a wry smile. "Were ye planning to check in with one of us first?"

Aislinn rolled her eyes. "Of course. I'm not that foolhardy." She walked past Gwydion into the hall and toward a staircase, figuring he and the animals would follow. It took time to wend her way down to the main floor of Fionn's manor house and through the great room furnished with wall hangings, Oriental rugs, paintings, and sculptures that museums would have fought over. At first, she'd been overawed by the richness and delicacy of crystal figurines and fine metal carvings. Today, she scarcely glanced at anything. Without Fionn, none of it was worth squat.

Another staircase at the far side of the great room led down into the kitchens. Fionn only used the large central room and pantry, but smaller rooms like the buttery lined both sides of it. She supposed it helped that he'd lived in a time without electricity and other modern contrivances because it made it easier to revert to using magic to cook.

"Where are the baby dragons?" she asked and wandered over to the stove to see what was in a large pot. Oatmeal plus nuts and dried fruit. She scooped a generous serving of the gelatinous mixture into a bowl, squirted honey over it, and made her way to the table.

"Outside with Dewi and Nidhogg and the other four adults," Bran replied.

"Och, lassie, and ye missed a hell of a fight." Arawn snorted.

"Let me guess," Aislinn said between bites. "Dewi and Nidhogg had it out over the Minotaur."

"I thought he was going to kill her." Gwydion shook his head and helped himself to the cereal mixture.

"Yeah. I heard some of it before I fell asleep, mostly Dewi bellowing for me to attend her, but I decided it would be a bad idea. I like Nidhogg, and if I'd shown up, I'd have been caught dead in the middle."

"Wise lass." Arawn nodded approvingly. "Would ye like coffee or tea?"

"Coffee's my first choice."

The god of the dead rose and poured fragrant, dark liquid from a silver carafe, placing the cup in front of her.

"Thanks." Aislinn smiled. "I don't suppose there's any milk."

"Nay, lassie. A cow or goat dinna wander into the yard during the night." Arawn returned to his chair. "Ye're damned lucky there're still coffee beans. One of us will need to teleport to South America before too much longer."

"Are the humans doing all right?" she asked.

Bran nodded. "Most of them are resting. We built pyres for their dead and saw everyone had food in their bellies." A sheepish look danced across his face. "'Tis the least we can do for our new allies."

"They're excellent fighters," Arawn said. "We will make certain to mention that at the next Celtic council gathering."

"I don't suppose an apology is in the cards?" Aislinn stared at the god of the dead.

"Probably not. We can be a stiff-necked bunch, and prejudice is a dicey thing, lass. No one has any control over their past actions." He winked. "Mayhap 'twould be better for all of us to look forward. We willna run out of foes anytime soon."

She recognized wisdom in his words and focused on her breakfast, eating mindlessly. Her spoon hit the bottom of the bowl, and she got up to get a second helping. "Have any of you heard from Fionn?" She kept her words casual, but hope flared hot within her—and died at the expressions on their faces.

"Nay," Gwydion said. "If we'd had word, we wouldna still be here."

It took a moment to sink in, but the meaning behind his words was clear enough. "You'd have left without me?" She slapped her bowl back on the table, surprised it didn't shatter.

"Mayhap." Bran spoke carefully. "Depends on where Fionn was and how hard it would be to extract him."

"So if it was very hard, you'd have left me here?" Aislinn persisted. She wasn't hungry anymore; the oatmeal tasted like glue, but she needed fuel, so she forced more of it down.

"That shouldna surprise you," Arawn said. "Fionn would skin us alive if we took you into danger, and ye dinna make it out alive."

She slugged back half her coffee, blew out a weary breath, and rested her chin on an upraised hand. It didn't make sense to dig deeper. She *was* weaker than them, but their penchant to treat her like a hothouse flower rankled.

"Do you have a plan?" she asked, switching tactics.

"The logical place to start would be the Strophades Islands in the Aegean," Gwydion replied.

"Aye, but it canna be that easy," Bran protested.

"True. Mayhap the dark gods are planning on us staging a rescue and have something unpleasant in store for us once we arrive." Arawn knit his dark brows together.

"Even if they do, that's not a reason not to go," Aislinn said.

"Relax, lass." Bran held out a hand, palm toward her. "No one is suggesting we leave Fionn to find his own way back, although he is more than capable of doing so."

Aislinn stifled a gasp, and a lead weight settled in her heart. "So you're saying if he wanted to return, he'd already be back?" Visions of him doing unspeakably twisted sexual things with the bird-woman pummeled her.

"Nay, I dinna say that at all," Bran shot a discerning glance her way. "Ye doona trust him."

"I do." Her voice wavered, so she cleared her throat and tried again. "I do, but he has…history with that thing."

"'Twas a time when Fionn had *history* with half the lassies in the Old Country." Gwydion arrowed a meaningful glance her way. "If ye canna get past it, mayhap ye'd be better served to pick one of us." A lascivious grin split his face, and his blue eyes glittered mischievously.

Aislinn drained her coffee. "Thanks, but you're still in love with my mother."

"I'm not." Bran leaped to his feet and bowed. "Neither is Arawn."

Rune scuttled out of the corner where he'd settled and pounced on something. A cacophony of squeaks later, he padded to Aislinn's side with a dead mouse in his teeth.

"Nice work," she said and stroked his rough outer coat. "Anytime you want to hire out as the castle cat, just holler."

"Not funny." Because his mouth was busy crunching through rodent bones, he switched to mind speech.

"When are"—she paused for emphasis—*"we* leaving?" Her gaze moved among the Celts.

"As soon as ye're done eating," Gwydion said.

"Oooh, I got lucky and get to come along?" Aislinn bit her lower lip. "Sorry, but if you think I'll grovel and thank you for including me, you're wrong."

"One caveat." Arawn held up a finger. "If we tell you to leave, ye must do so. Immediately and without argument."

Christ! It's like when I order Rune about. No wonder he hates it so much. "Are the dragons coming?"

"Ye're hedging, lass," Gwydion said. "Aye, Dewi and Nidhogg are coming with us."

"I wasn't hedging, not really." She cleaned the last dollop of cereal from her bowl. "Dewi can hide me in her body. She's done it before. So," Aislinn smiled brightly, "how about this? If one of you decides I'm not safe, I'll merge with the dragon."

"Ye dinna like it overmuch when she entertained the Minotaur," Gwydion noted.

"I'm not planning on her fucking anything on that Greek island," Aislinn countered. "Particularly now that Nidhogg is back."

Arawn stood. "Fine. We agree. More or less. Let's get moving. Getting Fionn back is far from the end of our problems."

FIONN'S BODY was soaked in sweat, and his legs shook with effort as he pushed toward his power with everything he had. The Harpies had locked his magic in some sort of dynamic prison. Each time he got tantalizingly close, it scuttled a few feet away.

"Fuck!" he sputtered. "They're wearing me down by inches."

He forced his outraised arms to his sides and took long, slow, deep breaths until his heart rate slowed. Obviously, his current strategy wasn't working. To pursue it further was a waste of valuable time, time when Aislinn might do something ill-advised, tell Gwydion and them to fuck themselves, and take matters into her own hands. He set his jaw in a tense line, teeth gritted together. God, but he loved that woman. If anything happened to her, he'd lay waste to the Harpies, the dark gods, and whoever else harmed his love.

The Celts had never gotten on particularly well with the Greek gods, but Fionn ran a mental catalogue of who might come to his aid if he asked nicely. Better to settle on one of them—as opposed to putting out a general distress call—since they often argued among themselves. After bouncing between Zeus, Hera, and Cronus, he kept returning to Cronus. One of the most ancient, he was Zeus' father. He may have devoured his children and taken control of the universe after killing his own father, Uranus, but Cronus had mellowed over the intervening millennia. He also had a strongly held sense of right and wrong.

Now. He dinna hold any such thing when he did away with his children to maintain a chokehold on his powerbase.

Fionn wasn't certain the god would respond to a direct summons. Perhaps a supplicant approach would buy him more. Though it grated, he sank to his knees and cried, "I call upon Cronus, lord of the world."

Head bowed, Fionn waited. He wasn't ready to give hours to this idea, but he'd wait a few minutes. The earth bucked beneath his knees, and his eyes flew open. Dirt rippled and formed fissures all around him. Fionn bolted upright and hastily climbed into the lower branches of a nearby olive tree. If the very firmament was about to implode, he didn't want to get sucked into Hades. Wind whooshed through the trees, tangling Fionn's hair. He pushed it out of his eyes and wished he'd taken the time to redo his braids.

A conical whirlwind formed a few feet away as dirt, stones, and dust from the open fractures flew toward it. The air was electric with magic. Fionn covered his nose and mouth with his arm and squinted against thickening grit in the air. After ducking to avoid a few good-sized rocks, one thumped him in the temple. Cursing roundly, Fionn reached blindly for power to shield himself—and found it. At first, he froze, not believing the barrier between himself and his magic had dissipated.

"Doona kick a gift horse in the mouth," he muttered and wound threads of magic into a ward. Apparently, whatever natural phenomenon was rearranging the landscape had also unlocked his magic. No matter what was behind it, it wasn't something to complain about. He'd sensed that whatever corralled his power wasn't strong, just wily and good at evading him. Once he'd protected himself, he chanted words to teleport out of this hellhole, but nothing happened.

What the fuck?

He faced the whirlwind, and it stopped spinning. Rocks, grit, and dirt spattered to the ground; Cronus walked from the center of the cyclone. His dark hair was woven with precious gemstones, and he was naked but for a crimson loincloth wrapped around his hips. His bronzed skin glistened as if he'd oiled it. He stared at Fionn, and his mouth opened in astonishment.

"The one who summoned me had no power. What have you done with him?" The god stood tall, and an ever-changing collage floated in his golden eyes.

"'Twas I who called you," Fionn said. "One of your Harpies separated me from my magic and stranded me here."

"But your power is intact," Cronus noted, looking puzzled.

"Aye, a recent development no doubt linked to the disturbance ye created traveling here."

A knowing leer split Cronus' face. With a high forehead, defined cheeks, and a strong, square jaw, he had an imperious presence. "A

Harpy commandeered you, eh? Well now, she must have had good reasons." He narrowed his eyes. "As I recall, you bedded one of them. Was it her?"

"Aye."

Cronus shrugged. "Mayhap she was lonely."

Fionn didn't give a flying fuck, but it didn't seem expedient to say so. "With all due respect, I would leave and return to my home and fellow gods. Earth is hard pressed just now and my absence is sorely felt."

Cronus tossed his head back and laughed. "Always were full of yourself, MacCumhaill. So long as you summoned me, entertain me for a bit."

"Ye're who kept me from launching my teleport spell."

"Great news, Celt! Nothing wrong with your mind. You win the virgin. I'll see if I can't gin one up. That should annoy the hell out of the Harpy." Cronus cackled as if he'd just made the finest of jokes. "What did you mean about Earth being *hard pressed*? Aren't most of the humans dead?"

At least he knows that part. "Lemurians and the six dark gods wish to claim Earth for themselves." Fionn stepped toward Cronus. "Look, mate, I havena the time just now, but I promise I'll return as soon as I can to fill you in."

"You haven't visited me in all these years, why would I believe you would do so now?"

"Because I give you my word. Besides"—Fionn walked closer until he was only about three feet in front of the Greek god and stared into his unsettling eyes—"nothing holds you here. Ye could come with me."

A surprised look washed across Cronus' face, as if he'd never considered hobnobbing with anyone outside the Greek gods' pantheon.

The air to the right of them brightened, and Aello stepped through. Her silver eyes widened in surprise.

"Cronus," she purred, and waddled to his side with her awkward bird gait. "I've missed you."

Fionn felt the blast of sexual heat from where he stood and was intensely grateful it wasn't directed at him. Working on the theory it was better to ask forgiveness than permission, he set a teleport spell in motion, and said, "If 'tis all the same to the both of you, I'll be taking my leave."

This time Cronus didn't interrupt his magic, and neither did Aeollo. The last thing Fionn saw before the island shimmered away to nothingness was the two of them locked in a heated embrace.

Better him than me...

CHAPTER 9

*A*islinn stuffed dried fruit, nuts, and a water bottle into a rucksack. Experience taught her it paid to be prepared, because these field trips frequently took much longer than anyone anticipated. She chewed on her lower lip, worried sick about Fionn. When he hadn't returned quickly, jealousy almost ate her up alive. He was a god, for chrissakes. If he wanted to return, he'd have figured it out. Unless the dark ones had imprisoned him—or he'd succumbed to Aello's milk-white breasts, cascade of blonde hair, and eyes like hammered pewter.

Don't go there.

Why not? According to Gwydion, Fionn fucked half the women in the U.K.

Her vision clouded with fury, and Aislinn slammed a hand down on the kitchen's stone countertop to get herself under control. It wasn't as if she'd been exactly virginal when she met Fionn, but the thought of him bent over another woman, kissing her, fondling her, and murmuring endearments was too much to tolerate. He'd moved to the States in the seventeen hundreds and was capable of English without a trace of a brogue, but he preferred the softened cadence of his native Highlands. At first it had driven her crazy when he switched between dialects, but that was because his brogue reminded her so much of her dead mother.

Tara Lenear was a direct descendent of Irish kings, except she'd never bothered to tell Aislinn anything about it. Along with her royal bloodlines had come linkages to both Dewi and Fionn. Tara hadn't loved Fionn, though. She'd loved Gwydion. To avoid a mess not of her own making, she'd fled Ireland as soon as she turned eighteen and used magic to bury herself in the Southwestern United States. Aislinn supposed her father, Jacob, had also been in the dark about Tara's roots. God knows, they'd never even discussed visiting Tara's Irish kin.

Surely, Dad didn't believe they were all dead...

"Are you coming sometime today?" Dewi's acidic tones blasted through a kitchen window.

"Be right there."

"I thought you were worried about Fionn, but I guess you'd rather while away the morning lost in the past."

"For Christ fucking sakes, stay out of my head." Aislinn tossed her rucksack over her shoulders and stormed up the stairs, across the great room, and out the front door.

Dewi waited at the bottom of the steps, her forelegs crossed over her red-scaled chest. "Humph. Thought that would light a fire under your ass."

Aislinn bit back a sharp retort. Dewi loved to argue and was a classic pot-stirrer. No reason to feed that part of her. She whistled, and Rune raced around a corner of the castle with Bella flying not far behind.

"Where's your brood?" she asked Dewi. Rune fell in next to her, tongue lolling. He and the raven had probably been hunting.

"Nidhogg is settling them with Kra and Berra back in our caves. Vaughna and Royce are standing by as well. Arawn even scared up a few Celts to keep watch until we get back."

Aislinn nodded and scanned the courtyard, which lay empty

beyond her, Dewi, and the two bond animals. "Are Gwydion and the others still coming?"

"Of course."

An exasperated breath blew past her lips. "Gwydion rousted me out of bed. You dragged me out here. I'm ready to leave."

"So am I." Dewi trumpeted loudly, and a dozen humans came running out the front door.

"Are we under attack again?" Daniel scrubbed his hands through his blond hair, looking like he'd just rolled out of bed.

Timothy, Eve, Corin, and the rest had their hands raised to summon magic.

Aislinn shook her head. "Stand down. All of you. Dewi's just cantankerous this morning."

"So what else is new?" Rune mumbled from beside her.

"I heard that, wolf," Dewi blew a tongue of flame his way, and Rune snarled, his hackles rippling to half-mast.

"We'll go back inside," Timothy announced.

"Call us if you need anything," Corin tossed in.

"Thank you." Aislinn watched the humans file back into the manor house, grateful for their support.

Dewi and Rune were trading growls, snarls, and fire. Aislinn opened her mouth to tell them to stop bickering when Gwydion, Arawn, and Bran loped out the front door, weaving their way amid the humans going the other way.

"We're ready," Arawn announced.

All three Celts wore battle leathers, even Gwydion. The buff-colored deer hides hugged their bodies like second skins, leaving virtually nothing to the imagination.

Aislinn gaped at the master enchanter and asked. "What happened to your robe?"

He held his arms out to the sides, the carved staff he was never without clutched in one hand, and twirled in a circle. "Do ye like what ye see lass?"

Aislinn snorted. "Please. If you're going to tell me you changed your wardrobe to seduce me with your Chippendale physique, don't bother."

Arawn nudged Gwydion. "Not sure if that was a compliment or not. Werena the Chippendale dancers gay?"

"Not the point," Gwydion smirked. "They were fine specimens of manhood."

Wing beats sounded and moments later, Nidhogg settled to the ground next to Dewi. He eyed the group with his whirling green gaze. "Sorry. That took longer than I'd anticipated. Our black youngling insisted on coming with me."

"What'd you do?" Aislinn grinned. "Knock him out?" In her experience, the black dragon didn't take no for an answer and pushed every limit in the book.

"Good question." Dewi glanced sidelong at her mate. "What did you do?"

"Made a bunch of unrealistic promises for after I get back." Nidhogg spread his jaws in a smile. "Isn't that what all parents do?"

Gwydion stepped forward, flanked by the other two Celts. "We need to get moving."

"No shit," Aislinn muttered under her breath. The air about twenty feet away took on a shimmery aspect and she felt the zing of magic, electric against her skin. Her gut tightened in anticipation of another wave of Lemurians, who'd had plenty of time to regroup. Rune stiffened where he leaned against her leg and growled louder.

Gwydion's eyes widened just before a broad smile wreathed his face. "Och aye, and 'tis one time procrastination worked in our favor." He strode toward the pulsating, multi-hued air and Aislinn relaxed. Surely he wouldn't be so cavalier if the magic belonged to the dark gods or Old Ones.

Arawn and Bran trotted after Gwydion. "He needs help," Bran noted tersely and power boiled around him, adding to the unsettled air.

"Whoever are they talking about?" Rune asked.

"Fionn, you dolt," Bella cawed. "He's trying to get back to us. Something must have siphoned off his power."

Aislinn's feet moved of their own accord as soon as Bella squawked Fionn's name. Shoving between Gwydion and Arawn, she rallied her own magic and threaded it in with Bran's, as she figured out how to enhance his summoning spell.

The god of prophecy turned to her and nodded approvingly. "Ye're good at this, lass."

"Comes from working with Fionn," she said through clenched teeth, her body vibrating with the effort of maximizing her magic. "What's wrong? It's almost as bad as when he barricaded himself in the *Dreaming* and I couldn't get to him."

"I doona think there is a problem," Bran countered. "Other than Fionn's magic having been thoroughly drained."

A portal formed in the air, glowing blue around its edges, and Fionn stepped through, shaking his unbound hair behind his shoulders. "No problem, lass. None at all." He strode forward and swept her into his arms.

She clasped him to her, barely believing he was back, and buried her face in the crook between his neck and shoulder, breathing him in. Her heart pounded against her ribcage, and her eyes sheened with unshed tears.

He smoothed a hand down her hair and spoke into her mind. *"Och, mo croi, ye're a sight for sore eyes. I was so worried the dark gods or Lemurians would attack."* He pushed her toward the house, still tangled in her arms.

"Hold up there." Gwydion grabbed Fionn's arm. "Afore ye disappear into your bedchamber with the lass, we want to hear what happened."

Fionn sputtered, but Aislinn let go of him, stepped away, and murmured, "We all want to know, so you may as well tell it once, rather than twenty times."

Fionn shut his eyes for a moment and took in a breath, blowing it out slowly. Dark smudges rode beneath his eyes, and lines that hadn't been there before carved into the sides of his mouth. When he opened his eyes, he scanned the group with his astute, blue gaze that didn't miss much, and frowned when he noticed Aislinn's rucksack.

"Ye were coming with them to find me?" he asked, his voice carefully devoid of inflection.

Aislinn knew what was coming. She squared her shoulders and studied him through narrowed eyes. "Of course. Is that a problem?"

Instead of answering her, Fionn stomped to Dewi and Nidhogg and demanded, "What were you thinking? You too." He raked Gwydion, Bran, and Arawn with a scathing glance.

"Why wouldn't they take me?" Heartily sick of being protected, Aislinn didn't move from where she stood.

"Mayhap because the Harpies kill humans who set foot on their island? Or worse, steal their souls, enslaving them." Fionn's harsh tones could have etched metal.

Gwydion scrubbed a hand down his face. "Och, and I'd forgotten that last part."

Fionn crossed his arms over his chest. "And did all of you forget about how predatory the Harpies are?"

"Not sure I ever knew." Nidhogg blew steam.

"Get over yourself," Dewi huffed at Fionn. "No harm was done. Even if you hadn't shown up, the five of us are more than a match for three Harpies."

"I do a fair job protecting myself," Aislinn cut in. Pain slashed and she looked down to find Rune's jaws around her calf.

Oops. Holy crap! Everyone's a prima donna today.

She dropped a hand onto the wolf's head. "Rune's damned good at protecting me too."

He let go of her then, and glanced up with his amber eyes. "Thank you, mistress, for remembering I exist."

"For Christ's sake!" She slammed a fist into her open palm, spun, and bolted across the greenway toward the moat. Life had been a whole lot simpler before Rune, Dewi, and Fionn. No one had any expectations of her then—

Except the Lemurians, once they suckered me into working for them.

Her pace quickened until she was running across the heath as fast as she could. The gates to Fionn's manor house flashed past. Something red flew above her and she realized Dewi was tracking her. "I'm not yours, either," she shouted.

"Ah, but you are," the dragon replied.

Footsteps pounded behind her. She didn't have to turn around to know it was Fionn. His energy was unmistakable. "Don't touch me," she screeched as he pulled alongside her.

"And why ever not?" he demanded, not sounding the least bit out of breath.

Aislinn ground to a halt. She'd nearly made it to the rocky beach fronting the sea. When she spun to face Fionn, it was all she could do not to gnash her teeth in exasperation. "We've had this conversation maybe twenty times. You have to stop trying to protect me." She gathered a measured breath. "It hurts my feelings that you don't trust I'm capable of taking care of myself. How the hell do you think I got through the three years after the Lemurians took over before I met you? It wasn't by being incompetent."

He extended a placating hand. "Now, lassie."

She shook her head. "Don't *lassie* me. How about American English?"

"All right," he said, with perfect diction, and dropped his hand to his side. His face twisted into something bitter. "I thought you'd be glad to see me, obviously I was wrong."

She ignored his barb. "What happened between you and that Harpy? You know, the Aello one you fucked before."

"Is that it?" He knit his brows together. "You're jealous?"

"Why the hell wouldn't I be?" She closed her teeth over her lower lip, chewing in consternation. "I know you didn't go there of your own free will, but you were gone for a long time. Why didn't you come right back?"

"I couldn't. Something separated me from my magic."

Aislinn blew out a breath and realized Dewi hovered above them, listening. She cast her gaze skyward. "Go away."

"What's the Maclochlainn's business is my business," Dewi informed her archly.

"Bullshit!" Fionn said. "You just want grist for the gossip mill. Go back to the house, Dewi. Please."

"Humph. No gratitude."

"I'm grateful to you for lots of things," Aislinn said, "but you wouldn't want Fionn and me listening in on one of your private conversations with Nidhogg."

Steam plumed from the dragon's mouth, but she turned and flapped her way back toward Fionn's home. Aislinn clasped her hands behind her back. "All this makes me tired. Cut to the chase, Fionn. How'd your magic suddenly reappear so you could find your way back here?"

"You noticed how weak it was—" he began.

She tilted her chin. "Not what I asked."

"All right. Aello left me by myself, and I tried and tried to reach my power, but couldn't. Since I needed help, I petitioned Cronus, one of the Greek gods—"

"I know who he is," she interrupted. "Just tell me what happened."

Fionn blew out an exasperated sounding breath. "I'm trying to, but you're not making this easy."

She unclasped her hands, drew them to the front, and made a beckoning gesture. When he took a step toward her, she shook her head. "Talk first."

"Fine." He nodded sharply, clearly hanging onto his own temper by a thread. "Cronus showed up in a cyclone that created such a psychic disturbance it severed whatever chokehold the Harpies had placed on my magic."

"Before that, did anything happen between you and that Harpy?" Aislinn held her breath. She didn't really want to know, but had to ask the question.

"No."

She tilted her head to one side, trying to mine for inflection beneath that one word. "Did you want to?" she persisted.

"For Christ's sake, Aislinn." Breath whistled from between his teeth. "Do you want to fuck the dark gods when they spray you with their libido fountain and flash their hard-ons?" She opened her mouth, but he waved her to silence. "Of course you do, but you don't act on it. That's the dividing line, whether we act on it, not whether someone gets our juices flowing."

Aislinn winced; he had a point. And a damned good one. She'd come within an angstrom of giving in to the dark gods, even knowing sex with them would freeze her from the inside out. Never mind the times she'd come when they flicked their knowing gazes her way, or masturbated in front of her. As if Fionn had been inside her mind—and he probably had—he walked to her side and gathered her into his arms. After a moment when she stiffened, she allowed herself to relax into his embrace. He ran his hands down her back, kneading tense muscles, before resting them on her ass and snugging her against his body where his cock stiffened between them.

Rune and Bella emerged from behind a nearby clump of gorse bushes. "Since they're going to make up," the raven quorked, "we may as well go hunting."

Aislinn turned her head to stare at her wolf and asked, "You were there all along, eavesdropping?" Rune batted his eyes at her and she snorted. "You're as bad as Dewi."

Fur flew as he shook himself. "I'm much stealthier and not nearly as likely to gossip."

She grinned. "Truer words were never spoken. Stay closer to the manor house than this while you're hunting."

"We will," Bella cawed, and the pair turned to leave.

"Does this mean ye've forgiven me, leannán?" Fionn's Gaelic inflection was back. Worried blue eyes sought hers.

"Since you didn't do anything wrong, I'm not sure *forgiveness* is part of the equation," she murmured.

"Och, I may not have sinned with the Harpy, but I admit I was flummoxed—and furious—when I understood the others were going to bring you to the Harpies' island."

"You can't keep me in a box."

"I know that, lassie." He tightened his hold on her butt. "Can we make up?"

He wriggled against her, and heat began in her belly, desire that spread until breath clotted in her throat.

She recognized a spell laced into his touch and giggled. "Wow! You must really want me if you're using a love charm."

"More than life itself," he murmured and tilted his head until his mouth rested over hers.

Aislinn squirmed from under him. "Before we get lost in each other, I have a piece of good news."

"And what might that be?" Heat from his blue eyes impaled her until she almost forgot how to talk.

"Dragons," she finally managed. "There are four more of them."

He rubbed his thumb over her lips. "Aye, I already know about them."

"How?"

"Bran and Gwydion spilled the beans." Fionn smiled. "Aye, likely there is much to catch up on, but it can wait, mo croi." Grasping the side of her face, he slashed his mouth over hers and kissed her hungrily.

Aislinn kissed him with a desperation that started in her toes. As she clutched him to her and opened her mouth beneath his, she wondered if they'd make it back to the house before lust got the better of them.

CHAPTER 10

Fionn sank his tongue into Aislinn's mouth, reveling in how sweet she tasted. They'd gone rounds before over his almost insane need to keep her out of harm's way, but he'd never be able to live with himself if something happened to her—something he could have prevented by... By what? Locking her in a Rapunzel tower deep in the woods, shrouded by spells?

She sparred with his tongue, sucking on it, and his stray thoughts shattered. He wanted the woman in his arms, pure and simple. Wanted her with an intensity and ferocity that shocked him. Fionn tore his mouth from hers. "I'm going to teleport us into my bedchamber," he said, his voice rough with need.

Her eyes shone with lust, and the points of her nipples pressed into his chest. "Is your magic recovered enough? I can help." She licked her lips lazily, her gaze never leaving his. Aislinn's eyes were golden, just like her mother's had been.

When Fionn thought about it, he felt like the worst kind of dolt for not recognizing the connection straightaway. Instead it had taken Aislinn running into a ward and nearly dying—and a trip inside her body to Heal her—for him to identify her MacLochlainn blood.

Before that, he'd suspected, but the connection had seemed so unlikely, he hadn't believed it.

"Earth to Fionn?" She smiled softly, fetchingly.

"I can get us from here to the house," he said gruffly, drew a spell, and counted through seconds while the greenery dissolved around them, exchanged for the whitewashed walls of his suite of rooms on the third floor of the manor house. He started pulling at her clothes as soon as he could and she responded in kind, unlacing the fastenings of his top and working on the buttons holding his faded jeans on his hips. He tossed her rucksack, jacket and top in a pile, and pushed her bra out of the way to suckle her breasts. She had the most amazing nipples, rose colored and the size of silver dollars. They puckered willingly under his ministrations, and she arched into his touch.

"Do you suppose we'll actually manage to get through this without being interrupted?" she asked, her breath coming in panting gasps as she wove her fingers into his hair.

He lifted his mouth from her breasts and grinned rakishly. "Good point." He shoved a bolt of magic at the door. "That should do it. If anyone knocks, we willna answer."

Aislinn pushed him backward until his legs hit the bed and he tumbled onto it. She unlaced his boots and tugged at them, jockeying them off.

"What about yours," he asked.

"Getting there." She pulled his jeans and shorts out of the way and captured his erection between both hands. Leaning forward, she licked around the glans, and he grunted at the sheer pleasure of her touch. Encouraged by his response, she took him most of the way into her mouth, working him with tongue, teeth, lips, and her hands. His cock jerked and shuddered under the attention and his breath came in harsh bursts as he rode a ragged edge of control. Every nerve in his body was on fire with wanting the woman bent over his body.

"Lass." He placed a hand on either side of her head and dragged himself from her mouth.

"Mmm?" Her golden gaze settled on his face, and the skin around the corners of her eyes crinkled with mischief.

"Lie next to me."

"But I was enjoying myself."

"Och aye, and I was enjoying you too, but I want all of you."

She wriggled onto the bed and arched her back, pressing her body against him. "Same problem I have. I always want to do everything with you at the same time. Lick, suck, fuck, kiss. And I never, never get enough."

"Goddess willing, ye'll always feel that way, leannán." He pushed to a sit and went to work unlacing her boots. Fionn made a clucking sound. "Ye're needing boots."

"Tell me something I don't know. Better yet"—she toed off the boot he'd unlaced—"don't tell me anything at all right now."

Fionn finished undoing her pants and jerked them down her hips, following them with her panties. The sweet musk of her arousal tantalized him and made his aching erection even harder. He traced a finger over the damp red curls surrounding her pussy, and she made a little mewling sound. He reached deeper and slid two fingers inside her, feeling her muscles clamp down on him immediately.

Aislinn shifted and gripped his upper arm, dragging him down with insistent pressure. Her nipples were tight buds of wanting him and her pussy rippled around his fingers. He pulled his hand out and knelt over her, stabilizing his cock so it pressed against the entrance to her body. She scooted forward and lifted her long legs until they draped over his shoulders, opening herself for him.

Just for him, only for him.

Fionn almost couldn't breathe. He'd never had this reaction to a woman before, where she held the power of life and death over him— or it felt that way. His life would be worthless without Aislinn by his side. With a groan of delight, he let himself sink inside her body. Surrounded by the liquid heat of her, he battled to stay the course. Coming immediately wouldn't be the end of the world, but he wanted to fly with this woman.

She settled her hands on his hips and tugged demandingly. Inchoate sounds burst from her, Gaelic mixed with goddess-only-knew what, but it didn't matter. He understood completely. Once they got going, their lovemaking was always cataclysmic as their bodies crashed together. He meant to go slow, but soon he plumbed her hard, over and over as she writhed beneath him. The contractions of her first orgasm were hard to resist, and he drew a bit of magic to make himself last. Watching Aislinn was like watching a goddess with flame-colored hair spread around her in a canopy of living flame. Her face and chest were splotched rosy with desire, and she drove her hips upward, meeting him stroke for stroke.

Somewhere between her third and fourth climax, his body rebelled and let him know that no amount of magic could hold back the tide. Semen boiled hot at the base of his cock. She lowered her legs until they were wrapped around his hips and pounded herself against him. Her eyes were closed and her head thrown back on a neck corded with passion.

"Yes," she shrieked. "Now."

He didn't know if she'd mixed magic in with the command, but his cock juddered inside her as he came. His vision wavered at the edges, and the only thing in the world was her slick sheath encasing him, urging him on. When he collapsed on top of her, there wasn't enough air in the room to serve his thundering heart. Aislinn closed her arms around him and stroked his back and hair, crooning low in her melodic voice.

Time passed before he came back into himself, still clasped in Aislinn's arms. "Gods but I love you," he said.

She laughed, and the sound warmed him. "Not nearly so much as I love you, and that's where we get into problems. I was blind with jealousy once I realized where you were—and that Perrikus had sent you there."

"Och, and I was blind with rage once I understood Gwydion and Dewi were hell-bent on dragging you into danger."

She twisted from beneath him until she lay on her side, so he turned onto his and faced her. Tracing the line of his cheek and chin, she said, "We're like that O. Henry Christmas story."

It took a minute for him to make the connection, and then he smiled. "Ye mean the one where he sells his watch for combs for her hair—"

"Exactly," she broke in. "And she sells her hair to buy him a fob for his watch."

Fionn blew out a breath. "There are worse things to be than crazy in love, mo croi. On a more serious note, we have to come up with something to immobilize the dark gods. That they can rally the Harpies to abduct me is worrisome."

She snorted. "You think? I didn't like it much when Perrikus showed up here gloating, either."

"I'm grateful that's all he did." Fionn shook his head. "Ye'll have to catch me up on what happened."

"I will. Lemurians attacked, but it turns out they were just Perrikus's puppets. They would have inflicted more damage, but we fought back. The humans helped—a lot."

He rolled his eyes. "Rub it in. We made an enormous mistake by not recognizing—and leveraging—their power earlier. Would ye like a bath?"

"That would be nice."

He kissed her forehead and cheeks, before brushing his mouth over hers. "Let's do that. Ye can fill in details while we clean up." He hesitated, mulling things over before adding, "I have an idea to float, but 'tis risky as sin, and I need to think it through a bit more afore I open my mouth."

She cocked her head to one side. "That was quite the teaser. Are you sure you don't want to say more?"

"Aye, quite sure."

AISLINN WOUND a towel around her wet hair. Fionn's manor house had a gravity feed spring which provided running water, and they could warm it with magic, so most of the creature comforts she'd associated with civilization were still available—at least here. In the underground dwelling where she'd lived in Utah, running water had come from a waterfall cascading down one rocky wall. Her cave was leftover from a deserted mining operation. It had been easy to hide with magic, but not very commodious. A wave of nostalgia swept through her. The few personal mementoes she'd kept from before the dark gods had killed her father were still in her cave. Though she might return there someday, it was looking less and less likely.

Buck up. They're only things.

She pulled on clothes. As usual, Fionn was quicker both dressing and bathing, and he'd left to rustle up some food for them in the kitchens. She gazed around his bedchamber. Nestled into a corner of the third floor of the manor house, huge beams ran through the ceiling, and a fireplace was set into the wall next to a door leading to a patio. Another door led into Fionn's study at the far end of the room. All in all, it was a simple, masculine environment. Nothing fussy. The headboard and footboard were carved, dark wood and they matched an armoire and several dressers scattered about. A round table and two chairs lay between the windows and the bed. Leaded glass panes lined the wall where the fireplace was and the wall nearest the bathroom. When she'd first seen this room, sunlight—a rare occurrence in Northern Ireland—had been bouncing through the windows, illuminating the room and adding both enchantment and mystery to it.

Scratching at the door jerked her from her reverie, and she sent magic spiraling across the room to unlatch it. Rune trotted in with the remains of a mangled rodent trailing from his mouth.

"Ewwww." Aislinn crinkled her nose. "Couldn't you have finished that outside?"

He dropped it onto the thick Oriental carpet and spread his jaws in a wolfish grin. "You've eaten worse."

"Yes, but only when I was starving. And I usually tried to cook squirrels."

"It's a chipmunk." Rune settled onto the floor with a *thunk*, and proceeded to munch on his treat.

"Where's Bella?" Aislinn dragged a sweater over her top.

"With Fionn and the dragons."

She headed toward the door leading into the hallway. "Are they outside?"

Rune made a chuffing noise and switched to mind speech. *"Of course. Dragons won't fit in the house."*

Aislinn wasn't so sure about that. They'd certainly fit inside the great room, but now that there were six of them, it would be a tight fit. "The babies?"

Rune shook his head and fur clumps flew every which way. *"Why do you think I'm up here? That little black one won't leave me be."*

"He's not all that little anymore." She bit back the rest of her words. The baby dragons were actually much bigger than Rune now, but she didn't see any reason to remind the wolf of that. She quirked a brow. "I'm going downstairs to eat something. Are you coming?"

He dropped the small corpse onto the carpet again. "If it's all the same to you, I'll stay here."

"Fine. I'll call you if I need you."

Aislinn let herself into the hall and made her way down two sets of stairs, across the great room, down more stairs, and to the kitchen. No matter what the Celts and dragons were hatching up, she needed food.

Bran stood over a pot on the stove, stirring. He turned and faced her, a smile on his face. "Can I dish you up a snack, lass?"

"That would be nice. Where's everyone else?"

"Somewhere between here and the moat. Fionn asked me to stay here and make certain ye had enough to eat."

She smothered a self-conscious grin. It was nice to be taken care of. No one had done much of anything for her since her father had been killed and her mother had gone mad. It was a harsh indoctrination into adulthood—and a quick one. She extended a hand for the bowl Bran held out to her. "Thanks."

"Doona mention it." He dropped a lid on the pot and turned to leave.

An idea formed. "Bran! Don't go just yet."

He focused his copper gaze on her; today his longish, blond hair was braided Celtic warrior style, and he wore his characteristic battle leathers. "Aye, lass. Can I get you aught else?"

Information, you can get me information. Unfortunately, the Celts were notoriously close-mouthed. Bran might be the god of prophecy, but if she wanted him to share anything with her, she'd have to proceed with stealth. His gaze sharpened, and red flared in the depths of his eyes. She built a quiet ward around her mind, hoping he wouldn't notice.

Fat chance.

Aislinn cleared her throat. "How much longer before the baby dragons can fight for us?"

"Mayhap only another few days." He made a grunting sound. "That is if Dewi allows them to fight at all."

"Could she make that choice?" Aislinn spooned a split pea and dried vegetable mix into her mouth. It wasn't bad. Sort of a stick-to-your ribs affair.

"She could. Nidhogg would fight her, though. So would Gwydion." Bran ran water into a glass at the sink and dropped it softly in front of her. "Ask what ye really want to know, lass. 'Twill save both of us a lot of time."

"Am I that transparent?" She winced.

"Och, I doona know about that." He shrugged. "But I've been reading minds for millennia."

"Great!" She smiled brightly. "Then you can tell me what I want to know without me saying a word."

His handsome face darkened. "'Tisn't a game. Sometimes I forget how young ye truly are."

That smarted. She dropped her spoon into her empty bowl. "All right. Your gift is prophecy. What have you seen about our war with the Lemurians and dark gods?"

He shook his head, his eyes flaring with compassion. "Some things are beyond my ken. Because so many varieties of magic wielders are involved, I canna see that particular future."

Her Seeker gift—the one that sorted truth from falsehood—twanged sourly. "That's not true," she blurted.

The air around Bran thickened, thrumming with magic, and she wondered if he'd teleport out of reach of her questions. Not much she could do if he did. She held her breath, waiting. If he left, she may as well go in search of Fionn and the dragons. Moments dribbled by. Finally, he strode to the table, used a foot to drag the chair opposite her out, and sat on it.

"Why'd you decide not to cut and run?" she asked dryly.

He narrowed his eyes. "And are ye determined to make me regret my choice? By the way, lassie, I never *cut and run*. I make decisions based on exigencies."

"You thought about teleporting out of here."

"Aye."

"So," she persisted, "what changed your mind?"

"Can ye remain silent long enough to listen?"

Aislinn chuckled. "Touché. Not one of my strong points, but I'll do the best I can."

"Prophecy isna like watching television." He folded his hands in front of him, lacing the fingers together. "I see bits and pieces of many different futures without knowing how they'll weave together."

"So you've seen snippets of what's coming?"

He nodded. "Of course. The dragons will be a great help, but there is a darkness there too that I canna interpret."

"Is there anything we can do to prepare?"

"Nothing beyond what we're already doing. We will continue to field attacks. If we're strong enough, we may prevail."

"Fionn said he had an idea."

"Did he now?" Bran's deep voice kindled with interest. "What was it?"

"I have no idea. He wouldn't tell me beyond describing it as risky."

"Och aye, and what isna risky in these times?" He splayed his hands on the table top and levered himself upright.

She gazed up at him. "Could you at least tell me about Fionn and me?"

His eyes twinkled. "Follow your heart. If that doesna work, Arawn or I would make more than adequate substitutes."

Aislinn made shooing motions with both hands. "Get out of here."

"Now she wants me to leave." Bran rolled his gaze skyward, laughing, and vanished. His laughter hung in the air after he'd disappeared.

CHAPTER 11

"The next one of you who tries to fly out of here will have to do some serious cave time," Dewi bellowed.

Nidhogg chuckled through steam and smoke.

"I fail to see what's so funny," Dewi snapped.

He turned his green gaze her way, and she could have sworn he winked, but it was tough to tell through the clouds of steam surrounding him. "This is why we raise them in caves, my dear. We can close off the entrance and they're not strong enough to escape for a while."

"We can return to your cave with them," Berra offered.

A cacophony of *nos* rose around Dewi.

"We just got back here," the black youngling announced. "We are not going back."

Dewi blasted him with flames, but they rolled off his scales. "You do not call the shots, youngling."

He sidled in front of her. His bravado would have been laughable, since he was less than a quarter her size, if it weren't so dangerous for him to make his own decisions.

"Soon, you won't be able to tell us anything."

Dewi didn't like the sound of that, but before she could ask for clarification, Nidhogg lumbered between her and their black offspring.

He bent and snatched the young dragon by the scruff of his neck and lifted him to eye level. "What did you mean by that?"

"N-Nothing." Face to face with Nidhogg, the youngster wasn't so bold.

Dewi joined her mate. "You can tell us," she said, her voice poisonously sweet, "or we can drag it out of your mind."

The dragon writhed in Nidhogg's grasp, but it didn't do him any good. He spit fire, and Nidhogg shook him hard.

"Stop that!" the Norse dragon growled.

Kra gasped; air and fire whooshed from him.

Dewi stared at the copper dragon. "What? Don't we have enough problems?"

"Apparently not," Kra muttered. He drew himself up to his full height, scales clanking together. "Since the two of you were dancing around the point, I looked inside his mind."

"And?" Nidhogg's tone could have branded a warning in plate steel.

"I'll talk," the black youngling piped up. "I didn't do anything wrong."

"We'll be the judge of that," Dewi said. "What did Kra see in your mind?"

A long, hissing snarl came from Kra, and then he said, "I'm counting to three. If you haven't told them, I will."

"Old Ones," the black youngling said. "They come into my dreams."

Dewi's heart plummeted into her feet. "Why haven't you pushed them out?" she demanded. "You're strong enough. Or you could have called one of us—"

"But they're in trouble," he broke in. "They hate the dark gods too. They want us to fight together. They said they'd come for me and my eggmates and give us everything we want if we'd just fight for them. We're almost old enough."

Dewi didn't know whether to laugh, slap her child, or lock him behind stone walls. "You believed them?" She shook her head, incredulous.

"Why wouldn't I?" her youngster asked. "After all, they were just doing the dark ones' bidding when they kidnapped our brother and sister." He hesitated a beat. "They were very sad about our sister dying."

"Let me tell you something." Dewi bent close and grasped the black dragon's head with a taloned foreleg. "I spent hundreds of years in a tunnel beneath Taltos spying on them. They invited the dark gods to Earth."

The black youngling nodded vigorously. "Yes, I know. They told me all about how they were dying and desperate for anything to help them survive. They said we come from common stock, that we have to stick together. Against everyone."

Berra had gathered the other six young dragons. "Have any of the rest of you been a part of this?" she demanded, her red scales vibrating with outrage.

"All of us," the black youngster said. "I already told you the Old Ones need all of us to help them fight the dark gods."

Dewi let go of her child and turned to Nidhogg. "I'm almost beyond words. What do you think?"

He narrowed his eyes. "No thinking to be done here. They must go to our borderworld and remain there until the fighting is done."

"But I don't want to—" the black dragon began.

"What you want doesn't matter," Nidhogg spoke over him.

"They need us," the youngster insisted.

"You've been duped," Dewi said. "Do you know what that word means?"

"Tricked." He sounded sulky.

She blew fire in frustration. "You're too young to know better, and you have a good heart, but what would have happened is once they had you, they would have tried to use you as a bargaining chip to get us to capitulate."

Royce clanked his jaws together. "Vaughna and I can see them safely to the borderworld and will remain with them until one of you tells us it is safe to return."

Fionn and Gwydion hurried around a corner of the manor and ground to a halt. "What's going on?" Gwydion asked, glancing from dragon to dragon.

Fionn muttered, "I fear we willna like the answer."

Arawn trotted after them and stood by Fionn's side, surveying the tableau. Dewi had always respected the god of the dead, and today was no exception.

He made his way to Nidhogg, laid a hand on the young dragon's head, and his face darkened. "Fuck!"

"What is it?" Fionn and Gwydion surged forward.

"Lemurians have done quite a thorough job corrupting this one." He slanted his gaze at Dewi. "Did the damage stop here?"

"No," Dewi said, her voice flat. "It's all of them."

"The Old Ones need us," the black dragon said in a wheedling tone, but he didn't sound quite as self-assured as he had before.

Maybe the fact that no one shared his worldview was sinking in. Dewi hoped so.

Fionn focused on Dewi. "What are we going to do?"

"We have it under control," she said. "They're going to our borderworld with Royce and Vaughna. And they'll remain there until the danger has passed."

"Or until there's no one left here," Nidhogg rumbled, "in which case, they'll live out their lives on our borderworld."

"That sounds horrible," a green youngster piped up.

"Yes," a red female chimed in. "Nothing but dirt and fire."

"How would you know anything about it?" Dewi eyed her brood. "You've never been there. The fire world has been good enough for dragons since the beginning of time. It's where we were forged."

"Old Ones said—" the green youngling began.

Nidhogg blasted him with fire. "Lies," he shouted, spraying everything within a fifty foot radius with fire. "They filled your heads with lies."

"How could all of you have been so stupid?" Dewi demanded, not really expecting an answer. They were young, naïve to the ways of the world. Of course they'd be an easy mark…

"We canna leave them here," Gwydion said, breaking into her thoughts. "They're a weak link in our defenses." He shook his staff at the dragon horde. "Why dinna any of you say aught?"

"I instructed them to remain silent," the brood's alpha said. "The Old Ones told us we couldn't tell anyone. They said you wouldn't understand."

"No shit," Fionn grunted. "They bought your silence because they knew we'd understand all too well."

"It doesna matter," Arawn cut in and focused on Nidhogg. "How will ye transport them?"

"It won't take long," Nidhogg said. "We'll teleport to a point where we're close, and then we'll power through the barrier separating Earth from our borderworld. He swept his gaze through his brood. "I expect absolute compliance from each of you," he said. "Dewi and I will be mind-linked to you, and if we sense so much as a stray thought we don't like, you won't make it to the borderworld. Do I make myself clear?"

Dewi winced at his tone. She wouldn't have been quite so harsh, yet she understood the necessity.

"Yes, sir," the brood's alpha dropped his head in deference to his father, and Dewi breathed a little easier. She wasn't sure if she could shoot one of her own children out of the skies.

Royce furled his black wings. "Vaughna and I are ready anytime."

Magic boiled around Nidhogg until the air was thick with the stink of ozone and dragons' fiery breath. He still held his son in an unbreakable grasp. Dewi laced magic in with her mate's casting and sent spells to tether each of her other six children.

"We'll be back within the hour," she told Fionn.

"Aye, and once we return," Nidhogg added, "we will convene a war council. This waiting around for them to strike next isn't working for me."

~

FIONN WATCHED as the four adult dragons and seven youngsters teleported away from his manor house.

Kra lumbered forward, followed by Berra. "What a goddess-damned shame," he said.

"We were counting on their help once they got a bit older," Berra seconded. She turned her golden gaze on her mate. "Do you suppose this happened while we had them in the caves?"

"Where else?" Kra replied.

Berra hung her head. In between steam and smoke, garbled words emerged. "I never left them alone for a moment, yet somehow this is my fault."

"'Tisn't." Gwydion raised his voice for emphasis. "The Old Ones are sly. Unless ye'd thought to establish a mind link to each youngling —and monitored it constantly—ye'd never have noticed the Lemurians' incursion. Or their cheap, empty promises."

Fionn sifted his hands through his hair, feeling inexplicably weary. "This isna good on many fronts. We needed the dragons' energy to help oust the dark gods. It has a healing aspect that would have helped Earth repel the dark ones."

"Do ye suppose the dark gods put the Lemurians up to trying to corrupt the dragons?" Arawn asked.

"Humph." Gwydion pounded the end of his staff into the grass. "I hadna considered that, but 'tis a strong possibility."

"What's a strong possibility?" Bran shimmered into being.

"Nice you could join us," Gwydion cast a sidelong gaze his way.

"I was in the house. What's a strong possibility?" Bran repeated, sounding annoyed.

"Listen for a bit and ye'll get the gist," Fionn told him, and then turned back to Gwydion and added, "Och aye, and we'll never know the answer to that one. I do agree with Nidhogg, though. I've been turning a plan about in my mind." He blew out a tense breath, and then another. "'Twill either be the death of us, or 'twill send the dark ones back to the hell they came from."

Arawn furled his brows. "Are ye going to say more?"

"It almost doesn't matter how risky it is," Kra broke in, puffing steam. "The time has come for bold and decisive action. I'm furious those spineless bastards would try to corrupt our young, and they did it with a perversion of the truth. If they'd lied outright, any dragon, no matter how young, would have dismissed them out of hand."

"Well then, there's the darkness I saw around the dragons," Brann muttered under his breath. He clamped his jaw into a tight line and moved closer to Fionn.

"What do you mean?" Gwydion asked Kra.

"One thing the Old Ones said was true. Dragons are, indeed, descendants of the Third Race, right along with the Lemurians."

Fionn caught his breath as surprise blew through him. "Dewi never told me that."

"Likely, she was ashamed," Berra cut in. "None of us wish to claim kinship with the Lemurians—for many reasons."

"We weren't the same species," Kra said, "but in truth the Third Race encompassed both dragons and Lemurians. Dragons breathed a collective sigh of relief when the histories didn't include us, likely because we left Mu before it blasted to bits."

"We have time." Gwydion leaned on his staff. "I would hear more of this, since 'tisn't a tale I'm familiar with, either."

"I know parts of it," Bran said, "but I'd be verra interested to hear it direct from a dragon's mouth."

The dragons exchanged glances, and Kra nodded once, sharply, his dark eyes whirling faster than usual. "We told Nidhogg and Dewi's brood that we were forged on our borderworld, but in truth, we are much older than that. Before Earth and the borderworlds formed out of the void, we shared the planet of Mu with the Lemurians. They built grand cities, and we excavated extensive cave systems. Though we both had reptilian characteristics, they always chose to hide theirs behind illusion. Over time, their wings became vestigial, and then disappeared entirely." He stopped to suck in a breath, and Berra picked up the tale.

"The Lemurians plundered Mu. We warned them time and time again, but they didn't listen to us. By the time they realized they were in danger of running out of clean water and had nowhere else to plant food because they'd burned up the soil's goodness, it was late in the game to launch countermeasures."

"Were either of you there?" Gwydion asked.

Berra shook her head. "No, but this is part of the oral tradition passed to every dragon, and we know it to be true."

"The Old Ones tried to enslave us," Kra said. "They needed our magic to save Mu, but we'd had a bellyful of them and had already decided to leave. When we didn't cooperate, they captured three dragons and would have killed them were it not for a valiant rescue. We killed ten of them, and didn't lose a dragon."

"Once that happened," Berra said, "we knew we had to find a different home, so we sent scouts through the universe and discovered Earth, a newly formed planet with a phalanx of borderworlds around it. At first, we moved to Earth, and shortly thereafter found a fiery borderworld that suited us perfectly."

"So you left afore Mu exploded?" Fionn asked.

Berra nodded. "At least two hundred years."

"We weren't happy once we realized the Lemurians had taken up residence on Earth," Kra said. "But there wasn't much we could do about them being here, other than stay out of their way—and keep the location of our borderworld hidden from them." He paused for a beat. "They settled on a continent and named it Mu, after their planet. It was only once they burned through that too, that they began construction of Taltos beneath Mount Shasta."

"Where'd they come up with Orione, that dragon guarding the passageways around Taltos?" Arawn asked.

"We never figured that out," Berra replied. "Dewi would be the one to ask, since she killed whatever it was so she could set herself up to take its place. It's possible the thing came from a Lemurian genetic manipulation. They were famous for them, even in our time."

"Fascinating," Fionn murmured. "Is there aught else?"

Kra nodded. "Unless they figured out a way around it, they poisoned their environment on the planet Mu so extensively, they could no longer reproduce." He blew smoke through his nostrils. "They're hermaphroditic, and have both male and female forms. They continued to cycle, but their eggs were lifeless."

Gwydion stitched his brows into a thoughtful line. "That would mean once this batch dies, there willna be any more."

Arawn nodded. "We already knew they were worried they were dying out. That's usually how it happens. No more young spells the death of any race."

"Good riddance," Bran chucked into the mix.

A thought rocked Fionn. "So they may have wanted the dragon brood for other reasons too. Lacking young of their own, they might have planned to raise these, indoctrinating them into their ways."

"And using them for breeding stock," Arawn said sourly. "They did those experiments blending human and Lemurian DNA and came up with viable results. Dragons are much closer to their own form, so they could have used the dragon brood to perpetuate their race."

"We got lucky," Berra spoke up.

"Whatever do ye mean?" Fionn asked, since he was feeling anything but lucky at the moment.

"If the brood's alpha hadn't shot off his mouth, we'd never have found out."

"Oh, we'd have found out all right," Kra cut in, "but not before a hell of a lot more damage occurred." He turned his gaze on Fionn. "I'd like to hear your plan."

"I'd say one's overdue," Bran muttered; Gwydion and Arawn nodded agreement.

"Do ye think we should wait until the dragons return?" Fionn asked.

Gwydion cracked a grin. "Aye, and we should include the humans and Aislinn, but if 'tis like most of your plans, 'twill require...refinement. Mayhap we could work on that with fewer of us. Decisions by committee are always ridiculously time-consuming."

Fionn huffed out a breath. "Thanks for the vote of confidence."

The master enchanter inclined his head. "Anytime. Now start talking."

 islinn and Rune walked down the manor house's broad front steps and across perpetual greenery toward where she heard the rumble of voices. They held an undercurrent of tension, which didn't bode well, and she wondered what had happened. Apparently Rune, who'd joined her, noticed it too because he growled softly and hackles stiffened beneath her fingers where they were buried in his neck ruff.

A dark form swooshed out of nearby bushes and Bella landed atop Aislinn's shoulder, digging in her talons to stabilize herself. "Ouch!" Aislinn yelped. "Fionn usually wears leathers. Your talons just bored a bunch of holes in my skin."

"Whiner," the raven cawed, and Rune snapped at her.

"For Christ's sake, stop it," Aislinn hissed and rotated her shoulder hoping to loosen the bird's death grip. "Where have you been?" she asked the raven.

"Eavesdropping."

The word held a particular supercilious tone that grated on Aislinn, but she bit back a snarky rejoinder. It wouldn't help.

"What did you hear?" Rune asked.

"You'll find out soon enough."

Aislinn ducked around a particularly thick stand of bushes and saw the Celts and two dragons. "Does what you overheard have to do with the dragons that aren't here?" she asked Bella, but the bird used her shoulder as a launching pad and flew toward Fionn. Aislinn reached inside her clothing to rub her shoulder and wasn't surprised to find she was bleeding. She quickened her pace, breaking into a lope, and sent Healing magic to her abraded flesh.

"Lass." Fionn inclined his head her way, but didn't smile. "Ye must have second sight. We were about to begin."

"Begin what?" she asked.

"Strategizing," Gwydion said succinctly.

"Mmph." Aislinn reached Fionn's side. "Were you planning to hatch up something without me?"

Fionn rolled movie star blue eyes. "Nay. I wanted to wait until Dewi and Nidhogg returned, but Mr. Gloom and Doom over there"—he pointed at Gwydion—"overruled me."

"Are Dewi and Nidhogg with their brood?" Aislinn asked, feeling like there were some major puzzle pieces that had passed her by.

"Aye," Arawn said.

"Stop right there." Aislinn made a chopping motion with one hand. "Something happened. I don't need every detail, but will someone please tell me why you all look as if Death just paid a visit?"

"Ye see, leannán," Fionn began in his most placating tone that made her want to scream, "'tis like this…"

A few minutes later, her anger dropped away, replaced by a sense of outrage and horror. How dare the Lemurians prey on the young dragons?

"Those bastards! Dirty, fucking, conniving bastards." She pounded a fist into her open palm. "They have no scruples."

"And are ye just now discovering that?" Bran arched a brow.

"Of course not."

"Is there any way the Old Ones can enter your world?" Rune asked Kra. "Or a way for the dragon brood to escape?"

Kra shook his head. "No to both questions. Only dragons can

penetrate the force field around our borderworld, and the younglings are not yet strong enough to marshal the magic to batter their way through."

"What if they combined their power?" Rune persisted. "I spent enough time with the black youngster. He's headstrong, determined."

Kra looked at Berra and she shrugged, her golden eyes thoughtful. "If they worked together," she said slowly, "they just might be able to pull it off, but not without collateral damage. Some would make it back to Earth, but maybe not all of them."

"Can ye communicate with Nidhogg, Dewi, or the others?" Fionn asked Berra.

Kra closed his eyes and Aislinn felt the bite of magic. Dragons hefted boatloads of power, and being next to them when they wielded it was similar to being in an electrical storm. Her skin tingled, and the fine hairs on the back of her neck rippled beneath her hair.

"I reached Nidhogg," Kra said after a few moments, "and warned him."

"How far away can you talk with one another?" Aislinn asked. She'd always figured the dragons operated a lot like the Celts, but apparently at least their mind speech had a much wider range.

"If he'd crossed over into the borderworld, it wouldn't have been possible," Kra said. "They'd just come out of their teleport and were getting ready to cross the barrier, so my timing was good."

Aislinn moved out from under the protective arm Fionn had curved around her shoulders and paced in a tight circle. She felt dirty, tainted. The Lemurians had spread their filth beneath everyone's noses—and nearly gotten away with it. "So what's this idea of yours?" she jerked her chin at Fionn.

"Ye sound about as friendly as an alley cat guarding a kill," he observed.

"Maybe because that's how I'm feeling," she said and shook her head. "It doesn't matter how violated I feel." She tossed her hands skyward, disgusted with herself for being weak.

The bastards tried something. So what? They didn't succeed. I should be rejoicing, but I can't pry myself beyond outrage.

"Lass," Fionn tried again, but she waved him to silence.

"I want revenge. For what they did to me. For almost killing Rune. For whatever twisted experiments they did on those humans where they blended human DNA with theirs."

Fionn narrowed his eyes. "'Tis as good a lead-in as I'm likely to get. My plan is simple, but dangerous because it will require us splitting our forces." He inhaled sharply and blew the breath out. "There are five dark gods left. We know where Perrikus and D'Chel live, and that they shuttle back and forth between one another's borderworlds. Tokhots may no longer be a problem. It depends how much damage the dragon's fire Dewi breathed into his lungs did. That leaves Majestron Zalia and Adva."

"No one's seen Adva in millennia," Gwydion noted.

"I've never seen him at all," Fionn said. "He's their god of portals. As such, 'tis critical to take him out of the equation. Once he's no longer a player, 'tis my belief the others will have no choice but to remain where we put them."

"Go on," Gwydion said.

Fionn nodded. "We target Perrikus, D'Chel, and Adva. Majestron Zalia is too dangerous, since she has the same poison blood as Tokhots, and all she has to do is bleed on humans to kill them. She canna kill us, but her blood could drive us permanently into the *Dreaming*."

"Easier said than done," Arawn cut in. "How do ye propose to corner them, let alone take them out of the action, since we canna kill them?"

"That's the risky part." Fionn's face could have been carved in granite, but for the muscle that twitched beneath one eye. "I propose we send one force to Perrikus's borderworld and another to D'Chel's. If we do our jobs properly, one or the other will tell us how to find Adva."

"What about the Lemurians?" Aislinn sliced into the discussion.

"What about them?" Fionn countered.

"Do we just ignore them?"

Fionn nodded. "They'll die out without the infusion of power they're getting from the dark gods. If we split our attention across too many fronts, we will exhaust ourselves with aught to show for it."

"Are ye thinking Majestron Zalia will go back to wherever she came from if we can somehow neutralize Perrikus, D'Chel, and Adva?" Bran asked.

"Aye." Fionn paused. "And if we doona get that lucky, she will have shown herself and we can take things from there."

"It might work," Arawn said, and he creased his forehead in thought. "Once Dewi and Nidhogg return, we can choose who will go to which borderworld."

Fionn held up a hand. "One other thing. Ye may recall that the dark ones escaped from Odin's dungeons. 'Tis my belief he'll join us, with at least some of the Norse gods."

"No!" Kra shouted, followed by fire that came so close it singed the ends of Aislinn's hair.

"We have no call to trust that one," Berra said. "He would have killed us were it not for Arawn's kind intervention." She blew steam toward the god of the dead and he sputtered.

"Exactly why I wanted to get the fine points hammered out," Gwydion muttered under his breath.

Fionn walked toward Kra and Berra and extended his hands. "I certainly understand why you might feel that way—"

"Save it, Celt," Kra rumbled. "The matter isn't up for discussion."

"Not until Dewi and Nidhogg return," Berra said. Her mate hissed smoke her way, but she continued. "If any of us have reason to hate Odin, it's Nidhogg. I want to hear his reaction to teaming up with the Norse gods."

"There are quite a few advantages," Fionn murmured.

"I don't care if they're a sure shot at victory," Kra said. "They didn't target you for death."

Rune made his way to the copper dragon. "May I speak?"

"You needn't ask my permission, wolf," Kra replied.

Rune lifted his head, jaws parting in what might have been a smile. "Since you will not like what I have to say, perhaps I do."

Kra narrowed his dark eyes, but at least he didn't try to immolate the wolf, and Rune went on. "Dewi tried to kill me—more than once. There were many moon rises before she and I figured out how we could work together."

"Why did you bother?" Kra grunted.

"Because we both love Aislinn." The wolf spoke with a simple dignity that arrowed right into her heart. "It wasn't in Aislinn's best interest for us to be at odds with one another."

"Well spoken." Gwydion nodded approval.

"Och aye," Bran cut in. "Desperate times create unlikely bedfellows."

Kra turned away, and Berra whispered something into his ear. Aislinn caught the words, but they were in Gaelic, never her strong suit. The copper dragon faced the group again. "I will try to keep an open mind, but it's not easy to fight side by side with someone you don't trust."

"Tell me about it," Aislinn said. "I fought for the Lemurians for two years before I met Fionn. I never trusted them, but it was fight for them or have them march me into their damned radioactive vortex."

"We've all been forced into unpleasant choices," Fionn said. "Moving the young dragons to the borderworld wasna part of my battle plan. I wanted to leverage their power—and their linkage with Earth magics."

"They'll return afore this is over," Bran said and then clapped a hand over his mouth. "Oops. I'm not totally certain about that. 'Tis but one of many possible futures I've seen."

Fionn stared at the god of prophecy. "Ye almost never share your visions. Why this one?"

Bran shook his head until the ends of his blond braids bounced. "I doona know. Mayhap I'm not totally recovered from when Perrikus and D'Chel trapped me and Gwydion."

Aislinn folded her arms beneath her breasts. She remembered that episode all too well. They'd all gone to Perrikus's borderworld to search for Bran and Gwydion. Along the way, Perrikus had killed her unborn child—the one she hadn't known about until it was too late. About the only bright spot from that incident was Dewi had finally freed Nidhogg from his imprisonment. Bran and Gwydion had returned. So had Fionn and Arawn, but they'd needed a bit of a hand since the only place open to them when they fled the borderworld was an obscure corner of the halls of the dead, one warded so well they couldn't get themselves out.

"Lass." Fionn waved an arm in front of her face, and she blinked.

"Sorry. I guess I got lost remembering what happened on Perrikus's world."

"Good thing," Gwydion said. "'Twill not be one whit safer this time."

"Or any more pleasant," Arawn added.

Breath whistled through her teeth. "Stop treating me like a child. Or like I'll break if all of you aren't riding herd on me every single second." She sifted her hands through her hair and draped it behind her shoulders. "I'm the one who got rid of Slototh. And the one who entreated Dewi to breathe fire into Tokhots when he was unconscious."

"No one said ye weren't tough as old leather." Gwydion slanted a wry grin her way.

Fionn shut his eyes for a moment. She wouldn't have noticed if she weren't looking at him. Thinking it was better to take a stand now before he gathered a perfectly rational argument and suggested she stay here, Aislinn planted herself in front of him. "I know what you're thinking."

"Do ye now, lass?" He trained his million watt smile at her, but it lacked conviction.

"Och aye," she aped his brogue, which was easy enough since her mother's Irish accent had been thick as porridge. "Ye're turning things round and round to come up with some reason to leave me here."

"Be reasonable." Fionn held out a hand to her, but she ignored it.

"I am reasonable. I'm also capable." She bit down on her lower lip until it hurt. "After Dewi brought me back from Perrikus's world, there were days when I had no idea if you were alive or dead. It was hell, and I'm not doing that again. We're stronger together. You admit it when there's no danger."

"And I'll admit it now," he countered.

"If the two of you are going to have a lovers' spat, I'll find some other way to occupy myself," Gwydion said.

"Us too," Arawn and Bran said almost in unison.

Aislinn clacked her jaws together. "Stay. There's nothing more to say. I'm a part of whatever's planned, and that's the end of it."

"We use our females in battle," Kra observed.

"Ye are not helping." Fionn shot a bitter glance at the dragon.

"Depends which side of things you're on," Aislinn argued.

"Enough of this." Gwydion raised his voice for emphasis. "There are five of us and four dragons. So Fionn, Aislinn, and two dragons will go to one borderworld. Bran, Arawn, and I will join the other two dragons and infiltrate the other borderworld. My assumption is Dewi and Nidhogg will go with Fionn and Aislinn, since I doona see Dewi separating herself from the MacLochlainn."

"When will we leave?" Arawn raised a questioning brow.

"Sooner is better," Bran said.

"Love the enthusiasm"—Fionn glanced around the group—"but there are a couple of niggling odds and ends here. For one, we need Dewi and Nidhogg to agree. And then there's Odin."

Aislinn didn't have to look up to know the hissing snarl came from Kra, who apparently hadn't warmed to the idea of including the Norse gods.

"Ye said ye'd keep an open mind," Fionn reminded him. "I doona think we can afford to cut ourselves off from any potential sources of magic in this battle."

"You said it so I don't have to." Aislinn squared her shoulders. "Where are the humans in this battle plan of yours?"

A sheepish look washed over Fionn's chiseled features, but he recovered quickly. "Holding down the fort here on Earth in case Lemurians get it in their heads to do something foolish."

"Mmph." She pressed her lips into a thin line. "There are a lot of humans. Surely some of them can assist us on the borderworlds."

"The lass has a point," Gwydion said. "They fought well in the prison in Arizona where Slototh barricaded himself."

"Thank you." Aislinn sent a pointed look his way.

"Anytime, lass." Gwydion half-bowed in her direction.

The muscles in Fionn's jaw worked, but what came out of his mouth was, "Once the dragons return, we'll include everyone in the discussion. I had thought stealth might work in our favor. If too many of us show up—"

"Nay," Gwydion interrupted. "The dark gods will know the second we breach their boundaries. The more power we have at our disposal, the better our odds."

"Goddess only knows what creatures they'll have at their end of things to deploy against us," Arawn muttered.

Aislinn thought of some of the abominations she'd squared off against here on Earth and hoped to hell she wouldn't have to face anything worse. Magic hit her in the solar plexus so hard she struggled to remain upright. "What the fuck?" she sputtered and raised her hands to summon power.

"It's just Dewi and Nidhogg," Berra said. "They're close enough to create a psychic disturbance."

Aislinn let her hands fall to her sides. "Why didn't it feel like this before when they came and went?"

"Two reasons," Berra replied. "This time they're in a hurry, and both of them are probably upset at having to leave their young so far away. We believe it to be the safest place, but still—"

Dewi's trumpeting cut her off, and familiar blood-red wings formed a hundred feet off the ground, followed by the rest of Dewi's body. Nidhogg emerged from the ether next to her. Both dragons spread their wings and fluttered earthward. Aislinn knew Dewi well enough to sense how distraught she was.

"We could hear you for a bit before we got here," Dewi said and blew smoke toward Berra. "Nowhere is safe. If I have to kill my children because those abominations filled their minds with lies—"

"You're overreacting." Nidhogg spoke sharply. "I asked for a war council. It appears everyone began without us." He focused his unsettling gaze on Fionn. "Catch us up fast so we can get moving. The sooner we fight back, the better I'll feel."

"That makes two of us," Dewi muttered. Her whirling eyes fell on Aislinn. "To my side, MacLochlainn. Or better yet, on my back."

Aislinn blew out a breath and straightened her spine. "I'm sorry for what happened, but just because you're hurting and furious, it doesn't open the door for you to order me around."

Dewi opened her mouth to spew fire; Aislinn held her ground and glared at the dragon. Fionn glided between them, but Aislinn sidestepped him and said, "Don't."

Steam mingled with smoke streamed from Dewi's mouth. "Plucky little thing, aren't you?"

"I wouldn't let the Lemurians push me around, and you can't, either." Rage left a bitter taste in the back of Aislinn's throat.

"Save it for the enemy," Gwydion snapped. "If the two of you are done pissing all over each other, I suggest we move to more productive ground."

Kra sidled in front of Nidhogg and inclined his head. "My liege."

"You don't need to abase yourself, Kra. What do you want?"

"Part of Fionn's plan includes Odin—" Kra began.

Nidhogg swiveled his long neck and stared at Fionn. "Really? Because he was part of my plan too. I invited him to leave Valhalla and lend us his assistance. Start at the beginning, Celt. I need to hear this in order."

"Gladly." Fionn walked close to Nidhogg, but Aislinn followed and gripped his upper arm.

"Wait," she said. Her tone was harsh, but no sharper than she meant it to be. "I'll round up the humans so we can do this together."

CHAPTER 13

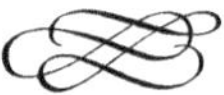

I t took longer than Fionn anticipated to get through the gist of things because so many people interrupted him. Finally, he glanced around the assemblage of Celts, dragons, and humans. "That's it. What do you think?"

Daniel, who'd been hunkered near Aislinn, pushed to his feet. "How many of us would you want in each away team?"

Fionn thought about it. "Mayhap four. That would give us six plus the dragons for one borderworld, and seven plus the dragons for the other. More than that and it might become unwieldy, particularly if Odin's people are there too."

Rune shook himself from head to tail tip and announced. "Bond animals will be included."

"Of course we will," Bella quorked from her place on Fionn's shoulder.

He smothered a groan. His bird was a gifted warrior, but she marched to her own drummer. *Rather like the dragons...*

Fionn jerked his chin toward Gwydion. "Ye're the warrior magician. Come up here and help craft a battle plan."

"Gladly." Gwydion strode to Fionn's side, but Fionn knew him well and read hesitancy beneath his smooth movements.

The master enchanter and warrior magician clasped both hands around his staff, centering it in front of him. "What about the other Celts?" he asked Fionn.

"And we never reached consensus about Odin," Nidhogg rumbled.

"Do the Celts and the Norse gods get along well enough to fight side by side?" Aislinn asked.

The corners of Fionn's mouth twitched. How like the lass to see straight through to the heart of things.

"Let's start with Odin and his crew," Fionn suggested. "If we canna agree about him…" He let his voice trail off.

"I can see the rationale for requesting Odin's help," Nidhogg said, "since it was his son's doing that freed the dark gods from Asgard. And I did ask for his help when I went there to reprimand him for forcing Dewi's dragons into hiding."

"What did he say?" Kra asked.

"That he'd gather his elite group of warriors and let me know when he was on Earth."

"But you haven't heard from him," Kra persisted.

Nidhogg shook his head until his scales clattered together. "No, but I've never known Odin to do anything quickly."

"I'll meet with a few key Celts, like Andraste," Bran said. "Just to sound them out."

"And I'll figure out if Odin's actually planning to do more than pay lip service to my request for his aid," Nidhogg said.

"We do need those two pieces of data," Fionn murmured. Magic bubbled around Bran and Nidhogg, and in moments both were gone.

"In the meantime"—Aislinn glanced around the group—"I suggest we practice fighting together. Fionn and I and Dewi and Nidhogg have at least had a bit of practice—along with Rune and Bella."

"Excellent suggestion." Eve strode toward Kra and Berra with her cat padding next to her. "Who fights by my side?" she called over one shoulder.

Fionn watched as Daniel and two humans he didn't know by name joined Eve. One had a hawk on his shoulder, so he must be another

Hunter. He nudged Gwydion and spoke into his mind. *"Why don't ye and Arawn work with them?"*

The master enchanter didn't answer. He snapped his fingers at Arawn, who looked annoyed to be summoned in such a cavalier manner, and moved toward the humans and dragons. The air thickened with combined magic and Fionn trotted to where Aislinn stood with Rune by her side.

"Thank you," she said softly.

"For what, lass?"

"Including the humans without giving me a raft of grief over it."

"They'll be a good addition. I'm ashamed I dinna think of it first."

She slanted a smile his way. "We should practice too."

"I was about to suggest the same thing," Dewi called across the fifty feet of lawn separating them. "We can funnel Nidhogg in when he returns. For now, I'll call the shots."

Fionn almost managed to stifle a snort, but enough escaped that the dragon glared at him and noted, "I have much more tactical experience than you."

"Ye are correct that we need a team leader." Fionn selected his words cautiously. "We canna determine who that will be until our final composition has been decided."

"For now, it will be me," Dewi insisted. She lumbered over to the group of humans. "Decide which four of you will throw in your lot with us. I'll be on the far side of the manor house so we don't get in the way of the other group."

The dragon spread her red wings and flew over the top of Fionn's home.

He exhaled slowly. "Guess we'd better not keep her waiting," he said to Aislinn and latched a hand beneath her arm.

Rune walked next to them making whuffly growls. At least Bella was silent.

They almost made it to where Dewi had set up a series of targets by pulling up bushes and moving them into ragged rows when Aislinn muttered, "I don't know why it grates so to have her order me around as if I were five."

"Does it make it any better that she does the same thing to me?" Fionn asked.

"Yeah, a little. It's not worth arguing over. I won't change her."

"Wise lass. Plus she wouldna understand why ye're so upset."

Timothy, Corin, and two male Hunters caught up with them. One had a wolf, who fell into step next to Rune. The other had a mountain lion like Eve's by his side.

"Tell us what you need from us," Timothy said.

"Indeed," Corin seconded. "It appears there are far too many chiefs in this operation as it is."

"Hush." Aislinn shook her head. "Don't let the dragon hear you."

"I hear everything," Dewi trumpeted. "Dragons have exceptional hearing."

"Tell us about the exercise you set up," Fionn broke in to divert her.

Smoke plumed from Dewi's open mouth. "This first drill will be masking ourselves so our energy doesn't leak through to alert the enemy. For the second, I scattered debris on the ground to teach us to use magic to muffle the noise we make. Of course it won't work nearly as well with this wet undergrowth as it would with the dry, dead plant material on the borderworlds, but we need to begin somewhere..."

By the time Nidhogg returned, Aislinn's body was streaked with sweat despite the chill, winter air. Dewi must have been a drill sergeant in a former life. She pushed hard, forcing each of them to go over and over each skill until she was satisfied it was acceptable.

"How about a break for something to eat?" Fionn said, sounding mildly short of breath. Dewi had borrowed from his magic to make tasks harder.

"Fine." Dewi clapped her forelegs together. "Back in an hour."

The humans faded toward the house, while Rune and the other wolf dove into thick brush, along with the mountain cat, no doubt in search of food of their own. Bella cawed her displeasure at something —maybe being left behind—and flew away, still cawing.

Nidhogg touched noses with Dewi. "Looks as if you've had a busy time here."

"They're coming along," she said, "but we have much to do before we're ready to face our enemy."

"What did Odin say?" Fionn asked.

"He wouldn't miss it for the world." Nidhogg blew steam.

Aislinn put her hands on her hips. "So what exactly does that mean? If he's showing up, when will he be here?"

"He's not coming here," Nidhogg replied. "He said he'd send forces to one of the borderworlds. If nothing's happening there, they'll move to the other one, and he understands the importance of locating Adva."

"But that means he won't be able to practice with us at all," Aislinn noted. Worry prickled down her spine, and she shivered. The gods were high-handed as it was. She'd been worried enough about working with the Celts, beyond the four she was used to. Adding God-knew-how-many Norse deities to the mix felt downright uncomfortable. Never mind if some of the other Celts decided they wanted to play too.

Apparently Fionn shared her reservations because he asked, "Do ye have any idea who will be part of Odin's *elite warrior* group?"

"Beyond Odin and Thor, unfortunately no," Nidhogg replied.

"So you don't know how many will come, or which borderworld they'll target," Aislinn cut in.

"That would be accurate." Nidhogg rolled his shoulders to the accompaniment of clanking scales. "I understand your misgivings," he went on, "but Odin was coming anyway. The only difference is that now he knows where we'll be concentrating our efforts."

"I don't like it," Dewi spoke up. "Kra pitched a fit before, and I guarantee you he'll like this even less."

"We all need food," Fionn said. "Dewi's idea about coming back together in an hour is a good one. By then, I'm certain Bran will have returned and we'll have all our data points mapped out."

"Hammering them into something other than a suicide pact will be a challenge," Dewi said sourly.

Nidhogg spread a wing and dropped it across her back. "Hunt with me. Fionn's right about everything looking better over a dead carcass."

Aislinn muffled a laugh and elbowed Fionn. "Not exactly what you said."

"It is in dragonspeak," he muttered. "Come on, lass. Let's hunt down our own carcass and talk about this."

She latched a hand around his arm. "Have the Celts and Norse gods ever joined forces before?"

Fionn paused for so long she didn't think she'd get an answer until he said, "Aye," in a reluctant tone, as if he had serious second thoughts about giving away even that much.

"Didn't go well, huh?" She raked her tangled hair back over her shoulders and chalked up a mental reminder to braid it before the next practice session.

"Ye might say that."

Aislinn stopped dead. Since she was still holding onto Fionn, he ground to a halt too. She walked in front of him and tipped her chin to look him in the eyes. "I am not dredging this out of you piecemeal. Tell me what happened."

A corner of his mouth twisted downward. "The good news is we always won."

"And the bad?"

"Ye might guess. They did what they wanted. So did we, and we tried not to fall over one another's campaigns."

She pressed her chapped lips together, not liking how they rubbed raw spot over raw spot. "I don't like the sound of that. For one thing, they're immortal just like you. This time, there'll be humans involved—and bond animals—all of whom can die." She clacked her teeth together, thinking. "No wonder Odin's not in any rush to join us. He probably has just as many qualms as you about merging efforts."

Fionn's gaze skittered away from hers. "'Tis one of the reasons I thought mayhap ye might like—"

"—to stay here," she finished his sentence. "Not on your life, buddy."

He closed the short distance between them and folded her into his arms. She tucked her head into the crook between his neck and shoulder and listened to the strong, steady beat of his heart. "We'll get through this," she mumbled, her words mostly lost against his body.

"I hope so." He drew back enough to look at her. "We doona have a choice. If we sit back, they'll continue to attack from different quarters and try to wear us out. We'll expend our energy in defending ourselves and never make aught in the way of progress."

She nodded. It was much the same way she'd felt during the time she'd fought for the Lemurians, like she was treading water and getting tired. She'd been afraid she'd do something stupid—once she wearied enough—and throw her life away because she didn't have the heart to go on fighting.

Fionn stroked her hair, catching his fingers in tangles that gave way when he pushed magic into them. "Sometimes thinking isna your friend."

"No kidding. The way I've gotten through the hard parts is by just powering forward. If I thought too much or too deeply, I'd probably never have left my cave."

"Aye, ye've told me that afore. If ye'd stayed put, ye'd never have found Rune. Or met me." He smiled crookedly.

"It's worse than that." She swallowed hard to buy herself the courage to go on. "My temper annoys you, but without anger, I'd have folded long ago. Before you and Rune, it was the only thing that kept me going. I'd picture Perrikus and D'Chel murdering my father at that Inca shrine in the Bolivian Andes. If that didn't work, I could always cull up an image of the Lemurian dragging my mother to her death. Between the two of them, I'd find the wherewithal to soldier forward.

Oh yeah, I forgot the Lemurians turning my house into an earthquake zone and making it uninhabitable." Her eyes burned, but she pushed the tears aside.

"Ye never told me that part." Fionn's voice was gentle, and he kept stroking her hair.

"Right after they took Mom, I was standing in the front doorway so filled with despair I almost couldn't breathe, and there was this huge, cracking noise. I bolted forward and turned to watch the house I'd grown up in crack in multiple places and settle into a ruin. About the only part left was the underground bomb shelter."

"Yet ye worked for them, even after they robbed you of everything."

She took a deep, snuffly breath. "At that point I didn't realize the Lemurians were in league with the dark, so I only blamed them for Mom and the house. But it wouldn't have made a difference. They dogged me after they killed Mom, and I said *no* over and over again until they made it abundantly clear one more *no* would land me right where they'd chucked Mom."

"Ye wanted to live."

"I guess I did." She shut her eyes for a long moment before opening them. "I'm glad our paths crossed. I don't know what I'd do without you and Rune."

His crooked smile got a little wider. "We both built a lot of walls, lass. Taking them down, admitting we need one another, isna easy."

"It would have helped if Mother had told me about you and Dewi."

"Would it?" He quirked a brow.

The tightness in her chest eased, and she found a smile to send back his way. "Not really. What normal kid finishing high school in Utah would believe her mother was descended from Irish kings and had both a dragon and a Celtic god at her disposal?"

"How would your father have felt about it?" Curiosity lined Fionn's question.

"He was a very open-minded man, and a scientist at heart. Remember, he spent his life studying the Harmonic Convergence and the surges associated with it. Somehow, I believe he would have taken it in stride. When we saw them in the halls of the dead and Gwydion was there, it was apparent Mom had told Dad about both of you."

"And he was quick to clasp hands with me." Fionn nodded, remembering. "Mayhap ye're right, leannán." He kissed her forehead. "How about a spot of food? Dewi's nowhere near done with what she wants to accomplish today."

"In that case," Aislinn brushed her lips over his, "we'd better get moving."

CHAPTER 14

Nightfall had arrived hours before, but Bran wasn't back yet. Fionn considered going after him more than once, but Dewi made it clear he was needed at their practice session. They'd covered basic evasive maneuvers, and working as a team to launch offensives. Fionn hadn't had a chance to check in with Gwydion or Arawn about how things went for their group, but planned to remedy that over supper.

It was both dark and cold when Dewi decided they'd done all they could for the day. The humans and Celts moved inside, and the dragons gathered in the courtyard outside the great room. Fionn held the kitchen door open for Aislinn and was pleased to see Gwydion, Arawn, and about twenty humans gathered around his large kitchen table. Pots bubbled on the stove, the heat powered by magic.

He ducked into the pantry and pulled out a bottle of mead, handing it to Aislinn, who drank deep. She gave the bottle back and swiped a grimy hand down her face, leaving dark streaks.

"Gods, but I'm tired," she muttered, strode to the sink, and flipped on the taps to wash her hands. Once they were clean, she bent forward and threw water on her face.

It looked like a good idea, so Fionn did the same once she was done.

"What would ye like to eat, lass?" Fionn pulled plates from a cupboard and rustled up forks. There weren't many left, so someone would have to wash dishes soon.

"I'll get my own." She joined him at the stove, took her plate, and piled it high with something from each pot. Fionn identified a grain and vegetable casserole, potatoes, and some variant of fowl, likely duck.

"Did someone find the time to hunt?" he asked the group.

Rune detached himself from a group of bond animals lounging in the far corner of the kitchen. "The meat is courtesy of our efforts."

Fionn bowed low, sweeping an arm in front of him before straightening. "I thank you."

"There are enough of us," Rune informed him, "that hunting is easy, and we killed far more than we needed on purpose."

Aislinn set her plate in front of an empty seat and made her way to Rune. She dropped into a crouch and wrapped her arms around his thick neck. The wolf angled his head and licked the side of her face. As Fionn watched them, he wondered where Bella had gotten herself off to this time. For one brief moment, he longed for a bondmate more like the wolf, but he squelched the thought before it could go anywhere. He and Bella had been together for hundreds of years. The bird was prickly and difficult, but she'd put her life on the line for him many times.

As if she were attuned to his thoughts—and maybe she was—she flapped through the kitchen door and landed on his shoulder.

"Get extra duck for me," she squawked. "I like it better raw, but I'll take what I can get."

Fionn turned back to the stove and added meat to his plate until the pressure of Bella's talons eased. "Where have you been?" he asked the raven.

"Spying."

Anger sent a shot of bile from his stomach to the back of his throat where it burned like a bitch. Fionn forced himself to walk to the table where he set his plate next to Aislinn's. She and Rune were still on the other side of the room, their heads bent together. Bella jumped from his shoulder to the table and buried her beak in a pile of succulent duck. He grabbed a fork and speared food, chewing and swallowing mechanically. If he waited long enough, the bird would tell him what she'd found, but if he gave in to his temper and rebuked her for going off alone without telling anyone what she was up to, she'd never say a word.

Aislinn settled beside him and placed a mead bottle on the table. He recalled leaving it on the counter next to the stove.

"Thank you," he murmured between bites and took a long draught. The liquor helped ease the fury that still burned in his gut. Conversation ebbed and flowed around him, but no one asked him anything, so he didn't have to pay attention.

They ate in silence, and he watched Aislinn sidelong. She shoveled food into her mouth like a starving woman; her appetite heartened him because she was far too thin. She'd dropped weight after losing their child and never gained it back. If he had his way, he'd swaddle her in layers of protection, see she had three decent meals every day, and keep her busy bearing his children. Realizing the absurdity of his fantasy, he snorted.

"What?" she asked, glancing up from her nearly empty plate. Before he could answer, she narrowed her eyes. "You and Bella are mighty quiet."

The bird had finished eating and moved on to preening her feathers. At Aislinn's observation, she lifted her head and focused her dark, avian eyes on Fionn. "It's because he'd like to wring my neck."

"Really?" Aislinn stroked Bella's wing feathers. "What'd you do this time?"

"Everyone was busy, so I did a bit of aerial surveillance." She fluffed her feathers, clearly proud of herself. "Ravens are common as goose grass here in Inishowen. No one paid me the slightest bit of attention."

"Are ye planning to tell us what ye found?" Fionn asked.

"I figured you'd get around to asking me sooner or later," the bird smirked.

Fionn ground his teeth together in frustration. Bella loved the limelight; maybe that would be a way to loosen her beak. He clinked his fork against the mead bottle and conversation died. Heads swiveled in their direction.

"While we were practicing," Fionn announced, "Bella did some scouting. She wants to tell you about it."

The raven flapped her way to the top of an industrial-sized, stainless steel refrigerator. The appliance was useless without electricity, but handy for mouse-proof storage, so Fionn hadn't bothered to move it outside. Bella folded her wings across her back and waited until everyone's attention was trained on her.

"Lemurians," she said succinctly. "Lots of them."

"How many?" a human asked.

The bird made a shrugging motion. "Numbers aren't my strong suit, but enough to fill the bottom floor of a deserted castle not far from here and more were teleporting in as I watched."

"Did ye sense any of the dark gods?" Gwydion got to his feet, leaning heavily on his staff.

"No, but that doesn't mean they weren't there," Bella said.

"Aught else?" Fionn asked.

"Isn't that enough?" Bella snapped her beak at him.

Fionn clamped down on a rejoinder and focused on Gwydion. "Any word from Bran?"

"Nay. If he isna back soon, mayhap one of us should track him down."

"My thoughts exactly," Arawn chimed in from where he sat at the end of the table.

"Would ye mind telling the dragons what ye just told us?" Fionn angled his gaze at Bella.

"Not at all." The raven flew across the kitchen and out the door.

Fionn scrubbed a hand down his face. "She is such a royal pain," he muttered.

"Hush." Aislinn poked him. "She'll hear you. She just likes to feel useful—like all of us."

"Maybe so, but—"

Aislinn shook her head. "She loves you. Her world's turned upside down right along with the rest of us, and she's figuring out where she fits. Because she lacks human social skills, you interpret her efforts as abrasive."

Fionn grinned in spite of himself. "When did ye turn into a bird therapist?"

"Since I discovered I held Hunter magic. Rune's the same way. Hell, Fionn, all of us need to feel valued. It's not unique to the bond animals."

"What do ye want to do about Bran?" Gwydion broke into Fionn's and Aislinn's conversation. "I've tried to reach him telepathically, and come up with aught."

Fionn rotated his shoulder blades, but his muscles still felt like bags of concrete. "I imagine our kinfolk are arguing—much like they always do—behind well-shielded warding. If it werena for the Lemurians, I'd leave things as they are, at least until morning."

Eve caught his eye from across the table. "We should set two hour watches." Dark smudges rode beneath her blue eyes, and her hair hung in tangled, dark mats around her face.

"Agreed." Fionn nodded briskly. "Mayhap 'twill yield an opportunity to test our developing battle strategies."

Eve shut her eyes and her shoulders drooped for a moment before she straightened them. "Thanks, Celt," she growled, and her eyes fluttered open.

"Doona mention it, lassie." He pushed to his feet, realizing he was weary too. Not just in body, but the continuing threat of attack dragged at his spirit. He much preferred open fighting, where he had at least some sense of where the enemy would strike next.

Gwydion stood and walked to Fionn's side. "Count off in fours," he instructed the group. "Ones will take first watch, from now until one in the morning. Second watch from then until three." He paused to take in a breath. "And so on until seven in the morning."

"Will we count too?" Rune asked.

"Nay." Gwydion smiled fondly at Aislinn's wolf. "Ye'll remain with your Hunter, bonded one."

"What about the dragons?" Corin asked.

"I'll speak with them and let them decide which group they wish to support," Gwydion said. "Four dragons. Four groups. Should be simple enough."

Fionn drew a two and Aislinn a three, but Daniel traded with Fionn so he and Aislinn could remain together. She got up, stumbling from weariness and plodded out of the kitchen with Fionn and Rune close behind her.

Gwydion caught Fionn while they were crossing the great room. "Hold for a moment. I would speak with you."

"All right." Fionn turned to Aislinn. "Go on up to our room with Rune. I'll meet you there soon."

Gwydion waited until woman and wolf had disappeared up the stairwell running along the far side of the enormous room. From there they'd go down a long hall to another set of stairs.

"Ye're worried," Fionn said, eying his old friend.

"No shit," Gwydion grunted.

"What do ye need me to do?"

"I wish it were that easy." Gwydion shook his head until blond strands of hair danced around his face. "This battle isna clean. I have no idea what will happen next. Hell, some days I wonder who's on which side. Having Odin pop up willy nilly willna help, and it may well hurt us."

"We've never fought well allied with the Norse gods," Fionn concurred.

"I feel responsible for the humans, like we need to protect them to make up for throwing them to the wolves earlier."

"It wasna quite that bad," Fionn murmured. "We dinna help them, but it wasna as if we wished them harm."

"Not the way they see it."

"Touché." Fionn gripped Gwydion's upper arm. "How about if ye spit out what's really bothering you?"

"In a hurry to get to the wench warming your bed?" Gwydion shot a meaningful glance at Fionn.

"Ye might say so."

"All right. I probably shouldna even mention it, since there's naught to be done, but what happened with the dragon younglings rankles."

"Aye, 'tis worrisome, yet we've done the best we can to corral the damage."

Gwydion raked a hand through his hair. "Not entirely. We could have one of us babysitting them, along with Royce and Vaughna."

"'Tisn't as if there are many of us to spare, unless Bran convinces a few other Celts to join the fight." Fionn loosened his hold on Gwydion. "That's tomorrow's problem. How about if we concentrate on getting through tonight without too many losses?"

"Humph." The master enchanter twirled his staff, which remained mercifully quiescent. When dark energy was near, it glowed red.

Fionn started for the stairs. "If ye find Bella outside, send her to my rooms."

"I'll suggest it." Gwydion's tone was dry. "Your bird isna any more compliant for me than she is for you."

Aislinn's words rattled around Fionn's mind. He stopped and turned back toward Gwydion. "If you tell her that, at least she won't feel left out."

"Oh, for goddess's-fucking sake. I canna command troops if I have to worry about people—or birds—getting their feelings trompled on," Gwydion sputtered just before he yanked the front door open and disappeared through it.

Fionn snickered as he plodded up the stairs. It was indeed a different world. The one he'd been born into had barely recognized emotions. People did what they had to because they had to. He pulled the door to his suite of rooms open and was greeted by clouds of steam. Aislinn must have drawn a bath. Good. He'd love to clean up too. Rune whined a greeting from where he curled in a corner and then tucked his nose under his tail again.

Fionn latched the door behind him and added a jot of magic to seal out the world before stripping off his clothes and draping them over a chair. He made his way into the Italian marble bathroom with its red and green-veined cream-colored tiles and sunken tub. Aislinn floated in the water with her hair fanned out about her like exotic sea anemones. She smiled lazily and patted the water's surface so ripples spread over it. "Come on in. It feels really good to be clean."

"I'll bet." He ignored the steps at one end of the tub and sat on its edge, lowering himself into steaming, scented water. "Teaching you how to warm water was a good investment."

"Thank you." Golden eyes twinkled at him and he waded through thigh deep water to sit next to her. She made a grab for the china dispenser where he kept liquid soap and pumped some into one hand. "Settle back and let me wash you."

"Best offer I've had all day, lass." Fionn settled his back against the tub's edge. He'd built the tub long before hot tubs came into vogue, but he'd had a similar idea: hot water that covered you to your shoulders.

He shut his eyes as Aislinn's strong fingers worked soap into his skin, kneading his tense muscles. When she shifted his body so he lay across her lap and washed his hair, he sighed with pleasure. "Best watch it, leannán. I could get used to this."

Claws clicked over marble and Rune nosed the side of Fionn's head. "Bella's outside. She says you told her to come up here and then sealed her out with magic."

"Crap!" Fionn followed that with a string of Gaelic curses, and pulled the power from his sealing spell. He turned his head and looked at the wolf. "Can ye undo the latch?"

"Of course." Rune trotted back into the bedroom, and Fionn girded himself for the flurry of feathers that barreled into the bathroom next.

"You locked me out," Bella screeched.

"Not on purpose."

"Then explain yourself."

Fionn squelched a desire to throttle his bond animal. He straightened and shook water out of his hair before meeting the raven's acrimonious glare. "I spelled the door to keep the world at bay for a short time. I apologize. I should have waited until ye were here, except I had no idea if ye'd heed Gwydion's words and come."

Aislinn stood, and water sluiced down her body. She stepped out of the tub and wound a thick blue towel around herself. "That's one of the problems," she told Bella, "when we never know what you're doing. Times are dangerous and we need you to be a little more forthcoming about your plans. We can't make decisions that include you if you don't include us in yours."

The bird cocked her head to one side. When she answered, her normally strident tone had softened. "Thank you. That was a good explanation."

Fionn considered pointing out that he'd said much the same thing —on numerous occasions, but wisely decided to keep his mouth shut. With a final dunk to finish rinsing soap that might still be clinging to his hair, he opened the drain and got out of the tub, funneling magic to dry himself.

Bella flew out of the bathroom, and Fionn knew he'd find her on her perch near the door that opened into his study. "Friends again?" he called after her retreating form.

"Friends," floated back to him.

He wrapped an arm around Aislinn, damp and fragrant from the bath. "Thank you."

She nodded. "That's why kids have two parents. Sometimes one's explanations sit better than the other's." Tilting her mouth invitingly in his direction, she pressed the length of her towel clad body against his. "Think we have time?"

"We'll make time." His voice roughened as desire shot through him, intense and demanding. Aislinn threaded her arms around him, and he closed his mouth over hers.

islinn dug her fingers into the bands of muscle cutting across Fionn's broad back. They'd made love countless times, but she never lost the sense of wonder that had filled her the first time they'd gotten naked together. Her body readied itself for him almost instantly. Everything tingled, from the top of her head down to her toes. Her nipples hardened, and her nether regions were awash with desire.

He plumbed her mouth with his tongue, and she nipped and sucked on it, loving the taste of him. His spicy, exotic, decidedly masculine scent rose around them, and she inhaled hungrily. Smelling Fionn was an aphrodisiac all its own. He tightened his hands on her towel-clad butt and tugged hard, wriggling so the thick terrycloth fell to the floor between their feet.

Without breaking their kiss, he swept her off her feet and carried her into the bedroom. She tore her mouth from his. "Put me down."

"Aye, lassie, that was the idea." He set her gently on the duvet atop the bed. For long moments, he stood, just looking at her. His cock jutted before him, rising proudly from a mat of golden curls.

She arched her back and raised her hands above her head to grip the edges of the headboard. "Like what you see?"

"So much, ye've damn near hypnotized me."

Rune rose and walked across the room, disappearing into the study.

Tilting her pelvis invitingly, she murmured, "Everyone's giving us privacy. Who knows how long it will last?"

He laughed and the sound warmed her heart. "Subtle as a sledge-hammer. There's my girl." He knelt between her legs and bent to kiss her breasts. When he took her nipples into his mouth, electric shocks blazed from them right to her core, and she moaned and writhed beneath his touch. Fionn kissed his way down her belly. By the time he settled his mouth over her sensitive center, the orgasm that had been building exploded, leaving her weak, wrung out, and aching for more of the same.

He licked and sucked, teased her delicate nub until she sent magic to muffle her shrieks. Finally, when the hollow place inside her was so desperate for his cock she couldn't stand it anymore, she slithered out from under him, flipped over, and got to her kees, hanging onto the headboard for support.

Fionn growled, the sound thick with need and planted his cock at the entrance to her body. She was so slick and wet from coming, he slid deep. She pushed her hips back and he bit her shoulder, and then wrapped an arm around her hips and rubbed her clit with knowing, calloused fingertips. She rocked, caught between his cock and fingers, but couldn't get him to give her what she needed.

"Move, goddammit." She butted her ass into his pelvis.

"How would ye like it, leannán?" he asked in a hoarse, panting whisper.

"Hard. Fast. Damn it, Fionn. Foreplay's over. I need the real deal."

He chuckled, breath warm against her neck. "I doona think I've ever been called that afore."

He rubbed her pussy harder and finally, finally began to thrust inside her. His cock was long, hard, and thick. It reached places no one else had even come close to. Another climax ripped through her, followed almost immediately by an even stronger one. Filled by uncontrollable lust, she summoned magic, formed it into tendrils and sent them to tickle his anus and his balls. A tortured sound burst from him and his cock grew even harder inside her. She made the tendrils move faster, sent them vibrating inside his delicate anal passage.

Another peak burned deep in her belly. The spasms of his climax would bring her over the edge one more time. Gasping, panting, slick with sweat, she felt him release inside her, felt herself join him, and leaned her back against his front as the world slowly came back into focus.

"Should have done the bath after," she said, once she could talk again.

"We could draw another."

He pulled himself out of her body, and she collapsed on the bed, still sorting out where she ended and he began.

"Nah. Probably need sleep."

He lay behind her, cradling her against him. "Ye cheated, using magic to make me come."

Aislinn giggled. "Guilty as charged." The grandfather clock in the corner struck one. "Boy, those last two hours flew by."

"Aye, my sweet, the next ones will too. I'll wake you fifteen minutes afore we report for watch duty."

She felt herself slipping toward sleep. "What happens if the Old Ones keep us too busy to launch our plan to go to the borderworlds?"

"We'll just have to kill all of them."

There was something so feral and bloodthirsty in Fionn's voice it sent sleep skittering to the four winds, and she turned on her other side facing him. "You really mean that, don't you?"

"'Tisn't a thing to joke about."

The skin around his eyes looked pinched in the faint light from his mage light that was suspended off to one side. Aislinn stared. With his face illuminated like that, no one would ever make the mistake of labeling him human. All the parts were there, but they were too perfect. His eyes gleamed with ancient knowing. Even the golden flecks in the irises seemed to vibrate, underscoring his *otherness*.

"What is it, lass? Ye're looking at me as if I grew a second head."

She bit down on her lower lip. "Nothing. Sometimes I'm more aware of you being a Celtic god. That's all."

"Having second thoughts?" He cupped her chin and forced her to look at him.

Well am I?

"No, not really. But I shouldn't make the mistake of ascribing too much humanness to you. You don't think like we do."

His face settled into stubborn planes she recognized, and she regretted her words.

"In the first place," he said, his voice laced with sarcasm, "ye're scarcely human yourself. Never mind, ye thought yourself so for most of your short life. In the second place—"

She laid a hand over his mouth. "Stop. I don't want to argue. I'm tired, and I misspoke. Of course I understand we need to wipe out all the Old Ones, and the dark gods too. It's not that I can't kill. I have. It's that I never quite warmed to the idea."

"Which is another good reason ye should remain here. Ye've been to Perrikus's borderworld. 'Tis fraught with danger, and 'twill be worse this time around because the dark ones know the odds have steepened—and not in their favor."

"While I waited to see if you and Arawn would return from there, I swore we'd never be separated again. I hated Bran and Gwydion for being the ones who'd returned first, and that was stupid. I should've bowed down and thanked every god and goddess in the pantheon that *any* of you were still alive."

Fionn drew her against his body and stroked her hair, crooning in Gaelic, until she murmured, "English, please."

"These are difficult times, mo croi. We have to get through each day as it happens. If the goddess smiles on us, 'twill come a time when things are easier."

And if she doesn't? But Aislinn kept that question to herself.

～

DEWI OVERFLEW the manor house and grounds, grateful for something to do to take her mind off her brood. It had damn near killed her to leave them on the borderworld. Not because she didn't think Royce and Vaughna would make good nannies, but because she felt she'd failed her offspring. It defied credibility that one of her blood would be so easily manipulated. And by a Lemurian no less. Stupid bastards with their hive mind mentality. For fuck's sake, it took at least three of them to make even the simplest decision.

Leave it. Just leave it. No matter how many ways I turn this thing around, I still won't like how it looks or smells.

She returned her attention to shadowed nooks and crannies, hunting for anything out of the ordinary. Humans and Arawn were patrolling on foot in a pattern that circled the manor every quarter hour. Since they staggered their line, nothing should be able to sneak through, but it wasn't wise to underestimate their enemy. She'd done so in the past with disastrous results. Fanning magic in a circle, she moved it from her level a hundred feet off the ground downward.

Wait.

Something didn't feel quite right, but it was subtle, so subtle Dewi ran her scan one more time, zeroing in on where she may have felt a tinge of wrongness. This time her magic pinged back clean, but she didn't totally trust it.

I'm jumpy as a March hare. The first time I was distracted, not paying close enough attention. No point in getting everyone riled up for nothing.

She flew two more complete circuits, but couldn't let it go. "Nidhogg."

"Yes, dear."

"Meet me up here."

He didn't ask for particulars, especially after Bella had identified their enemy so close. Soon his black form winged its way to her. "I know," his dear voice rumbled against her ears. "You got lonely."

She blew smoke, followed by fire. "If you want lonely, try believing you're the last of your kind for hundreds of years."

"I scarcely see that it's worse than having Perrikus holding me on the edge of life to siphon my power."

"Ouch. I didn't invite you up here to trade pity parties." She switched to telepathic speech. *Fly the circuit with me and scan with your magic. I thought I found something, but when I checked a second time, it wasn't there.*

"Why alert me and not the rest of your patrol?"

"Because I didn't want to look like an overreactive jackrabbit."

Nidhogg chuckled, but she felt his power sweep the area. Once. Twice. He kept coming back to the same spot that had bothered her.

Breath whistled through her open jaws. *"I didn't tell you where I felt the aberration, yet you found it anyway."*

"There's something there. We must land and alert the others."

Dewi and Nidhogg stopped near the moat and gathered the rest of the watch as they crossed that waypoint. Arawn moved between the dragons.

"What is it?" he asked in shielded mind speech.

"Is everyone here?" Dewi counted ten humans—two of them with bond animals: a hawk and a mountain cat. At nods, she drew strong wards around them, pleased when Nidhogg reinforced them.

"What the hell?" One of the human men asked.

"Something isn't right about a quarter league northwest of the manor gates," Dewi said. "I thought I felt evil, but wasn't certain, so I called Nidhogg to give things a second look."

"Ye felt it too?" Arawn gazed up at the black dragon, who nodded.

"It could be as simple as an outpost the Old Ones set up to spy on us and report back to the dark gods," Nidhogg said.

"Or it could be the start of another attack," Arawn grunted, shaking his head.

"It doesn't matter," Corin stepped forward. "We have to address it. I'll wake the others."

"We march as soon as everyone's up and ready," Nidhogg said. "It will still be dark, which works in our favor."

"Whatever it is, it's underground," Dewi cautioned.

"Let's do this," Arawn said. "The four dragons can attack from the air. Blast the holy fuck out of where you feel the evil. The rest of us will provide ground support." He looked as grim as the dead he commanded. "No prisoners. We kill every single thing that crawls out of the ground. Understood?"

"Do you suppose this is the same thing Bella stumbled on today?" Dewi asked.

"It better be," one of the human women said, "because if it isn't that means we have two problems."

"I'll get Kra and Berra," Nidhogg pulled magic from the wards around them.

"I'll roust Fionn, Gwydion, and Aislinn," Arawn said. "Everyone front and center in fifteen minutes or less."

Dewi waited, still as stone, in the dim mistiness near the moat. She'd been born for battle, yet she had a hard time finding the heart to move forward. She gave herself a good, hard mental kick. Feeling sorry for herself was an indulgence, one she could ill afford just now. It wasn't as if her brood was dead, and there were still the eggs percolating in her belly. After years of spinning her scales, they were finally moving into the endgame. She should welcome it, yet all she wanted to do was take Nidhogg and flee to some place where none of this could touch them.

Understanding smashed home.

When I had no one to love, and no one who loved me, it didn't matter. Nothing did. I took outrageous chances because I didn't care if I lived or died. That's all changed, but the world hasn't. There're still the dark gods to contend with, and those smarmy reptiles I spied on all those years.

Yes, and that will help because I know how they think even better than the MacLochlainn.

Dewi straightened. By the goddess, she had a role to play, and a damned important one. If what they faced were Lemurians—and it almost had to be—she was their best tactical leader, the only one who could outthink and outmaneuver the fucking things.

Kra, Berra, and Nidhogg touched down near her.

"Did Nidhogg fill you in?" Dewi asked.

"Aye," Kra clanked his double rows of teeth together. "It will be good to avenge ourselves for what they did to your brood."

"Assuming it is Lemurians," Nidhogg said.

"I suppose there might be a dark god in the mix," Berra said, "or some of those hideous Bal'ta things."

Dewi thought about the Bal'ta. Minions of the dark, they stood between five and six feet tall. With their sloping foreheads, matted hair, and ropy muscles, they looked like apes, except for their eyes, which glowed an unholy orange. "Pah. They're easy enough to kill. Least of our worries, really."

Arawn and Gwydion sprinted to them. "Never underestimate any of them," Gwydion said dourly. "I made that mistake with the human-Lemurian hybrids, and it almost sent me to the *Dreaming* forever."

"Where are Fionn and Aislinn?" Dewi asked.

"They'll be along soon," Arawn said. "I'm furious Bran's not back yet. He knows better."

The air took on a numinous quality by the manor house wall, and Bran stepped out of a glowing portal, followed by Andraste, goddess of victory. Wavy blonde hair fell to her waist and even in the muted light, her green eyes flashed fire. She wore a long buckskin skirt and a top of the same leather that hugged her curves.

Bran bowed toward Arawn. "Instructive what ye hear when people don't think ye're anywhere close."

"What took you so long?" Gwydion barked. "I was none too pleased with you myself."

"We got into an argument," Andraste said. "No one wanted aught to do with the Norsemen."

"If ye felt the same"—Arawn stomped to her side—"why are ye here?"

"Never could let a battle pass me by." One corner of her perfect mouth twisted downward. Her gaze settled on Dewi. "Where are your younglings? By my count they're nearly old enough to join us."

"On our borderworld."

"What?" Andraste squared her shoulders. "Why?"

"'Tis a long tale," Gwydion said, "and one which we havena the time for just now. Our first order of business is to wipe out something wicked that's taken up residence too close for comfort."

"I'm all for *wiping out darkness*"—the goddess's smile was as predatory as one of Dewi's own—"but why is it ye doona know exactly what ye face?"

"They're underground," Dewi said, "and we didn't want to look too closely. In fact, we should be shielding our conversation."

Humans trotted up in small groups, followed by Fionn and Aislinn. Dewi considered asking what took them so long, but her tone would've been snappish, and it would kindle the Maclochlainn's ire. Not the best idea on the verge of a major skirmish. Instead, she resurrected the earlier wards and outlined the plan. Before they moved out, she asked Bella if the location was where she'd found Lemurians.

For once, the raven looked rattled. "No. The group I found was in an old castle south of the gates, between here and the ocean."

"Hear that," Nidhogg cautioned the group. "Watch your backs. We have no idea what we'll find out there, and there may well be a second faction that's lying in wait to trap us."

CHAPTER 16

Fionn's muscles tensed with apprehension, and his nerves came alive like they always did when a fight loomed. He angled his head toward Aislinn's ear. "For once, do as I instruct. I canna split my attention, and if I'm worried half to death about you—or worse, doona know where ye are—it might prove tragic for all of us."

She tapped the side of his face with two fingers, and her face lit with a determined expression that made her look much older than her twenty-two years. "I'm not making promises I can't keep, but I will keep you apprised of what I'm doing if it deviates from your orders."

He swallowed the lecture that rose to his lips. No time, and it wouldn't make any difference. Lemurians may have trained Aislinn, but they'd trained her in guerilla warfare where she fought alone and made her own decisions. Nothing he could say would alter that.

The group around them melted into the night and the rush of dragons' wings created a torrent of wind until they were airborne. Aislinn took off at a lope, following a bunch of Hunters. Rune trotted next to her.

Bella's talons tightened on Fionn's shoulder to the point of pain.

"What are you waiting for?" the bird asked. "We'll miss the party."

Except it wouldn't be. "I have a bad feeling about this," he told the raven and bolted after Aislinn.

Bella switched to mind speech. *Since when does that excuse us from fighting?*

"It doesn't. Quiet. I need all my senses."

For once, the bird didn't argue, but he sensed her tension from the death grip she maintained on his shoulder. He reached the others in short order and noted the power circle they'd formed around the area Dewi had discovered. Fionn positioned himself next to Aislinn. Eve and her cat were on his other side. After a brief hissing and cawing match, Bella and Tabitha settled down.

The first bolt of dragon magic thundered down, and the ground shook beneath his feet. As they'd planned, the dragons piled charge atop charge with bare seconds in between. Fionn homed in on the patch of greenery before him, every nerve on edge. Something felt wrong. It was too silent, too devoid of life. Normally, small creatures —owls and rodents—would live in bushes like those, but they'd deserted it long since.

With an eerie, thrumming, cracking noise, the earth split open. Heather and gorse blew into the air, and an unholy, shrieking moan rose, grating against his ears and making his stomach clench. Bile blasted the back of his throat as he drew power, balancing it between his hands, ready to annihilate whatever rolled out of the hole.

Next to him, Aislinn's ragged breathing tore at his soul. Even though Northern Ireland looked nothing like the Andean mountainside where she'd lost her father, death had crawled out of a hole in the earth that night too. Sulfur and the rotten stench of road kill left in the sun to rot belched from the fault.

"What the holy fuck?" Aislinn snapped.

"We'll find out soon enough," Fionn ground out, ready for anything, but mostly wanting whatever it was to show itself.

The discordant cries rose in volume just before bodies pushed through the opening, and Fionn recoiled in horror as trolls and demons thrust their way through. Standing tall as mountain boulders, the trolls hefted cudgels and flails. With their bald heads, they resembled the stones they'd been formed from.

But they were far from the worst. Fionn gaped at the demon spawn. With hooves, tails, and claws, they wielded fiery scepters and had eyes like burning coals edged with gray smoke. Some were tall and humanoid, but others were perversions of animals, with double rows of teeth and razor shards where fur should have been. The smallest weighed at least a hundred pounds, and they moved with shocking speed. Winged abominations with sharp beaks and shiny, black, scaled bodies like flying dinosaurs emerged next.

The air around him blazed with magic as dark power met light in smoky, roiling fury. Between soot, grit, and stink, breathing became a challenge. Fionn released power and one of the animals with a lionesque head and a giraffe's lower body burst into reeking particles, showering him with filth that dripped down his head and burned like hell where it touched him. He stole a glance at Aislinn. Thank Christ she was still by his side and had the presence of mind to keep Rune right next to her. The wolf snarled like a mad thing, clearly furious she'd restrained him from leaping into the fray.

Truth flattened him like a steamroller. "Fuck! Goddammit!" Fionn didn't bother wasting magic on telepathic speech. "We played right into their hands. This is a portal straight into Hell, and we opened it for them."

Gwydion, Arawn, Bran, and Andraste materialized next to him.

"Next bright idea?" Gwydion wiped dark slime from his face where something he'd killed had exploded all over him.

"We have to close the hole," Andraste shouted, "before any more of those atrocities escape!"

"No shit!" Fionn glanced at the dragons, who were still circling. *"Dewi."*

But it was Nidhogg who answered. *"We understand. We'll join you on the ground. It's too crowded down there for us to keep blasting magic. We'll hit one of you by mistake."*

"Can ye undo the fault line?" Fionn hadn't expected an answer, and he didn't get one.

Anguished howls and screams rose all around Fionn, and he shouted, "Until we have some plan to stuff the crows back inside the pie, we have to help our allies." Magic blew through him until he felt like a lightning rod. Around him, the other Celts and Aislinn leant firepower, fanning out to at least try to maintain the integrity of the circle they'd originally formed around the dragons' blast zone. Bella clung to his shoulder like a shadow. The bird was savvy enough to understand leaving the protection of his warding would sign her death warrant.

Nidhogg settled to the ground in front of Fionn, fire streaming from his mouth. Explosions shook the ground whenever dragon fire met demon fire. For one black humor moment, Fionn wondered if that was where the phrase *fight fire with fire* had originated: with demons and dragons duking it out.

"We have to figure out some way to shut that thing." Aislinn's face was streaked with black and red ichor from whatever she'd killed.

Fionn rifled through his memories like a card shark shuffling marked cards, hunting for the one that would bail them out. He'd been to Hell a time or two. Once when he was very young—and incredibly stupid—he'd bribed Charon to give him a ride and had a nearly impossible time getting out. Different from Arawn's halls of the dead, Hell held those with wicked pasts, the ones who'd never played well with others. Abaddon ruled all nine levels with a steely will. It was because of him that his denizens remained caged.

They'd wanted out so badly when Fionn was there, he'd had to fight his way through hordes of atrocities, each of whom wanted a free ride out of Hell on his coattails. Had Abaddon made a deal with the Lemurians? Fionn annihilated a seven foot tall demon and one of its claws boomeranged back to impale his thigh. With a grunt, he pulled it out before it could poison him. Even after death, demons packed quite a punch.

Arawn sidled to Fionn's side, looking as degenerate and coated in grime and gore as Fionn supposed he did, but his dark eyes shone with battle lust, and power crackled around him, turning the air blue with its intensity. "The plot thickens," he spat.

"I was just thinking Abaddon crafted some sort of deal with the Lemurians," Fionn panted in between targeting one of the flying dinosaur things. He ducked so its spinning scales wouldn't take out one of his eyes.

"Optimist." Arawn snorted, spun, and took out two demons. "Somehow the dark gods infiltrated Hell. 'Tis the only rational explanation."

Fionn's heart stuttered in his chest as the truth in Arawn's words arrowed home. "One of them, probably Perrikus, fed us just enough false information to get us to do his dirty work," Fionn said. "It might have taken him months to get this portal open. It's the same thing the dark gods did when they teamed up with the Lemurians and coerced all those New Age idiots to chant and weaken the veils between the worlds. Without that, they'd never have been able to infiltrate Earth."

A demon hurtled toward them out of the murk. Fionn dodged sideways, pivoting to avoid the worst of the fire shooting from the creature's hands and mouth. Arawn spoke a word and it vanished.

"That's a neat trick," Fionn gasped. "What'd ye do?"

"Sent it back to Hell."

"Can ye do that for all of them?" Fionn stared at the god of the dead.

"Aye. How else could I rid my realm of those who sneak into it under false pretenses?" The god of the dead shook long strands of black hair out of his eyes. "It scarcely matters how many I return to their rightful place if they crawl right back out again. We must close the hole. The longer it remains open, the harder this will be."

"MacLochlainn," Dewi trumpeted from his right.

Fionn had a hunch what was coming next and he hastened to the dragon's side. "Ye are not taking her," he said.

"If you want us to negate our earlier magic, I need her."

"Figure something else out," he bellowed.

"There's no time." Dewi's tone was implacable.

"I never promised obedience." Aislinn straightened her shoulders. "All I promised was that you'd know what I was doing. Remember those times I told you about? The ones where I can't stop to think?"

"Aye, but leannán..."

"Well, this is one of them. I love you, Fionn, but I trust Dewi, and if she says she needs me, she does." Aislinn vaulted onto the dragon's back and summoned additional magic to lift Rune into her lap. "Whatever it is," she cried in a clear, ringing voice, "let's do this."

"Nay!" Fionn wanted to throttle the dragon. Fury and fear formed a burning knot in his belly. "If anything happens to her—" he began.

Something bumped his back so hard he staggered.

"Stop whining and ride me," Nidhogg said from behind Fionn. "What Dewi has in mind will require all of us."

"Go." Arawn shoved Fionn toward the dragon. "I'll cover things down here."

So much power bubbled around him, Fionn just rode it until he was settled on Nidhogg's broad back.

The black dragon spread his wings immediately and barked. "Hang on."

Bella was obviously listening because she tightened her hold on Fionn until he laid a hand over her feet to remind her to back off.

After the first lurching swing into nothingness, Fionn tethered himself in place with power. He hoped the air would clear as they gained elevation, but it did nothing but get worse. His eyes teared-up from the thick, smoky murk, and his throat and lungs felt scoured. He looked around for Aislinn, but didn't see her.

"What's the plan?" he asked Nidhogg.

"Just give me what I ask for."

Fion slapped a fist into Nidhogg's scaled hide. Pain lanced up his arm as the dragon's sharp scales cut into his hand. "That's not good enough. Goddammit it all to hell, I can't even see Dewi or Aislinn."

"They're here. *Be reasonable,*" Nidhogg switched to mind speech. *"Anything we say can potentially be overheard. There's a dark god some-*

where in this mess. I suspect Majestron Zalia. She's the only one wily enough to waltz into Abaddon's lair and seduce him with lies."

"If it was her, once she was done, Perrikus played us like suckers, luring us to blast a hole into Hell." Fionn bit down so hard he was surprised his teeth didn't splinter. *"As I recall, Majestron is quite the looker. Maybe it wasna just lies she fed Abaddon,"* he said sourly.

"It doesn't matter who she fucks. What matters is closing that rent and piling enough spells on it to keep it shut. Once that's done, we have to chase down whoever's still out and either kill them or send them back to Hell."

The dragon swooped and dove. At first it seemed random, but then Fionn recognized a pattern. The dragon was painting runic symbols in the sky. From time to time, Dewi, with Aislinn and Rune atop her, appeared through the gloom, apparently doing the same thing. Fionn played the configuration through his mind, but came up dry. Whatever the dragons were up to was a summoning he'd never tried—or even heard of, which didn't engender confidence. Not that he had an eidetic memory, but there were very few spells he hadn't run across at least once in his long life.

"Ready yourself," Nidhogg instructed, his voice harsh.

Fionn reeled in power until he couldn't hold any more. Bella threaded animal magic in with his, and he loved her for the effort. Clouds of black smoke billowed from below.

"Now," Nidhogg trumpeted. "Open yourself to me. Give me everything you can."

Fionn tossed his warding aside and gave the dragon entrance. Nidhogg's consciousness filled his mind and swallowed Fionn in a tidal wave of memories. Fascination trumped everything else as Fionn paged through thousands of years of history. Valkyries had ridden to battle where he sat. Hell, Odin had flown on Nidhogg. Farther back, much farther, Fionn gazed at an unfamiliar landscape with Lemurians lounging in front of golden buildings and gold-paved streets. Dragons wandered amongst the Old Ones under a sky with three suns.

Mu. It must be Mu. Unabashed wonder filled Fionn. He'd time-traveled to Atlantis before the volcano had decimated it, but he'd never been able to access Mu.

"Attention. I need your attention," Nidhogg dropped a chiaroscuro curtain over his memories.

"Anything." A grim smile split his face, and Fionn understood he'd been mesmerized by the ancient dragon.

"The first part of this is done. It laid the groundwork. The next is a closing spell. I will summon the dragon version, and you will call the Celtic one. They must weave together precisely. A piece of yours and then a piece of mine. Feed me the spell in quarters when I ask for it."

"Why did Dewi need Aislinn?"

"Because her magic is linked to the MacLochlainn and having Aislinn strengthens her. Focus. Give me the first part of your spell now."

Fionn visualized the spell, broke it into fourths, and gave the first to Nidhogg. The whole process went much faster than he imagined it would, which was good because judging from the anguished screams coming from below him, they wouldn't walk away from this confrontation scot-free.

"Hurry," he urged Nidhogg, but the dragon sucked up the last part of his spell without comment.

"It begins," Nidhogg said; tension thrummed through his scales. *"Timing is everything. Wait until my flight gets so rough you can't remain on my back, even with magic, and then teleport to the ground, but not too close to the rent or you'll get sucked into it as it shuts."*

"Does Aislinn know that?"

"I'm certain Dewi told her the same thing."

"Can ye fly close enough for me to include her in my teleport spell?"

"No. Be quiet or you'll undo everything."

Fionn forced a calm center by inhaling one smoke-tinged breath after another. A low, sonorous booming joined the screams from below. Nidhogg's body vibrated between Fionn's legs. What began as a slow bucking quickly turned into trying to hold onto greased lightning. The air around him exploded with light that seared his corneas, even through his closed lids.

"We have to go," Bella cawed, sounding frantic.

After two more jolting quakes that rattled his teeth, Fionn visualized a spot behind where he'd stood earlier and teleported there. The portal dissipated, and the stench of death—blood, shit, and entrails—enveloped him. Battlefields all smelled the same.

"Aislinn!" he shrieked, and then switched to mind speech and called her name over and over. He reached for her energy, but the air was so charged with bright magic colliding with dark, he couldn't get a fix on anything.

"Not here," Bella cawed.

"How do ye know?" he asked, filled with desperation and fury at Dewi for putting his love smack in the center of things.

"Because Rune's not answering, either."

Someone grabbed his arm. Fionn almost hit them square with a death blow before he realized it was Bran.

His battle leathers were singed and tattered, and he looked trashed. "Come on," the god of prophecy urged. "We need help. The hole in the ground's closed, but there are hundreds of those bastards yet to kill."

"Have ye seen Aislinn?"

A shadow flitted across Bran's begrimed face, but Fionn might have imagined it.

"Nay. I'm sure she's here somewhere, though."

"You found him!" Andraste punched Bran's arm before stalking to Fionn's side. Her hair was clotted with ichor and hung in tangled mats. Her buckskin gown had long rents in the skirt and a bloody hole over one shoulder. "Get moving. We need you."

"Aislinn needs me," Fionn countered. "There are plenty of you here to finish things off."

With his heart full of foreboding, he didn't stand around to chew the point to death. Something had clearly happened somewhere between Dewi's back and here. If he didn't find out what it was now, the trail would grow cold, making his task that much harder.

CHAPTER 17

Fionn put some distance between himself and the worst of the carnage. Once the interference from too much magic discharged in the same place cleared enough, he raised his mind voice and called Dewi.

Her peevish reply rattled his brain almost at once. *"What? I'm busy. While we're at it, where the hell are you? There are demons to kill."*

"Aislinn's gone."

Silence and then the thrum of wing beats. Dewi didn't even try for grace as she dropped to the ground so close to him she nearly knocked him over.

"How could she possibly be gone?" Dewi demanded. "She was on my back, left when I told her to—"

"We're wasting time. Ye're bonded to her. If ye're so certain she made it safely back, find her."

The blast of power from Dewi scalded him, and Fionn retreated a few feet, waiting. Part of him hoped for a miracle, but the other part knew Aislinn wasn't anywhere nearby. She had an unmistakable energy, and he'd know if she were here.

Dewi shuffled around until she faced him, her face etched with worry, lower jaw gaping open. "I don't understand."

Fionn shook his head. "Neither do I, but we have to find her."

The dragon's head drooped. "I haven't the faintest idea where to look."

"Narrows it down nicely." Fionn didn't bother to trim the rancor from his voice. "'Tis your fault. Ye put her at risk."

Dewi's dark eyes whirled dangerously fast. "Now you're the one wasting time." She took a step closer and shook a foreleg at him. "Life is risk, or haven't you noticed?"

Fionn swallowed hard. "Ye're right. Let's think this through rather than tear each other to shreds. The only way Aislinn could have vanished between your back and the ground is if someone else intervened with magic. There was so much power being jockeyed about, probably ye wouldna have noticed someone lurking nearby."

Criticism never sat well with the dragon. Fire streamed from her jaws, missing him by a narrow margin, but Fionn held his ground. "Get hold of yourself, Dewi. Aislinn needs us."

More fire. The dragon shook her head and a shrill, keening cry escaped her. "First my brood and now this."

Fionn gentled his voice. "I know ye love her, Dewi. I do too. We have to find her and Rune, who apparently got sucked into wherever Aislinn went."

"Should we go to Perrikus's borderworld?"

Fionn thought about it. "Probably not. 'Tis the first place they'd think we'd look. Nay, my bet is somewhere on Earth. One of the oldest strategies is to hide something in plain sight."

"So here in the Old Country, back in the States, or elsewhere? Earth's a big place."

Fionn watched the dragon. At least she was settling down since her eyes, while still whirling like pinwheels, had slowed. "They'll probably go where they have an established presence. Problem is I'm not all that familiar with the dark gods' history. I have no idea where they lived afore Odin imprisoned them in Asgard. 'Twas only after they escaped that they ended up on the borderworlds."

The dragon ground her teeth together, producing a gnashing noise that made Fionn want to punch her.

"We can ask Nidhogg. In fact, I will. Give me a moment."

Fionn shifted from foot to foot, anxious to get moving, but understanding that action without some kind of plan was worse than no action at all. He could blow through huge blocks of time and not get one angstrom closer to Aislinn. His heart twisted in his chest. Life without the only woman he'd ever loved wouldn't be worth shit. His immortality mocked him until it was all he could do not to race headlong into the demon throng and kick some serious demon ass. It wouldn't bring Aislinn back, but the purity of dealing out death would distract him.

"You still have me," Bella spoke low, her voice laced with pain.

He hadn't exactly forgotten about the raven, but she wasn't front and center in his mind, either. Guilt smote him and he stroked her feathers. "Aye, Bella. Doona think I doona appreciate it."

Wings thumped above them and Nidhogg crashed to the ground a few feet away. "Goddess's tits, but I'm tired." He turned his green gaze on Fionn. "You need Odin. I propose a compromise. Help us dispatch the rest of the demons, and I'll fly you to Asgard."

"But Aislinn could be dead by then," Fionn protested.

"She might be already," Nidhogg said, "and there are lives here you could help save."

"I don't need you to get to Asgard," Fionn countered.

"True, but Odin's more likely to help you if I ask."

Fionn recalled the enmity between the Celts and the Norse gods. Reluctant agreement curdled his stomach. "Fine," he ground out. "Half an hour."

"Good choice." The Norse dragon shot an appraising glance his way. "It shouldn't take much more than that."

But Fionn wasn't listening. He spun and bolted back the way he'd come, calling power as he ran. By the time he waded into the remaining demons, his vision hazed red with fury, and he handed out death with machinelike precision. Normally, he'd have enjoyed killing these bastards, but today all he could think about was Aislinn, her lithe body spread-eagled as someone tortured her.

Demon stench mingled with the coppery scent of blood and the sickly-sweet miasma of shit from ruptured entrails, but Fionn didn't waste power shielding himself. Blood from a falling dinosaur demon splattered him, but when he twisted to avoid the worst of it, a troll blew up, showering him with black ichor and chunks of stone. He wiped the worst of it out of his eyes and picked his next target. War was never pretty, and the sooner he mowed through the stinking rotters the sooner he could go after his love.

AISLINN CAME to with the back of her head aching and a nasty taste in the back of her throat. Momentarily disoriented, she listened for the battle she was certain still raged, but all she heard was the beat of her own heart. Something hot and wet licked her hand. Rune. She tried to stroke his rough fur, but her body was slow to respond.

"You're awake."

A feeble croak emerged, but the wolf nipped her and said, *"Mind speech."*

Aislinn struggled to focus, but her brain felt like mush. She pushed to a sit and forced her eyes open. A dimly lit room spread around her, with a rickety cot braced against one wall. A small, round table with two chairs butted against another. The walls were white plaster, and large wooden beams riddled with termite holes ran across the ceiling. Slowly, things registered. No windows. She gazed around the room, grateful beyond measure to see a door.

"Where are we?" she asked Rune.

"I don't know exactly, but a long way from where we sat on Dewi."

Aislinn digested the information and rubbed a lump at the base of her skull. No wonder her head hurt, but why take the trouble to hit her? Did whoever captured her not have magic?

She patted the narrow cot. Rune jumped up next to her and licked her chin. The cot creaked and swayed, but held. *"You slept long. I was worried."*

She pulled the wolf into her arms, reassured by the solid feel of him against her. *"Were you awake the whole time? Did you see our captors?"*

"Yes and yes."

"Did you recognize anyone?" Aislinn held her breath. Rune had met Perrikus, D'Chel, and Tokhots.

The wolf shook his head. *"There were two. A woman, who I believe is one of the dark gods from her smell. The other was a lackey, an underling. He obeyed her commands as if he feared her."*

Aislinn let go of Rune and pushed to her feet. Walking would help clear her head, so she paced from one end of the smallish room to the other and then back again.

Rune whined anxiously. *"You should sit, mistress."*

"No, I have to find a way out of here." Saying the words joggled her memory, and she reached for her magic, but gently. The last thing she wanted to do was alert whoever might be watching them. Rune's description of a female dark god had to be Majestron Zalia. Aislinn had come across her once before, the experience so disorienting she'd almost crapped herself. As strikingly beautiful as the male gods were handsome, Majestron radiated pure evil. Despite her waist-length black curls, midnight blue eyes, and tall, curvaceous figure, she'd been nearly impossible to look at. Just being within range had set Aislinn's teeth on edge and turned her guts to water.

She swallowed around a dry-as-dust throat and tried to suck moisture from her cheeks to help. Some thoughtful soul—or maybe just somebody who didn't fancy mopping up piss and shit—had chucked a bucket in one corner, but no one had left her anything else. Not that it was safe to drink or eat anything on the borderworlds—if that was where she was.

Her head pounded relentlessly, and she eased herself back next to Rune. Aislinn sucked a deep breath in, tasted the air, examined it, and blew it back out. Then she did it again. She might be wrong, but if they were on a borderworld, it wasn't the same one she'd been imprisoned on last time.

"How long did it take us to get here?" she asked the wolf. *"And did we go through that part where there wasn't any air?"*

"We got here fast. The time it takes for prey to run from me to a nearby den." Rune cocked his head to one side. *"No problems breathing. Not like when we traveled with Fionn and Dewi."*

Good news. That meant they were still somewhere on Earth, which made rescuing themselves easier. She pieced together what must have happened. Dewi had instructed her to wait until she couldn't hold on any longer and then to teleport to the ground. Because the dragon had been consumed by the spell running through her, she hadn't shielded her instructions.

Which means someone was close enough to listen in. Probably the same someone who'd manipulated them into opening Hell's gates. Aislinn shivered. For once, she'd left without her rucksack, and she wished for its contents. She always carried a water bottle, spare food, and an extra jacket. Rune leaned closer, draping himself across her and sharing his body heat.

"Are you ill?" he asked. *"It's not cold in here."*

How to explain to him that her spirit was shaken by knowing how close evil had come without her sensing it. If it was Majestron Zalia, the woman was smart. She'd taken full advantage of the plethora of different magics blasting every which way to hide herself.

"No, Rune. I'm all right."

"Can you access your power?"

"I think so." She pinched the bridge of her nose between her thumb and forefinger and then scrubbed the heels of her hands down her face. She'd checked her magic, and then gotten sidetracked by her fears about Majestron Zalia. Clearly, she wasn't firing on all cylinders.

Aislinn pushed toward the part of her that held her power and found the well depleted, but accessible. Obviously, her captors weren't concerned about her escaping, which meant there were some lethal booby-traps between her and freedom. She shook her head sharply. It would help if her mind was clearer.

"How long have we been here? You said I slept long."

The wolf hesitated. Time questions weren't his forte. *"After we got to Mount Shasta, the Old Ones came. Then time passed before they took us to Taltos. That's close to how long since they locked us in this room."*

Aislinn remembered that night well. *"Thank you. Means we've been here four hours, maybe five."* No wonder she was thirsty and getting hungry.

Rune nudged her with his snout. *"If you're well enough, we should leave while we can. It might be difficult out there, but at least we can hide."*

She didn't want to disabuse him of the notion, but it would be a neat trick to conceal themselves from someone with strong magic. If they were in a forested region with other wolves, Rune was home free, but she wasn't. She turned her thoughts inward, assessing just how low her batteries were. Dewi had slipped into her mind during the struggle to close the gateway, and had run through her power as if it were an inexhaustible resource. Still, a few hours had elapsed since then, and at least some of her ability was back online.

Aislinn clacked her jaws together. Anything was better than waiting like a tethered ninny for Majestron Zalia to come waltzing in. No matter what the dark goddess had in mind, it couldn't be good. She stumbled upright and tiptoed to the door, laying her ear against it. When she didn't hear any sounds coming from the other side, she paid out a tendril of Seeker magic to see if she could discover what held the door closed.

Wards. Layer upon layer held with intricate bindings that would take her days to unravel.

"No wonder they didn't post a guard," she muttered, not bothering with mind speech. Nothing could penetrate what she'd sensed, either in or out.

"Can we teleport?" Rune hadn't given up on telepathic speech.

"Not if this entire room is wrapped in the same stuff they have outside the door."

The wolf growled softly, walked to the far wall and hiked his leg. Urine splattered down the whitewashed plaster, and Aislinn grinned.

"Yeah, buddy, I'd like to piss all over them too."

An idea formed, raw and desperate. One of the five powers she commanded was Seer magic. Unfortunately, it was her weakest suit, but if she didn't screw things up, she could turn back time. Maybe not very far, but all she needed was a do over on being dumped in this room. She closed her eyes and reached for a calm center.

"What are you doing?" Rune demanded as he trotted to her side.

"Ssht. This is hard for me. I'm going to try to jump us to an earlier point in time. Hopefully one where we can alter the outcome."

"We'll still be a long way from home."

She knelt next to him. *"It's not like we have hundreds of options here. It will take me too long to untangle the warding, and someone would discover what I was doing long before I was done. I'm sure they set markers in their spell to alert them if I try to tamper with it."*

He licked her chin. *"Tell me what you need from me."*

"I will." She tried not to think about what might happen to Rune if this didn't work. Her own death was one thing, but for Rune to die because of his unquestioning loyalty was unacceptable. Anger straightened her backbone and cleared her jumbled thoughts. It had always been her ace in the hole, and it didn't fail her now as she laid the groundwork for her spell.

Fionn had tried to explain to her how Seer magic worked, but she hadn't fully understood him. Somehow, it bent the strands of time and allowed the user to reenter a scene or an event at a different point. She supposed it might work to travel forward too, but she'd never done that.

What was the best time to aim for? When she and Rune were still on Dewi's back would be optimal, but she wasn't at all sure she could buy herself that many hours. Second best was when she and Rune arrived at their current location and were being transported into this building. Someone had clonked her over the head to make it easy for themselves, which argued against there being more than the two people Rune told her about, and it was likely that the man had no power of his own.

"Rune. Send me an image of when they brought us here." No matter how impenetrable the wards, telepathic speech was still safer. The vision bloomed before her eyes, and ice chips congealed in her blood. It was Majestron Zalia, but looking far more beleaguered than on the other occasion Aislinn had seen her. Rather than a jeweled gown, she wore skin-tight black trousers and a low-cut black top. Lace-up black boots came to her knees. The mounds of dark, curly hair hadn't changed, nor had her cold, blue eyes or the harsh line of her perfect jaw.

No wonder she looks so furious. Her master plan to unleash Hell's denizens went sideways. Maybe Rune and I were a consolation prize, not planned for, but too good to pass up.

She placed a hand on Rune's broad head. *"Once I activate my spell—assuming it works—you'll see this same scene as if you're a spectator. Link to the wolf in the scene and run like the wind."*

"What will you be doing?"

"The same thing. We'll have a few minutes' grace before Majestron realizes what's happening. Rewinding time has a built in lag factor."

Another scene blasted her, thick timber choked with dense undergrowth. *"Head this way,"* he said. *"See the white-barked tree in the middle?"*

She nodded. *"Does everything outside look like that?"*

"Yes, but this is the only tree with light-colored bark. Sometimes their root systems are hollow and create underground hiding places for game."

Aislinn's throat tightened, and she hugged her wolf. *"I love you. If we don't manage to get through this, I wanted you to know."*

He wriggled in her grasp. *"Victory. Don't even consider anything else."*

"For Christ's fucking sake, you sound just like Fionn. I'm not certain Seer magic will do any better negating the warding than teleporting."

"Desperate times require desperate solutions."

Marta, the wolf's last bondmate, had been a highly educated physician and fluent in both Latin and Greek. She'd raised Rune and taught him an enormous amount, including classic quotes like the one he'd just spouted.

Aislinn laid her cheek against the wolf's head. *"Thanks, Ace."*

Rune swiped her face with his tongue and then did it again. If he was offering moral support, it worked, because confidence built in her chest, overshadowing her anxiety. She could be emotional later. Now was the time for action.

Aislinn chanted softly, taking care to deploy each step of the complicated casting. When the walls of her prison shimmered into nothingness, she held herself ready, every muscle tense as a drawn bowstring. For long moments, she looked out at darkness, but she was used to the void that was part of this spell. Time shifted; she felt it in the pit of her stomach. Light flickered and she watched herself being dragged between Majestron and her minion. The dark goddess had her arms, and the man her feet. Rune padded next to her.

"Why didn't you kill the dog?" the man asked.

"He's a wolf, and has magic of his own," Majestron replied. "Shut up. You don't ask the questions around here."

Aislinn turned to Rune's spectral projection and nodded, hoping he'd understand she meant they had to move now. She waited until Rune merged with his earlier self to launch herself into her comatose form. As soon as her astral and physical selves collided, she wrenched herself out of the hands that held her and ran for the white-barked aspen tree. Thick foliage covered her almost immediately and she tried her damnedest to be quiet, but twigs crackled and broke beneath her feet. She heard Rune ahead of her and let herself hope they might make it past this first gauntlet.

How much longer would they have? She held her breath, listening, and dove into the hole Rune had predicted would be beneath the tree. Slithering on her belly, she worked her way underground, following Rune's tail. In short order, the hole widened enough for her to crawl. While she hunted for a place to wait out the storm that was sure to blow over their heads, she called invisibility with her Mage gift and draped it over herself and her wolf. He curled into a tight ball and she sat next to him. Muted light from the hole filtered into their shelter. Aislinn hated to do it, but she deployed a short blast of power to seal their hiding place. Dirt filled the hole, cutting off the light and filling the air with dust and bits of grit and stone. She'd have to undo her work later—if there was a later.

A fury-filled shout sounded, followed by another.

Aislinn hunkered in the shelter Rune had led them to with her back against one damp wall. A grim smile split her face. They'd made it this far, by God. If they weren't discovered, she'd teleport them out of here as soon as her power recovered enough.

Doing the best she could to fine-tune the spell that hid them, Aislinn prayed to every deity she could think of to rain plagues down on Majestron Zalia so she'd leave them alone.

CHAPTER 18

Fionn followed Nidhogg's instructions to the letter and mixed power into their teleport spell as the dragon guided them to Asgard. It had taken far longer than the half hour he'd allocated to finish off the demons and their minions. He was filthy, his battle leathers singed and torn, and he stank, but he hadn't wanted to waste any more time cleaning up or changing. Bella had been shaken enough by the proximity of demons, she hadn't wanted to come with him, so he'd left her cleaning her feathers on one of the manor house balconies.

The golden walls of Valhalla formed before him, followed by the impeccably clean cobblestone streets of Asgard. As would befit a picture-perfect movie set, well-groomed Norsemen and women hurried in various directions, everyone brimming with purpose. Until they saw him and Nidhogg. Then they scuttled away, and the street cleared in record time. Fionn gazed about. The times he'd met with Odin had always been on Celtic territory, so this was his first view of the Norse stronghold. "Is it always this pristine?" he asked Nidhogg.

The dragon didn't bother to answer. Instead, he trumpeted long and loud. Fionn took a few steps away and inspected the black dragon. Nidhogg looked as ragged as Fionn with scraps of demon flesh impaled on his scales and splashes of blood and ichor decorating his hide like a psychedelic painting gone bad.

Odin burst through Valhalla's golden door and marched down its wide, golden steps. The Norse god always looked the same. Tall and burly, dressed in battle armor, with twin brass drinking horns criss-crossing over his broad chest. Blond braids fell down his chest, and a full red-blond beard spilled down until it tangled in the leather thongs holding the drinking horns in place. His sharp, blue-eyed gaze swept from Fionn to Nidhogg.

"I take it this isn't a pleasure call," he said and switched his attention to Nidhogg. "Let's see. This is visit number three after centuries of nothingness. What do you want this time?"

Nidhogg planted his powerful rear legs more firmly on the cobble-stones, and his green eyes spun faster. "I am the Norse dragon, and worthy of respect, but we're short on time just now, so I'll overlook your lack of manners. I brought Fionn MacCumhaill, Celtic god of wisdom, creation, and divination, because he needs your help."

Fionn bowed, sweeping a hand to one side. Odin rolled his eyes and muttered, "I remember you well enough. You're an arrogant whelp. Times must be dire indeed for you to seek me out. What could you possibly need from me?"

Fionn bit back a sharp retort. Throwing gasoline on a fire was never wise. He slanted his gaze at the Norse leader and said, "Other than your help when we storm the dark gods' borderworlds, I seek information."

"What kind of information?"

Odin narrowed his gaze, and Fionn recalled the Norse deity was an inveterate bargainer.

"Where did the dark gods live afore ye imprisoned them?"

"Humph. Simple enough." Odin smiled with all the warmth of a cobra and rubbed his hands together. "What's it worth to you?"

Flame shot from Nidhogg's mouth, landing just shy of Odin's leather boot tops. "Answer him," the dragon thundered, "or the next blast will take out your beard."

"What?" Odin smirked. "No breaking bread? No sharing a cask of beer or mead?"

"Those dark bastards stole my woman," Fionn broke in. "We're fresh from battling demons, and time grows short."

"You've been to Hell?" Odin broke in, leaning forward. "Now there's a tale worth the telling. And well worth the information you seek."

Fionn flexed his hands into fists, and exhaled sharply. "There isna time for this. I promise you a full explanation once I get Aislinn back."

"Odin." Nidhogg's voice held compulsion.

The Norse god's features softened, shifted, almost as if he'd been hypnotized. Fascination filled Fionn. He'd never realized the extent of Nidhogg's power and suspected it extended far beyond whatever he was doing now.

"Yes, of course," Odin murmured. "The dark ones built several fortresses in the Americas to avoid us harassing them, like we'd have done if they set up shop in the Old Country. You do realize this was long before the American continents were developed."

"How many fortresses and where?" Fionn cut in.

"Three. One was in the American northwest, maybe ten leagues east from Seattle's current location. Another was near Mexico City, and the third lay in the Tierra del Fuego."

"Any idea if they're still standing?" Nidhogg asked.

Odin grinned broadly. "You always were one for coming up with defining questions. The Mexico City one was wiped out by an earthquake. The one in the Tierra del Fuego got avalanched into nothingness." He rubbed his hands together. "Best I know, the one in the northwest of what used to be the U.S. still stands."

Nidhogg averted his gaze, and Odin shook himself. He glared at the dragon. "I did not appreciate that."

"You didn't give me much choice. We'll be on our way."

"Thank you," Fionn said.

"You owe me a tale, Celt."

"Aye, and I'll make good on it, but not just now."

Nidhogg was already pulling power and magic sizzled around him, electric to the touch. The fine hairs on the back of Fionn's head stood at attention and he closed the few feet between him and Nidhogg.

"Ye doona have to go with me—" he began.

"Nay. We'll see this thing through."

"I want to come." Thor catapulted down Valhalla's steps, battle axe in hand. He looked so much like Odin, they could have been brothers. The only difference was more of a red cast to Thor's hair—and the lack of drinking horns around his neck.

"Grand idea," Odin seconded and crossed his arms over the drinking horns. "We'll both accompany you."

Fionn hesitated, feeling torn. While it might prove handy to have more firepower, there'd be no hope of stealth. He looked up at Nidhogg. "What do ye think?"

Smoke steamed from the dragon's open mouth, and a deep, booming laugh shook the ground. "Brilliant. I'd love to have Thor and Odin fighting by my side again. After all, I am the Norse dragon."

"Our first concern is Aislinn's safety," Fionn cautioned, finding it difficult to latch onto Nidhogg's enthusiasm.

Thor clapped him on the back so hard it was a struggle to maintain his balance. "Celts!" he sputtered. "What a bunch of pussies you always were."

"Really?" Anger flared red hot, and Fionn felt like he was back on the battlefield outside his house. He reached for magic, intent on wiping the smirk off Thor's Nordic features.

"Enough," Nidhogg roared. "We leave now."

Before Fionn could lodge a protest, the world whirled and dropped away to nothingness. He pulled his ragged emotions into some sort of order. Pounding Thor into the dirt wouldn't help them find Aislinn, and it would piss Odin off. Time dribbled by. Even with teleporting, it took a while to cover the longer distances, and the journey gave him time to think. Odin and Thor would never agree to follow his orders, but they might follow Nidhogg's.

He reached for the dragon's mind and, surprisingly, found it still open to him. *"What happens once we get there?"*

"We use magic to locate them and do whatever we have to in order to free Aislinn and Rune."

Fionn swallowed hard. *"Do ye believe they're still alive?"*

"Probably."

"Say more."

"This is conjecture on my part, but we did a fair job foiling the plan to loose Hell's minions—once we fell headlong into it."

"The plan being tricking us into opening a portal into Hell?"

"Exactly. Once whoever was orchestrating things realized we were onto them, and were about to shut the gateway, they scrambled to salvage something. There'd have been no point in bothering with hostages, if they just meant to kill them."

Understanding rose, dragging hope along with it and Fionn said, *"Makes sense. If whoever took Aislinn and Rune was close enough to kidnap them, they could just as easily have killed them."*

"Now that I've had a chance to think things through, it's the same conclusion I came to," Nidhogg agreed. *"I realize I said she might already be dead earlier, but once the words were spoken, they didn't ring true."*

Fionn didn't bother mentioning they'd certainly *rung true* for him, but that was because he was incapable of rational thought when it came to Aislinn. So long as Nidhogg appeared inclined toward conversation, Fionn tackled tricky ground. *"Once we get there, will ye take on leadership of the group?"*

Dragon laughter nearly deafened Fionn and he shook his head to stop the ringing in his ears.

"Never fear," the dragon said once he stopped hooting with mirth. *"I'll never tell anyone that you offered me ascendency on the battlefield."* He paused for a beat. *"If the unspoken question is whether I can encourage Thor and Odin to be assets, I believe I can. You've fought alongside them. For all their stubbornness, they're skilled fighters, and damn near fearless."*

The gray of the teleport tunnel lightened around its edges indicating they were nearing whatever destination the dragon had selected. Moments later, a portal formed and Fionn walked through into thick, wet greenery. He brushed his hands over a dripping bush and wiped them across his face, probably smearing the hell out of the grime coating him, but it felt refreshing.

Thor and Odin trotted out of the same portal, followed by Nidhogg who spewed fire at the gateway and blasted it into oblivion.

Fionn smothered a wry grin. He chanted to close portals, but fire was much faster.

Odin lifted his head, scenting the air. "Gods, but it's good to be outside Asgard."

"We should leave more often." Thor slapped his father on the back, tilted a drinking horn from around his father's neck, and drank.

"None of that." Odin dragged the horn out of his son's grasp. "You can drink once this is over."

Fionn wisely remained silent, but he was relieved beyond measure that someone was riding herd on Thor's legendary alcoholism. "Do ye know where the old one's fortress is?" he asked Nidhogg.

The dragon's nostrils flared. "That way." He jerked his head to the right. "And not very far."

Thor and Odin started in the direction Nidhogg indicated, but the dragon called, "Hold up a moment. You can't go marching in there as if you've got the rest of your warriors at your beck and call, or the Valkyries ready to ride to your defense."

Odin turned to face the dragon. "Humph. Good point. I'm open to your thoughts."

Fionn set his jaw in a hard line. Clearly Odin was used to command, just as Fionn was. He turned his attention to Nidhogg and hoped to hell the dragon's plan would be something he agreed with. He had a feeling Odin would fight anyone who disagreed with *his* dragon.

"First," Nidhogg focused on Fionn, "do you sense Aislinn?"

Fionn narrowed his eyes and sent tentative magic spiraling outward, doing his damnedest to mask it from their enemy. So far, they held the element of surprise, but that could evaporate in a hot second. Because he expected to latch onto Aislinn's energy, and didn't find it, shock rattled him, followed by disappointment.

"I guess I was wrong," he muttered. "She isna here."

"Just because you can't feel her doesn't necessarily mean she's not here," Nidhogg said. "She might have escaped and is shielding herself."

"Nay. If she escaped, she'd have left."

"Maybe. If she still had enough magic. Or her captors could have her stashed behind wards." Nidhogg blew steam, and it made the damp air even soggier.

Odin moved to Fionn's side. "Your woman has magic? Fascinating. What kind?"

"Human magic, but all five skills."

Thor joined his father. "That's impossible," he said flatly. "Humans don't possess magic."

"They dinna," Fionn said, "until the dark gods stormed Earth. I'm not certain how it happened, but when the Lemurians weakened the veils between Earth and the borderworlds, they opened the possibility for human magic to sift through. Some weren't sensitive to it, and the Lemurians slaughtered them. Of those who remain, most humans have two gifts, one primary and one weaker. Aislinn has them all."

"What are these gifts?" Thor asked.

"We doona have the time—" Fionn began, but Nidhogg shook his head.

"We'll take the time," the dragon said. "Thor and Odin must know what Aislinn can do, in case they're the ones who find her."

Fionn counted off on his fingers. "One is Mage magic. It confers ease with casting spells. Two is Seeker magic. It ferrets out truth. Three is Hunter magic. Hunters bond with animals and working as a pair, they fight evil. Four is Healer magic, which is self-explanatory, and five is Seer magic." He paused to take a breath. "Aislinn is the only human I've ever known with Seer abilities. She isna verra proficient, but she can travel backward in time to alter outcomes."

"Can she read the future?" Odin asked.

"'Tis part of the gift, but I dinna have a chance yet to teach it to her," Fionn replied.

Thor grinned knowingly. "Sounds like quite a woman. Are you wed?"

"What difference does it make?"

Thor shrugged, his blue eyes dancing with mischief. "I don't cuckold married men, otherwise, she's fair game."

"The hell she is." Fionn grabbed Thor's arm and spun him so they faced one another.

"Let's focus on seeing if she's even here," Nidhogg broke in, sounding beleaguered. "One more thing. She has a wolf bondmate named Rune. Like all bond animals, he talks—and has a mind of his own."

Thor wrenched out of Fionn's grasp, still grinning like a gargoyle.

"Why don't I sense any people nearby?" Odin asked.

"Because the Lemurians killed millions these past three years," Fionn said. "Tens of millions, actually. Ye really should leave that stronghold of yours more often."

"Grand idea, Celt." Odin slugged him in the shoulder, and turned to Nidhogg. "What's this plan of yours?"

The dragon slanted an appraising look his way. "Maybe you're gaining wisdom. There are two possibilities. Either Aislinn is here hiding, or we guessed wrong, and she's not here at all. If she's sequestered herself somewhere, she's likely buried herself in as strong an invisibility spell as she could muster. Or worse, she's hidden behind warding not of her own making."

While Fionn listened to the dragon, he asked his magic a different question and cast a wide net. "At least one dark god is here," he muttered.

"I'd come to much the same conclusion," Nidhogg said. "If a dark one is all the way out here, it's a good bet Aislinn's here too. The fortress is a short distance to the northeast of us. We need information, so I propose we corral whoever we can find and encourage them to talk."

"That willna work well if it's a dark god," Fionn said.

"I have my ways," Nidhogg said smugly. "Plus I have the best backup in the world." Fire belched from his mouth, but the soggy greenery just smoldered. "I'm hoping for Perrikus or D'Chel. I'd love to dish out a hundredth of the misery they foisted onto me."

"Another tale I'd love to hear," Odin chimed in, looking hopeful.

"Later," Nidhogg said. "Frankly, I don't see the point wasting magic on stealth. They'll know we're here the moment we poke our heads into their territory."

"Let's get going." Fionn turned in the direction Nidhogg had indicated and was joined by Thor and Odin. "You coming?" he asked Nidhogg.

"Certainly, but I'm flying. It's an advantage to be able to see what we face from the air." The black dragon spread his wings, flapped them a few times, and rose off the ground.

"I'd forgotten how much I love that black bastard," Odin said and loped forward. Fionn and Thor paced him, one on either side.

Fionn kept his magical senses deployed, so he felt when the small birds and animals thinned out and then disappeared. "We're getting close," he cautioned. "Slow down."

"Why?" Thor asked, barreling forward. "Fuck!" His beefy body bent backward and power arced off his chest.

"That's why," Fionn snapped. "The place is warded. 'Tis likely the first of several perimeter guards." He sent power auguring into the ward to figure out its intricacies.

Thor rubbed his chest. "Hold up, Celt. If we mix our magics, we should make short work of this barrier."

Thor's prediction turned out to be a shade on the optimistic side, but it didn't take more than ten minutes to chop a hole in the warding. Of course that meant they'd announced their presence as surely as if they'd ridden in on Nidhogg's back. Perimeter wards weren't worth a damn unless someone was monitoring them.

"Hurry." Fionn gestured and broke into a run. "I want to be closer before the greeting party intercepts us." Adrenaline poured through him, making his heart pound and his muscles fluid.

This time it was him who ran into a ward circle. Because it was constructed similarly to the first, it took much less time to untangle. Moments later, a large house came into view. It looked like a southern mansion with pillars supporting an upper floor. Sitting in the middle of a clearing in the forest, its white paint and shiny glass windows shone invitingly.

The air in front of Fionn split open and Majestron Zalia waltzed through a black-tinged portal. "Hello, boys." Her full mouth opened in a parody of a seductive smile. "Nice of you to drop in. I've been lonely."

"Bitch!" Odin spat on the ground. "Last time I checked, your blood was poison. Anyone who fucks you dies."

"But they die happy." Her grin widened. "Now, who can I thank for the pleasure of this visit?" Her midnight gaze settled on Fionn, and she licked her lips appreciatively. "I've lusted after you for years, Celt. I suppose you're here because you didn't like my little joke."

"The one where ye got the dragons to open the gates of Hell for you?" Fionn eyed her warily.

"Speaking of dragons, I notice one's flying about up there." She waved her hands skyward. "He's welcome to land. Poor thing," she clucked. "He's very old, and he must be exhausted. Wouldn't want his heart to give out."

"Nidhogg?" Fionn glanced up.

"I'll stay where I am, thank you," the dragon replied dryly. *"Watching out for my weak heart and all."*

"You may as well talk out loud. I can hear you," Majestron Zalia simpered and arched her upper body to push her breasts toward Fionn.

"Give it up, whore," Fionn snarled. "I came for Aislinn. What have ye done with her?"

"I could make you much happier than that weak excuse for a human. Besides," she shrugged, "I seem to have misplaced her."

"Ye mean that *weak excuse for a human* managed to elude you." Hope speared Fionn, so poignant he struggled to keep focused on Majestron Zalia. Aislinn was not only alive, she was still thinking, still fighting back.

"As long as we have you in our sights, sweetheart, we shouldn't lose the opportunity." Odin tugged his axe from its holster and faced Majestron. Fire shot from his blue gaze.

"If my blood touches you, you die too." The dark goddess danced on the balls of her feet, her hips swaying in clear invitation.

Fionn kept his distance; he wasn't sure about the effects of Majestron's blood on any of them. The Norse deities were immortal, just like the Celts. He had no idea if they had some iteration of the *Dreaming* hidden away in the bowels of Asgard, and now wasn't the time to ask.

Odin glared at her. She glared right back.

"Your precious dragon can't kill me, either," she said. "Fire won't hurt us."

"Not true," Fionn cried. He may have let the blood gambit pass, but he wasn't about to ignore this one. "I watched while Tokhots burned from the inside out."

An unreadable expression flitted across Majestron's face. He'd called her on her bravado, and she didn't like it. He opened his mouth to follow up on his advantage when Aislinn blasted into his mind. She didn't know he was there, but her energy was out in the open. The dark goddess felt it too because she spun, intent as a hunting dog on newly released prey.

"I doona care how ye manage it"—Fionn latched gazes with Odin —"but keep her here. I'm going after Aislinn."

CHAPTER 19

*A*islinn huddled beneath the tree with Rune while Majestron vented her fury by screaming in Gaelic and a couple other languages Aislinn didn't recognize. But anger was anger and it bled through despite the unfamiliar words. After Majestron finally stopped ranting, Aislinn waited a whole lot longer, barely breathing. Thirst was a constant, nagging companion. The more time that dribbled past, the drier her throat got until the sides rubbed together painfully.

"We can't stay here forever." Rune nudged her.

A breathy sigh escaped. *"I know. Let me see if I have enough juice to teleport from down here."*

It was always harder to activate the teleport spell from underground. She'd done it a time or two when she'd been fresh. Now she was anything but. She needed food, water, and rest. Panic had fired her use of Seer magic, and she'd blown through any reserves that had built while she was unconscious in Majestron's lair.

Aislinn took inventory. No matter how she sliced it, there was no way she could transport herself and Rune twenty feet from where they were, let alone far enough away for her to recover enough to bring them home.

"We have to go outside."

"I figured as much." The wolf shot from her side, his jaws crunching as they closed over some small, hapless creature. He twisted sideways and dropped a still-twitching mouse in her lap.

"You caught it, you can have it." She smoothed his fur.

"I'll find another. You need liquid and energy. Drink its blood. Suck the meat from its bones."

Her empty stomach twisted in rebellion, but the wolf was right. It wasn't as if she'd never eaten raw rodents, but they were far from her favorite sustenance. While she stared at the mouse, Rune skittered away from her, and she heard violent rustling and several outraged squeaks before he returned, carrying three more mice in his mouth.

Nothing for it but to do it. She pulled the knife that always hung from leather cording around her waist free of its sheath, surprised Majestron hadn't taken it from her, slit the rodent's neck, and sucked blood from its carotid artery. Thick, copper-scented liquid slid down her dry throat soothing her inflamed tissue, and her squeamishness faded. Once no more blood came from her insistent sucking, she split the belly, tossed the gut sack to Rune, and field stripped flesh from the tiny bones, eating hastily.

Rune nosed another mouse her way and said. *"Two for each of us. It's not enough, but it will do until we get some distance from here."*

Because she'd gotten past the mental part of eating raw rodent, the second one tasted better, and she wished for a third and a fourth. Wiping a hand across the back of her mouth, she said, *"I'm ready. First thing I'll do is clear the entrance. As soon we can, we'll climb out and I'll teleport us away from here."*

As she readied the spell to punch through the dirt she'd plugged the tree's root hole with, she wondered about a destination. The teleport spell required one. She couldn't just say *take us as far as my power will stretch.* Since she had no idea where they were, it made it difficult to come up with a location within the limited reach of her worn out magic.

Maybe when I see what's outside, it will give me some clues. Her reasoning was weak, but it would have to do.

"Are you certain you don't have any idea where we are?" she asked Rune. *"Can you remember smelling something that might give me a clue?"*

"We're probably not far from where we found Taltos."

Aislinn set her spell preparation aside and stared at him. *"What would make you think that?"*

"The mice. They're the same kind we had at Marta's and around Mount Shasta."

"You're telling me they have a different strain of mouse near Fionn's house?"

"Why is that so hard to believe? Get us out of here." He closed his jaws around her ankle for emphasis.

All right, then. I'll just aim for Marta's and call it even. If we're in the western U.S., we can't be all that far from Ely, Nevada.

Aislinn picked up the threads of her spell and reversed what she'd done earlier. Because she didn't want to create any more warning of her intent than she had to, she pulled the dirt downward and crawled over the mounds it formed. Fresh air tantalized her as she moved cautiously upward, stopping when her head was level with the opening.

"Why are you stopping?" Rune laid his head on her butt.

"To make certain no one's waiting to snatch us, and we have at least a short window of opportunity. It takes a few minutes to make a teleport spell, and then a couple more to pull us into it. I'm going to remain in the dense brush around the tree bole. You stay near me."

She sent the barest wisp of Seeker magic outward. When she didn't find anything, she extended her range a little. Hope burned a hole in her heart as she scrambled the rest of the way out of the hole, staying low, and immediately started the incantation to teleport them the fuck away from Majestron's lair. She hadn't dared let herself think about Fionn, but his face wavered before her now, and she longed for the feel of his arms around her and the sound of his deep voice crooning in Gaelic.

Can't go there. Got to concentrate.

Her spell formed, and then skittered away. Rune eased out of the hole in the ground and lay next to her. Aislinn bit down hard on her lower lip and tried again. Being frantic and forcing magic to do her bidding had never worked well for her. She let go of her warding to free up power to teleport.

Rune pushed into her mind. He'd done it before when she needed an infusion of strength. Suddenly, she saw the world through his eyes, and her senses became far sharper. She realized she'd been siphoning off needed energy to listen for danger. With Rune's hearing on board, she redirected additional power into her spell.

Finally, finally, it seemed to be coming together for her. Another few moments and a portal would form. Once they had that part, they were all but gone. She nudged Rune and pointed to where she expected her gateway to take shape. *"Once you see it,"* she instructed. *"Jump through. I'll be right behind you."*

"I've done this before." He sounded hurt.

"Yes, but not when I'm this trashed. I'm trying to cover all the bases."

The portal blinked, wavered, and dissipated.

Fuck!

She scrubbed a hand across her face. What was she doing wrong? Before she could resurrect the spell, this time writing each step in the dirt to make sure she wasn't missing one of them, Nidhogg's unmistakable voice blasted into her mind.

"Grab the wolf. I'll transport you to my back, and then we'll leave."

Her gaze shot upward. Even though it sounded like the dragon, she suspected foul play. Surely the dark gods could mimic anyone. Relief so staggering it brought tears coursed through her when she saw the Norse dragon hovering a hundred feet above them. It didn't matter how he'd found them. What mattered was help was at hand. Rune wouldn't die. Not today, and neither would she.

Rune jumped to his feet, his tail pluming furiously. Thank Christ he didn't start barking. Aislinn sidled to him and wrapped her arms around his thick body. The blast of magic that lifted them to the dragon's back was so powerful she could have kissed it.

"How'd you find us?" she asked once she'd settled Rune across the dragon's back.

"Later," Nidhogg growled. "Fionn's here with Odin and Thor. I need to tell him I've got you, and they can find their own way home." Magic bubbled as the dragon reached for Fionn's mind.

She opened her mouth to say she wanted to be with Fionn, needed to fight by his side, but common sense kicked her in the teeth. She wasn't in any shape to be anything other than a liability—to anyone. Hell, even something as simple as a teleport spell had eluded her.

"Thank you," she told Nidhogg. "If you could take us back to Fionn's, I'll be in your debt forever."

"Our lives are linked," the dragon said solemnly, "because of your bond to Dewi."

"Lass," Fionn's voice bloomed deep in her mind. *"I love you. Stay in the manor house where ye're safe, and I'll join you presently."*

She had just enough time to tell Fionn she adored him before Nidhogg swept them into a portal and she fell against his neck, exhausted.

"It's good you didn't argue with me," Nidhogg rumbled. "I'm not in the best of moods, and I'd hate to have to hurt you. Dewi might never forgive me."

"What'd you expect me to do?" Aislinn asked.

"Teleport off my back to Fionn's side."

Heat swept from her chest over the top of her head. She'd come perilously close to doing just that. And she might have if she'd trusted her magic was intact.

"Never mind, child. Rest. I'll see you and Rune safely home."

"What about Majestron Zalia?"

"The men will do what they can to neutralize her."

Aislinn's weary eyes snapped open. "But that's dangerous. She's got the same poison blood Tokhots did." Her tired brain pedaled in slow motion. "How does that work? Could she kill Fionn or the others?"

"Nay, they're immortal, but she could force Fionn deep into the

Dreaming, where it would take someone like Gwydion to draw him back."

"What about the others? Do the Norse gods have somewhere to retreat to when they're hurt?"

Nidhogg snorted. "You're quite the question girl. I thought you'd be so grateful—and so tired—you'd lean on my neck and wink out." He paused. "Your wolf's asleep."

She placed a hand on Rune's side and he made a soft, whuffly, growling noise. "As if I could sleep while we teleport," he muttered.

Aislinn turned Nidhogg's last words over in her mind and said, "I asked you about the Norse gods and got a bunch of fluff. You don't want to tell me."

"Smart wench. I can't. It's classified."

She wrapped her arms as far as they'd go around the dragon's neck. Lethargy dragged at her, exacerbated by hunger and thirst. "How much longer?"

"Soon, child. Dewi's been pestering me ever since she knew I found you. I swear, the two of you could drive a man into his cave for eternity."

Rune woofed softly, and Aislinn knew he was laughing.

Fionn felt like turning cartwheels. Aislinn was alive and on her way to Inishowen. If anyone could see her safely home—besides himself, that was—it was Nidhogg. He felt buoyant, as if a million tons of worry had just lifted off his heart.

Majestron Zalia.

What to do about her? Odin was correct that this was too good an opportunity to pass up. They actually had her where the odds were three to one. No one had raced out of the house to stand by her side, and he didn't sense anyone else here beyond the four of them. At least no one with power. Maybe that was why no one had shot to Majestron's rescue. She was here by herself.

A shrill battle cry split the air, followed by another. Fionn raced toward where he'd left the two Norsemen and the dark goddess. Immortality was great on his side of the equation, but deucedly inconvenient when it came to the dark gods. What he wanted to do was batter their sorry asses into dust and feed them to Hell's demons.

Thumping, pounding, and the crash of trees falling shook the ground. Fionn burst into the clearing and saw Odin hacking and slashing at Majestron while Thor held her pinned from behind. She hissed and writhed, shifting into a snake, and then back to herself. Both the Norse gods dripped blood, but were still on their feet. Maybe they were immune to her poison, or maybe it just took longer to act than it had when one of Dewi's brood had bitten Tokhots.

"Care to join the party?" A feral grin lit Odin's face, and he slashed downward with his axe, severing one of Majestron's arms. It fell to the ground, but bounced upward immediately and hovered next to her body trying to reattach itself. Majestron chanted furiously in a language Fionn didn't recognize.

"They spent long years in your dungeon," Fionn said. "Do ye know how to kill them?"

"If I did, they'd have been dead long since," Odin growled.

The dark goddess's arm was almost fully reattached. She twisted her head halfway around on her neck, something she shouldn't have been able to do.

"Watch out!" Fionn shouted, understanding she planned to sink her teeth into Thor's neck.

He had good reactions and thrust her away before she could strike. Once freed, her form began to shimmer. Fionn darted forward, shuffling through spells as he sought one that would interrupt her magic. A few more moments, and she'd teleport beyond their reach.

Odin whipped a golden rope from somewhere in his battle armor and wound it around her neck.

"Bastard!" she snarled, showing teeth that morphed into fangs.

"It won't hold her for long," Odin cried. "Precious metals dull their power."

Fionn held out a hand for Thor's battle axe. "Give me that." As soon as he had it in hand, he hefted it in a huge, sweeping blow that severed Majestron's head from her shoulders. Fionn pulled wards to shield himself from the splattering blood and booted the head as far from the body as he could.

"Always loved a rousing game of kickball." Thor wrested his axe from Fionn and dropped it back into its sheath.

"Excellent!" Odin kicked the still spurting, headless body, and turned to Fionn. "Summon fire. I will too and we'll burn her. It won't kill her, but it should move her out of the action for long enough to tackle the rest of her tribe."

Fionn dropped his warding to call mage fire. It burned blue and braided itself with Odin's orange-colored flames. Thor chanted low in the Norsemen's tongue, his hands extended toward the growing conflagration. As if they fed one another, the twin fires blazed upward forming an inferno. Majestron's body bubbled and smoked, but didn't turn to ash.

"Better drop the head in too," Odin instructed.

Fionn trotted in a wide circle, hunting where it had landed. Black ichor smudged the ground, leading him right to it. He picked it up gingerly by the hair and Majestron's blue eyes snapped open. Fionn froze.

How was this even possible?

Her wide, seductive mouth opened in a grin displaying vampiric fangs. "You haven't won," she said.

Fionn had seen a lot in his long life, but having a severed head talk to him was so wrong it rattled his brain. Slowly, the head swung toward him, jaws snapping.

"MacCumhaill!" Odin's voice cut like a whip. "The fire. Her head goes in the fire."

"No shit!" Cursing in Gaelic, Fionn covered the distance to the flaming pyre and dropped Majestron's head atop her body. That had been much too close a call. The bitch had hypnotized him because he dropped his guard, figuring she wasn't a threat anymore. He pushed the creep-factor aside and kicked himself for being sloppy.

Odin gripped Fionn's shoulder. "She's strong, that one."

Fionn watched as Majestron's head moved incrementally toward her shoulders, sidling through the fire. He pointed. "What happens once she's whole again?"

"Won't happen if we do this right." Odin snapped a hand downward and a lightning bolt added juice to the blaze. After one more rocking push, the head fell to the side. Her eyes opened one last time and she bared her teeth at Fionn. "We are not done, Celt."

"The hell," he snapped.

"We'll stay until the fire goes out," Odin said.

"You probably want to get back to that woman of yours," Thor cut in. "Too bad the dragon made off with her before I got a good look. Loved all that red hair, though."

"Ye can love it from a distance." Fionn looked from Odin to Thor. "Why didn't Majestron's blood affect you?"

"She scratched me once when I got too close," Thor said. "It was my own fault. I was slumming in the dungeons, and she bared her breasts." He made a snorting noise. "Never seen a set like them before or since. I felt like I'd die if I couldn't touch them." He shrugged self-consciously. "I'd no sooner got my hands on her overheated flesh when she dug her nails into me. They must've been tipped with her own blood. I was unconscious for a long time. Months. One of our most competent healers dosed me with various combinations of herbs until she hit on one that neutralized the toxin."

"Once we found an antidote," Odin picked up the tale, "we all took it as a precaution in case Majestron or Tokhots got loose."

"Majestron must not have known," Fionn said, "or she wouldn't have been so bold when we cornered her. She just assumed her blood would protect her."

"No way she could have known," Thor concurred. "We never told her." His head whipped around. "Goddammit! Who's there? Show yourself."

Fionn twirled in the direction of Thor's voice in time to see a slightly built man creep from behind a broad evergreen tree. Black hair fell untidily to the middle of his back, and he had the wide brown eyes of a frightened mouse. A quick scan told Fionn the man was human and didn't appear to have any power at all. How had he escaped the Lemurians' purge?

"Who are you?" Fionn stepped into his path.

The man raised a trembling hand and pointed at the smoking pyre. "Is she dead?"

"Nay," Fionn replied. "Ye canna kill those such as her. But it will be long afore she causes any more trouble. Who are you?"

"Christian Jones. Her manservant." He glanced nervously about. "If she's not watching me, that means I can go home. My family must think I died."

"How long have you been here?" Thor asked.

The man narrowed his eyes. "Better than ten years."

Fionn blew out a breath. "I have bad news. Things have changed a lot since Majestron shanghaied you into her service."

"I'll tell him what he needs to know," Odin said. "Go find your woman."

"Best not to leave them alone for too long." Thor laughed. "Women, they get ideas when you're not there to correct them."

Fionn didn't bother telling Thor just how headstrong and stubborn Aislinn could be. He walked to Odin and held out a hand. The Norse god clasped it. Then he did the same with Thor.

"Three down and three to go," Fionn said.

"Aye," Odin nodded, and his eyes lit with anticipation of battles to come. "See you on the borderworlds and we'll knock out Perrikus and D'Chel."

"Surely once they're out of the running, Adva will pack up shop," Thor said

"Love your confidence. I hope to hell you're right." Fionn clapped him on the back and summoned a teleport spell to take him home to Aislinn.

CHAPTER 20

Fionn aimed for his bedroom. Once the teleport spell spit him out, he glanced around, surprised to find his rooms empty. Where the hell was Aislinn? She had to be exhausted, so why wasn't she in their bed? Sudden fear gripped him. Had something happened to Nidhogg en route? Too beat to do anything elegant, Fionn opened his mind seeking Aislinn's energy. Relief weakened his knees when he located her easily. It still didn't explain why she wasn't in their bed, but at least she was close.

He caught a glimpse of himself in a wall mirror and groaned. So much crud begrimed his face and streaked his hair, he barely recognized himself. He wrinkled his nose at a rank smell, and then realized it came from him.

Makes sense. I reeked when I left here. No reason I'd smell any better now.

Got to find Aislinn, then I'll clean up.

His bedchamber door crashed against its stops, and Gwydion, Arawn, and Bran rushed in.

"Told you he was back," Gwydion crowed and smoothed dark blue robes down his body. His blond hair was still damp from being washed.

Bella flew through the door in their wake and latched onto Fionn's shoulder where she pecked his head gently. He ruffled her feathers, happy to see her.

"I'm glad you're back," she quorked.

"Yeah." Fionn turned to look at her. "Me too. Thanks for the welcome."

"Whew." Arawn made a face at Fionn. "Ye're pretty ripe."

"Never mind that," Bran broke in. He and Arawn were still in battle leathers, but clean ones. "What happened? Nidhogg told us ye cornered Majestron Zalia."

"Where's Aislinn?" Fionn asked.

Gwydion trotted past him, staff clasped in one hand and his robe fluttering around his ankles. His perennially bare feet slapped the wooden floor once the warrior magician got near the door leading to a small patio. He crooked two fingers above one shoulder and Fionn followed him. Once they were outside, Gwydion pointed downward.

Fionn trained his gaze in the indicated direction and smiled. Dewi lay curled in the grass bordering the manor house with her body splayed protectively around Aislinn. Nidhogg sat nearby, keeping watch over both of them with Rune by his side.

Dewi must have sensed his presence because she glanced up and said, *"I'll let you know when she wakes. The child is exhausted. She was filthy, half-starved, and badly dehydrated when Nidhogg returned her to me."*

Fionn opened his mouth to protest that Nidhogg had actually returned Aislinn to him, but he thought better of it. Dewi was grieving about not having her brood close to hand. If she wanted to transfer her maternal instincts to Aislinn, he wouldn't stand in her way. *"Thank you for taking care of her."*

"You're quite welcome." The dragon winked lazily. *"It will give you a chance to clean up. I can smell you from here."*

Fionn rolled his eyes and walked back inside with Gwydion behind him. "Since everyone thinks I stink," he said, "I'm going to draw a bath. I can wash up while I tell you what happened."

Arawn and Bran dragged chairs into the bathroom, and Gwydion commandeered the bath stool. All three listened without interruption as Fionn relayed what had transpired after Nidhogg left.

"Ye say her head actually moved independent of her body?" Arawn made a sour face. "How unsettling."

"Even worse"—Fionn dipped his head backward and rinsed shampoo from his tangled hair—"was when she managed to hypnotize me with only her head." He stood with water running down his body, stepped out of the bath, and grabbed a towel, which he wrapped around himself.

Bran bent and pulled the drain plug; the rank water gurgled as it left the tub. "I assumed ye werena saving it for aught." The god of prophecy arched a brow in Fionn's direction.

"Thanks. I'm tired. 'Tis been a long couple of days."

"Aye"—Gwydion clasped his hands together in front of him—"but look at what we've accomplished."

"Time well spent," Arawn agreed. "We turned what could have been a disaster into a victory, since it netted us Majestron Zalia." He followed Fionn back to the bedroom. "Do ye think the Norse gods would share the formula that protects them from the dark ones' poison blood?"

"'Twould be convenient," Bran agreed.

Fionn pulled a pair of soft, stonewashed dungarees over his legs and tucked his cock out of the way to button them. He followed the pants with a faded sweatshirt emblazoned with *Go Bears* and set to work with magic and a comb untangling his hair. Because it would be easier seated, he carried a chair back from the bathroom and plopped onto it. Bella, who'd only reluctantly left his side while he was in the bath, took up residence in his lap.

"Why do we need the formula?" Fionn countered. "Tokhots and Majestron are out of the way."

"For now, maybe"—Gwydion perched on the side of the bed—"but from the sound of Majestron's body parts finding one another, I'm wondering just how long either she or Tokhots will remain sidelined. Or Slototh, for that matter."

"Mister Cheerful." Fionn jabbed him with an elbow and went back to unsnarling his hair.

"I prefer to label myself as Mister Practical." Gwydion jabbed him back. "On a more serious note, I'm encouraged that fighting side by side with Odin and Thor went so well."

"Och aye, I was worried about it," Bran said.

"When do ye want to gather forces and leave for the borderworlds?" Gwydion asked.

"We'd have been gone already were it not for the demon problem," Arawn noted.

"Mmph." Fionn set his comb down. His hair was good enough. He'd braid it once it dried. "What was the casualty count?"

"Ye mean from the demon skirmish?" Bran asked. When Fionn nodded, he steepled his fingers together and shut his eyes as he recalled numbers. "Eight humans died, and one bond animal. Around twenty were wounded badly enough we made an infirmary out of the ballroom on the second floor. It was nip and tuck with a couple, but all are recovering nicely."

Breath whistled from between Fionn's clenched teeth. Their losses were worse than he'd anticipated—much worse. "We have to do a better job protecting them."

"I thought the same," Gwydion said, "yet they dinna wish our help. When we were under attack, I offered to shore up wards I sensed werena strong, but they shooed me aside."

Bella tightened her talons where they dug into his thigh, but he didn't chide her. Fionn rubbed the back of his neck and funneled magic to his right temple where a headache pounded. "Looks like we need another meeting. We shouldna need their permission to help them."

Gwydion rose to his feet and crossed his arms over his chest, leaving his staff propped against the bed. "When do we leave for the borderworlds?" he repeated. "Majestron will have a way to communicate with the others, and I fear they'll whip up some unpleasant surprises if we leave them enough time."

Fionn's eyes widened, and he pounded a fist into his open palm. "Goddess's tits but I was stupid. Stupid."

"What did ye do this time?" Gwydion shot a bemused look his way.

Fionn ignored the barb at the end of Gwydion's comment. "When Majestron's head and body were sitting in fire at our feet, Thor, Odin, and I discussed meeting up on the borderworlds." He shot to his feet; the abrupt movement elicited an unhappy squawk from Bella, but Fionn was so annoyed with himself, his empty stomach twisted into a heaving knot of snakes.

"For fuck's sake, people engulfed in fire are supposed to be dead," he sputtered, but his excuse sounded pathetic because he'd known she wasn't. Holy crap, she'd even spoken to him from the fire, never mind nearly sinking her fangs into him while he held her head suspended by her hair.

"'Tis unfortunate ye dinna keep your mouth shut," Arawn said slowly, "but it simply means we leave sooner rather than later."

"The rest of us have had a spot of rest," Gwydion said. "We'll gather the humans and give them a pep talk on battle strategy."

"I'll help," Fionn muttered.

"Nay." Gwydion nailed him with his blue gaze. "Ye'll sleep a spell and have a meal. We need you at full power, not barely functioning."

"I am not *barely functioning*," Fionn growled, and then understood he wouldn't have underestimated Majestron, spilling information in front of her, if he hadn't spent the hours before in a pitched battle to seal demons back in Hell. "Never mind," he muttered. "Point taken."

"We'll do all the spade work," Gwydion said, "including sending Nidhogg back to Asgard to let them know our timetable."

Fionn glanced out a window, but it was so overcast it was impossible to find the sun. "What time is it?"

"Midafternoon," Bran said.

"We'll leave tomorrow at dawn," Arawn announced.

"Do ye think it wise to wait that long?" Fionn asked.

"It will take us that long to get everyone whipped into shape," the god of the dead said grimly. "I doona wish to drag human corpses back from the borderworlds, and we canna leave them there."

Something bright tugged at the edges of Fionn's weakened magic. Aislinn. Her energy was on the move. When she waltzed through the door seconds later, he understood how badly depleted he was. She'd obviously been on her way upstairs for several minutes before he felt her psychic emanations. He opened his arms and she dove into them.

Gwydion cleared his throat. "We'll be leaving now," he said, and he, Bran, and Arawn walked out the door.

For long moments Fionn and Aislinn just held each other. She felt so good in his arms he almost couldn't believe she was real, and they were together again. "I was so afraid I'd lost you," he murmured against her hair. "When I teleported to the ground and couldn't find you, I wanted to tear the world stem to stern. And when I cobbled together what must have happened…" He let his words trail off. "I've never felt so helpless."

"You found me." She tilted her head back and met his gaze, her golden eyes sheened with tears. "How'd you do that? Dewi snatched me from Nidhogg the moment we got here, stripped my clothes off, and gave me a steam bath. Then she forced food and water and mead into me until I was afraid I'd puke it all back up, and wouldn't let me ask any questions."

"Why not?"

"She said I'd been *upset enough*."

"Och, leannán, she's compensating for not having her younglings."

Aislinn hissed out a breath. "I know that, but I don't need another mother, particularly when Dewi and the one I had hated each another. You still haven't told me how you found Rune and me."

"Nidhogg took me to Asgard. Odin knew where the dark gods' fortresses were located. They'd only built three. Of those, only one was still standing." He traced the line of her high cheekbones with his thumb. "When we got to where I was convinced you had to be, and I couldna sense ye anywhere, I panicked."

"I was underground, warded, and scared shitless Majestron would figure it out. Except she never did."

"I begged the goddess to watch over you." Fionn tightened his hold on her and kissed her forehead. "Mayhap she heard me."

RUNE TROTTED through the room's still open door and nudged the back of Aislinn's leg. Bella cawed a greeting and fluttered to his back.

The wolf pressed his snout into Aislinn's side and said, "They tell me we're leaving soon. I need to hunt."

She let go of Fionn and hunkered next to her wolf. "I never got a chance to thank you properly for taking care of me."

He solemnly licked her chin. "That's what bondmates do," he informed her. "We make sure we don't die."

Her heart squeezed painfully in her chest at the thought of losing her wonderful wolf. "No," she said, her throat thick with emotion, "we don't die. Be careful hunting. Stay inside Fionn's wards."

He licked her again. "Promise."

"I'm going too," Bella said.

Aislinn watched Rune trot out the door with Bella on his back and then moved to close it. She took in dark smudges beneath Fionn's eyes and a whole new network of fine lines radiating from them. "You haven't slept since before the demon battle, have you?"

"Nay, lass, but just looking at you is all I need to revive me."

A soft smile curved her lips. God but she loved him. "That's sweet and romantic, but I could have sworn I heard Gwydion telling you to rest."

"Ye have ears like a lynx since he said that afore ye entered the room."

Aislinn cocked her head to one side. "Maybe I sat outside for a bit, listening. It's amazing what I learn that way. I even heard about what you did to Majestron Zalia. When I asked Nidhogg, he didn't know."

Fionn grinned. "Nidhogg left afore the fun began. Ye dinna tell me ye were a regular James Bond."

"Please. Emma Peel."

"Och, and I liked *The Avengers* too." He crooked a finger her way and patted the bed.

"Gwydion said rest." Her body ached for him, but she could see how tapped out he was.

"I'll rest better with you in my arms."

She couldn't come up with even the teensiest argument against that, so she closed the distance between them and jerked his sweatshirt over his head. Once his bare chest came into view, she ran kisses from the hollow in his neck down to where both nipples puckered, surrounded by their fine scattering of golden hair. He groaned when she licked his nipples and buried his hands in her hair.

Aislinn busied her hands undoing his jeans. He preferred the button closures, probably because zippers hadn't been invented when he was young. The bulge of his cock pressed against her hands as she fumbled to get his pants open. Now that she was this close to him, her fingers shook and her breath came faster. She tugged his ridged flesh out of his snug pants, not bothering to try to get them off. Instead, she moved down, kneeling before him, and took him into her mouth, kissing, sucking, nibbling the way she knew he liked.

He murmured something in Gaelic that she was pretty sure meant stop, but she ignored him. This wasn't the time for long, drawn-out lovemaking. This was a celebration they were both still alive. His penis grew even harder under her ministrations, and she reached between his legs and tickled his anus with a fingertip, urging him to let go. He cradled her head between his hands and drove himself into her mouth, making decidedly male sounds that sent every drop of moisture in her body straight to her crotch.

Just when she was certain he couldn't possibly get any bigger, his cock swelled even more and jerked as he came. She sucked hard, willing him pleasure, and kept working him with her hands and mouth until she was certain he was done.

"I love you, Aislinn," he managed between gasping for air. "Ye're my heart, my life."

She pulled his still-erect cock from her mouth and grinned up at him. "At least that was in English."

"Ye'd understand the Gaelic." He reached beneath her arms and pulled her to her feet where he closed his mouth over hers, kissing her with an intensity that stole her breath.

She wound her arms around his body and pressed her engorged nub against his thigh. He moved so she could straddle him and cupped her ass with both hands, holding her tight against him. It was how she'd come the first day she'd met him, riding his leg between both of hers. The memory of it drove her over the edge. Spasms coiled from her belly lighting every nerve on fire, and she held onto Fionn as the world dissolved around her.

When she could breathe again, she gazed at him. "I vote for the bed."

"Och, lassie, I thought ye'd never ask." He let go of her and pulled his pants up enough to hobble to the bed. Once there, he sat on the edge, and pushed his trousers all the way off.

Aislinn wriggled out of the oversized sweat pants and top Dewi had rummaged from somewhere for her to put on and dropped them over a chair. Fionn had pushed the duvet aside and she crawled beneath it to join him. Wrapped in his arms and lulled by the even cadence of his breathing, she fell asleep almost immediately.

CHAPTER 21

A cold, wet nose pressing into Aislinn's face woke her, and she opened her eyes to see Rune staring down at her. His hind legs were on the floor, but his front ones splayed over the duvet.

"Gwydion sent me to wake both of you." He swiped her from chin to nose with his tongue. She peered out the window at darkness, but that didn't mean much in the northern realms where it didn't get light until midmorning.

Fionn rolled against her and ruffled Rune's fur. "Where's Bella?"

"Right here." The raven settled on Fionn's side of the bed, digging her sharp talons into the duvet.

Fionn scooted until he sat with his back against the headboard and gazed at wolf, raven, and Aislinn. "'Tis the last private moment we're likely to have," he said. "I'll be brief. You're my family, all of you. My only goal for the coming days is for all of us to survive. So"—he drew his blond brows together into a straight line—"if I tell ye to do something, ye will do it without question. I canna fight if my attention is split three different ways worrying about you. Understood?"

Aislinn nodded solemnly. They'd had this discussion before, and she'd never paid much attention to it. *Yes, and look where it's gotten me.*

Rune lifted his head. "My allegiance is to Aislinn. I will do whatever is needed to protect her."

"There is rarely time for talk during the thick of a battle," Fionn said. "Ye must trust I wouldna instruct you in an action that would put her at risk."

Sensing things would only go downhill from there, Aislinn laid a hand on Rune's head. "We'll be good soldiers. I don't want to end up in the dark gods' clutches again—ever."

"You don't have to worry about me," the raven muttered. "I never wanted to be a hero."

"But you have been." Rune gazed at the bird. "You've launched diversionary tactics and put yourself in danger for Fionn."

Bella twisted and pecked gently at his snout, the bird's way of saying thank you.

Aislinn hated to leave the warmth of the bed. Fionn had nailed it when he said they were family. It was a long time since she'd had one, and the thought of losing any of them tore at her heart. Her throat swelled with suppressed emotion, and she blinked back sudden tears, hoping no one noticed.

"Och, mo croi."

Fionn reached for her, but she slipped between the wolf and the bird and got out of bed. If she let herself be held, cuddled, she'd devolve into a syrupy mess, not something she needed this morning.

The floor felt cold against her bare feet, and she hurried to dress, pulling on layers. Last time she'd been to the borderworlds they hadn't been cold, but who knew if the dark gods could control the temperature. Black wool pants were followed by a black, stretchy, long-sleeved shirt, a thick, synthetic green jacket she'd filched from their time at Marta's house, thick socks, and her battered boots. By the time she reached for her rucksack, intent on making certain she had food, water, a hat and gloves, Fionn had snugged into fresh battle leathers, and Bella was attached to his shoulder.

He walked to her side, kissed her forehead and said, "See you downstairs. I'll dish up whatever's made for breakfast."

Aislinn nodded, still too emotional to trust herself to talk. Rune watched her from a spot near the door. He sat, ears pricked forward, and tail stretched behind him. She hefted her rucksack, draping it over a shoulder, and looked around the room wondering if she'd ever see it again.

Crap! When did I get so morose?

But she understood. Before Rune, before Fionn, she'd had nothing to lose, nothing precious to her. That had changed. She didn't want to go back to her solitary existence in the abandoned mineshaft in Utah, but life had certainly been a whole lot less complicated then. She shuttered her feelings, burying them deep, and marched out the door with the wolf right behind her. As an afterthought, she sealed the door with magic. It wouldn't hold forever, and it wouldn't keep one of the Celts out, but the space was hers and Fionn's, and she wanted to lessen the odds of someone wandering in.

Two flights of stairs and the great room passed in a blur. By the time she pushed the kitchen door open, holding it for Rune, she was back in warrior mode. It had taken longer this time to clear her mental debris aside and focus, which worried her. Maybe her time with Majestron had scarred her in ways she had yet to discover.

Or maybe I'm just tired and sick of fighting. Foes you can't kill are a bitch. God only knows when they'll pop up again.

"Come eat, leannán. I poured you coffee too." Fionn patted the place next to him at the table. A few humans ranged at the table's far end, but no one Aislinn recognized readily.

Grateful, she sat next to him and dug into a barley and dried fruit mixture, eating methodically. "How long before we leave?" she asked between bites and swallowed scalding coffee. It was black and bitter, the way Fionn liked it. She preferred it sweetened, but wasn't about to complain.

"As soon as we finish. Everyone else is out in the front courtyard."

"I'm mostly done." Aislinn scraped two more bites out of the bottom of her bowl and drained her coffee before getting to her feet. She rustled through the pantry and dropped nuts and dried apricots into a cloth bag, adding them to her rucksack, along with a generous flask of water. "Are you taking anything with you?" she asked Fionn.

He shook his head. "Nay, lass. We willna be there that long. At least I doona believe so."

"Doesn't matter. Every time I don't plan ahead, I'm always sorry." She shouldered her pack and buckled the waist belt. "Lead out. Who's going with our team again?"

"Nidhogg, Dewi, Bran, and about ten humans. We decided to take more than the original four who trained with us after that mess with the demons. Andraste threw in her lot with the other group, which is why Bran will be part of our effort."

"How many bond animals?" Rune asked.

"Not sure," Fionn replied. "Eve is in our group, so her mountain cat, Tabitha, will be along. Beyond that, I couldna tell you."

Fionn angled his head and glanced at Aislinn. "Ye dinna ask the most important question, lass."

She met his gaze, mystified. "What? It doesn't matter which borderworld we're going to."

"I meant about the command hierarchy."

She snorted. "Yeah, that would be important to you. Remember, for a long time I worked by myself, only checking in with the Lemurians when I had to."

"It needs to be important to you too." His voice held a stern note. "Nidhogg is in charge, with Dewi second, me third, and Bran fourth."

"That's going to piss the humans off," she observed.

"So far, they seem grateful for our help."

Aislinn bit her tongue. Fionn probably mistook reluctance to engage in arguments so close to their departure on an extremely dangerous undertaking for gratitude. She cleared her throat. "Which world are we going to?"

"The same one ye were on afore. It makes sense since several of us were just there, plus it's the same place Nidhogg was imprisoned for hundreds of years."

She remembered the dry, dead air and the ominous stillness of the borderworld. The atmosphere was dying, since Perrikus had killed off all the trees. "Do you suppose it will be worse than the last time we were there?"

Fionn blew out a tense breath and followed her outside the manor house. It was still pitch black, probably around six in the morning. "If ye're asking about how hard it was to use our magic there, it shouldna be that much worse. It hasna been all that long since our last visit."

She walked to where Dewi, Nidhogg, Bran, and a group of humans stood. The dragons glowed, lending muted light to the gloom. On the far side of the courtyard, Kra, Berra, Gwydion, and Arawn stood in a similar cluster with Andraste at its center. The low hum of her voice held a grim note.

"Will we be able to communicate with the other group?" Aislinn asked.

Nidhogg shook his head. "We'll be on our own. The plan is to return here as soon as our job is complete. If no one has yet returned from the other group, whoever's back will attempt to offer aid."

"So that could be them or us," a human said.

"Yes." Nidhogg raised his forelegs. "Quiet until I'm done. We will aim for the spot on the borderworld where Perrikus's stronghold is. If he's there, he'll know the moment we break through the barrier between Earth and his miserable excuse for a world, so there's no point in setting down far from our target and then having to teleport a second time."

Steam hissed through the dragon's open mouth. "Your magic will not work as well where we're going. It will be slow to respond and take a whole lot more effort to achieve the same results."

"We won't exactly have time to experiment," Eve mumbled.

"No," Aislinn broke in, "we won't. Since my magic is closer to yours than the Celts, I can tell you it took roughly double the wattage for me to do anything."

"I requested silence until I was done," Nidhogg reminded them. Side conversations that had bloomed died away. "Good lead-in to my second point, though. I command this group. Dewi is my second. That means if something happens to me, she takes over. It also means if I'm not close enough to see what's happening where you are and she is, you listen to her. Fionn is third in the command structure, and Bran fourth."

"What if we don't agree with something?" Eve squared her shoulders and walked dead center in front of Nidhogg.

"You won't agree with everything," Dewi replied, "but if each of us is fighting our own war, we may as well not go. The dark gods are quick to recognize dissention, and they'll play it to their advantage."

"Any other questions?" Nidhogg glanced around the group.

Aislinn repressed a shudder. Now that it was upon them, the last place she wanted to go was back to Perrikus's world. It was where the dark god had killed her unborn son, and where Fionn had almost died, or done whatever it was the Celts did when they were so badly hurt their bodies couldn't go on.

Rune nudged her side and she buried a hand in his thick neck ruff, grateful for his warm, animal presence. He pushed into her mind.

"We will remain linked," he told her. *"My senses are sharper than yours."*

"Come close to Dewi and me," Nidhogg instructed. "There is no air between here and the borderworld. Try not to panic, we'll finish this teleport as fast as we can."

FIONN'S LUNGS BURNED. Traveling between Earth and the dark gods' borderworlds was painful because an airless void eddied between them. It reminded him of when he and Arawn had barely escaped Perrikus's world. It had taken a week afterward before his lung tissue stopped hurting every time he inhaled. Rather than being on his shoulder, the raven was cradled in his arms, and she had her beak tucked inside his leather top, presumably taking advantage of an air pocket. He wished he had something like that to tap into.

Hell, he wished this was over with. All of it. He wanted nothing more than to settle in with Aislinn and watch over her while her stomach swelled with their children. He'd made a huge mistake not telling her about impregnating her the first time, and he still mourned the son who would never be.

Next time, he vowed. *There has to be a next time.*

He felt lightheaded from lack of oxygen, and the muscles in his legs threatened to cramp. Just when he was wondering what the holy hell Nidhogg was up to, the unremitting black around him shaded to gray at its edges, and he knew they were closing on their destination. Anticipation shot through him, along with a healthy jolt of adrenaline. If they did their job well, the dark gods' threat would be eradicated. At least for a long time. Leaving Majestron Zalia a smoking heap of melted flesh had been a coup, and an unexpected one.

Fionn rolled out of a rough portal, landing hard. He shot to his feet, scanning everything at once, intent on ferreting out any immediate danger. The dragons were already there, holding the gateway open with their magic. Bella gave a muted squawk, wrenched out of his hands, and took up her customary spot on his shoulder. Fionn watched anxiously as humans dribbled through the gateway. Where were Aislinn and Rune?

Dewi nudged him. "She's here. Don't worry. You're not the only one watching out for her."

Fionn narrowed his eyes. "'Tis scarcely the place to fight over who Aislinn belongs to. There's enough of her to go around."

"My sentiments exactly," Aislinn said and walked to him, with Rune by her side, having exited the portal when Fionn wasn't looking. "Damn it! I always forget something." As she talked, she worked her hair into sloppy braids and reached into a pocket for a black watch cap that she pulled low on her head, tucking her hair under it.

"How far are we from the place Perrikus held Arawn and me prisoner?" Fionn asked.

"Less than a mile," Nidhogg said. "Be grateful we're not going where I was detained." He blew fire into the stale, dead air, and a nearby tree lit up like a firecracker, cracking and popping.

"Not much remains of that hellhole," Dewi noted, satisfaction evident in her voice. "I didn't leave anything for them to salvage when I rescued you."

Bright light flashed behind Fionn when Nidhogg shot fire at the gateway to seal it. "We march," the dragon said. "Except Dewi and I will fly."

"I'll see everyone gets there." Fionn hooked a hand through Aislinn's arm. After a quick look over one shoulder to make certain everyone was watching, he set a quick pace. Dragon wing beats whooshed above him, rustling his hair and clothes with the dragon equivalent of prop wash, and branches crackled as humans and bond animals hurried after him. He'd counted three Hunter companions in addition to Rune and Bella: a wolf, a mountain cat, and a hawk.

Bran caught him up. "Have ye looked about?"

"Nay. I prefer surprises." Fionn glanced sidelong at the god of prophecy.

"I dinna feel any of the dark ones here, but they could be shielding themselves."

Fionn set his jaw in a determined line. "If they're not here, we'll destroy the stronghold and move on."

"The dark gods aren't the only bad things here," Aislinn said.

Fionn recalled the oversized beaver-like animals that had nearly been the death of him. One on one, they were trivial, but there'd been hundreds, maybe thousands of the toothy bastards.

Nothing says the dark ones havena imported something even worse.

A wave of magic hit him in the solar plexus. He could have powered through it, but Fionn stopped and sent his own magic spiraling forward.

"Hurry," Dewi's mind voice blasted him. *"At first the ground around the fortress was empty, but then it cracked open. Nothing's come out of it yet, but I wouldn't hold my breath."* A pause and then, *"Goddammit!"*

Fire flared through the dead trees, and the acrid stench of smoke etched into his throat and lungs. Fionn assumed something must have crawled out of the ground, and the dragons were doing what they could to kill it.

Since Dewi had cut off communication, Fionn didn't waste time pestering her for details. He turned to the row of humans behind him. "We're under attack. Send it down the line. Full power. Magic ready. Fan out when we get there. Kill first, ask questions later."

Nerves thrumming with anticipation, Fionn surged forward. Despite the stink and dirt and hardship, he loved battle. It was dark and gritty and real. One of the last places a man could pit himself against his fears and find out what he was made of. And then he glanced at Aislinn's grim, drawn face. Gods but he adored her. He tried to thrust her behind him, shield her with his body, but she moved back to his side.

"Stop it," she hissed. "I can't fight if I can't see."

He opened his mouth to protest, and snapped it shut. She was here; she wouldn't let him protect her, so the best he could do would be to kill everything in sight before some stray minion of the dark harmed the woman he loved.

The dead trees thinned out. "Form a line," Fionn barked. "Watch your aim."

"Give it up, Celt," a human muttered. "This isn't my first battle."

"Christ! You're all touchy as scalded cats."

"Maybe that's because—" Aislinn began, but her words trailed to nothingness, replaced by, "Shit!"

As the last line of trees dropped away, Fionn stared at a scene straight out of Dante.

No, he corrected himself. *Worse.*

The sky lit with fire as the dragons fought something else with wings. When Fionn funneled magic to sharpen his vision, he realized they were griffons.

CHAPTER 22

*A*islinn stared. When she'd been held captive by Perrikus and D'Chel, she'd never seen the outside of her prison since they'd teleported her inside, and she'd teleported out. What stood before her was a blocky, medieval-looking fortress made of gray-black rocks mortared together. It rose four floors with a substantial central building and two lateral wings jutting off to each side. Round towers marked each junction. There weren't many windows, and those that were there looked as if they'd never been washed. A putrid moat circled the structure with water the color of old blood; its rusty drawbridge was down, or maybe it didn't work anymore. Nothing grew between the house and the forest of dead trees they'd passed through, not so much as a weed or blade of grass.

Someone had cut gouges in the ground with surgical precision, and two runic appliques split the dry earth. When she tried to look at them, decipher their meaning, her vision blurred and her heart pounded against her ribcage. With no warning, the runes flared bright red. Large beaver-esque animals with double rows of wicked-looking teeth poured out of one, and something that must have shared kinship with the Harpies from another. With avian hindquarters and the upper body of a grotesquely large hunting hawk, the things lacked the human faces Harpies had, but keen intelligence shone from their black eyes. Orange claws jutted from stunted arms and their back feet, digging divots into the dirt.

Where were Dewi and Nidhogg? She heard the crackle of fire and looked around. Smoke rose from three huge mounds, twisted and burned beyond recognition. "What were those?" she yelled at Fionn.

"Griffons. Ye'd best pray there are no more. No matter what, doona let them get close to you."

The stronghold's front door thudded open, stone ringing against stone. Three more griffons lumbered down the steps on their leonine hindquarters before spreading their eagle's wings and taking to the skies. Aislinn pushed down horror coiling through her midsection. How could things she'd only seen in fable books as a child be real? A sickly sweet smell wafted over her, making her suddenly lightheaded.

"Their breath will put you to sleep." Rune growled and closed his teeth over her leg biting, but not too hard.

"How do you know?" She was too rattled to use mind speech, even though it would have been easy since he was in her head.

"Marta and I fought them once."

Magic rained around her, yet she stood like a starstruck dimwit. She knew fear, had lived with it so long it was like an old, unwelcome friend, but this was the first time it had immobilized her. Rune bit harder. It helped. She stared at the fortress wondering what perversion would waltz through the door next.

It doesn't matter. I need to kill what's in front of me. Now.

She raised her arms, called power, and blasted a line of beavers to grisly chunks of gore. Next she targeted one of the harpy-lookalikes. It proved much harder to kill. She had to dial up her power—and move closer, dodging fire blasting from its beak—before it finally exploded.

"Leave those to Fionn and me." Bran danced around her, light on his feet, his hands alight with power.

She eyed him askance. What was it with the Celts and war? They came alive when they killed and got even larger than life.

Next to her, a human male shrieked and folded to the ground when a griffon nailed him from the air with a dark, smoking spear. Where the hell had the weapon come from? She hadn't seen the winged horrors carrying anything. Aislinn knelt next to the man, laid her hands on his chest around the spear, taking care not to touch it, and sent Healer magic inward to see if she could fix the damage. His green eyes caught hers, and he shook his head. "Save your magic," he said, his voice low and gravelly. "If I'm still alive at the end of this, you can Heal me."

"But—"

"No buts. Pull the thing out. It burns like there's no tomorrow, and I'll see what I can do to help myself from there. Maybe I can crawl back to those dead trees and they'll shield me." He sucked in a gurgling breath. "If we don't win, none of us will leave this accursed place."

Shielding her hands with magic, she grasped the spear, lifted it easily, and tossed it aside. Red welts raised on both her palms. If she hadn't taken precautions before touching the spelled piece of metal, it would have burned her down to bone.

"Ye canna touch their weapons." Fionn stood over her, his face dark as a winter storm.

"I figured that out."

"Do ye need us?" Fionn asked the man, but he motioned them away from him.

Fionn nodded tersely and hauled Aislinn to her feet. "I need you over there." He pointed. "We've lost two people."

"Thank you," the man called after her, but she didn't look back.

Aislinn filled in the space in their line and killed beavers until she could barely hold her arms up, but they still kept coming. Rune killed them too. He grabbed them, twisted their necks until they snapped, and then grabbed another one. It was like a ghoulish comic book where everything you killed recycled itself and came at you again. The rare times she took her eyes from the field and glanced up, Dewi and Nidhogg were trading blows with griffons. More streamed out of the stronghold whenever one of their brethren fell from the skies. They were beautiful in a macabre sort of way with their ten foot wingspans and bald eagle coloring. She noticed they tucked their leonine hindquarters under in the air, and then realized her mind was wandering.

Aislinn scanned the field. They'd been fighting for hours and made zip in the way of progress. At this rate, they'd exhaust themselves for nothing. She imagined Perrikus—or D'Chel—sitting inside laughing their asses off. Because whether another fifty beavers died seemed irrelevant, she made her way to Fionn and said, "This isn't working."

"Because they were ready for us."

"It doesn't matter why. We should leave, or at least fall back. Figure something else out."

He shot an appraising glance her way. "I was just coming around to the same conclusion. Let me talk with Nidhogg and Dewi."

"They're having a grand time ducking and weaving in an aerial ballet," she observed. "They're welcome to stay if they want."

An idea caught her attention, and she stared at the runes. "Fionn! The creatures can't move beyond a certain distance from those runes. Somehow magic from them is what's powering them. I wondered why they weren't chasing us, and that has to be it."

"Brilliant!" He sent power arcing at the hole in the ground, targeting it rather than the Harpy-things streaming out of it. The air around the rune caught fire, burning a sickly red-orange. Fionn upped the ante on his spell, and Aislinn chucked power in behind his. An explosion shook the ground beneath her feet, followed by another. Smoke and bits of grit swirled through the air, making it even harder to breathe. Gravel scored her face, stinging, burning, and she tasted blood dripping from abrasions on both cheeks.

Bran loped over and added his magic to their mix. Time dribbled past. Her lungs were raw, her mouth painfully dry, and her legs shook with the effort of pulling still more power in this dead world where nothing worked very well.

"Aye!" Bran punched the air with a fist as the runic symbols dissolved. "We got that one. How'd ye figure out we needed to target the runes and not the creatures?" he asked Fionn.

"'Twasn't me, but her." He hooked a thumb toward Aislinn.

Normally, she'd have enjoyed the glory, but she was bent over, hands on her thighs, sucking air like someone tossed out of a plane at thirty thousand feet. Her vision swam and her ears rang insistently. She didn't have any more power to target the second rune. She'd run herself dry.

"Aislinn?" Fionn gripped her upper arm.

"Don't mind me," she panted. "Get rid of the other one."

She slipped her rucksack off her shoulders and gulped half of one of her water flasks, following it with handfuls of dried apricots and some almonds. If she got some sustenance into her, she'd boost her reserves. While she crouched in Fionn's shadow, grateful to have him standing in front of her for once, she watched the second rune—the beaver one—smoke, catch fire, and fold in on itself. Maybe Bran and Fionn had gotten more proficient, because that one was much easier.

A dark form plummeted from above. She didn't have time to yell so she barreled into Fionn's body from behind, targeting the backs of his knees so he'd go down. A split second later, the ground vibrated as if a bomb had gone off and a griffon landed scant inches from where she lay atop Fionn.

"What the fuck?" he pushed her off him, saw the griffon still twitching in death throes with blood gushing from a rent in its furred abdomen, and grinned. Raising a hand, he sent a short blast of magic into the thing to stop its heart. Still, it opened its beak and issued a snarling challenge.

Bella, who hadn't left Fionn's shoulder since they arrived, launched herself at the griffon and pecked out its eyes.

Fionn snorted. "If my magic willna kill it, at least it's blind." He scrambled to his feet.

Aislinn followed him. She shouldered her pack, her mind still a jumble.

The humans drew near, milling about. Aislinn did a quick nose count. Other than the man she'd tried to help, they were short two. Not bad, considering. She shook her head to encourage rational thought. Actually, any losses were unacceptable.

I'm not thinking straight. It's the evil here. It perverts everything.

The dragons dropped heavily to the ground. Aislinn wondered if they'd killed all the griffons. She didn't see any in the sky, but that didn't mean anything.

"We have two choices." Nidhogg eyed them. "The stronghold gates are open—probably on purpose. We can leave, or we can storm the fortress."

"What other surprises do they have in store for us?" Eve asked. Tabitha snarled low in her throat. Blood smeared her snout and whiskers, and she looked fierce.

"Truthfully," Dewi said, "I have no idea. I understand you're tired and this world drains your ability. Nidhogg and I won't make this decision for you."

"How about if I make it," a clear, melodic voice cried. "Welcome to my humble abode."

Aislinn cringed. D'Chel. She'd know his voice anywhere. Christ! She'd listened to him enough, either seducing her, or screaming epithets when she wouldn't cooperate. She squared her shoulders and saw him framed in the open door of his fortress. Silky dark hair flowed around well-defined muscles and bronzed skin. Copper eyes leered at her. Thank God he was dressed for once, but his buckskin top and pants fit him like a second skin.

She girded herself for the rush of sexual energy, but it still caught her unprepared, staggering in its intensity. Damn the dark gods. They all wanted to use her for breeding stock, and her sexual response to their energy amused them. Visions of D'Chel's huge, perfect cock danced before her eyes, and her breath quickened in her throat.

"Human." He smiled lazily. "I've missed our visits."

"Leave her out of this," Fionn growled. "Last time ye wanted me to trade her for Bran's and Gwydion's freedom. It dinnna work then, and it willna work now. She's not part of the equation—now or ever."

"Fine." D'Chel half-bowed, his eyes alight with intensity. "She wants me, though. I can smell her…interest from here."

"Only because ye bespelled her." Fionn curled his hands into fists and stepped between Aislinn and D'Chel.

"If you're here"—Nidhogg faced the dark god—"then where's Perrikus?"

"Sorry, old chap, er old dragon, but that's classified."

Aislinn moved to Fionn's side. "Since he invited us in, I think we should take him up on it." She clapped a hand over her mouth. "I didn't say that. It wasn't me."

Fionn shot her an incredulous look. "So long as he's shown himself, he can come the rest of the way out—or stand in the doorway —to talk. The only reason to risk ourselves in his lair would have been to flush him out."

Rune whined anxiously, and Aislinn leaned toward him. *"Out of my mind. I don't want him to hurt you."*

The wolf developed a mulish look and drew his upper lip back in a snarl, but he obeyed.

Something subtle altered the air around D'Chel. He was up to something, but she had no idea what.

Rune stood by her side, hackles raised, sending a foul stare at the dark god. If looks could kill—and if D'Chel weren't immortal—he'd be dead.

Fionn jerked her behind him again. Aislinn bit back a string of harsh words, and Dewi shot a stream of flame at the god of illusion. It ran down D'Chel's body and smoke roiled about his feet. Nothing burned, not even his clothes. He must have spelled them in some way.

"He's cooking something up," Nidhogg said, "and we're playing right into his hands by standing here."

~

FIONN SHIFTED from foot to foot. They should move forward, all of them, and attack. D'Chel couldn't hold them off forever, not by himself. He caught Nidhogg's eye and jerked his chin toward D'Chel, but the dragon shook his head.

"Why not?" Fionn asked in carefully shielded mind speech.

"Because that's what he wants us to do. Something's in the fortress with him. I feel its energy, but can't determine what it is."

"We canna just stand here. If we're not moving forward, we should retreat."

The humans had formed a tight group, talking among themselves. Suddenly, with no warning, they broke and hurtled toward the house, magic streaming from them, while Fionn watched horrorstruck.

"They're not going in there alone," Aislinn cried, and took off after them with Rune at her heels, growling and snapping.

Fionn pelted after her. So much for a coordinated approach. This was what came of fighting with troops you hadn't trained much with. The smile on D'Chel's perfectly sculpted face broadened, and he didn't lift his hands to defend himself.

"Stop!" Fionn yelled. "'Tis a trap. Once you get close enough—"

Sound cracked like a hundred whips snapping against one another.

"Retreat!" he shrieked and grabbed Aislinn, throwing her behind him. "Flee," he told her. "Back to the dragons."

"I will not run."

"We're right behind you," Dewi said.

Magic flashed past Fionn and Aislinn whooshed onto the dragon's back. At least she'd be safe there, so long as she stayed put.

Rune ran to him. "Get her back," the wolf demanded. "She wants to be on the ground with me."

"I've got bigger problems just now," he told the wolf. "Stay close to me."

Bran and Nidhogg dove into the group of humans, pushing, pulling, yelling. Some obeyed, others ran pell-mell toward D'Chel, who was grinning like a Cheshire cat who'd just cornered an entire nest of mice.

A wave of magic rolled past, and the front row of humans got sucked into a vortex that spun them upward. So that was why D'Chel needed them close. Something about the fortress, or where he stood, concentrated his magic. Sowing chaos and destruction was a real power hog, but the dark god looked as fresh as if he'd just wakened from a nap.

Nidhogg flew into the vortex, interrupting its flow. His black scales gleamed golden as magic bounced off him. He caught three of the four airborne humans on his back and made a grab for the fourth with a foreleg, catching him handily. Huffing smoke and fire, Nidhogg flew back to where he'd overseen the earlier battle.

Fionn made certain Rune was still with him and turned to follow the dragons. Once he caught up to them, he'd insist they return to Earth. No point in remaining to provide sport for D'Chel. As he ran, the air felt thick, prickly, just plain wrong. He stopped and made a grab for Rune. "Something is amiss. Until I figure it out—"

"Nothing to figure out, human." Another dark god with cropped red curls and brilliant green-gold eyes dropped from nowhere, blocking Fionn's path.

Fionn narrowed his eyes. "By a process of elimination, ye must be Adva."

"Brilliant! You're quite the brain-boy." Adva straightened his broad shoulders and mock bowed. Unlike his fellow gods, he wore a pale linen shirt and dark trousers, with a blue silk tie hanging loosely around his neck.

"I do all right." Fionn eyed the god of portals. "I'm thrilled you showed up. Saves us a lot of trouble finding you."

"You won't be so thrilled when you discover I've shut off your exit route."

"Ye're bluffing."

Adva's green-gold gaze glazed over with pure evil. He wasn't smiling anymore. Nor was he bothering to maintain the illusion that made him appear human. Sharp planes bisected the lines of his face and his teeth lengthened into fangs.

"I never bluff, Celt," he hissed.

"Is this where ye turn into a vampire and—"

"Fionn!" Aislinn's shriek tore into his heart. When he spun and looked for Dewi, her back was empty.

CHAPTER 23

$\mathcal{D}$ewi's screech nearly flayed the skin from Fionn's bones. Rune howled and leaped into the air, snapping his jaws over and over. To the accompaniment of Nidhogg's booming trumpeting, Dewi shimmered and vanished. Fire flashed from Nidhogg, cutting a wide swath.

"What's the matter, Celt?" Adva sashayed to his side. "Lose something?"

Fionn twisted, light on his feet, and smashed his fist into Adva's face. He heard the crack of bones breaking and drew his arm back to do it again, but the dark god jumped out of the way. Blood and snot ran down his face, but the damage began to repair itself immediately.

In a shower of fiery sparks, smoke, and steam, Nidhogg dropped to the ground a few feet from Fionn, his green eyes whirling furiously.

"Goddamnit!" More fire flashed from the black dragon. "I told Dewi not to use the MacLochalinn bond to follow Aislinn. Ordered her not to, but she ignored me. Now she's trapped too."

Nidhogg plodded toward Adva with fire blasting from his mouth. It rolled off the dark god like water, but his shirt and trousers smoldered. "You control portals," he thundered. "Where are Aislinn and my mate?"

Adva shrugged. "Who can say? These things are…complicated."

Nidhogg moved faster than Fionn imagined he could and swiped a taloned foreleg around Adva's neck, lifting the dark god off the ground.

"Uh-uh." Adva shook a finger at the dragon. "You need me. This isn't the way to secure my cooperation."

"What happens next depends entirely on that *cooperation*," Nidhogg replied, his voice viciously sweet.

"Put me down this instant." Adva wriggled, fighting the circle of the dragon's talons. Fionn felt him deploy magic, but Nidhogg was impervious to it because nothing changed.

"He says he closed off the portals," Fionn told Nidhogg. "All of them."

The Norse dragon cocked his head to one side. "That could be good news. Closure works both ways. If, and that's a huge supposition, this piece of shit is telling the truth, that means Dewi and Aislinn are still somewhere on this world."

"I resent that," Adva sputtered, and opened his mouth to say more.

Fionn spoke over him, addressing his words to the dragon. "Can ye sense Dewi?" he asked, not daring to let himself hope, "because I canna feel Aislinn's energy."

Rune howled mournfully. "I can."

A bitter smile split Fionn's mouth. This wasn't the first time Hunter magic had trumped his own.

Eve sprinted to where they stood with Tabitha pacing her. She tossed her long black hair over her slender shoulders and her blue eyes were pinched with worry. "What's next?"

"How many of your people sustained injuries?" Fionn asked.

"One is dead. Bran helped two more who were injured, or they'd be on the far side of the veil right along with poor Freddie."

"We doona need numbers anymore," Fionn said. "Take your people and return to my manor house. We'll be along presently." He thought about how things had unfolded and added, "'Tis possible ye'll find the other contingent already returned. All the action appears to have unfolded here."

"But they were supposed to join us in that case," she protested.

"Mayhap they couldna." Fionn sent a harsh glance Adva's way and followed it with, "Ye will allow my troops safe passage."

"Oh I will, will I?" Adva smirked. "The Geneva Convention scarcely applies here."

Nidhogg shook the god of portals until Fionn heard the rattle of teeth.

"Ye have a smart mouth," he observed. "'I'm surprised it hasna landed you in trouble long since."

"One of the benefits of immortality," Adva muttered through gritted teeth.

Nidhogg tightened his grip, and then snugged it up some more. Adva's face turned an unattractive tomato color, and the dark god's breathing degenerated into gurgling gasps.

"If I'm unconscious, I can't open the gates around this world," he panted.

"Aye, I'm betting if he's unconscious, 'twill be naught to hold his spell in place." Fionn watched Adva carefully to see how close he'd come to truth.

"Same bet I'd make," Nidhogg rumbled and hoisted Adva another foot in the air.

"Stop talking." Rune bit Fionn's calf hard enough to draw blood. "We have to go after Aislinn."

The god of portals tried to thrust his hands beneath Nidhogg's talons, but couldn't budge them. His face was purple now and his pupils dilated. Fionn figured he'd pass out soon.

"Stop." Adva motioned with both hands. "You win. I'll let them go."

"Gambit well played." Fionn grinned at the dragon and then turned to Eve. "Gather everyone, including your fallen comrade. At my signal, open teleport spells and return home." He blew out a breath. "Home doesna mean ye get a holiday. Ye may well have to defend the place from Lemurians."

"What about you?" she asked.

"I'm not leaving without Aislinn, and I'm betting Nidhogg feels the same way about Dewi."

"Do you even have to ask?" the dragon opened his taloned foreleg and Adva dropped to the ground with a *thunk*.

He rubbed his neck, but didn't make any motion to get to his feet. "It's done," he said sulkily.

"What's done?" Fionn asked.

"What you asked. The gates guarding the borderworld are open. I'd hurry if I were you, though. You didn't say how long I had to keep them that way." Adva opened his mouth in a hissing snarl that would have done Tabitha proud. The cat saw it as a challenge because she lunged at the dark god, and Eve had to call her off.

"Good Hunting." Eve bowed slightly and took off at a trot for the queue of humans.

"Same to you," Fionn called after her.

Rune bit him again. Fionn yanked his leg out of reach.

Bella fluttered her wings. "Stop that," she told the wolf. "Fionn's got his hands full just now."

A snort blew past Fionn's lips. Having the raven defend him was something new. He toed Adva in the ribs with a booted foot. "Where's D'Chel?"

"Last I looked he was on the raised platform in front of the drawbridge."

"Yes, well, he isna there anymore. Second guess?"

Nidhogg leaned close hissing fire. "This accursed world tries my patience. Answer him."

"If I were D'Chel, I'd have gone back inside." Adva managed a smirk; his face was still colorful, but white splotches had formed in between the reddened parts, sullying his casual elegance.

"What exactly is inside, besides D'Chel?" Magic caught at Fionn's senses, and when he glanced over his shoulder the humans were gone. He hoped to hell Adva hadn't played fast and loose with them. Portals were tricky things. Just because the humans left this world was no guarantee there'd be a clear shot to Earth. Adva could have made certain the only route off this world led to another of the border-worlds—or somewhere much worse, like straight into Hell.

If that happened, the humans could go home from there, assuming one of them understood why they'd had an extra stop stuffed into their itinerary.

Bran loped to Fionn's side and stared down at Adva. "I saw the humans off. Did that one"—he jerked a thumb at the dark god—"tell you aught?"

"Not yet," Fionn replied, "but the day is young."

"We waste time," Nidhogg said pointedly. "We need to go inside. I'll join with Fionn."

Fionn's eyes widened, but then he understood there wasn't any other way. The dragon was much too large to squeeze through interior doorways. Besides, it wasn't as if Nidhogg hadn't done the same with Gwydion while they'd hunted him and Arawn in the halls of the dead.

The dragon watched him carefully. "Warming to the idea, are you?"

"What do we do with him?" Bran nudged Adva with his boot.

Power flared so bright Fionn shut his eyes. When he opened them, Adva was gone.

"Shit!" He pounded a fist skyward. "He's gone to warn D'Chel."

"What did ye expect?" Bran shrugged. "He probably communicated with him telepathically before he left. We'll do the best we can. Dewi's a powerful adversary when her dander's up."

Nidhogg blew steam and blasted into Fionn. The sensation rocked him to his roots. Having the dragon share his mind was one thing, but housing his physical essence felt like swimming in a tank of eels. Power ricocheted from one side of him to the other.

"Steady." Bran took his arm. "Takes a bit of getting used to."

"How would ye know?" Fionn grunted. Even his mouth felt alien, and forming words took a ridiculous amount of effort.

"Gwydion described it. Let's move. I suggest we teleport. While we've been standing here, yon moat's grown and things are swimming in it."

"Are they real?" Fionn asked, recalling D'Chel was the god of illusion.

"Does it matter?"

"No," Rune answered and took off for the fortress at a dead run.

"Come back here," Fionn shouted. "We're teleporting. I doona want to have to tell Aislinn ye died because an imaginary sea serpent bit you in half."

Rune wheeled, his claws tossing up clods of dirt, and stalked back to Fionn. "Do it now," he growled, "or I'm going after her myself."

Admiration warmed Fionn. The wolf was a courageous companion. "Aislinn is lucky to have you."

"I used to feel that way about you before you turned into a procrastinator."

Fionn felt the dragon restless within him. *I agree with the wolf. Either start the spell, or I will.*

"Did ye hear that?" Fionn glanced at Bran.

"Aye. It appears the animals have spoken." He chanted low and Fionn joined power with him.

They needn't have bothered. At the midpoint of their casting, Nidhogg took over and the parched, dead world fell away, replaced by whitewashed castle walls.

A FORCE so powerful she couldn't fight against it jerked Aislinn from Dewi's back. It cut right through both Dewi's warding and her own as if it weren't there. Behind the physical force, desire licked at her, hot and urgent.

D'Chel.

No wonder he'd stood there watching her so intently. He was working on untangling her warding—and the dragon's, once Dewi stepped in and scooped her up. She curved her hands into fists so hard her nails bit into her palms. Maybe it was good Rune wasn't with her. It would just be one more place D'Chel might exploit her. Fionn would watch over her wolf. They'd both be there when she got out, unless they did something foolish and tried to follow her.

If I get out.

Her heart jolted in her chest. She'd beat Slototh because he wasn't expecting her attack. When she'd tried the same tactic on D'Chel, it hadn't worked, which meant she had to come up with something else —and goddamned fast. Her bones rattled as she dropped onto a carpeted floor. On her feet in a flash, Aislinn extended her hands to call power—if it were even possible in here. She backed into a corner because at least then her backside was covered.

Sure enough, D'Chel wavered into view and bowed low. "Like it?" he asked and swept his arms to the sides. She glanced at a lavishly appointed bedchamber. A bed sat on a raised dais surrounded with red silken curtains that appeared dusty and unused. When she looked closer, the entire room was covered thickly in dust. It coated the carpet, the armoires, chests, and table and chairs that butted against one wall.

"What happened to your last victim?" she snarked. "Looks like this room hasn't seen much use."

"Maybe I kept it special just for the two of us."

"Bullshit! This isn't even your house."

He shrugged. "Then perhaps Perrikus kept it for you." D'Chel winked lazily. "He and I whiled away many a pleasant hour imagining what it would be like to share your body."

For the second time in a few minutes, Aislinn's body reeled from shock as Dewi rolled into it. They'd done this before, and the sensation was never pleasant.

"I'll take things from here," the dragon informed her archly.

"No, we'll make joint decisions," Aislinn shot back, but she doubted Dewi took her seriously.

D'Chel drew back, and his stunning face twisted into something much less attractive. "How'd you get past my wards, dragon?"

Aislinn fought against it, but Dewi dragged her body much closer to D'Chel. Close enough she sprayed him with spittle when she said, "The MacLochlainn bond persists beyond death. Why wouldn't it be able to defeat your simple-minded warding system?"

D'Chel crossed his arms over his chest. "How controllable is she?"

"Who are you asking about?" Dewi had taken over Aislinn's vocal chords, and didn't appear inclined to cede them.

He narrowed his eyes. "I was asking Aislinn about you. Any chance you'd let her out to play?"

"Not very fucking likely," Dewi snapped.

The dark god clasped his hands behind him and paced in a small circle, obviously thinking. Aislinn was certain he hadn't envisioned this possibility. Tension built in her nether regions, sexual heat so intense it hurt.

"*Do something*," she shrieked at Dewi. "*Sex is how they establish control.*"

"*He'll never control me*"—the dragon sounded over-confident in Aislinn's opinion—"*but what he's doing feels quite nice. We could let him finish.*"

"*No we can't, you oversexed hussy.*" Aislinn remembered when Dewi had forced her to share the Minotaur's ridiculously-sized cock. It was the darkest, kinkiest sex of her life, and she had zero desire for a repeat performance. She thought quickly. "*Nidhogg would be soooo disappointed in you.*"

"*The only way he'd find out is—*"

"*If I tell him,*" Aislinn finished sweetly. She writhed. It was torture not to touch her engorged nubbin.

"*You wouldn't.*"

"*Try me.*" Aislinn paused for emphasis. "*Remember how upset he was about the Minotaur?*"

While she and Dewi traded barbs, D'Chel was getting into things. He'd moved still closer to them and stripped off his leather top. Aislinn blinked against his undeniable beauty. All the dark gods were perfection incarnate, but D'Chel's skin was a bit more golden, his body a shred more perfect. Planes of muscle cut through his broad shoulders and flat stomach, and his copper colored nipples were puckered with lust. He stroked the tented front of his leather breeches and started on the laces.

Dewi did something because the sexual sensations bombarding Aislinn fell off abruptly.

"I am not happy about this," the dragon muttered.

Too bad, but Aislinn kept her mind mouth shut. No point antagonizing Dewi. She'd seen what the dragon could do when her dander was up. She could shatter every bone in Aislinn's body going after an enemy. Not on purpose, but because she was used to her dragon form and simply assumed Aislinn's human body was more robust and didn't break quite so easily.

D'Chel gazed lazily at them. "What, no more games? You were enjoying yourselves."

"No more games," Dewi said. "We're leaving."

"I don't think so. You may have gotten through my wards because of some magnetic attraction you have with the girl, but she's here with you, which means you don't have a ready exit route."

"Is he right?" Aislinn asked, frantic. At the moment, she wasn't sure which was worse: sharing her body with the dragon, or being stuck in the same room with D'Chel.

"Unfortunately," Dewi mumbled. *"Never fear, I'll think of something."*

"While you're thinking, I want my voice back."

"Why?"

Aislinn wanted to punch something, but she didn't have any more control over her fists than she did her tongue. *"Because I'm not some child for you to pull rank on. I didn't ask for you to come barreling into my body."*

"Next thing, you'll be telling me you didn't need rescuing," Dewi said acidly.

"I didn't. Not yet, anyway."

"Girls, girls, this is instructive, because I'm beginning to understand your relationship, but let's not argue."

"What? I suppose you'd rather sit down over a meal and chat?" Aislinn was shocked when her words emerged and sent silent thanks to the dragon.

"We'd have much more fun in bed," D'Chel smirked, but at least he'd stopped unlacing his breeches. "Besides, food's a bit thin here. You may have noticed nothing grows on this world."

As she listened, a plan bloomed. The reason she'd failed last time with D'Chel was because she didn't have enough magic. With Dewi inside her, her power was practically limitless—if the dragon would cooperate.

A ragged-looking man she didn't recognize burst into the room, slamming the door against its stops so hard plaster chunked off the wall. His face was streaked with bloody mucous, and fury radiated from him in palpable waves.

D'Chel rounded on him. "I told you not to disturb me."

"We need to talk. Out there." The man jerked a hand toward the open door.

D'Chel tossed a lascivious grin her way. "Keep that fire burning for me, girls. I'll be right back."

Breath whooshed from Aislinn as the door thundered shut. *"Who the fuck was that?" she asked Dewi.*

"Adva."

She should have been frightened, but Aislinn's spirits soared. The missing dark god. Maybe their luck was turning after all. It was only a matter of time before Fionn, Rune, and Nidhogg did something brave and foolhardy to rescue them.

If she and Dewi didn't beat them to the punch and escape on their own.

CHAPTER 24

"Keep your power muted," the young black dragon hissed at one of his eggmates.

"Sorry." The green dragon didn't sound the least bit repentant. "Told you we needed more practice."

The black male stood in the middle of a circle of his siblings. Royce and Vaughna had finally gone hunting and left them alone. At first, the adult dragons had spelled them to sleep before hunting, but a few days of good behavior lulled them into believing their charges would behave.

"I still don't understand quite what we're doing. Or why it will take all of us," a red female whined.

Fire spewed from the black dragon's mouth. They were beginning to name themselves. His name was Nidhogg, just like his father, since he'd grow to become the Norse dragon. Still, it felt pretentious to call himself that quite yet. He lassoed his annoyance and started over.

"We don't have much time. We have to go now while they left us alone. If we don't, goddess knows how long it will be before we get another chance."

"Where are we going?" the green male asked. "Tell us why again."

"I made a big mistake when I let the Old Ones into my mind. This is a way to make amends and build back trust. Mother and Father need us. They're on one of the dark gods' borderworlds."

"How do you know?" the red female asked, crossing her forelegs over her scaled chest.

"I overheard Royce and Vaughna talking."

"Not what I meant. How do you know Mother and Father need us?"

Young Nidhogg cast his attention inward. Because he was the next Norse dragon, he had a link with his father. It wasn't precise, but his mind was filled with images he presumed he shared with his father, and the one where his mother raced off like a crazy thing to join Fionn's red-headed girlfriend had burned into his brain. Because he suspected the others might not believe him, he tried a different tack.

"We are old enough to fight now that our scales have hardened. I know Mother and Father are in trouble because…he told me."

The cave filled with steam as the other six dragons huffed disbelief. Nidhogg junior winced. He hadn't thought they'd go for it—and they hadn't.

"Please." He infused compulsion into his tone. "I need all of you because our magic will feed on itself if we're together. I'd go alone, but I'm not strong enough."

"Have you ever teleported?" the copper male asked. "By yourself?"

"No, but I know how." He shut his eyes for a moment and came to a decision. Sometimes you had to take chances and he needed the others' cooperation. "I will be the next Norse dragon, so I hold many of father's memories. It's how I know he needs us."

A collective *ahhhhh* whooshed through the cave. The challenges he expected never materialized, and he blew out a relieved breath at not having to fight his siblings.

"If this goes bad"—a red female shook her head until her scales clattered against each other—"there'll be hell to pay. They'll probably lock us on this world and throw away the key."

"They wouldn't." The copper male straightened, furling his wings.

"We need to go. Now," the black urged. "If we don't, the choice will be taken from us. Who's in?"

Silence hung in the cave, lasting so long, he figured he'd lost. Finally, one of the three green males shuffled nearer and muttered, "I may regret this, but me."

After that, everyone except one red female said they'd go with him.

"We can't leave you here," Nidhogg the younger said.

Smoke poured from the other red female. "No shit. Once Royce and Vaughna return, they'll torture the truth out of you."

The reluctant red female winced. "We're not supposed to use bad language." Her shoulders drooped. "All right. I'll go, but I do not have a good feeling about how this will turn out. We're safe here."

"The world is at war," the black dragon informed her. "Soon no one will be safe anywhere. Besides, do you want to spend thousands of years here? I know it's our world, but it's not very interesting. Fire and sand and mountains."

"You won," she grumbled. "Let's go before I change my mind."

Tamping down triumph, the young black dragon furled his wings wide. "Come close," he instructed, "and mind link with me. We'll be gone from here very soon."

"Will we go directly to Mother and Father?" the copper dragon asked.

Young Nidhogg considered it. "No. It would be faster, but since this is our first time, we'll go from here to Earth and see if we need to fine-tune anything before we tackle the dark one's realm."

Dragon magic rose in a glittering arc, a blend of all their colors. The black dragon dug deep, plucked the memories he needed, and guided them into the teleport spell.

KRA, Berra, Gwydion, Andraste, and Arawn exchanged glances with Odin, Thor, and an assortment of Valkyries, and Norse warriors. The humans and bond animals had formed small groups, grumbling among themselves. A foul wind blew hard, bringing the odor of a charnel pit with it, and Gwydion knew this world was about to change yet again. The same putrid smell that twisted his stomach into a pounding knot of nausea had presaged the other shifts too.

The borderworld had looked like a reincarnation of the movie *Waterworld* when they'd arrived, switched to a darkened cave, complete with a damp, dripping, low-hanging ceiling, and then formed a barren desert. Hideous animals had come with each iteration, but the sea serpents had been the worst, because they had a nasty way of winding themselves around your body in a hammerlock. His magic didn't work as well underwater—especially not in this world—and he wasn't interested in testing it in that environment again.

"I doona believe the dark gods are here," Gwydion said.

Andraste shot him a long-suffering look. "I told you that an hour ago, but ye dinna believe me."

"I know the plan was to return to Inishowen, but I believe we should go directly to Perrikus's world afore we get mired in another battle with whatever crawls out of the ether next time the landscape changes," Arawn muttered.

"It's as if someone's trying to hold us here," Kra said, blowing an irritated looking cloud of steam. It dissipated instantly in the dry air.

"We're more than ready to go," Timothy said. "I speak for all of my kind. We discussed it—thoroughly. At least we haven't lost anyone, but I fear if we remain, our luck won't hold. That last attack from whatever those things were was much more vicious than either the serpents or the slimy things in the cave."

Gwydion clacked his jaws together. Those *things* had been fear gortachs. Hunger ghosts straight out of Irish legend. They fed on humans, taking up residence in their bodies in times of famine. Because all of their group were well fed, the gortachs had been easy enough to defeat. There'd been a few acepheli too, but the headless ones were more nuisance than problem. And some acheri, Native American spirits in the form of small girls who brought illness.

"What I'd like to know," Gwydion muttered, "is why we're facing horrors from diverse mythologies. Ye'd think they'd stick with one."

"Why?" Arawn asked pragmatically. "If I had the ability to cull help from different times and different cultures, I'd do it too."

"We can debate philosophy later." Andraste rolled her eyes.

The reeking wind blew harder. "None of this matters. We waste time." Berra blew steam and added, "You Celts always were prone to endless discussions."

Gwydion glanced about and his gaze landed on Odin. "Ye've been quiet."

"Aye." The Norse god nodded and narrowed his eyes in thought. "I can see the wisdom in checking the other borderworld, yet I believe some of us should remain here. For one thing"—he swept his mail-clad arms wide—"we're killing things that have no right to live, no matter what world they inhabit."

"Are ye volunteering?" Arawn asked.

Odin nodded. "If the magic behind the changes here dies down, and we can see the bedrock world and assure ourselves no further threat exists, we'll join you."

"And will ye remain here forever, otherwise?" Gwydion cracked a very thin smile.

"Of course not. If we don't see you before you return to Earth, find me in Asgard, and we can compare tales. And share a few tankards of ale as well."

"Good enough," Arawn said and the air around him took on an incandescent aspect as he built a teleport spell.

"We'll go together," Gwydion said and motioned to the humans and dragons to move close. He stuck out a hand; Odin clasped it and then moved up so they held each other's forearms. He let go, and Thor did the same thing.

"Until later," Gwydion said. "Victory in battle."

"Until later," the Norse god echoed. "Glory in battle to us all."

The other Norse warriors and Valkyries took up the chant. "Glory in battle to us all!"

The last thing Gwydion saw as the borderworld dimmed around them was it shifting into dense jungle and Odin and his troops fanning out to deal with whatever might crawl out of the thick undergrowth. The master enchanter suppressed a shudder. He'd dropped by Southeast Asia briefly while the United States was fighting the Viet Cong. Between heat, mold, bugs, and a booby-trapped jungle, it hadn't impressed him.

At least 'tis familiar. He wondered what the hell lay in store for them on Perrikus's world. Despite not flushing out any of the dark gods, D'Chel's world held a carefully choreographed aspect. If both the dark gods were on the other borderworld, how much worse could things get? Deciding he didn't want to know the answer to that question before he had to, Gwydion closed his eyes and waited out the teleport spell.

Fionn stood in a large, rather barren hall with Rune and Bran flanking him. Two ratty chairs sat in a corner with a table made from stone blocks between them. Nidhogg snuffled, borrowing Fionn's nose until the mucous membranes ached. The dark gods had a moldy smell that permeated the place and made him feel dirty. Grubby rugs were scattered over the stone floor, and the ceiling rose in a curved arch until it flattened above their heads. He tried to get his bearings and figure out how the fortress was laid out.

"She's that way." Rune jerked his chin toward the wall to his right. "Where are the doors?"

"There don't seem to be any," Nidhogg rumbled through Fionn's vocal chords.

"Or windows," Bran noted. "Look at this." He walked to an oval mirror leaned against one wall.

It was about six feet tall, and when Fionn joined Bran to get a better look, he realized there were actually four matching mirrors spread out at ninety degree angles to one another. While the surface looked silvery, like a looking glass, it didn't reflect his image.

"Do ye know what these are?" he asked Nidhogg.

"Gateways. I'd be careful touching them if I were you. We could get sucked into somewhere we don't want to be."

"Did ye hear that?" Fionn touched Bran's arm.

The god of prophecy nodded, and his features screwed into an exasperated scowl.

"There's no way out of this room." Rune trotted back to Fionn. "Teleport us to where I sense Aislinn."

"Send me an image." Fionn felt tired and edgy. It was possible this would be as far as their magic would move them into Perrikus's stronghold.

"Got it," Nidhogg said. *"Let me control the spell this time."*

Fionn almost pointed out that the dragon had controlled it last time, but he nipped his reservations in the bud. No point casting doubt. Magic was sensitive that way, and believing in the outcome was almost as important as the spell itself.

The air glittered. Rather than another of the stronghold's rooms, Fionn ended up back outside, but much nearer the moat this time. A prehistoric-looking monster reared a black, triangular-shaped head and bared triple rows of four-inch, red teeth.

"Goddammit!" Fionn followed the English curse with a string of Gaelic ones. If Nidhogg couldn't bend his magic to move them where they wanted to go, it was unlikely either he or Bran could do any better.

Bran grabbed his arm and dragged him backward. "I doona like the looks of that water," he mumbled. "At best, 'twill burn if it touches us. At worst, it could be poisoned."

A wrenching sensation shot through Fionn, turning his nerves into live wires and Nidhogg formed to one side. "Christ!" Fionn glared at the dragon. "Next time, give me a bit of warning, eh?"

"Sorry. Wasn't thinking." Nidhogg shook himself and furled his wings. "Apparently, we can't use magic to get any farther inside the fortress. My spell was flawless."

"If it was flawless, why are we back outside?" Bran quirked a brow.

"Excellent question." Fionn gritted his teeth.

"I just told you." Nidhogg sounded pissed, his voice full of sharp edges. "There's something inside that subverted my casting."

"Mmph. So even if we waltz back through the front door, how well will our magic work once we're in there?" Bran asked.

Nidhogg clacked his teeth together. "It's the mirrors. They gather power, hold it, and turn it back on itself."

"Let's go back inside and break them," Rune said.

"If it were that easy," Bella pronounced from her perch on Fionn's shoulder, "we would have done it the first time."

Fionn winced at the raven's highhanded tone. "We dinna know," he chided her. "Even if we'd suspected, Nidhogg said not to touch them."

"Glass breaks," the wolf persisted. "Throw something at it."

"Those mirrors don't break," the dragon said. "It took me a while, but I recalled where I saw their like."

"We doona need a history lesson," Bran said.

"Och aye, just tell us how they work," Fionn cut in.

"They're how you travel inside the fortress, but I'm certain they lead to other worlds as well. The trick is what you do once you're inside them."

"Say more." Bran stepped closer to Nidhogg.

The dragon's eyes whirled faster. "I fell into one thousands of years ago. I'd followed Odin and Thor into Persia to wage a campaign against the Infidels. After months of battle, we established a fragile truce and the Persian ruler invited us to share a meal. I didn't trust him, but Odin said we must go or it would look like bad faith..."

Fionn curled his hands into fists; he felt like chewing a hole in his cheek. Aislinn was trapped inside that hall of mirrors hellhole. Maybe D'Chel was having his way with her even now. He latched gazes with Nidhogg, silently urging him to get to the point.

"...and so my tail brushed up against one of the mirrors and suddenly I found myself in a place I'd never been. A hideous place filled with fell creatures and bloodsucking undead humans." Fire belched from the dragon. "Fortunately, between my size and my thick hide, they gave up after a while, and I could focus on getting myself out of there."

"What made it difficult?" Bran asked.

"My magic was bent, perverted by the glass. I had to find where the threads twisted and set them right before my teleport spell worked."

"You said the mirrors were also gateways into other parts of the stronghold." Fionn rolled his shoulders, but tension etched into them, holding him rigid. "How do we manipulate them to remain in the stronghold and not get catapulted to a different world?"

"Too bad Odin isn't here," Nidhogg said. "He understood how the mirrors—but he called them silvers—worked."

"We have to do something," the wolf whined.

Bella cawed agreement and Fionn snorted. Apparently, the bird was done siding with him.

"Can you talk to Aislinn?" Fionn asked Rune.

"No. It stretches the Hunter bond to find her."

"Has she moved?"

The wolf shook his head. "Not since I located her." He bit the air in frustration. "What good does it do, knowing where she is, if we can't get to her?"

Good question. Fionn hunkered next to the wolf and placed a hand on his shoulder. "I will find her, laddie, if 'tis the last thing I do."

As if it understood his words and rose to the challenge, a sea serpent hooted from the moat, blasting nasty-smelling red water their way. It fell short, but not by much. The ground smoked where rancid water splattered it, and the air filled with a burned stench.

"I say we go back inside, by way of the front door," Fionn said. "If all roads lead to the room where the mirrors are, so be it, but at least this way we'll know. Once we're back inside, we can pick which mirror to tackle."

"Brace yourself." Nidhogg blasted steam and smoke just before he merged with Fionn.

The sensation wasn't quite as unpleasant as it had been the first time, and Fionn loped toward the fortress. When they got near the moat, he lobbed a jolt of power at the serpent, still coiled well above the waterline with its jaws gaping. Nidhogg fused power with Fionn, and the monster exploded in a haze of blood mixed with bits of bone and scales. Another rose to take its place, but warding glittered around it.

"Doona waste your magic on these watchdogs," Fionn snarled and pounded across the drawbridge.

The front door had shut, but it creaked open on stone hinges. While the fortress had wooden beams, no doubt a carryover from when this world still had living trees, most of it was constructed of stone, including the door. The front hall was lined with portraits of the six dark gods, looking like well-fed royalty dressed in archaic finery. Because there were no choice points, no doors leading off from where they walked, Fionn followed the wide hallway. It disappeared beneath an arch, and he found himself back in the room with the mirrors.

When he spun to look, the doorway leading into this room vanished, shutting them inside. Rune growled, hurtled himself against where the door had been, and pitched up against a solid wall. He glared at the wall and snarled.

"Neat trick," Bran muttered. "Next time I design a castle—"

"Not now," Fionn snapped. "Help me figure out what to do with these mirrors."

"Nidhogg"—Bran faced Fionn, but addressed the dragon—"what happens once we're inside?"

"Try projecting an image of where you want to go. Since we've never seen the rest of the interior of this building, perhaps holding images of Aislinn and Dewi will be the best we can do." The dragon borrowed Fionn's vocal chords to answer and jerked Fionn's head from side to side as he looked from mirror to mirror. "It's not accidental there are four," he said at last. "We must pick the correct one."

Fionn shut his eyes for a moment. When he opened them, he had to unclench his jaws before he could talk. "How do we do that?"

"*Carefully,*" Nidhogg said into his mind. "Let us get close to each, and I will try to sense its specific purpose."

Fionn chafed at the time dribbling by as Nidhogg moved them to the nearest glass and sent magic cautiously into it, but if they screwed this up, Aislinn had no chance at all. He reminded himself Dewi was with her, but were they a match for the dark gods? He and Arawn had nearly been lost forever, would have been if Arawn hadn't led them into the halls of the dead through an obscure, hidden route.

I have to believe this will turn out. I'll drive myself mad otherwise.

Nidhogg dragged their shared body to the next mirror. Fionn wanted to ask what he'd found at the first one, but kept quiet. If the dragon had anything to tell them, he would have.

CHAPTER 25

*D*ewi's restless energy set Aislinn's teeth on edge and made her want to scream. "There's room for you to take your own form."

"Not really." Dewi jerked Aislinn's neck around as she scanned the room.

"How long do you think D'Chel will leave us alone?"

The dragon snorted, and steam rolled through Aislinn's nostrils. *"The crystal ball's a bit cloudy today."*

"Goddammit." Aislinn pounded her fist into a nearby wall. "I am not a dragon. No smoke, fire, steam, or anything else."

"So, have you ever actually fucked him?" Dewi asked, with an undernote in her voice that Aislinn recognized all too well.

"No. And I don't plan to. Can we teleport out of here?"

"Doubtful. Let me work on it."

Aislinn doubted it too. It would have been stupid for D'Chel to nab her if she could spell her way to freedom. Her crotch was damp from his idea at courtship, and a mixture of fury and fear twisted her stomach into a knot of apprehension. Adrenaline gave her a boost to fight or flee. When all she could do was twiddle her thumbs, it left a sour taste in her mouth and made her legs shaky.

"Well?" she asked Dewi as the walls of the bedchamber shimmered, but reformed again and again.

"Do you even have to ask?" the dragon retorted. *"If I could have freed us, I would have."* She paused for a beat. *"I don't understand. We get to where the spell should develop its own momentum, but then it just fritters through my talons."*

Aislinn thought she understood just fine. "Doesn't that mean we have to find whatever casting he has around this room and blast through it?"

"I tried that first. There isn't any shielding around this particular room. Whatever's holding us is coming from elsewhere."

Aislinn switched to mind speech and took care to shield it. It might not keep D'Chel or Adva out, but it was the best she could do. *"If we can't escape, we have to fight them. I still think that would go better if you were in your own form."*

"What do you have in mind?"

"Pour fire down their throats like you did with Tokhots."

"You think they'll just lay themselves at our feet and let me do that?"

"Of course not. We'd have to knock them out somehow first, which is another reason we're better off with you in dragon form."

Aislinn felt a wrenching sensation in her belly as Dewi exited. Her insides felt raw, exposed. Despite that, being queen of her own body again was worth it. The dragon took up half the floor space in the bedchamber and her head reached the ceiling. Smoke and steam curled from her jaws, and scales clanked as she stretched.

"When they come back in here," Aislinn said, *"we give them everything we have. No talking, no bargaining, nothing. We fight, plain and simple."*

"D'Chel controls illusion. He can shape shift, and he will once he sees me." A tongue of flame joined the smoke. *"It will get a bit close in here with two dragons, or something else that's the same size I am."*

"I'll try not to get underfoot."

"You do that." Dewi chucked softly. *"I do love you, child. We'll find our way back to the men somehow."*

Aislinn swallowed hard, but her throat was dust dry. She couldn't think about Fionn now; it would just get in the way. Once she'd started down that road, though, she wondered why no one had shown up in their prison. She sent magic auguring out and found Rune easily, but when she tried to talk with him, the Hunter bond reared back and slapped her magical center.

"What the fuck?" she shook herself, not believing the electrical sensation that had just scalded her.

"What happened?" the dragon narrowed her eyes.

"I used the Hunter bond to find Rune."

"And?"

"Found him fine, but then something odd happened. The bond blew up around me and bit back."

Dewi nodded. "Pretty much the same thing that happened when I tried to teleport us out of here."

"What's wrong?" Aislinn fought terror. It was one thing not having her magic work at all, but quite another for it to turn into something unrecognizable and unpredictable.

"They held you here before, didn't they?"

"I think so, unless there are two places like this here. I never saw the outside of the building then, only the one room they kept me in."

"I'm guessing it wasn't this one." At Aislinn's curt nod, Dewi went on, "There's some sort of vortex here that perverts our magic. Likely it doesn't affect the dark bastards, or they'd never tolerate it. If I reach deep, I can almost wrap my mind around the source, but it's a very ancient magic, maybe even older than me, and it stymies me every time."

"Well, it wasn't here last time. There were tapestries on the walls that muted my power. Once I took them down, I was able to escape."

The door snicked open, and D'Chel strolled through, flanked by Perrikus. "Surely you didn't think we'd be so sloppy as to leave you the same exit route you used last time?" D'Chel inquired and furled his perfect, dark brows.

Perrikus's long auburn hair flowed around him, and his green eyes danced merrily. He wore a long, pale green robe, and a golden torc circled his neck.

"Welcome to my castle." He mock bowed, his gaze never leaving her.

Dewi pushed between Aislinn and the dark gods. "Address yourselves to me," she trumpeted and blasted them with smoke mixed with fire. A small wooden wall hanging smoldered before catching fire.

D'Chel made a sound between a snort and a grunt. "I was trying to ignore you, dragon. I liked it better when you were catching a ride inside Aislinn."

Perrikus shrugged. "I'm not so sure about that. Dragons are quite useful. I've missed that one we kept here. Handy fellow, and brimming with power."

"That you siphoned off to keep this world alive," Dewi cut in. "I don't plan to be your next patsy."

"He didn't plan on it, either," Perrikus pointed out smugly. "Look where it got him."

"Best laid plans and all that," D'Chel agreed with a shit-eating grin that made Aislinn's blood boil with fury.

"This isn't what we agreed on," Aislinn reminded Dewi.

D'Chel rolled his eyes. "Save your magic. I can hear every word. What exactly did you agree on? I'd love to know."

"If you can *hear every word*"—Aislinn squared her shoulders—"then I shouldn't have to tell you." She tried to move past Dewi's bulk, but the dragon blocked her.

She peered around Dewi and eyed the two dark gods warily, wanting to attack, but not wanting to be foolhardy. Something about this world sapped her magic, and her anger, which had always been her ace in the hole.

"Stay behind me," the dragon instructed. *"Don't let them close enough to get their hands on you."*

Neither Perrikus nor D'Chel flinched, so maybe D'Chel's boast about cutting through their warding like a hot knife through clay was empty rhetoric.

Fire blasted from Dewi, along with strong jolts of magic. Perrikus and D'Chel staggered backward, batting at their burning clothing. Both mages spewed a language she'd never heard, probably profanities from the inflection. She wanted to help, lend her power to the fight, but the dragon took up the entire room between the wall and the bed.

The bed.

Aislinn skittered along the back wall, dove into the bed curtains, and rolled off the other side of what felt like a straw-filled mattress. If Dewi turned fire on it, it would incinerate like a bonfire, and then the room would fill with smoke and… *Not a good idea*. She hated to siphon off any power, but she strengthened her wards before calling attention to herself.

She landed light on her feet on the narrow strip of floor between the bed and the far wall and moved cautiously forward. Dewi cursed her, but Aislinn didn't bother to answer. She had to concentrate to draw power, focus it, and launch it at Perrikus, who was closest to her.

He turned to face her, his perfect face drawn into a snarl. "You've always been more trouble than you're worth."

"So?" She shrugged and sent more power his way. Once she warmed to the defensive magic, it got easier, even here. "By the way, what happened to Adva?"

"He's doing what he does best. Manipulating gateways." Perrikus blasted magic her way, but she sidestepped him and wished she had more room to maneuver.

Dewi had pushed so much fire, smoke, and raw power toward D'Chel that he was backed into a corner, but no matter what she bombarded him with, his warding held.

"What does *manipulating gateways* mean?" Aislinn danced from foot to foot, looking for an opening where she might break through Perrikus's magical perimeter.

"Did your grasp of English slip?" White, jagged lightning shot from his fingertips, and she rolled beneath it, shocked by how the floor shook when it landed where she'd been standing seconds before.

Maybe Dewi had been right, and she should have remained behind her. She could retreat, but it wasn't her style. The last thing she wanted to do was let these bastards know how rattled she was.

"I figure it has something to do with why we can't teleport out of here," Aislinn panted and lobbed power back his way. Never mind it did nothing but roll off his warding.

"Smart girl. Too bad you're not a shade more cooperative."

"Isn't it?"

The next lightning bolt came at her from the front and forked to both sides, cutting off her escape. She clenched her jaws and hoped to hell her wards held. They did. Sort of, but a stinging burn flared up one arm. She was afraid to look away long enough to assess the damage, but hot liquid dripped, so he must have drawn blood. Fury boiled hot, and she drove power along the floor, telling it to creep beneath his robe and singe his dick off.

Dewi showered Perrikus with flames at the same time, but he just laughed and shrugged his burning garment off, displaying his amazing body. He pointed a finger at her ground strike, and it skittered to one side, not touching him at all.

Aislinn's breath clotted in her throat, and arousal tightened her belly. She tried to look away from his golden skin and perfect form, but couldn't even manage to close her eyes. Incredulity cut deep. It was unthinkable he'd divert her with sex. Unthinkable she could be diverted.

Why? He's the original one trick pony.

Heat built in her loins until she couldn't think, and a climax tore through her. Like it always went with the dark gods, her arousal didn't recede much with release. "Stop it," she screamed. "Just stop it."

"Why should I?" Perrikus stroked his growing erection. Like the rest of his body, it was masculine perfection. Huge and beautiful.

Aislinn spun away so she might have a prayer of reestablishing her mind as the leader of the pack, but even when she wasn't facing him, the dark god's amazing physique still mocked her. Because it was a small task, something she couldn't fail at, she sent Healing energy to the jagged cut running down her left arm.

"Playing hard to get?" Perrikus taunted.

"Just trying to get through the day." She turned and faced him. "What do you want with me?"

"The same thing D'Chel and I have always wanted. Children from your bloodline. We made a mistake when we killed your father that night in Bolivia." He shrugged. "How were we to know? We'd just arrived, and the key to all successful campaigns is decisive action. One expects collateral damage, but those stupid Lemurians made incredibly poor choices. We're living with the fallout."

His words cut through the sexual haze her brain had become. "It was hard to lose my father when I was eighteen, but why'd you say it was a mistake?" She wanted to know, and maybe if she could get him talking, he'd dial down the libido juice.

"According to Adva, the Harmonic Convergence exerts a significant effect on gateways, both on Earth and the borderworlds. Your father was almost the only person knowledgeable about the Convergence. There was one other, but the Old Ones killed him."

"You were looking pretty chummy with them in Inishownen." Aislinn took a few steps back to get more distance between her and Perrikus.

"If they trust us, it will be easier to annihilate them."

"What are you doing?" Dewi shot a look her way. She still had D'Chel pinned in the corner, but beyond that, whatever was happening looked like a stalemate.

"It doesn't matter." Aislinn fought weariness, inertia exacerbated by the borderworld. "We have to get out of here."

"That's not going to happen," D'Chel smirked. "Your rescue party is lost in a labyrinth. Or they will be once Adva works his magic."

"Besides wanting to use me as a broodmare, what else do you have in mind?" Aislinn asked, still parleying for time to think. There had to be a way out of this, but probably not with Perrikus and D'Chel breathing down their necks. Blood still dripped down her arm, but the flow had slowed and the sting of the injury had lessened.

"That depends on your level of cooperation," Perrikus replied.

"If you're a total bitch about this, or keep trying to escape, we'll have to kill you." D'Chel spread his hands in front of him as if to indicate it was unfortunate, but what choice would they have?

"You missed your calling," Dewi said, her tone acerbic. "You should have been on stage."

"Many have told me that." D'Chel smiled prettily. "Of course, we hadn't bargained on you."

"I'll bet you didn't." Dewi puffed flame his way. "You trapped Nidhogg because you caught him unaware."

"We'll figure out something, some neat little surprise for you." Perrikus strode to D'Chel's side. "I think she's hurt we haven't tried harder to immobilize her."

"Indeed. Maybe jealous we put so much more effort into her mate." D'Chel sent a disingenuous glance at the dragon.

Perrikus's gaze sharpened. Something passed between him and D'Chel that Aislinn couldn't decipher. He looked from Aislinn to Dewi.

"Ladies. I'd say our first skirmish ended in an impasse. Be patient. We'll return for round two once we've taken care of some urgent business that just came up."

The air around both dark mages blackened, turned opaque, and they were gone.

The breath swooshed from Aislinn and she fell into a chair. "We have got to get out of here," she told the dragon.

"State the obvious, why don't you," Dewi said acidly. "Now look here, child. When I give you orders, they're for a reason. If you'd remained behind me, you wouldn't have been injured, nor fallen prey to that lecherous scum."

The anger that had eluded her earlier cut a path from her head to her toes, and Aislinn stomped in front of Dewi. "Funny. You didn't think it was so wrong when D'Chel was handing out the sex cookies."

"Stop!" Dewi held up a foreleg. "This is exactly what they want us to do. While I had D'Chel pinned, I pushed into his mind. Not as far as I wanted, but far enough. The reason my magic is uncooperative is there are Persian mirrors here."

"Huh?" Aislinn scrubbed her hands down her face. "What the fuck are they?"

"I wish I knew more about them, but they serve as gateways, usually to other worlds, but I suppose someone like Adva could manipulate them to make it hard to get in and out of this fortress."

"Persian? Like from the Arabian Nights?"

"No, more like from the Sufis, the mystical branch of Islam." Dewi's eyes whirled faster. "None of that matters. I could tell you everything I know, and it would be a waste of time and breath, because I don't know all that much. Nidhogg got trapped in one once—"

"Wait." Aislinn held up a hand. "How can you get trapped in a mirror?"

"Because they only look like mirrors." Fire flashed from the dragon. "Anyway, he had a hell of a time getting out, but I'll be damned if I can remember what he told me about it."

"That's not helpful."

They stared at one another, and Aislinn shrugged her pack off to get water. Her stomach was too tense for food. "If we can't get out of here"—she wiped the back of her hand across her mouth and put the water flask back in her rucksack—"we need a better plan for when they come back."

"I have one." Dewi showered her with compulsion. "Since both men want you, and I'm an inconvenience, let's switch what we did earlier."

Aislinn shut her eyes for a moment. "I'm a little slow on the uptake here, but switch what?" And then she understood. "Ohhhh. Like when you fucked the Minotaur with me inside you."

"No Minotaurs here"—Dewi's jaws lolled in a grin—"so you're fairly safe."

Despite reservations, Aislinn could see advantages—lots of them. She straightened her spine. "No sex with any of the dark gods."

"Agreed. You were right to terminate that event."

Aislinn's eyes widened. "No shit. I was right about something?"

"Oh, stop it. If you're willing, come close and we'll do this thing. We can hammer out the fine points once we've merged."

CHAPTER 26

Fionn stood in front of the last mirror while Nidhogg looked through his eyes. When the dragon didn't say anything, Fionn prodded, "We must pick one and be gone. Too much time has passed."

Bella spread her wings and flew to a table where she landed and looked up at him. "Not going?" Fionn asked.

She shook her head. "None of them feel right to me."

"'Twould appear Nidhogg is having the same problem," Bran noted sourly.

Fionn felt steam rise from his lungs and he blew the heated air through his nose and mouth. "Don't bait him," he told Bran. "My throat's raw from dragon effluvium as 'tis."

Nidhogg pushed their shared body back to the last mirror. *"This one."*

"What do we do once we're inside?" Fionn asked.

"I won't know until we get there."

"Not particularly comforting," Bran muttered.

"You're taking me." Rune had been sticking to Fionn's side like a stubborn shadow.

The dragon borrowed Fionn's voice. "It may well be the death of you, laddie."

"I don't care." Rune's tail plumed. "I'm the only one here who can find her."

"Yon wolf has a point," Fionn said and reached into a pocket for the length of leather he often used to tie his hair back.

"Here." Bran handed him more cord. "That isna long enough."

"Thanks." Fionn hastily fashioned a collar with a loop he could hang onto. Rune eyed him balefully, but didn't protest when he snugged the device around his neck.

"We must stay together," the dragon cautioned. "I'll use magic to bind us, but the pull inside the glass is strong, and it only takes seconds to get swept away."

"Will we be able to talk in there?" Rune asked.

"I don't know," Nidhogg replied.

"Let's find out." Fionn chafed to be gone. Sharing his body with the dragon was taxing, and he wanted to get into the thick of things, rescue Aislinn, and be gone from here. Once she was safe, he could return and make short work of the dark gods. Or maybe just blow their dead, rotten borderworld out of existence. Hours had passed since Aislinn and Dewi's disappearance. Despair riddled him if he let himself think about everything that could have happened to Aislinn in all that time.

"Here we go," Nidhogg said. "Follow my lead."

Fionn gripped Rune's leash and stepped through the silvery surface. It rippled around him and pressed hard, as if it were trying to crush him. Rune grunted, but didn't yip.

"Ooph, not exactly pleasant," Bran muttered.

They still weren't through the glass; the sensation of being crushed intensified. "Pull us the rest of the way through," Fionn told Nidhogg, struggling to breathe through compressed lungs.

"I did this on purpose." The dragon didn't sound much better than Fionn felt. "Once we're through, we're at its mercy."

"We have to control it," Fionn ground out. "We'll never do that half in and half out."

With a wrenching tug that made a wet, slurping sound, the dragon moved them to the far side of the glass. As soon as they were through, the dark haze before Fionn's vision cleared, and pulsating, iridescent tunnels spread in three directions. He dug in his heels and anchored himself to the dragon's magic to avoid being sucked into one of them.

Bran wove magic in with his, and clutched Fionn's arm. "Which way?"

"Rune?" Nidhogg's deep voice echoed and the tunnels pulsed harder.

The wolf whined; something about the ultrasonic frequency in the vibrating walls hurt him—probably his ears because they were pinned back against his skull. Fionn felt the wolf deploy the Hunter bond. Thank fucking Christ it didn't boomerang back and hurt him further.

"Middle," the wolf said. He whined again and added, "Hurry. This is hard."

And it only got harder. The magic didn't want them in the middle tunnel, which told Fionn the wolf had chosen wisely. Power buffeted them from behind, pushing them to the right, then the left. Even with the dragon's magic linked to his own, Fionn moved forward at a glacial pace, as if he were plowing through thigh deep quicksand or snow. Bran's hand tightened on his arm and the rough sound of his breathing joined Fionn's own.

Deep in Fionn's mind, Nidhogg cursed, first in Gaelic and then in the dragons' language. Fionn considered asking where he thought the other tunnels led, but didn't want to disturb his concentration. Maybe they didn't lead anywhere fixed. The thought of mutable passageways that shifted depending on who was in them was even more unsettling than Majestron Zalia's head had been.

He lost all sense of time. The pressure surrounding him ebbed and flowed. Once the wolf yelped piteously and Fionn picked him up, holding him awkwardly and shielding his ears.

"Will this get better once we reach the tunnel?" Fionn asked Nidhogg.

"Probably."

"Can we hurry?" They'd been crossing the fifty yards between them and the center passageway forever, or maybe time ran differently behind the glass. Fionn snuck a glance over one shoulder and couldn't see the backside of the glass. How would they find their way out?

I canna worry about that.

Rune wriggled in his arms and he whispered soothing Gaelic into the wolf's ear. Finally, just when Fionn was within a hairsbreadth of telling Nidhogg they had to go back, that the pearlescent tunnel would suck the life out of them, things got easier. And easier still. Rather than thigh-deep quicksand, it was just knee-deep, and then mid-calf.

"'Twould appear we survived the first leg," Bran observed. "Would ye like me to carry the wolf? He must be heavy."

"I can walk," Rune said, so Fionn set him down and they covered the final few feet to the rounded opening of the center passage.

"Hang on," Nidhogg said. "Things may go very fast once we pass beneath the lintel."

YOUNG NIDHOGG DID a quick nose count. They'd all made it back to Earth handily. In truth, he'd been impressed by the amount of power they'd been able to concentrate. It was triple what he'd expected.

"That was fun," the copper male crowed.

"What's next?" one of the green males asked.

"We move to the borderworld," Nidhogg junior answered. "It will be harder, but we can do it, and we need to move fast, before Royce and Vaughna track us."

"Yes, it would be bad for them to haul us back now," the copper male said.

"Once we're heroes," the green male said, "they won't be able to punish us."

The black youngling, understudy to the Norse dragon slot, wasn't so certain about that. He was fairly sure there'd be hell to pay once one of the adults caught up to them, but until then they'd keep going. His link with his father came and went, and he hadn't liked the last bit he'd seen. Something about a place of shifting sands and illusion that crushed and pulled.

"Ready?" he asked and scattered what magic he could to obliterate signs of them having passed this way. It might fake out Royce and Vaughna. Maybe.

"Do we have time to hunt?" a red female asked.

"No. Heroes eat after victory, not before."

"Who made that rule?" the copper dragon grumbled.

"My father," Nidhogg junior answered. "Now let's go. There's no air for this crossing, so fill your lungs well."

To the accompaniment of huge sucking breaths, Nidhogg borrowed magic shamelessly from his eggmates and formed the spell that would take them to the borderworld. They tumbled through a gateway so fast he was certain he'd done something wrong, but before he took them back to Earth to start over, he sent his magic spinning outward.

"This is an ugly place," one of the red females said.

"Yes, and it stinks," the copper male cut in.

"Not much lives here," a green male said, "but there's lots that's dead and decayed."

Nidhogg junior exhaled sharply. Despite his doubts, he'd led them to the right place. Clear traces of his father and mother lingered in the stale, lifeless air.

"Do you suppose they're in there?" The copper dragon inclined his head toward a sprawling building.

"Well, they're not out here, and I sense them close, so it's logical," young Nidhogg replied.

"How do we get inside?" the copper male asked. "Should we teleport again?"

The black dragon shuffled the idea through his father's memories. "Not a good idea. We have to get inside, but there's a barrier once we get in there. Everyone else went through the front door and ran into problems. Let's look for another entrance. Maybe one where we won't get trapped by whatever crushed Father."

"Is he all right?" one of the red females cried anxiously.

"Yes. Bad choice of words. There was a crushing sensation, but he got through it."

"Is Mother with him?" a green male asked.

"No. I don't have the same link to her that I do with Father. She's inside, and alive, but I don't know anything further."

"I know where she is," the red female who'd been reluctant to come with them spoke up.

He eyed her and was suffused with sudden understanding. "You're the next Celtic dragon god."

She snorted fire. "Unfortunately, yes. It's a shit job and I don't want it."

He wanted to slap her, tell her to quit whining and grow up. Instead, he swallowed his irritation and said, "You'll have a long time to get over that. I suspect Mother will live a few thousand more years." He spread his wings. "Fly with me. All of you. We've come this far. Let's get to where we can do some good."

As he pumped his wings, forcing the air to support him, young Nidhogg hoped to hell they could find a way inside. He feared the way his father had taken might well be the death of them. It had taken most of his father's wisdom—and power—to lead himself, Fionn, Bran, and the wolf through the bad place. As he flew, he sought Nidhogg, trying to pinpoint where he was in the rambling structure beneath him.

"You!" detonated in his head, nearly blowing his brains out his ears. *"I thought I sensed you. What in the hell are you up to?"*

Young Nidhogg hastily erected wards. He should have done it

before, and he sent orders down the line to his eggmates to do the same. The last thing he needed was their father ordering them home. Not when they were so close to their chance to become heroes.

As he flew in an arcing circle, something caught his attention. Toward the rear of the building, a collection of other structures linked to the main house by a partially submerged walkway. Surely that was how servants had gotten inside. Those entrances were probably never warded.

"Look there," he sent to the other dragons. *"A way in."*

"Not a moment too soon," the copper male sent. *"A portal just opened on the other side of the building, and I sense more dragons."*

Crap! Must be Kra and Berra. Or even worse, Royce and Vaughna.

"Hurry," Nidhogg urged his eggmates and scattered magic to obliterate any evidence of their presence on this world.

Gwydion stepped through a gateway and waited for the others. He forced magic outward to reassure himself they'd come out at the right place, and was gratified when he sensed Fionn's energy, along with Dewi's and Nidhogg's. He sheathed his power. No reason to do a headcount of everyone who'd been here. He gazed at the dry, dead landscape he remembered from earlier visits. Not the last one where his astral self had been locked away in a bell jar deep within a dungeon. He'd never seen the outside of his prison then, since he'd teleported both ways.

Gradually, Arawn, Andraste, and the humans and dragons emerged. "No one's here," Arawn observed. "They were, and not all that long ago, but what happened to them?"

"Do you suppose they're in there?" Timothy motioned toward the fortress.

"'Tis as good a guess as any," Gwydion muttered.

Kra trumpeted and blew smoke. "The dark ones are here. I feel them."

"You and I can stand watch while the others go inside," Berra said. "We could merge with them, but it would be foolhardy to not guard our exit route."

"Thank you." Andraste blew a kiss at the dragons.

"Shall we?" Gwydion jerked his chin forward, grasped his staff, and took off at a lope. If the dragon was right about the dark gods—and there was no reason he wouldn't be—why wasn't his staff glowing red? Normally, the staff wasn't influenced by wards. Maybe the magic-muting effect of this world had something to do with it.

Arawn chugged around him and across the drawbridge. "Charming." He pointed at two sea serpents coiled beneath them in the moat.

Andraste caught them up, mumbling, "We should have annihilated both these borderworlds a long time ago."

"A use for us already." Kra screamed a battle cry and bathed the serpents with fire. Berra joined him. The inferno blazed orange before it rolled off the serpents' scales, but at least it kept them from squirting poison upward through slats in the drawbridge.

Gwydion let magic guide him through the entry hall, past portraits of the dark gods and into a dead end.

"What the fuck?" He turned in a circle and saw the doorway into the room vanish as the last of them entered it.

Arawn walked briskly to one of the mirrors and tapped its surface, except it swallowed his fingers. The god of the dead yanked his hand back. "Goddammit!"

Gwydion joined him. "Persian mirrors, huh?"

"'Twould appear so."

"Aye." Andraste spat on the floor. "They bite back."

Timothy made his way to their side. "What are they?"

"Gateways," Arawn said, his voice grim.

"Look, Celt." Timothy crossed his arms over his chest. "You're going to have to do better than that. Gateways to where?"

"I'm not certain," Gwydion answered, "but, 'tis a sure bet Adva is here. He's their god of portals, and I'd bet my ass he brought these with him."

"Is that a guess, or are ye certain?" Arawn asked.

"As certain as I can be. I only tangled with him once, and he nearly had my hide because of these fucking things. He lured me inside, chasing him, and I got lost—horribly lost. 'Tis like a hall of mirrors inside with nothing firmly anchored."

"How'd you get out?" Timothy asked.

"I verra nearly dinna. But I learned how to counteract their power." He blew out a tense breath. "Let's hope I recall exactly how I did it."

A tall human female with a hawk on her shoulder spoke up. "Is it safe for the animals in there?" Her black hair was pulled back into a queue, and her dark eyes reflected worry.

"Probably not," Gwydion said.

"Humph." She pressed her lips together. "There are five of us Hunters. We'll wait outside with the dragons."

"How?" Timothy asked. "The door into this room got absorbed by something, probably the mirrors' magic. If I pay attention, I can feel it like a scratchy undercurrent."

Andraste drew magic experimentally, and a portal glittered before her. With a sharp nod, she scattered her spell. "Ye can teleport," she said. "Mayhap not far, but at least out of here."

A corner of Arawn's mouth turned down grimly. "Aye, the mirrors are glad enough of us leaving their domain, but they guard the rest of this building—and goddess knows what else."

The Hunters formed a tight ring with their bond animals. The dark-haired woman chanted low until a gateway formed and all of them walked through it. Gwydion waited until the magic winked out, then he turned and faced the others. Besides himself, Arawn, and Andraste, there were five humans.

"Listen closely," he said. "Once we're inside, 'twill feel as if something is crushing the verra breath from your body. We will face choices on the far side of the glass. 'Tis imperative we pick the correct one, or 'twill take us so long to return here we will be useless to Fionn and the others."

"How will we know?" Timothy asked. "My magic isn't as strong here as it is on Earth."

Gwydion shot him a wry smile. "The choice that fights back is the one that will lead us into this stronghold. I sense Fionn in this room, Bran too. We may be able to track them once we're behind the glass, but doona count on it."

"Does every mirror work the same?" A human female with short, curly brown hair asked.

Arawn shook his head. "Nay. We must pick the correct one to enter, and then the correct choice once we're within."

"The first choice is easy," Gwydion said and walked to the far side of the room. "This is where Fionn went through."

"How can you be certain?" Timothy asked. "I sense him—and Nidhogg—in front of each mirror."

"As do I," Gwydion concurred, "but the energy moves forward here, and not with the others."

"How do we know Fionn chose the right one?" the brown-haired female asked.

"Because he had the dragon with him," Andraste said. "Nidhogg is many things, but he isna often wrong. Gwydion and I will draw a spell to hold all of us together. Ye all must weave your power in with ours to avoid being swept away once we cross the barrier."

"Have ye ever passed through Persian mirrors?" Gwydion asked Arawn.

"Nay, but I've read about them."

"Have you?" he asked Andraste.

"Aye."

Gwydion snorted. "Excellent. I'll take all the help I can get. Build this spell with me and we'll be on our way."

A rustle from a distant corner of the room had him spinning in place, hands raised to summon a death blow. Bella stalked from behind a mirror. "Son of a bitch," Gwydion swore. "Why aren't you with Fionn?"

"The mirrors felt bad."

"Why dinna ye show yourself afore?" Arawn demanded.

The raven's head drooped. "I didn't wish to shame myself before the other animals."

Gwydion chewed on his lower lip. "Ye showed yourself to us now for a reason. And it must be damned important. What is it?"

Bella rustled her feathers. "You picked the right mirror. Or the one Fionn took, anyway. Rune went with him. Don't let anything happen to him."

"I hate to take the time," Andraste said, "but tell us what happened here. Just hit the high points."

"Won't take long." The raven sounded like her old, sulky self. "One of the dark gods nabbed Aislinn right off Dewi's back. Dewi went after her. Nidhogg freaked out, and he, Fionn, Rune, and Bran went after the women."

"What happened to the humans?" Timothy asked.

"They went to Inishowen to keep watch over Fionn's manor and fight Old Ones."

"Aught else?" Arawn walked to where Bella was.

"Adva's here, and I saw D'Chel too, but not Perrikus."

"'Tis a safe bet all three are here, since the other borderworld held booby-traps but no master of ceremonies." Gwydion clacked his mouth shut.

"Would ye rather wait for Fionn here or outside?" Arawn asked the bird. "Kra and Berra are keeping watch."

"Outside. There are no guarantees Fionn will return by the same route." Bella settled her wings across her back. "I can teleport myself. Go. Make sure nothing happens to Rune."

"Doona ye wish me to watch out for Fionn too?" Gwydion furled his brows.

"He can take care of himself."

The master enchanter grasped his staff and turned away. The bird was a sour number, but Fionn was bonded to her and there was no undoing it. Over centuries, they'd established a brittle détente, but

Gwydion was mightily grateful he didn't have to deal with Bella. He'd have throttled her long since.

As soon as the bird was gone, Andraste rolled her eyes. "That," she intoned, "is why I never bothered with a bond animal. Too much trouble."

"Never mind about that," Gwydion said. "Let's get moving or we may miss our opportunity to help anyone."

$\mathcal{A}$islinn got as comfortable as she could inside the dragon and tried to ignore Dewi's rich mind. Before, when she'd shared Dewi's form it had been tempting to help herself to what amounted to a comprehensive library and history of the world, but there'd never been time.

And there isn't now, either.

"We need a better plan," she told the dragon.

Dewi cocked her head to one side, listening. "Might be a tad late for that," she grunted and swung her large body toward one of the unadorned walls moments before the room dissolved into blackness around them.

Aislinn wanted to call power, wrench herself out of whatever they were being sucked into, but Dewi commandeered all their joint magic to ward them.

"What's happening?" She felt like screaming, but her mind voice sounded the same as it always did, not entirely barren of inflection, but almost.

"What do you think, child? Adva is moving us somewhere. Let's hope it's a larger space where I can maneuver a bit."

"He can do that? Without even being present?"

"It's their world. They can do whatever they like here and you'd be well-served not to forget it. Nidhogg couldn't get away from them, even with all his magic."

Desolation spread through her. If it was that hopeless, why not just give up? The black void shifted to gray and then to pallid, yellow lighting from smoking wall sconces, and a huge cavern formed around them.

"Are we still on the borderworld?" she asked Dewi, worried about Fionn and Rune.

After a long pause, the dragon said. "Yes. Probably beneath the fortress. All these places had dungeons, and— Shit! Things are going to get ugly fast. Give me access to your power. *Now.* And don't distract me with questions."

Aislinn tensed and stared out through the dragon's eyes. The cave's ceiling disappeared in darkness. The floor was dirt. Other than the smoldering torches, the space was devoid of furniture or ornamentation. *"Can we teleport from here?"* she asked

"I said no questions. Be quiet. Something's coming. Can you feel it?" A quick intake of breath, and then, "If Adva dumped us here—and it pretty much has to be him—there's no teleporting out of here until his scheme plays itself out."

Aislinn's sense of desolation deepened. It was all too much. There was no way they'd ever win. Why keep fighting? Just lie down and be done with it. Easier that way.

"Shield your mind," Dewi hissed. "D'Chel is planting suggestions."

Horror filled her, pushing despair aside.

I need to get angry. I should be pissed off as hell that slimebag invaded my thoughts.

But when she tried to shove him out, he just laughed at her. It gave her the incentive she needed. Riding fury's coattails, she chivied him out and slammed her mental gates behind him. How the fuck had he gotten inside her mind in the first place? Must have happened before he left the bedchamber. Maybe he used the cut Perrikus had opened in her arm to send something into her body.

The thought creeped her out and she shivered, even inside Dewi's warmth. The dragon tensed, and Aislinn did too. Whatever was coming would be easier to deal with now that her mind was her own again, and it was a hell of a relief to be shut of her despairing thoughts.

I cannot relax my guard. Nothing actually got better. We're still trapped.

Maybe so, but if I go out, it will be in a blaze of glory, goddamnit.

Fiery portals burst into view, surrounding them. Demons poured from the gateways, looking just like the ones that had escaped from Hell next to Fionn's house in Inishowen. Aislinn counted a dozen, but that was just in front of her. She felt their fell energy from behind as well.

"Can we kill them?" she shouted.

"Yes. They're not like the dark gods. Any doubts I had about them joining forces with Abaddon just vanished. How else would they have imported Hell hordes here?"

Dewi sent magic spinning in a half circle. It incinerated everything it touched, but more demons waltzed through the portals. Six-and-a-half feet tall with cloven hooves, taloned hands, and fangs, they had eyes like old smoke and barbed tails they swung like whips. One struck the dragon's side, and she bellowed in pain.

A rush of energy blasted them from behind, and demons hurtled onto Dewi's back and dug their sharp talons into her scales. She screeched her outrage and charged toward a wall intent on scraping them off. Some fell, but not all, and she stomped on the ones scrambling to their feet in the dirt.

Demons closed from all sides. Dewi pounded them with fire and magic, but more kept coming, and they sent fire of their own right back. It didn't bother the dragon, but the temperature inside her began to climb. If it got much hotter, Aislinn would have to leave or she'd incinerate. As it was, sweat poured down her and she was panting.

"Dewi, do something. It's hot in here."

"Nothing I can do. Gut it out. It'll get hotter before we're done."

Demon bodies piled around them, but fresh atrocities just used them to try to leap onto the dragon. She'd learned from the first bunch, though, and managed to keep her back clear.

It was so hot inside the dragon, Aislinn felt consciousness slipping. She slapped a lid on her power, redirected it, and wrenched herself out of the dragon. Better to die on her feet than roasted to death, helpless.

"Told you it would work." The sleazy tones of D'Chel's honeyed voice grated against her ears. She flipped around to face him, magic at the ready, only to feel arms close around her from behind.

Perrikus.

"Bastards!" she squealed. "You planned this."

"You bet we did, sweetheart." Perrikus nipped her ear. "Be nice, and I won't hurt you."

"Fuck you." She writhed in his grasp, kicking, scratching, biting, but his grip only tightened.

Dewi pushed toward her, but demons blocked her. "Fool," she screamed. "I told you to stay put. I can't help you now."

"Goddamned dragons!" Perrikus shouted. "Nothing but trouble."

"The demons will take care of her—eventually," D'Chel said.

Because he was close enough, Aislinn aimed a kick and caught him square in the groin.

"Ooph." He cupped his genitals. "You little bitch! That does it. We're moving to Plan B."

"What's that?" she inquired sweetly through clenched teeth.

"We kill you, cut out your ovaries, and use your eggs that way." D'Chel's expression was so chilling he was hard to look at.

"We've wasted enough time." Perrikus sliced downward with one of the hands he had wrapped around her, and heat gushed down her belly, soaking her clothes.

Blood. Hers. A lot of it.

Pain filled her, hot, white, blinding as he wrenched something from deep inside her. The taste of bitter ashes flooded her mouth and she vomited bile.

Fear battled fury. She was going to die in this underground hell-hole on an alien world. And there wasn't a damned thing she could do about it. She directed Healing magic inward, but the extent of the damage was enormous. Tears clouded her eyes. Fionn. Rune. Maybe once she was gone, the dark gods would let them go.

"Please." She clung to consciousness so she could ask.

"Look at that," D'Chel chortled. "Dying brings out the best in her."

"We should have jumped on that bandwagon a long time ago," Perrikus cut in. "Saved ourselves a lot of trouble."

"Please." More blood sheeted down her stomach. "Let Fionn and Rune go back to Earth. You have what you want from me. It's a fair trade. A good one." Her vision was shading to black.

"We'll think about it," D'Chel said. His mocking laughter, and the dragon's outraged scream, were almost the last things she heard as consciousness slipped away. Just before she let go, she thought she heard Rune howling, but it must have been a trick of her dying brain, neurons firing willy-nilly as she faded into the nothingness of death.

"Close," Rune howled mournfully. "Aislinn's hurt. Hurry."

Fear closed a fist around Fionn's heart. "How bad?"

"She's dying." The wolf howled again just as they burst into an enormous cavern. Fionn had no idea where they were. It might be beneath the fortress, or on another world. Or in Hell from the piles of demons stacked around Dewi.

Nidhogg ripped his way out of Fionn, trumpeting his rage, and cut a path through the demons. Rune sprinted away from Fionn and launched himself at Perrikus, sinking his fangs into the dark god's throat.

"This way." Fionn told Bran and hurtled toward Perrikus, D'Chel, and Aislinn. She'd been sagging in Perrikus's arms until the wolf attacked him, but now she lay on the ground. Blind fury drove Fionn and he wrenched a metal pikestaff from a dead demon's hand and drove it through D'Chel, pinning him to the wall.

Rune must have taken Perrikus by surprise. The dark god pushed power at the wolf, but Rune held firm. He'd ripped a six inch length of both jugular and carotids open along one side of Perrikus's neck. Blood geysered everywhere, and the dark god was weakening.

"Take care of them," Fionn snarled at Bran and knelt to gather Aislinn into his arms. Was she still alive? Praying to every god and goddess in the pantheon, he sent magic auguring into her, relieved beyond measure when he found a weak heartbeat. He retreated to a corner and rocked her against him, deploying Healing magic to try to keep life in her body.

"Leannán," he whispered. "I love you. Doona leave me. Fight this."

He poured magic into her, but she didn't rally. Blood. She needed blood. She'd lost too much. He ripped the dirk from her waist sheath, intent on cutting into a vessel to feed his own blood into her, but Dewi lumbered to his side.

"Bran has the dark gods under control. I breathed dragon fire into them. Nidhogg is taking care of the demons. Give me the MacLochlainn." She bent low and held out her forelegs.

"Nay!" Fionn gazed at the dragon, and his soul twisted with anguish. "She will die in my arms, not yours."

A blood-coated Rune raced to Fionn's side. "She yet lives. Can the two of you fix her?"

"I'm trying," Dewi said grimly. "Fionn, give her to me. Hurry. We're running out of time. If you let me have her, she won't die."

"Please." Rune nipped him. "If there's a chance. Any chance at all..." A desolate howl burst from him.

Fionn handed Aislinn's boneless body to the dragon. It might have been his imagination, but she was already cooler than she'd been when he picked her up.

"Thank you." Dewi's eyes flooded and a pile of gemstones clattered to the dirt at her feet. She crooned in the dragons' tongue and turned one of her talons to her own breast where she cut through scales and flesh. Once her blood, a deep red-black river, began to flow, she angled Aislinn's wound beneath it and let her blood seep into the gaping hole that had been Aislinn's stomach.

"Do you understand what she'd doing?" Rune asked softly.

"Not entirely. I was on the verge of doing much the same. Giving Aislinn my blood."

"What she needed was mine," Dewi said and handed Aislinn back to Fionn. "It is done. She will live." The vertical tear in Dewi's chest closed as if it had never been there.

"Dewi!" Nidhogg bellowed. "I could use a spot of assistance."

"Take care of her." Dewi's voice was as gentle as Fionn had ever heard it. "Coming," she called over her shoulder and waded back into the battle.

Bran made his way to Fionn's side. "I heard most of that. Dewi may have fixed one problem, but we're a long way from out of the woods. The only one having a good time is Nidhogg. I swear, that dragon thrives on battles. Those damnable demons are pouring in here as if we're having a fire sale on pitchforks, and he's killing them and laughing his head off. I'd hoped when we took Perrikus and D'Chel out of the action, those portals into Hell would close."

"Why would they?" Fionn asked. "Adva's the one controlling them."

"Och aye. I hadna exactly forgotten about him, but he wasn't at the top of my mental list, either. Where the hell do ye suppose he is?"

"I'll watch over Aislinn," Rune said, "if you need to fight."

Fionn wanted to teleport them all the hell out of there, but he couldn't leave the dragons to face Hell's denizens alone, not after Dewi had saved Aislinn's life. He experimented with the teleport spell, but it bounced back at him. Apparently, Adva was still controlling the game with his warped house of mirrors.

Aislinn moved weakly in his arms. "Fionn? Or did I die and I'm dreaming you?" Her voice was the barest whisper.

"Nay, love. I'm real enough. Ye dinna die, but it was much too close for my taste."

"Put her down," Rune demanded. "I want to clean her wounds."

"Rune?" Aislinn twisted her head to look at her wolf. "Aw, Rune."

Her eyes flooded with tears, and Fionn's heart shattered at how close he'd come to losing her.

Smoke and fire thickened in the cave. Fionn caught glimpses of other fell creatures: incubi, succubi, gnomes, trolls. Kneeling, he placed Aislinn in an alcove. "I have to fight, love. I'll return as soon as I can. Rune will keep watch."

"Nothing will harm her," the wolf said with a simple dignity that touched Fionn beyond words.

"Where…" The single word trailed off, and Aislinn tried again. "Where did all these things come from?"

"Hell," Bran said shortly. "'Tisn't enough to kill them. We must subvert Adva's spell and shut the gateway."

A flash of light nearly blinded Fionn, and he shielded his eyes with one hand. "Shit! Fuck! We do not need more demonic bastards in here."

"'Tisn't," Bran said, and a grin bloomed on his face. "By the goddess, 'tis the baby dragon horde come to bail us out."

"I knew you were out there somewhere," Nidhogg roared at his brood. "You wanted war. This is war. Dive right in. No one's stopping you."

"But they're my babies," Dewi wailed and shot a swath of fire through a dozen undead who incinerated in a stinking flare of ghoulish bits.

"They were old enough to join their power to escape from Royce and Vaughna," Nidhogg said. "This is their birthright, Dewi. Dragons were born to rid all worlds of evil."

With the black dragon leading the troupe, the seven younglings fanned out. Fire and magic spewed from them in a mix so potent, it cut through at least fifty demons before they gathered themselves enough to fight back.

"I'm impressed," Bran cried. "Go younglings!" He fist pumped the air, pulled magic, and three trolls blew up, scattering rock everywhere.

"See?" Nidhogg shouted at Dewi. "Our brood will be just fine."

"Shut up and fight," Dewi growled, and cast her gaze Fionn's way. "Speaking of which, Celt—"

Fionn grabbed Bran's arm and they waded into the fray. Somehow, they had to track Adva down, but maybe if they dished out maximum destruction, the god of portals would get discouraged and leave. Behind him, twin flares went up, lighting the cave bright as day, and he knew it was Perrikus and D'Chel, burning form the inside out, courtesy of the seeds of dragon's fire Dewi had breathed into them.

CHAPTER 28

Gwydion gnashed his teeth in frustration. The blasted Persian mirror tunnels had led them to three dead ends, but their current path looked like it might pan out. They'd passed this point in the central tunnel before. He recognized it because he'd carved a gash in the flesh-like material lining the passageway last time they'd been there. It had really pissed off whatever breathed life into the passageway because the damned thing had ejected them back to the room they'd started from.

"If I ever get my hands on that fucker Adva, I'll choke the life out of him."

"Same thing I was thinking," Arawn mumbled. "There's a battle. I feel it in the pit of my stomach, and we keep walking around it."

"We just passed where we've been stymied before," Timothy said from behind him.

"Tell me something I doona know." Gwydion pushed power through his staff until it glowed brightly. "Hold a moment. Tell everyone to concentrate as much magic as they can and focus it there." He jabbed the tip of his staff forward. Power bubbled so sharp and bright, the tunnel walls actually retreated a foot.

The walls turned silvery, and then pink. Suddenly the tunnel fell away to nothingness and they were in an enormous chamber full of smoke and flames and littered with bodies.

"Goddess be praised! We hit the mother lode. Finally." Gwydion stabbed the air with his staff and hurried into the melee. It was hard to see much of anything until he fine-tuned his magical senses.

"Holy crap!" He came to an abrupt halt, surveying the impossible. "What the hell? How'd they get here?" he muttered.

Arawn pitched up against his back. "Why'd ye stop?" the god of the dead demanded.

"Of all of us, ye should be able to see in the dark."

"I can. I was fixated on the dragon brood. How do ye suppose—" Fire flashed past his head, and Arawn ducked.

"The mystery will keep till later." Gwydion focused power through his staff and sent lethal energy into a troll, a gnome, and a pair of undead glued to one another in the throes of sexual ecstasy. It looked as if someone had emptied Hell into this cave, and he cursed Adva for creating a portal.

"Fight well." Arawn loped into the fray, with Andraste on his heels keening a battle cry.

Gwydion scanned the room to see what was needed. Demon spawn poured from half a dozen gateways. A young dragon had stationed itself in front of each and was dealing death to whatever popped through. The black youngling circulated among his eggmates, urging them on and killing at the same time. Damn, if he didn't look like a junior version of his father. Gwydion smiled wryly, recognizing truth in his thoughts.

If a new Norse dragon's been born, it bodes well for the world.

Fionn, Andraste, Arawn, and Bran traded blows with trolls and demons. Nidhogg and Dewi had split up their brood and looked like they were providing backup and encouragement and doing their damnedest to make certain nothing happened to any of them. It made sense—this was their offspring's first major battle.

The humans had fanned through the room killing whatever stepped into their path. Where were the dark gods? And Aislinn and

Rune? Gwydion let his power guide him to a spot a little away from the worst of the fighting. Looking pale, but determined, Aislinn sat with her back against a wall. Rune sat by her side, ears pricked forward and his gray-black fur drenched in the dark gods' blood.

Gwydion tried to breathe through his mouth. The dark gods' blood had a nauseating stench: decayed flesh mingled with rotten grease. Because the battle seemed to be moving along all right without his immediate assistance, he sat next to Aislinn. "What happened, lass?"

"Long story. I was certain I was dying. Tried to Heal myself, but there was too much damage. D'Chel got tired of trying to fuck me and decided to carve one of my ovaries out."

Fury roiled through Gwydion at the atrocity of it. "That son of a bitch. I'm surprised ye remember aught."

She nodded, her golden eyes somber. "I am too. Something shifted once I passed out. It was like I'd moved to my astral self, but the color leached out of the world. It looked like how I always imagined *death's dream kingdom* from some poem I read in high school." She twisted her head to meet his gaze. "It isn't important, but who wrote it?"

"T.S. Eliot. What did ye see in your astral form?"

"Fionn had me, was doing everything he could to Heal me, but he ran up against the same roadblocks I found. Once over half the blood in a body is gone, it's impossible to reverse things. Dewi showed up and ordered him to give me to her. At first he didn't want to, but Rune sided with the dragon." Her eyes fluttered shut for a moment. "I would be dead—actually, I think I was—except Dewi gave me her blood."

Gwydion tried to mask his surprise, but even in her current condition, Aislinn was sharp. She narrowed her eyes and asked, "What aren't you saying?"

He eyed her appraisingly. "Ye must be feeling pretty chipper."

"I am, and I don't understand it. If Fionn wouldn't kill me for joining the battle, I'd be on my feet fighting."

"You are staying right here," Rune said. "If you try to leave, I'll bite you."

She ruffled his fur and then brushed her fingers together. "Ick. Your fur is full of sticky blood."

"I killed Perrikus," the wolf announced with more than a tinge of satisfaction. "I jumped on him and ripped the side of his neck out."

"Yes, I saw that part." She stroked her wolf. "I'm proud of you, honored you're my bondmate." He turned and nuzzled her, bloody snout and all.

"Is that him and D'Chel over there?" Gwydion asked and tilted his head toward twin pyres burning fifty yards away. He was grateful Aislinn hadn't asked more about why Dewi's blood gift had been a shock. It was the dragon's place to tell her, not his.

Aislinn nodded. "Dragon fire. After Rune attacked Perrikus, Fionn pinned D'Chel to the wall with a steel pike and Dewi moved in to finish them off—as much as they can be finished off, that is."

"How'd the little ones get here?"

"You mean the baby dragons?" At his nod, Aislinn smiled. "I think they invited themselves. Their parents sure weren't expecting them."

A demon sashayed close and Rune leaped at him, closing his jaws over his neck. More blood spewed, drenching all of them with black ichor.

"Why the fuck can't they bleed red like the rest of us?" Aislinn muttered, wiping gore out of her eyes.

"I'm going to join the others, lass." Gwydion patted her thigh. "We have to get those gateways closed afore we have a prayer of winning the day."

He scrambled to his feet as Timothy made his way to them.

"Fionn sent me," Timothy said. "He wanted me to make certain Aislinn doesn't require further Healing."

"I'm fine," she said and made shooing motions with both hands. "Both of you help finish this so we can go home."

"If it's all the same," Timothy murmured as he settled next to her, "I'll just do a quick scan. Fionn will want a full report."

Gwydion strode to where Fionn, Bran, and Arawn fought. Andraste glittered like the golden goddess she was, dealing death from a few yards away. Fionn had been there when Dewi shared her blood with Aislinn, yet he'd sent a Healer, which meant he didn't know the legend—or the power—of dragon's blood, particularly from a dragon bonded to you. Gwydion pointed his staff at a pesky phalanx of gnomes that were closing on him, annihilating the front row. At least it slowed them down. It was possible Fionn, who'd never been much for study, and who was one of the younger Celtic gods, had no idea what had transpired between Dewi and Aislinn, or what the gift of dragon's blood meant.

Gwydion clapped Fionn on the shoulder and moved between him and Arawn. He burned to tell his friend what he'd figured out, but that was Dewi's task, not his. "How's it going?" he asked Fionn.

"Och, we're holding our own, but we need a different strategy."

"Like finding Adva and disabling him and his wretched portals?" Arawn suggested.

"Any idea where to look?" Gwydion asked.

"Nay," Fionn grunted, looking like he wanted to rip the world apart. "We've been kicking that can down the road for a while now. The bastard is a master of hiding in his own tunnels, and they're such a rat hole of a maze we could hunt from now until the world ended and not find him."

Gwydion gazed around the demon-filled cavern and counted at least ten of the fell creatures for every one of them, with more emerging from new gateways that were forming fast. They needed to do something, but what? The young dragons moved to cover the newer gateways, but there were twice the number of gateways as dragons now, and Hell's hordes burst through, ready to fight.

THE YOUNG BLACK dragon spit fire in frustration as another gateway opened. He retreated to where his father stood, blasting everything within range with a potent combination of fire and magic. He ducked behind the range of Nidhogg's fury and said, "I have an idea."

"Spit it out."

Nidhogg junior swallowed hard. He'd imagined an easy victory where he and his eggmates waltzed in and saved the day, but there were hundreds more of the enemy than he'd envisioned. It didn't matter how many they killed, more blatted through new openings every few minutes.

"Behind every new portal that opens, there has to be a master portal developing new branches."

Nidhogg twisted his head and looked down at his son. "Interesting concept."

"So," he hurried on before his courage failed entirely, "since we're small enough to fit, I say we follow one of the portals until we find the main one and destroy it."

The elder Nidhogg's eyes whirled with admiration. "I like it. Furthermore, it just might work." He leaned close. "Don't tell your mother. She'll have a fit. Worse, she'll want to catch a ride inside one of you."

"So I have your permission…sir?"

Nidhogg roared with laughter. "You must be terrified, or you wouldn't have asked."

The young dragon shook himself and drew himself up to his full height, which was about half his father's. "I am not *terrified*, just…cautious."

"Once you're inside the portal isn't the time for *caution*," Nidhogg warned. "Your path will be set then, and you cannot retreat." He bent so his head was at eye level with his son's. "Are you certain about this?"

"It's my idea isn't it?"

"Indeed it is. Have you told the others?"

"Yes. But it's dicey enough, I wanted to get your blessing."

"You have it, and more."

The black youngling clasped talons with his father, then turned and clumped into the murk, calling his eggmates telepathically. They gathered in front of the largest portal. "Once I tell you"—he gazed from dragon to dragon—"weave your magic with mine and we'll go inside. It may take a while to locate the source tunnel so we can bombard it."

"What happens after that?" the copper male asked.

Nidhogg cracked a quick smile. "I have no idea. We're making this up as we go. We have Father's approval. Mother doesn't know, so when she starts screaming, ignore her. Keep your warding up so she can't catch a ride with any of us."

He twisted on his haunches and launched himself into the tunnel with his mother's furious trumpeting ringing against his ears. At least she didn't try to follow them, but then she couldn't, because she'd never fit. Young Nidhogg scattered demons as he went. It took too long to kill them, so he stunned them enough to let him pass. The passageway was smaller than he'd anticipated, barely large enough to accommodate him. The walls were made of a pink-gray ectoplasm that seemed to be alive, which was encouraging. If it lived, they could kill it. The beating walls curved in a downward spiral, and Nidhogg hoped the damned thing didn't go all the way into Hell.

If he'd been wrong about his *master tunnel* theory, he'd just signed his and his siblings' death warrants. No going back. Unless the tunnel widened, there wasn't room to turn his blocky body around. Nidhogg grabbed at the fleeing edges of his courage. He'd seen this clearly, it had to work.

Unless the reason I saw the vision was because one of the dark gods planted it.

Stop! I have to believe in myself and my magic. It's the only way.

"How much farther?" someone called from behind him, but Nidhogg didn't answer. He didn't know and didn't want to insult anyone's intelligence by guessing.

Time rushed by in a haze. The occasional demon blocked their path, but they'd thinned out. Perhaps someone had spread the word to take another route. After three tight spirals where his body scraped against the clammy ectoplasm, the tunnel spit him into a cavern. His first thought was relief because he could finally maneuver his body.

He dialed up his night vision and found what he'd hoped for. "Yes!" he trumpeted. Before him was a much larger opening, and ranged behind him were over a dozen portals like the one he'd just come through. He may not have found the master tunnel into Hell, but they were close enough.

"Now!" he shrieked at his eggmates as they joined him in a tight row. "Blend your power and target that huge hole right in front of us."

Two trolls swaggered through the opening, took one look at the line of dragons and turned back the way they'd come.

Young Nidhogg took the time to braid their magic into an invincible mosaic. Once he was satisfied, he launched it into the opening and instructed it to detonate after a slight delay.

"Will we blow up right along with it?" a green male cried.

"If we did, it would be for a good cause," the copper male said.

"More magic," Nidhogg demanded. "I'm going to teleport us back to Mother and Father before this blows up in our faces."

Try to, he amended silently as he gathered power from his brothers and sisters. Roaring filled his ears and the creepy, gray tunnel dissolved around him. For long moments, he didn't know if it was because he'd teleported them to safety or because he was now bits of nothingness joined to the universe.

He peered through emptiness, willing his vision to clear. When it did, shock flattened him. They weren't in the cave where the battle was raging, but outside the fortress. Kra and Berra converged on them.

"Where did you come from?" Kra shouted, sounding furious. He latched a taloned foreleg around the roots of one of Nidhogg's wings.

"I told you they'd never stay put on our borderworld," Berra cut in.

"Well, they're going back just as soon as we finish things here," Kra said, winding bands of power around the brood to contain them.

"Stop it!" Nidhogg junior wrenched himself out of Kra's steely grasp. Pain shot through his wing, but he couldn't elude the invisible barrier the dragon was constructing around them.

"Stop what you're doing," the copper male echoed. "We're heroes. We blew up the master tunnel into Hell."

"Fucking great," Kra muttered. "You've lost your mind." He rounded on Nidhogg. "See what your folly has cost? You should be ashamed. I'll see you locked on our borderworld for the rest of your days."

Nidhogg's temper snapped and he shot fire at Kra. "Father knows we're here. He gave us his blessing. We've been beneath the fortress fighting. Copper is right. We are heroes."

Kra shot fire back, but it rolled off Nidhogg's scales.

"I'd like to hear this tale from the beginning," Berra said, eying her mate.

"Why?" Kra countered. "It's nothing more than a bucket of week-old fish guts."

The red dragon faced down her mate, golden eyes blazing with determination. "And I say we listen. I sensed truth in what little we heard."

Fire spewed from Kra, but since he hadn't contradicted his mate—a bad idea in young Nidhogg's limited experience—maybe it might be all right to tell them what happened.

"I'll begin," he told his eggmates. "Feel free to jump in if I miss something."

CHAPTER 29

An ominous booming roar filled the cavern. Fionn twisted from side to side trying to determine the new source of attack. Magic at the ready, he balanced power until he could get a clear shot at whatever was after them now.

Nidhogg's triumphant trumpeting rose above the din of battle, and Fionn hurried to his side. "What's going on?"

"Look." Nidhogg jerked his head toward the scraggly row of portals that were winking out of existence. Only three remained, and they fell in on themselves as Fionn watched.

"Did someone locate Adva and corral him?"

"No." Nidhogg's chest swelled as if he were bursting with pride. "My son and his eggmates went into one of the demon's portals and followed it until they found the main tunnel leading up from Hell. Then they blew it up."

"Brilliant." Fionn slapped Nidhogg's side and winced as scales sliced into him. "How'd ye know to do that?"

"It wasn't my idea. The black youngling came up with it."

"Quite a genius." Fionn beamed and dragged a hand through his hair to get it out of his face.

Nidhogg trumpeted again. "He should be. He's the next Norse dragon."

Fionn cast an appraising glance at Nidhogg, realizing he should have known. "Regardless, that little bastard is too smart for his own good. He just impressed the hell out of me." Fionn looked about, but didn't see any of the brood. He fought a sudden, sinking feeling that they'd gone on a suicide mission. It didn't seem like Nidhogg would be quite so cheerful if that were the case, but still... "By the way, where're he and the rest of them?" Fionn kept his tone casual, while peering through smoke and murk searching for flashes of color that would signal the young dragons' presence.

"Excellent question," Dewi shrieked as she lumbered to where they stood. "You sent my babies to their deaths," she wailed. Tears gushed from her eyes, forming a king's ransom in jewels at her feet. "How could you do such a thing?"

Nidhogg grabbed her foreleg and shook it hard. "Get hold of yourself. They're fine. They're outside with Kra and Berra."

"How do you know?" Her dark eyes whirled like deep, perilous pools.

"Because Kra reached me telepathically. Mostly to apologize. He was quite harsh with our brood when they showed up in front of the fortress."

"How dare he?" Dewi's despair shifted to outrage so fast it made Fionn's head whirl. "Our children are magnificent, splendid. Heroes."

"Yes, but they also snuck away from our borderwold," Nidhogg cut in.

Dewi shrugged. "They're young, experimenting with life—"

"Hold the argument until later." Fionn exhaled briskly. "Once we mow our way through what's left here, we're done. Let's get to it. I want to take Aislinn home."

"Adva's still very much alive," Nidhogg reminded him.

"I suspect he won't hang around once he realizes he's the only one left." Fionn cracked a grim smile and trotted to where he'd left the other Celts to tell them what happened.

The rest of the battle was fast and bloody. Once the demons realized their physical exit route had been cut off, a sizable contingent, probably all those who had enough magic at their disposal, teleported out of there, leaving their fellows to fend for themselves. Fionn grabbed a battle axe from a fallen troll and cut his way through swathes of demons, trolls, and gnomes. Killing with the axe was more satisfying than killing with magic, and he gloried in the crunch of bones as he connected with enemy bodies.

He'd loved battle in the early years after his birth in 1048. It was simple, personal, with just him, his horse, his broadsword, and magic when he needed it. Modern warfare, where you killed millions with a bomb from an airplane, lacked the personal touch that created warriors. No wonder humankind had sunk into such a depraved state that they'd been swayed enough by empty rhetoric to open their world to darkness.

He laughed at his foray into philosophy, and then laughed some more at the joy of victory, of using body and brain to rid the world of wickedness. As he killed, he worked his way to where he'd left Aislinn and Rune. At first he didn't see them, but that was because they'd moved. Not far, but she perched atop a fallen troll, presumably to give herself a better view of the battlefield.

Rune stood, his tail pluming. The wolf was barely recognizable through blood that covered him from nose to tail tip. Fionn ruffled his fur and got splattered with gore. Not that it mattered, since he wasn't any cleaner than the wolf. He hunkered in front of Aislinn. "How are ye feeling, mo croi?"

"Fine. I'm fit enough to fight. I could finish this with you."

"Not on your life." He laid a hand over her stomach and sent magic into her. His eyes widened when he found the damage completely Healed—minus her missing ovary. "I doona believe it," he breathed. "Timothy must be one hell of a Healer."

"He checked me over, said I'd done a fine job Healing myself, and left."

"Then how?" Fionn moved his hand to her cheek, leaving bloody fingerprints on her skin. "Did ye Heal yourself once I left you here?"

She shook her head. "I think my miraculous return from the far side of the veil is because of whatever Dewi did."

"We'll have to ask her." Fionn straightened and swept Aislinn into his arms. "The ones who are left can finish mopping up. We're verra nearly done, and I'd like to take you out of here." He tightened his grip, drawing her as close as he could. "Gods, but I love you."

She snuggled against him. "I love you too, Fionn. My last thoughts, or the ones I was certain would be my last, were of you and Rune." She hesitated. "Once I knew I was dying, I asked Perrikus and D'Chel to spare both of you."

"What'd they say?" Fionn stared down at her.

"That they'd think about it, but I didn't believe them and was sick I'd abased myself by groveling."

He shifted her in his arms and smoothed hair back from her face, leaving more gore in the wake of his fingers. "It doesna matter. They're out of the way for now, and we still have each other."

"Since we're leaving, can we teleport?" Rune broke in. "Or will we be stuck trying to find that rotten tunnel we took in here?"

Fionn liked the feel of Aislinn cradled in his arms. When he thought how close he'd come to losing her, it curdled his blood. "I doona know," he told the wolf, "but I aim to find out."

Aislinn wriggled against him. "Not that I don't adore being held, but you stink of demon. I probably do too. Put me down and let me help get us out of here."

If it were up to him, he'd never let go of her again—ever. Even if it meant chaining her to his wrist with magic.

As if she'd read his thoughts, she squirmed harder. "No boxes. Not for either of us. Remember?"

"Aye, lassie, all too well." He set her on her feet, kept a protective arm around her, and grabbed the lead that still hung from Rune's neck with his other hand. The thick smoke that had filled the cavern was finally clearing. Fionn crafted his magic into a teleport spell, added a silent prayer it wouldn't boomerang them back into this infernal cave —or somewhere worse—and pulled them through.

They emerged into the pallid light that passed for day on the borderworld; the fortress rose behind them. The sea serpents hissed and lunged, but they were far enough away it didn't matter. Bella flew from goddess-only-knew where, attached herself to Fionn's shoulder, and pecked his head.

"Happy to see you."

"I'm glad to see you too," he told his bird.

Rather than staying put, she opened her wings and fluttered to Rune's back. "Tell me everything," she demanded. "I was worried about you."

Fionn watched them move off to one side and chuckled. "Och aye, and my bird appears to have switched allegiance."

Aislinn rolled her eyes. "They're close. It's fine." She lowered her voice and spoke near his ear. "Bella's figuring out where she fits now that it's not just you and her anymore. It's a process, but she's finding her way."

Fionn hoped so. The bird could be the original bitch on wheels when she felt slighted. He turned as Kra and Berra closed on them, followed by the seven young dragons. Fionn blinked. The younglings were half the size of the adults, or even a little bigger. Christ, but they'd grown fast.

"Is it finished?" Kra asked, his dark eyes spinning.

"Almost," Fionn said. "The dragon brood truly saved the day. What moxie. Racing headlong into a demon portal like they did. Not that I wouldna have, mind you."

Aislinn snorted. "You're disappointed you didn't think of it first."

"Aye, that too."

Gateways popped open around them, and humans spilled through, followed by Andraste, Arawn, Bran, Gwydion, Nidhogg, and Dewi. The Hunters and their bond animals, who'd sat out the battle, surged forward to meet the newcomers.

Once everyone was accounted for, Timothy called to Fionn. "We're leaving. See you back at your manor house."

Fionn trotted to his side and shook his hand. "Thank you for all your help. I hope there aren't many more battles, but I'd be honored to fight by your side again."

After a long pause, Timothy smiled, and his hazel eyes glowed with warmth. He gripped Fionn's hand harder. "The feeling's mutual, Celt."

Gwydion leaned his staff against his body and dusted his hands together as he watched the humans summon teleport spells and disappear through portals. "It appears the gateways are functioning again."

"Which means Adva packed up just like I predicted." Fionn grinned.

"He isna gone," Arawn said. "None of them are."

"Excellent." Andraste squared her shoulders. Her blonde hair was matted with black and red gore and her face streaked with grime. "I'd hate to run out of battles. What would I live for?"

"Ye'll have to find another foe," Fionn said. "I suspect the dark gods will be quiescent for long years after this." He kissed Aislinn's forehead and walked to the young black dragon. Once there, he bowed. "I thank you for your courage and quick thinking."

The youngling bowed back. "Appreciated."

When Fionn straightened, the dragon winked lazily. "There were a few tense moments."

"There always are," Fionn said. "Times when ye're almost certain ye made a fatal mistake." He sent a knowing glance at the dragon's whirling eyes and waited to see if he'd find out what really happened.

"Yes, but those are the times it's important to believe in yourself." The dragon winked once more, clearly not wanting to say anything further. Whatever had happened in that tunnel would remain between him and his eggmates.

Mayhap, 'tis how it should be, Fionn thought. He'd never been particularly forthcoming about the details of victories, preferring to hold them close to the vest.

Fionn grasped one of the dragon's forelegs in an effort at a handshake. The dragon gripped his hand, watching where his sharp talons landed. "Ye did well," Fionn said. "I'll look for great things as ye continue to grow."

The black youngling threw his shoulders back, and his scales clattered against each other. "We"—he cast a wingtip to encompass his eggmates—"are Earth's hope. Today was just the beginning. There is much damage to undo. It will make a life's work—for all of us. This was foretold. I saw it in Father's memories."

Nidhogg snorted, blowing steam. "That's one advantage of a fresh pair of eyes. He was able to pick through millions of bits of information and sort dross from gold."

Dewi hustled to Fionn's side and eyed her hatchlings. "I'm proud of all of you," she said, "but next time, tell one of us what you're doing."

"How?" The black youngling stared his mother down. "You'd moved us far away."

"I was trying to keep you safe," she protested.

"We weren't born to be safe." One of the red females came forward. She bowed stiffly in front of her mother. "I railed against that fate, but I've come to accept it."

"Pull up your head," Dewi instructed sharply. "Dragons bow to no one."

The red female raised her snout and met her mother's gaze. "I bow to you, Mother. I will be the next Celtic dragon god, and I have a lot to learn."

A slow smile split Dewi's jaws, and smoke bubbled through her nostrils. "Daughter. It bodes well that the future has shown itself to you. I'd be honored to be your teacher."

Nidhogg's rumbling laughter filled the air. "It seems both our understudies are in place. You and I can take a long vacation."

"I don't think so," young Nidhogg piped up. "You have lots to teach me, and there's no time to waste."

"Definitely your son." Dewi snorted fire. "Pushy, sure of himself."

"You fell in love with me." Nidhogg sidled next to her.

"Guess I'm one sick bitch since I like pushy, arrogant men." Dewi smiled fondly at her mate.

A portal burst forth, fiery in the dead air of the borderworld, and Royce and Vaughna leaped through spewing fire.

"There they are!" Vaughna trumpeted and moved as fast as she could to the black youngling. "You should be horsewhipped." She blasted him with fire.

Royce joined her, fastened his talons around young Nidhogg's neck, and lifted him off the ground. "I demand an explanation."

The black youngling dipped his head. "And I owe you one. I am sorry—"

"Sorry doesn't cut it," Vaughna screeched. "We went all the way to Taltos looking for you."

"And rammed a broad swathe through those foul reptiles," Royce broke in.

Nidhogg trudged over and inclined his head toward Royce and Vaughna. "I apologize for my offspring. What they did was wrong, but they've redeemed themselves since arriving here." He cleared his throat. "Please put him"—he jerked a talon at young Nidhogg—"down, and tell us what happened in Taltos."

Royce dropped the young dragon, who landed with a solid *thunk*, and said, "We blew it up."

"How?" Dewi moved closer and hauled young Nidhogg to his feet. He dusted himself off and faded back into the group of his eggmates.

"We were in that tunnel beneath Taltos, grabbing Lemurians who wandered by and torturing them until they told us what we needed to know about the dragon brood," Vaughna said. Her jaws parted in a self-satisfied smile.

"Once we were quite sure the younglings weren't there," Royce added, "we tuned in to a harmonic running through the tunnel, experimented a bit, and changed the frequency."

Vaughna snorted, blowing smoke. "We thought we'd just give those slimy bastards a bit of a headache. No one was more surprised than us when the whole damned place began going off like a firecracker. We barely had time to teleport out of there."

"Why'd you come here?" Dewi asked. "Rather than back to Fionn's?"

"We weren't certain we'd find you here," Royce said. "If we didn't, we'd have checked the other borderworld, but we had to report in and let you know we'd failed and your children were missing."

Nidhogg nodded slowly. "Thank you for your loyalty." He swiveled his neck around and eyed the next Norse dragon god. "You owe a huge apology to Royce and Vaughna. I order you and your eggmates into their service for six months after we return. Anything they need, you will provide for them, including hunting for their food."

"That's scarcely necessary—" Vaughna began, narrowing her copper eyes.

"Yes, it is," Dewi broke in. "Even though what my brood did had a good outcome, the way they went about it was wrong, and this is a way to teach them they must take responsibility for their mistakes."

"How about if we all go home?" Gwydion shouted to be heard above the din of dragon voices.

"What do ye think?" Fionn made his way back to Aislinn, Rune, and Bella.

"I'd love to go home," Aislinn said, "but first Dewi has some explaining to do." She focused her golden gaze on the dragon, and Dewi looked away.

Oh-oh. Fionn's gut tightened. *This canna be good.*

He made one more trip to stand in front of Dewi and Nidhogg, with Aislinn in tow this time. "What magic did ye wield to Heal her so quickly?" he demanded, never taking his eyes from the dragons.

"It is generally forbidden—" Nidhogg began.

"You couldn't have stopped me if you'd tried." Dewi spoke over her mate.

"Which is why I didn't," Nidhogg said.

"Whoa!" Aislinn looked from one dragon to the other. "You're talking in riddles. What did you do to me, Dewi? How did you Heal me so fast, and without any other magic from you? I may have been unconscious, but my astral self saw you drop some of your blood into my open wound. That was it. Then you gave me back to Fionn."

"My blood *is* magic," Dewi said, still not looking at them.

"Ye're hedging," Fionn cut in. "All of us hold power in our blood. What aren't ye saying? And why did Nidhogg say what ye did is forbidden? By whom and why?"

"You ask a lot of questions," Dewi groused.

"At least so far, you haven't answered a one." Aislinn pushed closer and shoved her shoulders straighter. "It's my body. I have a right to know what you did. Will I turn into a dragon? Have dragon babies, if I can even have children at all?"

Fionn winced. "Ye have one ovary left, lass. We should still be able to—"

"Ssht." She waved a hand to silence him. "Not my point." She narrowed her eyes and stared at Dewi. "I'm waiting."

"You may as well tell her." Nidhogg sounded resigned.

"Tell me what?" Aislinn screeched.

Fionn felt like burying himself in Dewi's mind and digging until he found the truth, but when he pushed into her head, she blocked him.

"If a dragon shares its blood with a human, and there's a bond between the two before the blood is shared," Dewi said, drawing each word out until Fionn wanted to throttle her, "the human becomes sort of, er, immortal."

Aislinn drew back as if she'd been slapped. "Im-Immortal," she stuttered. "What does *sort of* mean?"

"Not exactly immortal," Nidhogg said, "but you'll live as long as we do, so thousands of years without aging, or at least very little."

A smile started in Fionn's heart and spread to his face. "But that's marvelous news!" He picked Aislinn up and swung her around before putting her back on her feet. "Why wouldna ye wish to tell us that?" he asked Dewi.

"Because the creed that binds dragons forbids us to interfere with the natural order of things. If we saved every single human who was near death, it would play hell with Earth's population."

"But ye said ye had to be bonded for it to work," Fionn pointed out. "Surely a bond like the MacLochlainn one is rare."

"Any human who receives dragon blood will live for at least a thousand years," Nidhogg clarified. "The few with bonds to dragons live much longer. You can see how that sort of power could be easily abused." Smoke plumed from his mouth. "If humans found out—especially once they had magic of their own at their disposal—they'd have laid traps for us, kidnapped us, kept us alive much like the dark gods did with me here, and fed off our blood, probably selling it to the highest bidder. Not that they'd have had an easy time of it, but they'd have made our lives hell evading them."

Dewi nodded. "If that didn't work, they'd have tried to kill us outright." She eyed Fionn and Aislinn. "You can never talk with anyone, outside of those here, about what I did." She hesitated. "Most of the Celts know the legend. I'm not sure how it bypassed Fionn. Gwydion figured out what I'd done quick enough. He nagged me to tell you and Aislinn every time he got close to me during the battle."

"We held the secret for long years," Nidhogg added. "Once it appeared dragons might die out, a few of us breathed a collective sigh that we'd successfully avoided dealing with at least this one problem."

Fionn pressed his lips together. "Did the dark gods know?" he asked Nidhogg.

"I don't think so, or they'd have siphoned my blood and sold it."

Aislinn stood off to one side, her head bowed in thought. Rune padded to her side and licked her hand. Bella still rode on his back, her talons tangled in his bloody pelt.

"That seems like good news," he said gravely.

Aislinn nodded slowly. "Maybe, but I feel just as used as I do whenever one of them"—she swung her hand in a wide circle—"manipulates me."

"Would you rather I'd let you die?" Dewi asked.

Fionn sensed uncertainty roiling through Aislinn. He wanted to whoop, turn cartwheels that he'd have her by his side for much longer than he'd thought, but he restrained himself. Immortality, or anything close to it, was a huge pill, one that stuck in the craw of any thinking person. And one that took a lot of getting used to.

After a long silence, Aislinn turned and faced the dragon. "I'm grateful you saved my life. I wasn't ready to die." Her throat worked as she swallowed. "I realize there wasn't time for me to make a choice, and maybe I wasn't in any shape at that point to even think this through, but it would have gone down easier if you'd asked, rather than just forging ahead."

"I understand." Dewi nodded. "Even if there'd been time, I'm not certain I would have asked your leave, but it's a moot point since you were unconscious. I had no idea your astral self was standing on the sidelines, watching."

A faint smile curved the corners of Aislinn's mouth. "I know. That's most of what bothers me, but I'll get over it. You acted because you love me, and I can't fault you for that." Walking forward, she wound her arms around the dragon, and Dewi bent to lay her head atop Aislinn's, breathing steam over her.

At length, Aislinn let go and moved to Fionn's side, clucking to Rune. "Could you take us home?" she asked Fionn, and her eyes sheened with tears. "If I never see this borderworld again, it will be too soon."

"I thought ye'd never ask, leannán."

Fionn wrapped his arms around her and sandwiched wolf and bird between them. He summoned the magic to return them to Inishowen and cautioned, "Doona try to breathe. There's no air between here and Earth."

Aislinn snorted. "I haven't forgotten, but it seems minor after everything else that's happened."

"I love you, lass. We'll be there afore ye know it." With his arms around the woman he loved, Fionn loosed the spell to take them home.

A month later

Aislinn twisted before the glass in Fionn's bedchamber, trying to see her back. She'd picked through the trunks in the manor house attic and come up with a gorgeous ivory gown made of silk and seed pearls. It was cut low and fit her torso like a glove. Long, sheer sleeves fell from the open neckline. The skirt hit her just below the knees because its previous owner had been much shorter. Fionn couldn't recall just who it had belonged to, but he'd assured her it wasn't leftover from one of his previous marriages. Even though it was ridiculous, that mattered to her. She didn't want to stand by his side and recite marriage vows in the same dress an earlier bride of his had worn.

She stared at her bare feet. She may have been able to scrounge a gown from the trunks, but what few shoes there'd been were inches too small. Aislinn wriggled her toes and smiled. "Barefoot it is then," she murmured, not about to stuff her feet into her falling-apart leather boots, even if she could find them. They'd disappeared a couple days before. When she asked Fionn about them, he'd shrugged and borrowed a pair of leather slippers from Bran. They were big on her, but not as oversized as Fionn's would have been.

Satisfied with her dress, she picked up a brush and went to work on her hair. After twisting it this way and that, she settled on a simple French braid. It pulled her hair away from her face and let it trail down her back. A faint scratching at the door told her Rune was in the hallway.

She sent a bolt of magic to slip the latch holding the door closed, and her wolf padded in. His fur was still damp from the bath Fionn had threatened, and he glowed as he pranced into the room.

"You look beautiful." Aislinn beamed. "Guess that bath wasn't as bad as you feared."

"Worse." The wolf snorted and shook himself. Black and gray hair scattered.

"Regardless." She eyed him. "You survived. How do I look?" She twirled in place.

"Absolutely ravishing," Gwydion said as he swept into the room. Today he wore white robes sashed in teal. When she looked closer, runic writing crawled up the robe's lapels. The warrior magician winked broadly. "Still time to change your mind, lass, and choose one of us."

A smile tugged at the corners of her mouth. "It's a charming offer, and I'm flattered, but I've waited a long time for you to marry Fionn and me." She cocked her head to one side. "Are we ready?"

Gwydion nodded. "Aye, the guests are arriving, and Fionn sent me to fetch you."

"Actually he sent me," Rune chimed in. "Gwydion just came along for the ride."

"Och, so that's how 'tis." Gwydion grinned broadly. He extended a hand. "Arawn and Bran fought over who would give you away."

"Who won?" She quirked a curious brow.

"Arawn. Bran will be Fionn's groomsman." He paused for a beat. "Actually, Nidhogg offered too, but Dewi vetoed it since you could hardly walk the length of the great room on his arm. 'Tis crowded what with all the chairs we set up in there."

"I thought we were holding the ceremony outside," she said.

"Lass!" Gwydion pointed at a window. "Have ye looked outside this last hour?"

She shook her head and walked to the window, not surprised to make out rain falling from the night-dark sky. "Rain in Ireland. What a surprise," she murmured and turned to face him. "What about the dragons?"

"They'll be outside. Close enough to hear, and see through the windows."

"Not good enough."

"What are ye thinking, lass?" Gwydion asked. "We dinna wish to disturb your preparations, so we worked things out the best we could."

A few long strides carried her to the armoire that held her clothing, and she reached in and grabbed a red jacket with a hood that she draped over one arm. Aislinn narrowed her eyes. "Do you happen to know where my boots are?"

An uncomfortable look crossed Gwydion's face. It was gone so fast, if she hadn't been looking right at him, she'd have missed it. When he said, "No. Why would ye ask?" she was ready with her Seeker gift and heard the falsehood behind the words.

She crossed her arms beneath her breasts. "I thought it odd when they disappeared. I've looked everywhere. If Fionn took them to have someone make me a new pair, or scrounge me some from a deserted house, I need them now." She tossed her head back. "We're having the wedding where everyone can be a part of it. Dragons too. That means we'll be outside, rain and all."

A grudging look of admiration lightened his face. "'Tisn't every woman who'd volunteer to recite her marriage vows in bad weather, and I told Fionn ye'd figure it out about the boots. Come on downstairs, lass." He stared at her bare feet. "Ye might want to bring socks."

Aislinn rooted in a dresser and withdrew a red pair to match her jacket. She waved them in his direction. "The best dressed brides," she pronounced, "wear red and white. Saves time if something untoward attacks. All that blood will blend right in with—"

Gwydion was by her side so fast it stole her breath. He clamped a hand over her mouth. "Nay, lassie. Doona tempt fate by even thinking such a thing." His blond brows drew together into a harsh line.

"Joke," she mumbled from behind his hand. "I was making a joke."

He dropped his hand. "When ye've lived as long as we have, ye willna joke about such things."

"Maybe not. Ready?"

He turned and led the way out of the third floor bedroom. Rune followed him, and Aislinn came last, closing the door behind her. The next time she returned to this suite of rooms, she'd be a married woman, something she'd never expected.

Rune waited for her one flight down in the second floor hallway. "Are you happy, mistress?" He nuzzled her palm.

"Happier than I ever expected." She dropped to a crouch next to the wolf and hugged him to her.

He pulled away. "Your dress," he protested. "I'll get fur all over it. Slobber too."

"People you love are more important than clothing. Always," she reassured him and kissed the top of his head before straightening.

Aislinn stopped at the top of the final staircase leading into the great room. The men had done an amazing job transforming the room into an impromptu wedding chapel. At first they'd thought to use Gwydion's manor, which had a real chapel, but she'd wanted to be married in her and Fionn's home.

Most of the furniture had been pushed to the side, and rows of chairs lined the room. People—humans and Celts—milled about with glasses in their hands, and the din of conversation rose to meet her. Odin had sent his apologies, and she and Fionn had promised to plan a long visit to Asgard soon. Andraste happened to glance up, or maybe the goddess of victory had sensed Aislinn's energy. She stuck two fingers in her mouth and whistled loudly.

"The bride," Andraste announced, smiling up at Aislinn.

Rune nudged her from behind. *"With that kind of a proclamation, you'd best get moving,"* he said, switching to mind speech.

But Aislinn stood, surveying the growing crowd. "There's been a change of plans," she said, using magic to make her voice carry. "I know it's raining, but I want the dragons to be a part of this wedding, so we're moving the party outside, at least until Fionn and I have said our vows."

Applause began in one corner of the room and spread through the group.

"Excellent," Andraste said once the clapping died down. "We willna melt. 'Tis a sound decision."

Aislinn scanned the crowd. She picked out Arawn, Bran, and a few other humans and Celts she knew. Others she recognized, but didn't know their names, and a few she'd never seen before. There must have been a hundred people, and more were still arriving. "Where's Fionn?" she asked.

From the bottom of the stairs, Gwydion turned. "Och, lassie, mayhap he got cold feet."

Bran slugged him in the arm. Both he and Arawn wore buff colored battle leathers trimmed with rich embroidery. "Ye canna see the bridegroom afore the ceremony," he informed Aislinn. "'Tis bad luck."

She giggled and made her way down the remaining steps. Once Bran said it, she did recall that particular custom. With her socks and jacket tucked beneath one arm, she made her way from group to group exchanging pleasantries until Gwydion tapped her shoulder and waggled a pair of beautiful brown boots in front of her. "Would ye like to try them on, Cinderella?"

She shot him a bemused glance. "If they fit, does it entitle you to stand in for Fionn? Oh, wait. You can't, since you're the minister today."

He smiled. "Never saw the use in shoes myself, but come sit a moment, lass. 'Tis raining harder, and we should get started afore everyone gets drenched after a turn outside."

Aislinn moved to a couch that had been shoved near a wall, sat, and pulled on her socks. She held one of the boots for a moment and breathed a silent prayer it would fit before sliding her right foot into it. "Yes!" She bent to the laces. "They're awesome. How did you manage it?"

"'Twasn't me, but Fionn," Gwydion said, and handed her the other boot. "We hunted through the local deserted manor houses and castles using your boots for a model. Actually, we located three pairs and shaped them with magic so they'd be perfect."

"Three?" she squealed, and then clapped a hand over her mouth. "I have three new pairs of boots?" When he nodded, she jumped to her feet and hugged him.

After a moment, he hugged her back. "If all it took was footwear —" he began, but she shushed him and got the other boot on.

She shrugged into her jacket, stood, and said, "I'm ready. Let's do this."

"That's the same phrase I've heard ye use afore a battle." He eyed her appraisingly.

"And I'm just about as nervous." She shifted from foot to foot. "I love Fionn to distraction, but I'll feel better once this is done. It's been mighty quiet since we got back from Perrikus's borderworld."

He narrowed his blue eyes. "Ye havena had any long stretches of quiet since the dark ones breached Earth's veil, have ye?"

"No. Makes it hard to trust this one."

"Trust it, lass. I doona sense evil anywhere near."

"I hope you're right." She switched to mind speech. *"Dewi!"*

"Yes, child."

"We're having the ceremony outside. Where are you and the other dragons?"

"Right outside the great room windows on the terrace." The dragon paused a beat. *"It's raining. Are you certain?"*

"Yes. I want you and Nidhogg and your brood and the other dragons to be a part of my joy."

Aislinn heard Dewi's trumpeting through the thick manor house walls. "See." She tilted her chin. "I just made her very happy. Come on." She clucked to Rune and made her way to the front door where she turned. "Outside, everyone," she cried. "I want to get to the feast, and that cake."

"Nay, you just want to get to Fionn's body," someone called.

"That too," she said, spun, and marched down the stairs and into a light drizzle. Dewi spread her wings and Aislinn took up residence beneath one as the men went to get Fionn, and the guests deployed themselves near her and the dragons. Light spilled through the manor house windows from candles, and mage lights bobbed all around her, adding illumination to the terrace.

"Happy?" Dewi bent her head around so she was looking at Aislinn.

"Very."

"Good. We might have…dalliances," the dragon said sagely, "but they can't take the place of our one true love."

Aislinn considered sniping that if anyone should know, it was Dewi, but she kept her mouth shut.

The black youngling, who'd grown to two-thirds the size of his parents, made his way to her. "Thank you for wanting us next to you and not on the far side of that window." He pointed with a wingtip.

"How could I not?" She smiled at him. "I remember you from when you were this"—she held her hands a foot apart—"big."

"And I remember playing with your hair," he countered. "I loved it because it reminded me of fire."

Aislinn felt Fionn's unique energy and glanced up, seeking him. Gwydion led a processional with himself in the lead, staff in hand. Fionn and Bran came next, and Arawn stopped next to her.

"Lass?" He held out a hand to her, but she was fixated on Fionn.

He was dressed in pure white leathers with gold runes embroidered along the neckline and cuffs. His hair was braided, showing off the classic lines of his timeless face. Bella rode in her customary place on his left shoulder. Her black feathers glistened with rainwater.

Once he, Bran, and Gwydion reached a point at the head of the courtyard, he turned to face her, his glacier-blue eyes alight with love and hope, and his lips parted in a slight smile. Aislinn felt the quick, hot prick of tears. He was so impossibly beautiful, she couldn't quite believe he wanted her.

"Lass?" Arawn said again. "'Tis time."

With a hand that only trembled a little, she tucked her fingers beneath the crook of his elbow and let him lead her to Fionn's side. Rune padded next to her.

Gwydion nodded approvingly and began to chant in Gaelic once she stood on Fionn's left side. The Celts ranged behind them picked up the chant, as did some of the humans who were fluent in Gaelic. The dragons chimed in at intervals, and Aislinn was grateful she'd insisted on keeping the wedding outside. The rain wasn't that bad. She barely noticed it because of the fire burning brightly in her heart.

Gwydion completed the initial part of the ceremony and switched to English. He took her right hand and placed it in Fionn's. The heat from him seared her, but it was the joy streaming from Fionn's entire body that almost undid her, and she blinked back tears.

"Leannán?" Fionn said softly. "Are ye all right?"

She nodded. "Just happy. So happy it's spilling over."

"Do ye," Gwydion asked, "take this man to love and cherish forevermore?"

"I do." Aislinn tightened her hold on Fionn's hand.

"And do ye," Gwydion asked Fionn, "promise to love, cherish, and protect this woman so long as ye shall exist?"

"I do," Fionn intoned.

"What?" Aislinn shook her head. "Don't I get to protect him too?"

Gwydion stifled a snort. "And would ye protect him, then?"

"Of course." She smiled at the master enchanter. "That's what lovers do. Watch each other's backs."

Gwydion chanted in Gaelic with his staff raised above their heads. It glowed a brilliant blue white as it blessed their union. Finally, he fell silent.

Fionn gathered her into his arms and crushed his mouth down on hers, kissing her hungrily. Oblivious to the crowd around them, she flung her arms around him, clasped him close, and kissed him back. Hoots, catcalls, and clapping rose around them before she came up for air with Fionn smiling at her as if he were the happiest man in the world.

She cupped the side of his face with a hand. "God willing, we'll always feel like this," she murmured.

"We will." He leaned into her hand.

"How can you be so sure?"

"Because we'll take care of the moments, each and every one. When we do that, the hours and days will take care of themselves."

"I like the sound of that." Aislinn was grinning like a fool, but she couldn't stop herself. "Hey." She glanced up and saw an almost full moon peeking from behind the clouds. "It stopped raining."

"So it did, lass."

Cries of, "Food. Mead. Whiskey. Cake," came from all quarters.

"Let's bring our plates out here, at least for a while," she said. "That way the dragons can visit with us."

"I'll dry some benches with magic," Bran offered.

"Before we go inside for food," Bella said, "I'd like a private moment with Aislinn."

Fionn glanced at his bird. He looked worried, but didn't say anything as she fluttered to Aislinn's shoulder and the pair moved a few feet away.

"Thank you for being part of the ceremony." Aislinn stroked the bird's damp plumage.

"What I wanted," Bella said, without preamble, "is to tell you I'm glad Fionn married you. You're perfect for him, and he is for you." She pecked Aislinn's head softly. "I know I'm not easy to get along with, but Fionn's needed a good mate for a long time. Your mother, she wasn't right for him, but you are." The bird tightened her talons. "That's all. You can go inside and get dinner now."

Aislinn felt the bite of tears again. She reached up and plucked the bird off her shoulders, bringing her around so she could look at her.

"Thank you so much," she said. "That's one of the nicest things anyone's ever said to me." Bending, she kissed the tip of Bella's beak.

The bird twisted in her grip. "Now don't get all maudlin. This is your wedding day. Let go of me."

Aislinn did, and the raven flew back to Fionn. He angled his head to talk with her, clearly interested in what had transpired. Aislinn got back in time to hear the raven say, "That's between Aislinn and me," in her usual smug tone.

Stifling a giggle, she looped an arm around Fionn's waist. "About that wedding feast? Looks like most of the guests have gone back inside. If we don't hurry, we won't get a thing to eat."

He cast his million watt smile her way. "We could just retire to the third floor—"

"We could," she agreed and grinned at him, "but it's not every day a girl gets married, and I'd like to savor a little more of the celebration before we get lost in our own private world."

"We'd like to savor it with you," Nidhogg rumbled from a few feet away.

"Indeed," Dewi concurred and made shooing motions with both forelegs. "Go get dinner and come back and sit with us. There are plans to be made."

"Like what?" Aislinn asked, genuinely curious.

"Well, for one thing," the dragon began, "you still need years of practice with martial skills, fighting from my back."

Rune growled low from the shadows, and Aislinn laughed. "Not today," she said. "No talk of war, fighting, battle strategies, or any of that. It's my wedding day, and I want to enjoy it."

"I couldna have said it better myself." Fionn threaded an arm around her and together they walked up the steps and into the house.

"Husband," she said, enjoying the way the word rolled around on her tongue so much, she said it again. "Husband."

"Aye?" Mild amusement underscored the word.

"Nothing. I just like the sound of it."

"Would any husband have done?"

She elbowed him. "Of course not, silly. The only husband I ever wanted was you."

He turned her to face him just inside the front door. "That was the right answer," he said, and tilted his head to kiss her.

306

You've reached the end of the Earth Reclaimed Series
Thanks so much for sharing Aislinn and Fionn's journey with me.

ABOUT THE AUTHOR

Ann Gimpel is a USA Today bestselling author. She's also a clinical psychologist, with a Jungian bent. Avocations include mountaineering, skiing, wilderness photography and, of course, writing. A lifelong aficionado of the unusual, she began writing speculative fiction a few years ago. Since then her short fiction has appeared in a number of webzines and anthologies. Her longer books run the gamut from urban fantasy to paranormal romance. She's published over 50 books to date, with several more contracted for 2018 and beyond. A husband, grown children, grandchildren and three wolf hybrids round out her family.

Keep up with her at www.anngimpel.com or http://anngimpel.blogspot.com

If you enjoyed what you read, get in line for special offers and pre-release special reads. Sign up for Ann's newsletter on her website or her blog.

BOOK DESCRIPTION: HIGHLAND SECRETS

If you enjoyed this blend of urban fantasy, high fantasy, and romance, you might like my Dragon Lore Series. Read on for a sample.

Highland Secrets, A Dragon Lore Prequel and the first book in a four book series that includes:
Highland Secrets
To Love a Highland Dragon
Dragon Maid
Dragon's Dare

Furious and weary, Angus Shea wants out, but no matter how he feels, he can't stop the magic powering his visions. The Celts kidnapped him when he wasn't much more than a boy and forced him to do their bidding. He's sick of them and their endless assignments, but they wiped his memories, and he has no idea where he came from.

Dragon shifters are disappearing from the Scottish Highlands, and the Celtic Council sends Angus to investigate. He meets up with

Arianrhod, legendary virgin huntress from Celtic myth, in Fire Mountain, the dragons' home world.

Arianrhod prefers to work alone, mostly because she harbors a dirty little secret and guards her privacy for the best of reasons. She's not exactly a virgin, and she'd be laughed out of the Pantheon if the truth surfaced. Despite the complications of leading a double life, she's never found a lover who tempted her to walk away from her fellow Celtic gods.

Attraction ignites, hot and so urgent Arianrhod's carefully balanced life teeters on the brink of discovery. Angus is everything she's ever wanted, but he's far too close to her Celtic kin to keep her secret safe. Angus wants her too, but she's a Celt. He's hated them forever, and she's part of everything he's lain awake nights plotting to escape from.

Can they risk everything?

Will they?

If they do, can they live with the consequences?

HIGHLAND SECRETS, CHAPTER ONE

Angus Shea stroked beneath icy waters off the northern tip of Ireland, blending his energy with a pod of Selkies. The sea creatures cut through choppy waves in front, behind, and above him. He'd rather dive and play in the deeps with them—and if it were any other day, he would have—but he needed to keep an eye on the skies, so he edged toward the surface, pushing his head free.

Celene, a coal black Selkie he'd done more than swim with, drew close enough her lush pelt stroked his skin. He draped an arm around her, and she nuzzled his neck with her snout.

"Where have you been?" She spoke deep into his mind. Accommodating vocal chords were part of her human form, not her seal, and he'd never learned the Selkies' lyrical language.

"I spent a little time at my home in Scotland, but mostly I've ranged far from the Irish Sea."

"That doesn't tell me anything." She nipped playfully at his shoulder with her squared-off teeth.

"Prying ears are everywhere." He leaned into her warmth, enjoying a respite from the cold water.

"We could go where no one would hear."

He was tempted, so tempted he toyed with saying yes and taking a break from watching for the dragon he expected. Dragons interpreted time in their own way, and the damned thing might not show up today or tomorrow or even this week. If it showed at all.

How much could he tell the Selkie?

An answer crowded on the heels of his question.

Nothing.

Angus shuttered his mind, so the creature swimming by his side couldn't read it. Much as he yearned to talk with someone, anyone, about the impossibilities the gods tasked him with, prudence won out. Not that this assignment was worse than any of the others, but he'd finally figured out they'd never end.

I could say no. Tell them I'm done.

He cut off the bitter laugh that wanted out. Whoever had the balls to refuse the Celts risked swift and certain punishment. He could hear Gwydion, master enchanter, or Ceridwen, goddess of the world, laughing their heads off—before they cut out his tongue or killed him on the spot.

"You don't have to say a word." Celene went on, almost as if she'd peeked into his thoughts before he took care to protect them. Selkie laughter buffeted him, spraying him with a warm, rich melody mixed with salty water. *"I'm curious, but I miss your body."*

He missed hers too. She'd been his only break from solitude for more years than he wanted to admit. He cast another glance skyward. Though he tried to be subtle, he heard a smug murmur near his ear and knew he hadn't fooled the Selkie.

"You wait for an Ancient One." The tenor of her mind speech shifted as she shielded it from anyone who might be close. Without stopping for him to corroborate, she forged ahead. *"We can take up the banner and watch for you. My kin will let us know."*

Angus picked his way carefully, as if he walked through a field of unexploded ordnance. "I appreciate the thought, but no one can know of my comings or goings, lass."

"We know more than you think." Celene batted him with a flipper. *"In*

truth, very little escapes us, but here isn't the place to share what I heard about your latest mission."

Concern rippled through him. If the Selkies knew, who else might? Hell, he didn't know much beyond his assigned meeting place with the dragon, and they'd be heading into danger.

What else was new? Danger was so second nature, his adrenaline pumps barely flinched at anything these days.

"Come with me." Either Celene was oblivious to the turmoil rumbling through him, or she ignored it. She swam from beneath his arm and herded him toward shore. *"There's a secluded glade deep in marsh grass. No one will find us, and my kin will keep watch for the dragon. I already asked."*

The Selkies would do their best—and maybe today it would be enough—but they were no match for evil that had sunk its roots deep into the fabric of the Old Country and the rest of this world. It was why the gods stooped to using him—half-mortal, half-divine, or whatever the hell he was—to do their dirty work. Arawn, god of the dead, revenge, and terror, caught him skulking in the time-travel tunnels when he wasn't much more than a boy and trapped him, cutting off any possibility of return. To make certain Angus remained, the god altered his memories, so he had no idea where he came from.

Now almost twenty-five years later, Arawn and the others still came up with enough for him to do that a life to call his own was out of the question. The carrot they dangled was the truth about his birth, but they never came close to divulging it. The stick was his fear of what they'd do, if he told them he was done.

Over time, he'd stopped asking about his origins. He cared, but it wasn't worth the energy to run up against their stony faces and cunningly crafted half-truths that revealed exactly nothing. Despite his reservations about a quick dalliance with Celene—and maybe missing his rendezvous with the dragon—he was sick of his self-imposed isolation.

She chivied him into shallow water. Once she was certain he'd follow, she drew ahead easily. As if the other Selkies understood, the pod dispersed. When he peered through gray-green water for their multi-colored pelts, they weren't there.

By the time he clambered onto the rocky shore, Celene had shucked her skin. In human form, she opened her arms to welcome him. Long black hair shrouded her almost to her feet. Violet eyes gleamed in welcome. Her generous breasts peeked through the curtain of hair, their copper-colored nipples already pebbled with wanting him.

Angus had tucked his clothes beneath a rock before joining the Selkie pod. Because he swam nude, nothing was in the way as he plunged into Celene's offered embrace. God, how he'd missed the touch of another against him, skin to skin. Celene's body felt warm against his chilled one. She closed her arms around him and ran her hands down his back, lingering over the curve of his butt.

He hugged her in return. The scent of her, salt and mint, flooded his mind with images of their lovemaking, and his cock hardened between their bodies. He trailed his fingertips down her smooth skin, marveling at how different she felt from a human woman. Velvety and charged with electricity. Some Selkies walked among humans, even took permanent partners. Angus didn't understand how they eluded discovery.

Celene closed her mouth over the junction between his neck and shoulder, licking, sucking, biting. He moved a hand from her back to cup the side of her face and lowered his lips over hers. Desire engulfed him. Hot, urgent, desperate, he sank his tongue into her waiting mouth.

She grappled with his ass, pulling his body hard against hers as her hips writhed and breath hitched in her throat. Tearing her mouth from his, she gasped. "Too long. It's been too long."

Liquid heat trailed the path of her mouth as she licked her way down his chest, stopping to tease his nipples. He kissed the top of her head and wove his fingers into her long hair. Every nerve came alive with wanting her, but it ran deeper than that. Touch was such a basic need, and he'd denied that essential part of his humanity—along with every other comfort.

For what?

No matter how much he gave the Celts, they took every shred— and him—for granted. He wanted to get a job, blend in with humans. Something mundane like driving a cab, or flipping burgers in a grill, but his requests were denied. The Celts provided for him. So long as they housed and fed him, why would he need to clutter his time with anything as humdrum as earning a living? What if they needed him, and he was in the middle of washing dishes in some nameless restaurant? He could almost hear Gwydion's voice. See the master enchanter with a long-suffering look on his face—

He wiped his Celtic masters from his mind. This time was for him and Celene. No one else belonged in his head. Just because he'd chosen a semimonastic existence was no reason he couldn't give her everything she needed. Months had passed since they'd last been together, maybe as much as a year. He moved back enough to fill his hands with her breasts, rubbing her erect nipples before he bent to suck on them, remembering the little biting motions she loved.

A low, guttural moan escaped her, and she threaded her fingers through his hair. Holding him against her breasts, she began to sing as he loved her. A series of low, sweet notes rose in cadence and intensity as she lost herself in his touch. He'd asked her about the music once, and she told him it was how sea people vocalized their joy. The music filled him with unbearable hunger—poignant, mind-bending need for another person's touch.

Although he'd never done it before, he raised his voice and joined her song. The change was instantaneous. In that moment, he sensed her loneliness and isolation, twin to his own and recognized that both of them needed more kisses, more touches—even more than they needed sex.

"Lay on your belly." His voice rasped with wanting her. He tore tufts of marsh grass and arranged them to make her a bed on a sandy stretch between rocks.

She lay down, continuing to sing. Angus sang too, as he straddled her and ran his hands down her back rubbing tension from her muscles. He followed his hands with his mouth and strung kisses across her shoulder blades and down the line of vertebrae from her neck to the curves of her ass. Between their song, the feel of her skin beneath his fingertips, and his cock getting stiffer by the moment, waiting became almost painful, yet he held back, not quite sure why.

The rhythm and cadence of her song shifted as he alternated his mouth and hands across the sculpted planes of her back. The intense pressure in his balls receded almost as if he'd reached a peak, though he hadn't come. Maybe she sensed his need for warmth, contact, much as he'd sensed hers.

"Move off me so I can look at you." Celene flipped over to face him, kneeling above her. Rose and gold splotched her pale skin, and a broad smile split her exotic, high-cheek-boned face. "Today was different. You sang with me. You've never done that before."

He shrugged, suddenly self-conscious. "It felt right. Even though I wasn't inside you, what happened between us felt right."

She cocked her head to one side and trained her gaze on him. "Are you sure you don't have sea blood?"

A flicker of annoyance at the Celts' staunch refusal to disclose anything about his birth narrowed his eyes. "I have no idea what I am." He ticked what he did know off on his fingers. "I'm not immortal, but I'll live well beyond human lifespans. My magic is closer to seer and witch than anything else, yet I'm neither of those. The covens acknowledge me as one of theirs, but only because the local witches are too kind to tell me to go away. The time-travel portals accept me." He shrugged again. "I don't suppose knowing more would make a hell of a lot of difference."

"You're not from Scotland, even though you live there." She stated it baldly, as fact.

He frowned. "Why would you say that?"

"Your speech. There's something about the lilt of Scotland that's impossible to rid yourself of. You don't sound Irish or British, either, at least not from the time we live in." Her nostrils flared. "Maybe that's it."

"Maybe what's it?"

"You could be from the past, and not just a few years back, perhaps hundreds—or even more. I'm not old enough to recall what human speech sounded like then, but some Selkies are."

"Fine." Frustration tightened his chest, like it always did when the mystery of his origins became a point of discussion. "My first memories are when the god of the dead dragged me out of a time-travel portal when I was fifteen."

"I'm sorry." She draped a hand over his hip, cradling it. "I've upset you."

He started to protest, but she silenced him with a look. "Don't insult me with a lie, Angus, but you don't have to talk about it, either. Such a pretty man." She stroked hair back from his face. "With your deep brown hair and amber eyes. Did you know they shade to dark gold when you're angry?"

She was trying to divert him with flattery, but he wasn't buying it. "You have no idea what it's like not knowing—" He shook his head, and the rest of his words died unspoken. It didn't matter what she knew or didn't know about him. She'd never be more than an occasional lover, and both of them knew it.

"It could be more," she said softly, obviously having been in his mind.

Angus took her hands in his and gazed at her. "You get more of me than anyone, and you see how pathetically little that is. There's nothing more to give."

"There could be," she persisted. "You could refuse next time they send you on—"

He bent toward her and laid a hand over her mouth. "I'm not free. Not now. Not ever."

"I don't understand." She pushed his hand away and closed very white teeth over her full lower lip.

He smiled crookedly. "Not sure I do, either. Every man has a life's work. No matter how I feel about it, this appears to be mine."

Even though it wasn't wise, he started to ask what she knew about his current assignment, but a flash of unusual energy drew his gaze skyward. He leapt to his feet. A copper-colored dragon circled to land not far from him. Maybe the Ancient One had seen him with Celene and decided to be considerate.

Not very fucking likely. Dragons were a force unto themselves.

"I have to go," he said. "Let me walk you to your skin, so I know you're safely on your way home."

A sad expression crossed her face, creasing the skin around her eyes into a network of fine lines. "It's right here." She scrambled to her feet and gripped both his upper arms, forcing him to look at her. "Thank you."

"For what?"

"Being you." She brushed her lips over his and moved to a marsh grass thicket. In moments, she'd dragged her pelt over her human body. Transformed into a seal, she waded into the surf.

Before it engulfed her, she turned to gaze at him. *"Be careful, and think on what I said."*

He didn't answer, just watched her head bob in the waves before turning toward his clothing. It wasn't far from the place Celene had led them. His body felt vibrant, alive, and he still tingled from her touch. He longed for a woman of his own, children, a home, before he stuffed the impossible so deep under wraps he couldn't mourn the loss.

Angus moved the large rock he'd placed over his clothes to protect them from the wind. He pulled a ragged dark blue fisherman's knit sweater over his head and stepped into thick, black woolen trousers. Settling on a log, he pulled on socks and laced up stout leather boots. Though the breeze was raw, he'd worn neither hat nor gloves.

Ready as he figured he'd ever be, he covered the fifty yards to where the dragon had settled up the beach. He didn't recognize this one, but he'd only met a bare handful of the hundreds living in Fire

Mountain and on other worlds as well. When he drew near, he stopped and bowed his head respectfully, waiting for the dragon to speak first.

"I don't like this any better than you do," the dragon muttered. "Come close enough I don't have to broadcast our business to the world."

Angus walked closer. He could've suggested the dragon use telepathy since all the Ancient Ones were conversant in the technique, but he kept his mouth shut. The dragon was smaller than many he'd seen. Copper scales shaded to burnished gold on its chest, and dark eyes with golden centers whirled so fast they held a hypnotic quality. Lethal, six-inch-long red claws tipped its stubby forelegs. The dragon stood upright on hind legs tipped with the same sharp claws and kept its gaze averted, not saying anything.

What the hell? Every other dragon he'd met was proud, imperious, and quick to remind Angus of his inferiority. This one seemed young, but was it? After another long few minutes, Angus tossed respect—and caution—to the winds.

"What's your name? And what are we supposed to be doing? All Ceridwen told me was to meet you here."

The dragon opened its mouth, and a gout of flame landed scant inches from Angus's boots.

He frowned and drew his brows together. "If we're going to work together, I need to know what to call you." He sent a speculative gaze across the air between them. "If you annihilate me, they'll just assign you a new partner, and I'm a hell of a lot easier to get along with than any of the Celts."

"Tell me something I don't know," the dragon rumbled and belched smoke.

Frustration in its voice struck a note in Angus's soul, and he gestured with both hands. "You may as well tell me who you are and what we're supposed to do together." He infused his words with subtle persuasion. If the dragon didn't care for the Celts, either, they'd likely get along well enough.

"Why? What I should do is leave." The dragon sounded sulky—and scared.

"If you could, you'd already be gone." Angus was as certain of that as he was of anything. The dragon needed him for something, and whatever it was, the Ancient One wasn't particularly proud of it. "What happened? Am I some sort of punishment for you?" Tension settled like a steel bar across his shoulders, and he curled his hands into fists before he realized what he'd done.

"Oh I'd be gone, would I?"

The dragon ignored Angus's questions, and it mimicked his tone with eerie precision. It furled its wings and flapped them a time or two. Dirt swirled; small pebbles slapped Angus in the face. The creature belched steam and looked so distraught, he felt sorry for it.

"My life's not exactly a picnic, either," he ventured, on a hunt for common ground. "I'm a permanent mercenary, with no time off and no possibility of parole."

That got the dragon's attention, and it focused its whirling gaze on him. The golden centers of its eyes deepened with fiery motes that looked like little shooting stars. "Why would you want a respite from being a warrior?"

Good question.

"Because I'm tired. I'd like what most men have."

"What's that?" The dragon raised its brows, and its scales clanked against each other in a dissonant tinkling.

He shook his head. "It doesn't matter. The sooner you spit out whatever you need to say, the easier it'll be. The worst part about holding something you're ashamed of inside is it eats at you until you're nothing but a hollow shell."

Wings flapped, and those intense, whirling eyes shifted to the rocky beach. "I'm not *ashamed* of anything. I've been banished. Ceridwen said if I worked with you—and we were successful—I might be able to return."

Angus kept surprise out of his voice. "Banished from Fire Mountain?"

Steam puffed from the dragon's open mouth. "No. Idiot. I could live with that. They've banished me from the Highlands. My home."

"What happened?"

"It doesn't matter." The dragon threw his words back at him. "We have to go to Fire Mountain, where I'm to find one of the First Born. Once we have him—or her—"

"One of the six First Born dragons?" Angus broke in, scarcely believing the dragon's words. "They'll never show themselves—unless it's in their best interest."

Another wing flap and a defiant head toss. "There are actually ten. One of them was my father."

"When's the last time you saw him?" The words slipped out before he could stop them. Dragon males frequently didn't hang about once mating was over with, but the trembling mass of scales in front of him likely didn't need to be reminded.

"Never. Mother said he was too immersed in battles on another world to return for our hatching."

Angus unclenched his fists and hunted for something soothing to say that wasn't an outright lie. Dragon energy poked past his wards and into his mind. He tried to block it, but couldn't.

"You believe locating a First Born is hopeless." The dragon sounded resigned. "I may as well throw myself into a crater at Fire Mountain. I'll never see the Highlands again—or my mate." More wing rustling and the dragon rose a few feet off the ground, clearly intent on leaving.

"Hold on." Angus loped forward until he was right beneath the dragon. "I didn't say that—or think it, either. I don't know enough to make any sort of judgment. How about if you start at the beginning? If we're going to work together, I deserve that much."

The dragon circled a few times, indecision stamped in its erratic flight pattern.

"I know what it is to be alone." He kept his voice gentle. "And to not have anyone who cares if I live or die."

Maybe it wasn't totally true. Celcne might shed a tear or two, but she'd be the only one. He kept his gaze trained on the sky, relieved the dragon wasn't putting distance between them. Something about the creature's pain tugged at his heart and made it feel like a kindred spirit.

The copper dragon folded its wings and settled heavily to earth a few feet from where Angus stood. It straightened its shoulders and tipped its chin defiantly.

"My name is Eletea," the dragon announced, revealing its gender.

"Angus Shea, though you likely know that."

"Yes, I do. I killed a mage, who fancied herself a dragon shifter." Eletea's eyes whirled faster, as if she dared Angus to say something.

He crinkled his forehead as he dredged up what he knew about dragon shifters. "Don't mages take their chances when they show up seeking a dragon to pair with?"

She nodded once, sharply. "The mage seduced one of us into believing her. I saved him by killing her, but he turned on me. Reported me to the Dragons' Council, and they roped the Celts into deciding my fate, since the one I killed had Celtic blood." Eletea's scales rippled in the dragon equivalent of a shrug. "I don't understand why they're bothering. It's not like I went after one of the gods. They're immortal. The one all the fuss is over barely qualified as a Celt."

Angus kept his expression neutral. "Celtic blood aside, I thought mages only bonded with same sex dragons."

"That was another problem," Eletea said, sounding vindicated. "No one saw it but me, though."

Sensing the worst was out on the table, Angus settled on a nearby rock and invited, "Start at the beginning. We have time."

"No, we don't," Eletea protested. "We should've been at Fire Mountain yesterday." She hung her head. "I didn't know what I wanted to do, so I flew and flew and flew. I almost didn't land this afternoon."

Angus did his best to project optimism. "Let's open a time-travel portal and be on our way to Fire Mountain." At the dragon's reluctant nod, he went on. "I understand you have your own ways of returning home, but if you travel with me, you can fill me in as we go."

What he didn't say was it probably wouldn't matter when they arrived at the dragons' home world. First Borns wouldn't give them the time of day, whether they showed up early, late, or right on time. He held many concerns, such as what would a First Born do, assuming they could locate one? But he held those cares inside for now.

He could've dreamed the future. Instead, he summoned a spell to take them to a time-traveling portal. Once the undulating gray-pink tube admitted them, he gradually paid out questions.

Reticent and quiet at first, Eletea finally began to talk.